CRITICAL MASS

TOR BOOKS BY WHITLEY STRIEBER

2012

The Grays

The Wild

Catmagic

Critical Mass

CRITICAL MASS

WHITLEY STRIEBER

A TOM DOHERTY ASSOCIATES BOOK
NEW YORK

This is a work of fiction. All of the characters, organizations, and events portrayed in this novel are either products of the author's imagination or are used fictitiously.

CRITICAL MASS

A Forge Book
Published by Tom Doherty Associates, LLC
175 Fifth Avenue
New York, NY 10010

www.tor-forge.com

Library of Congress Cataloging-in-Publication Data

Strieber, Whitley.
Critical mass / Whitley Strieber.—1st ed.
p. cm.
"A Tom Doherty Associates book."
ISBN-13: 978-0-7653-2253-1
ISBN-10: 0-7653-2253-6
1. Nuclear terrorism—Fiction. 2. Terrorism—Prevention—Fiction. 3. Islamic fundamentalism—Fiction. I. Title.

PS3569.T6955 C75 2009
813'.54—dc22

2008050412

First Edition: February 2009

Printed in the United States of America

0 9 8 7 6 5 4 3 2 1

This novel is dedicated
to the men and women
who are engaged in the
lonely and dangerous struggle
to protect the Western world
from nuclear terrorism.

ACKNOWLEDGMENTS

I would like to acknowledge the help of technical specialists, Arabists, and so many others who were kind enough to contribute their time and expertise to this project. I wish that I could acknowledge each individual personally, but various circumstances obviously prevent that. Any errors are, of course, my own.

But the day of the Lord will come as a thief in the night; in
which the heavens shall pass away with a great noise, and
the elements shall melt with fervent heat, the earth
also and the works that are therein shall be burned up.

—2 Peter 3

'Tis light makes color visible: at night
Red, green, and russet vanish from thy sight.
So to thee light by darkness is made known . . .

—Rumi, "Reality and Appearance"

CRITICAL MASS

1

NIGHT RIDE

Jim Deutsch was driving much too fast, but it was urgent that he interview the children before they died. He was not close to the end of this investigation, and they almost certainly possessed crucial information. If he did not get it, he had not the slightest doubt that more people were going to be joining them in death—many more, and soon.

What he had to find out was something he was very much afraid he already knew: why these little children, just smuggled in from Mexico, were radioactive. He had spent his career in counterproliferation, and the sudden appearance of radiation-sick kids in a border town was a definite worry. Of course, they could have been brought over in a truck full of smuggled X-ray isotopes, or gotten into some other innocuous material. But he doubted that. He had to get solid evidence and work it up convincingly, in order to get the massive search going that he feared was needed.

When the speedometer moved through a hundred, he forced himself to let the car slow down. He took a deep breath, held it, then let it out. He loosened his hands, and felt blood rush back into his fingers.

The South Texas countryside rolled past, a wilderness of mesquite brush, the sky to the west deep orange. To his Connecticut eye, it was almost hellishly ugly. But his was a war fought in nightmarish places, and this terrain was certainly better than dry, stripped Afghanistan, or the lethal, magnificent mountains of Iran.

When the brush gave way to threadbare fields, he glimpsed cattle staring and old oil wells pumping with a lazy sensuality. He could imagine the Texans of the past racing up and down this road in their Cadillacs and Lincolns, whooping. Wildcatters, they had been called, those buccaneers of the oil fields.

He had been in many of the world's isolated places, and felt here the same disappointing and reassuring silence. Cities with their bustle and promise lured him, and also repelled him. He liked to hang out at Dom u Dorogi in Moscow listening to blues, or Sway in New York, with its Middle Eastern decor that always drew him into his memories. In the end, though, he would need the night and the silence where he had made his life. He would need the danger, foolish addiction that it was.

Ahead, a figure rode a horse right down the middle of the highway, a silhouette against the late sky. With foolhardy and trusting slowness, the old man walked his beast onto the shoulder. Jim shot past him at a distance of no more than thirty feet, glimpsing a narrow man on a tall roan. He seemed so needful, slouching along in the last sun, that Jim wished he had prayer left in him.

Again, he let his rented Taurus ease back to eighty. Mesquite brush whipped past, now. To the west, the sky faded. Texas Highway 57 was as empty as any road he'd known in Siberia or Afghanistan.

He considered the dying children, ahead in the border town of Eagle Pass. He wanted to believe that they'd been brought across with some piece of smuggled radiological equipment. But that was the sort of thing that the suits at Langley would want to think, and that was what they must not be allowed to think. On his end of the intelligence community, you survived by expecting the worst. On their end, he who made waves was in the most danger. But their danger was demotion. His was death.

His fear was that a bomb had come across and it was in motion, right now. He needed to find it, or at least find its trail, and he thought it must start with these poor kids. If he got lucky, they'd have some specific information. If not, he'd take what he got and go from there.

He wished that he trusted the system, but he was far too experienced for that. If he had, he would have called this thing in the second he heard about those kids. But he had feared what would happen—he'd find himself looking at orders not to waste his time. Wrong orders, and they would result in catastrophe.

The front face of the intelligence community appeared formidable, but that was the work of media experts, not a reflection of reality. It was the filter of analysis in the secret rooms that didn't work, and not understanding that—or not accepting it—had been his potentially fatal mistake. He had assumed that the system would absorb the information that he and his strings of agents gathered, and respond correctly.

But that hadn't happened when he was in Afghanistan or Pakistan or Siberia, so here he was in Texas, chasing after nukes that should have been caught before they left whatever benighted place they had come from. Instead, they were here, and the Mexican border was now the front line of a battle that belonged twelve thousand miles away.

Something had been wrong out there, very wrong. The CIA had extensive operations devoted to monitoring the nuclear materials black market. He had been part of that, operating out of U.S. embassies, and available to do things like penetrate storage facilities and inventory their contents. He was also good at finding people and obtaining information. He was good at running, too. He'd escaped across many a border in his time.

But he shouldn't have needed to do that sort of thing. He shouldn't have been compromised, not ever. After 9/11, there had been a number of decoy companies created by the CIA to draw the interest of terrorists and smugglers by operating things like false weapons sales organizations.

But there had been dissention about these fronts. They hadn't attracted their targets because they'd been too far from the centers of Muslim extremism—all except one, Brewster Jennings, which had operated in the Middle East and had been effective.

However, Jim had believed since he had first engaged with it in 2002 that it was penetrated by somebody. Soon after he began working with this organization, his life had become dangerous. People knew. Turkish intelligence had him identified. Friends in Pakistani intelligence warned him that they were building a dossier on his activities.

Then had come the Valerie Plame affair in 2003, and the name of her front operation, which was Brewster Jennings, became as famous a name as Microsoft or Toyota.

The result of all this was simple: too many men like him had been compromised. Some must have lost their lives. He, who had been working halfway across the world, was now working in the United States, because there was now fissionable material in Mexico, possibly in Canada, too, and it was on its way here, no question.

As he sped toward the dying children, the fear he lived with every second of his life rose up in him, the sick, desperate urgency that dragged him awake nights and haunted his days. He was in the dark and he was falling, and he could not stop falling.

Somewhere along the road, every intelligence agent meets a demon question, one that absolutely must be answered but that has no answer, and Jim's fear told him that his was lying in the hospital at the end of this road.

His stomach forced acid into his throat as he churned down the two-lane highway, speeding through silent towns called Batesville and La Pryor. Between them, he pushed the Taurus hard. Surely there wouldn't be a highway patrolman hiding along here, to come out with his lights flashing and entangle Jim in delay. His car was waking up buzzards asleep on the roadside, for God's sake.

He operated out of Dallas, where he officed in a little cell in the Earle Cabell Federal Building, just down the hall from the FBI. He was now a CIA contract employee, his status a fiction that allowed him—allegedly—to work within the continental United States. He suspected that his activities were not legal. He suspected that if he ever ended up under the bright lights of a congressional hearing, he would be alone.

He'd been transferred here from Kabul six months ago, after a quarter ton of U-235 had been intercepted on its way into Laredo and his supervisors had finally understood that the danger they had been fighting in distant places had arrived on their doorstep. He liased with the FBI Weapons of Mass Destruction coordinator in Dallas, which was another problem. The Office of National Intelligence might have improved interagency cooperation at the top, but the old "stovepipe" system still operated when it came to the nuts and bolts of intelligence gathering. His FBI counterparts shared only what they were legally required to share. Or did they? Did he, for that matter?

To counteract his lack of eyes and ears, he'd requested the right to recruit in the field, but had been turned down. These past few months, he could have used some good agents along the border, really used them.

Maybe then he would have been on top of this case before children lay dying. Maybe he would have made an interception. But this was going to be a chase, because whatever had been on its way across the border was now in country and being positioned.

U-235 didn't matter. This would not turn out to be about uranium. In fact, he thought the U-235 that had been brought over before was a test carried out to see how U.S. safeguards worked.

Nuclear materials are hard to detect if they're properly shielded. The most reliable detection systems react not only to radiation but also to the presence of the kind of bulk necessary to conceal it.

Whatever he was chasing now had been highly radioactive, and it had been brought across with illegals, probably in a truck. Could it be plutonium dioxide, perhaps, ready to be transformed into a metal, or intended to be used in some sort of low-yield bomb? It was shipped as a powder, which could have leaked. But if that was the case, why hadn't the radiation detectors on whatever bridge it had crossed screamed bloody murder?

Maybe, while the truck was on the bridge, there had been nothing to detect. No leaks. But the new systems were designed to see shielding as well as emissions, and there were new brand-new detectors in Eagle Pass; he'd seen the installation reports. They would have seen a bomb, surely.

But for whatever reason, they hadn't.

At this morning's meeting, the regional Weapons of Mass Destruction coordinator, Cynthia Spears, had read a report from the Laredo Field Office about the radioactive kids. "They are illegals aged ten, eight, and four, believed to have been off-loaded by coyotes when they got sick."

The moment he'd heard those words, he'd booked a flight to San Antonio, then been compelled to drive from there because of the lack of air service to Eagle Pass. He knew little about the community. In 2007, the mayor had refused to allow Homeland Security surveyors to enter the town to survey for the wall. Later, it had been built, but it was of no concern to Jim. Walls had no relevance to him. The things that concerned him came across bridges in disguise, not through the river under cover of night.

The more he thought about it, the more certain he became that he was dealing with plutonium and that these children had somehow been exposed during handling, after it had crossed the border.

Plutonium was potentially much more of a threat than highly enriched uranium. It took far less plutonium to make a bomb, and therefore it was more portable. But it was also harder to make plutonium go critical and explode. If the builders had the right parts, though—well, it was possible. You could even get a low-yield plutonium bomb out of a simple gun-type detonation system of the kind used with uranium bombs.

Every country that had ever produced nuclear weapons materials had experienced some loss. Most highly enriched uranium and plutonium that had been lost by Western governments was accounted for in one way or another. But that was not true of Russia. During the collapse of the Soviet Union, highly enriched uranium and plutonium had gone missing and so had numerous critical parts.

He drove harder than ever, pushing the car relentlessly. In the movies, he would have had access to a government-issue Gulfstream or something. In the real world, no chance.

He fought the illusion that the road was actually getting longer, stretching away in front of him like an expanding rubber band.

This came from the desert lights phenomenon, the sense that distant lights weren't getting closer. For a fair amount of time, he'd seen lights ahead—but at least it was a city, and not the dim cluster of lanterns that marked most settlements along the ragged edges of the world.

"Come on," he muttered. *Were* the lights receding?

Nah, the Global Positioning System now had him twelve miles out. Experimentally, he opened his cell phone. Nope. Okay, noted. At least he was not going into some squat Kazakh burg full of bored sadists in threadbare uniforms who would thoroughly enjoy a night of waterboarding an American.

Gradually, the lights resolved into individual buildings, an Exxon station, a trailer back from the road, and he was soon moving through the outskirts of Eagle Pass.

But no, this was the middle of town. Eagle Pass appeared to be all outskirts, but it was low-slung, that was all, and quiet at this hour. A peaceful place.

Towns like Ozersk and Trekhgorny and Seversk, where he'd worked from time to time, might be isolated, but they were more lively than this at night. Drunk Russians—which after a certain hour in Siberia is, essentially, everybody—do not go gently. But here in this little border town, you sensed a peace, the same peace you felt throughout the developed world. He called it profound peace, soul peace. Eagle Pass enjoyed the same soul peace that blessed the rest of America. People felt safe here, which was another reason that things like 9/11 were so destructive. They slammed the American spirit right in the face.

Of course, human and drug smuggling were big business on the Mexican side of the border, and the violence involved was certainly known to cross over. Still, this was very certainly not the third world.

In cities like Islamabad or Kabul or Tashkent, you can smell the old, sour stench of hate, and see the fear that lives in people's eyes, the blood-soaked remembrance of crimes long past, and waiting retribution. You come back to this country after a few years of that and you want to kiss the ground.

Then he saw it ahead, the outline of a big building just visible in the last light. The hospital. Inside, maybe a key that would save a million lives and, with them, the way of life now called freedom. The dying children and, God willing, some clues.

He drove into the parking lot, pulled the car in between a weathered Toyota and a Ford truck. How deeply American was this place, how kind and how very ordinary.

He got out of the car and hurried toward the great, dark building to challenge its secrets.

2

DELIVERANCE BY DEATH

As he approached the hospital's wide main doors, instinct made him check the locations of fire escapes and exits, count the stories, and note whether or not you could get off the roof. He had no reason to be concerned; it was just habit.

The lobby was large, the floors white and polished. There were people sitting here and there in the chairs, some reading, others simply waiting. He passed the gift shop and a row of plantings, and approached the information desk. There was faint music, no hospital smell, a sense of order.

He remembered hospitals like great broken skeletons, echoing with the voices of the unattended.

"I'm Dr. Henry Franklin," he lied to the receptionist. "I have an appointment to visit the Morales children."

She punched at a keyboard. "Uh, uh-oh, they're critical. I'm afraid they're in intensive care, no visitors."

"I'm from the Centers for Disease Control," he said, the falsehood emerging with practiced smoothness.

She made a call, spoke Spanish. "There's a guy out here. I think it's a reporter. He's claiming to be from CDC."

He was a fair linguist, which was one of the reasons he had been an efficient case officer. He rarely let people he dealt with know when he spoke their language, and he didn't do that now.

"May I see some identification?"

He drew out his wallet and showed her the CDC card he'd armed it with. As a nominal CIA operative, he had access to a variety of false IDs, some of which he could use legally, all of which could survive an in-depth background check . . . he hoped.

"Please, Doctor, come with me," a nurse in green scrubs said. She'd appeared silently, a young woman whose dark looks reminded him of his former wife, the gorgeous Nabila, still present in his heart. She was furiously complex and needed urgently to be cherished—too Arab, in the end, to endure an unruly American husband such as himself.

The implacable demands of his work kept him away from her too much, and this made her feel unloved, and, in the end, she had walked out of the marriage. He was still heartsick at the loss and grieved as if she were dead.

People raised in the restless Western tradition understood nothing of what it was like behind the doors of Muslim households, of how right it could feel to be enclosed in deep tradition and intimate privacy. She had made coming home an entry into another, better world, gorgeously peaceful. Sentiment aside, though, he was an old rogue puma. Home is the hunter, home from the hill—except not him. This hunter only came home on leave, assuming he was close enough to manage it.

He missed her now, as he followed the nurse up the corridor. He watched the dark hair, the fluorescent overhead lights glowing on the olive skin, the smooth surge of her private body, and imagined her private ways.

Then they were at the entrance to an intensive-care unit. The doors opened onto a forest of equipment, patients enveloped in technology, nurses in their greens, a group of doctors conferring quietly at the foot of a bed. Again, he was reminded of other hospitals, where he was sometimes the only person present with even rudimentary medical knowledge, sitting with men of courage who were dying in squalor, able to offer them nothing more than a hand. The edges of the world may seem tattered and ugly and corrupt, but there are heroes there.

"She's in and out," Nurse Martinez said. "Rodrigo is conscious now."

"Has the FBI been here?"

"Just the border patrol, to take them back if they survive."

"The parents?"

"No parents."

"But they know they're illegals?"

"Sure." The sudden clipped tone reflected the quiet fury of the Mexicans, their disdain for the whole process that was unfolding at the border, the way it reminded them of ancient defeats, and made them cling even more fiercely to the bitter certainty that being Mexican did not make you less.

She stopped before three shut green curtains, then drew one back.

And there he was, a shocking picture of childhood gone wrong, a little boy festooned with IVs, his vitals monitor indicating a temperature of 105, a blood pressure of 171 over 107, and an oxygen exchange number that Jim knew was ominously low.

A drain, black with blood, led from the boy's mouth. Mouth bleeding: 300 REMs exposure. Probably fatal in a healthy adult. This scrawny boy was already dead.

"Can he speak?"

"If he will."

"Hello, my son," Jim said in Spanish, causing Nurse Martinez to glance at him. "Will you tell me where you sat in the truck?"

They had been brought across Bridge 1 right here in Eagle Pass, Jim felt sure of it. He would not ask the boy direct questions, though. Jim had done too many interrogations to try that. Only the stupid were direct. Only the stupid were violent. He prided himself on being able to extract information without the subject realizing that he was being interrogated.

The boy's eyes met Jim's. Mahogany, sad as a dying animal's, waiting blankly. His throat worked, his mouth opened, and the interior was red, as if filled with tomato soup. "It was in the front."

"Do you mean with the driver?"

He shook his head.

So they'd been in the body of the truck, pushed up against the front wall. "And what was there with you? A box, perhaps?"

Rodrigo shook his head. His skin, mottled from burst capillaries, looked like colored tissue paper, as fragile as if it could be ripped by the friction of a thumb. There was internal hemorrhaging as well, Jim thought, and soon that blood pressure would start crashing, and that would be the end of this poor damn kid. The eyes settled on Jim's face, and he knew the look, defiant: *I haven't told you everything.*

"No box, then, Rodrigo. But there was something there." Sick fear swayed Jim. There was a question now, to which the answer, at all costs, must not be "yes." "Rodrigo, was the thing round, and it had lots of wires?"

Rodrigo's mouth opened. There was a deep sound, gagging, bubbling, as if his guts were boiling. Consciousness ebbed.

"Can we bring him back?"

"You're not a doctor."

"Can we bring him back?"

"What's this about? Who are you?"

"Nurse, I have to get him to answer my question. Reduce his morphine drip."

"I can't touch that drip!"

Jim reached up and turned it off.

"How dare you!"

Jim stood to his full height, causing him to loom over her. "This is a national security matter. You will cooperate."

"I—"

Rodrigo groaned. Jim went back down to him, laid his hand on the poor little guy's sweating brow. "What did it look like?"

"Black," the boy said. "We sat on it."

"Round? Black and round?"

Rodrigo frowned a little.

"Was it a box, Rodrigo?"

He nodded—and Jim knew, suddenly, what had been done. These children—in fact, everybody in that truck—had been used as a human shield. The bodies were there to confuse the mass detector and, hopefully, absorb enough radiation to get past the particle monitor.

But that wouldn't work. It might help, but the instruments were too sensitive. And, in any case, why in the world hadn't Customs and Border stopped a truck obviously loaded with illegals?

Jim wanted to scoop this little guy up into his arms and take him away, but he had no key to heaven. He had no kids, but he hoped that he would, one day, and if so, they would be cherished with this man's whole soul, to make up for the horrors he had seen across the shuddering mass of the third world.

"Where were these children found?"

"On Main, a couple of blocks from the bridge. The police brought them in."

In an adult, radiation exposure at this level would cause immediate fatigue and nausea, followed by a few days of recovery, the so-called walking-dead phase. Rapid and irreversible decline would then commence.

"Has there been a dosage evaluation?"

"We're estimating three to four hundred REMs for the older children, a bit less for the little one."

He'd get a satellite lookdown of the area from the National-Geospatial Intelligence Agency. From Nabila's brother, Rashid, who worked in their reconnaissance unit. If he was lucky, Rashid might actually find a picture of the truck. With the computers they had available, whether or not a truck had stopped in the street near where the children had been found could be determined in an hour or less. If they were lucky, they'd get the make, the year, conceivably the license plate and a visual of whoever had taken the kids out and laid them on the sidewalk.

Interesting to see if Nabila and Rashid were on speaking terms again. Rashid had been against the marriage, called it an abomination. He'd been right, but for the wrong reasons. He and Nabby were among a tiny handful of Muslims in the intelligence community, and they were there only because of political pull. At a time when you could not understand the enemy without at least understanding Arabic, American's clandestine services had locked arms to keep Arabic speakers out. In Jim's opinion, that made Nabby and Rashid crucial personnel—but they were nevertheless treated with suspicion, and their activities were carefully watched.

Silently, Nurse Martinez closed the curtain around Rodrigo's bed. "I won't be able to rouse him. It's not a coma, but the sleep is profound."

It would, Jim knew, turn into death, and he thought that could happen at any time. But the boy had done all that was needed of him. He had informed Jim that he had crossed the Rio Grande in a truck with a plutonium bomb for a companion. So the burning question now became, how could that happen? Who in the world could miss a thing like that? Even if the detectors failed, they searched all vehicles, especially trucks.

Then the nurse opened the curtain around the little girl's bed, and Jim did not understand what he was seeing, not at first. Then he realized that she was under a tent of lead.

"She's emitting," the nurse said.

He contained his shock. There was only one way the girl could be that radioactive, and the knowledge of what that was drew a coldness into his belly. She had been made to carry unshielded plutonium or plutonium dioxide on her person, in her rectum, her vagina, her stomach. Poor damn little thing! The stuff was so heavy, she couldn't have carried much.

"These kids were the only victims found?"

"Yes."

"No other cases of radiation sickness in the area? At all?"

"I don't think so."

"I'll need to know the exact spot on Main where they were found."

"Of course." She drew him a little map.

He left the hospital, trying not to run. The moment he got to his car, he threw open the trunk and unlocked the silver case that held his detection equipment. His standing orders required him to contact the FBI Weapons of Mass Destruction Directorate in the event he became aware of the presence of a nuclear weapon inside the United States. He wasn't actually sure of this, though. The situation was highly suspicious, to say the least, but he needed harder evidence if he was going to get a massive interdiction response.

Among his tools were brushes and a vacuum to gather dust, cameras, an ultrasensitive GPS device, a Geiger counter, and a device that could detect the kind of high-explosive materials likely to be used in nuclear detonators.

He put the Geiger counter on the front seat beside him, and headed for the address the nurse had given him.

A nuclear bomb could be loose in the United States. If it was, it would be on its way to its target right now and they would be wasting no time. Certainly anybody capable of injecting a plutonium nuke across the U.S. border understood U.S. detection systems well enough to know that it was going to be found, and soon.

So they would be moving as fast as possible. If he was lucky, there were maybe a few days until the thing was detonated. But for all he knew, it could be in the air right now, approaching Los Angeles or Denver or some other vast concentration of innocent Americans.

He left the parking lot, forcing himself to drive as carefully as possible, forcing himself to continue to think clearly and calmly.

The thing was out there. Oh yes. He just needed to lock down a little more evidence to make sure the whole system took notice, and this was treated like the emergency that it was.

3

RESSMAN AIR SERVICE

Todd Ressman was beginning to think his business might actually work. Last year, he'd cleared a little money, and so far this year, every month had seen positive cash flow. It had been a long haul, very long, since he'd been laid off during the death of Eastern Airlines in 1991. But what's nearly twenty years in a guy's life?

He'd done charter work, off-the-books work, piloted for discounters, worked in Africa and Asia . . . and in the end gotten together enough cash for a down payment on his cargo-modified Piper Cheyenne. He'd put down sixty grand, all of his savings. He wasn't going to move people, not after all his years in the damn airlines. Cargo didn't complain, and had few other alternatives. If you were going to get something moved out of Colorado Springs fast, he was the go-to guy, and tonight he was taking a machine tool and a crate of frozen chickens to the Pahrump Valley Airport in Nevada. He was slotted for flight level 18, and at economical cruising speed he expected to land just after midnight.

The flight would cost him $3,118.23 and would generate revenue of $5,004.19. If he got something in Pahrump, the run would be even better. What he might get there he couldn't imagine, however. The town's chief industry was sod, followed by prostitution and gambling. And speaking of chicken, the Chicken Ranch airport was one of the drop-ins, for God's sake, but not for a cargo operator, obviously. Nevertheless, he'd learned in the years he'd been running his service that the worst thing you could do was anticipate. His business ran on the unexpected.

The tool he had, for example, looked like some kind of disassembled drill press. It was heavy, but not heavy enough to take up all of his poundage. The chickens in their sealed crate had been a late addition.

Who would spend all this money to move a drill press, or, more fantastically, chickens that couldn't be worth but a few hundred dollars?

He knew the answer, which was always the same: folks had their reasons.

He'd take off in a few minutes, into what promised to be a gorgeous night. This was why he did it, why at fifty-eight years of age he was still going up every day of his life. He never got used to it, never tired of it. Back on Eastern, he'd flown sixes, then sevens, then twenty-sevens. He'd seen Eastern in its glory days and in its Lorenzo days. The death of that airline had not been pretty, nossir. Frank Lorenzo had destroyed it surgically, pulling off one valuable part after another, until there was nothing left but a lot of wretched old planes and men and women who would not quit until the thing was simply liquidated, which was what had happened.

Well, that was groundside stuff. Todd wasn't really interested. What he wanted in his life was his two PT6A-28s roaring on the wings of his lovely, quick airframe, his glowing instruments before him and the stars in the sky.

He got aboard and checked his stow, making certain that all the tie-downs were secure. Thirty years in the air had taught him that the sky had a lot of ways to hurt you and the best method of dealing with that was to respect the fact that airplanes that usually wanted to fly sometimes decided not to do that anymore.

He could have been flying with another pilot, but why spend the money? Generally, he rented ground crew by the hour. He was based out of Colorado Springs but really would take anything anywhere in the United States, Canada, and, less willingly, Mexico. He spent two or three weeks flying, usually, then went back to C.S. and his house and Jennie, whom he had met on the old LaGuardia–Pittsburgh run pushing twenty-eight years ago.

He looked over his manifest. The drill press was from Goward Machines, destined for some outfit called Mottram Repair. They must need it bad, to move it like this. As for the chickens, they were going from Blaylock Packers to an individual, Thomas Gorling. Todd could figure out most of his cargoes, but this one had him stumped. He had it back against the bulkhead, well secured. You always had to ask yourself, what happens if this airplane turns upside down? Given a small plane and a big, violent sky, that could happen. Had happened. In fact, in his years in the air just about every damn thing had happened. He'd experienced fires, crazy passengers, every known malfunction you could imagine. Usually, the Cheyenne was a pretty tolerable traveler, but she could get obstreperous when she was running heavy and there were crosswinds about.

He went into the Fixed Base Operation. A couple of other pilots were hanging around, guys waiting for their jetsetters to get poured out of their limos. He could have made steady money flying bigs, but he wanted to be his own man and no way could he afford a jet. It was a struggle to make the payments he did have. But it was his plane. His life. He went when he was ready to go. Or not.

Nobody said anything when he came in. Why should they? They knew what he was, a guy on the bottom rung, fingernails dug into his airplane, scratching through the sky on fumes and maxed-out credit cards.

He checked his flight plan, then went into the hangar. He was looking for something, he supposed. Not really thinking about it directly. Just looking.

There were a couple of mechanics there. "Hey," he said. "I'm the guy moving the chickens."

They were heads into a Citation that looked like it had a hydraulic leak in the left-wing leading-edge controls. That would've made for some complicated landings, for sure.

"Yeah," one of them finally responded.

Todd didn't want to crack the cargo, but the truth be told, it was bothering him. He'd four-one-oned Pahrump and hadn't located anybody called Gorling. Of course, maybe he was staying at one of the whorehouses or a motel, who the hell knew?

But chickens? Come on, the guy was paying close to a thousand bucks, here.

"Who brought them in?"

"Christ. Lemme think. Coulda been—yeah, a fridge truck."

"Mexican fellas?'

"White men, all."

He went back inside, spoke to the FBO operator, a girl of about thirty, dark and tired looking, with a name tag that said: "Lucy." "I need a phone number for this chicken guy," he said. "Lemme see the manifest."

No phone number for the receiving party. So what was supposed to happen? He just dumped the crate in Pahrump and good-bye, Charlie? He'd been paid; that wasn't the problem. But he liked things to work right. There were no tracking numbers in this business, and there wasn't one damn thing about Mr. Gorling on this manifest.

"The hell with it," Todd said.

"Isn't there a Chicken Ranch in Pahrump?" Lucy asked.

"Funny girl."

"Chickens are a funny cargo for you guys. I could understand caviar or wine, but not chickens."

"Unless it's not chickens."

There was a silence, then. The two pilots lounging in the ready room both perked up. Everybody knew the rules. You had to report suspicious cargo. But was it suspicious? Todd had five hundred dollars of his profit riding on the poultry, so he didn't want a bunch of FBI crew cuts out here fisting the cavities. On the other hand, he was damned if he was going to move illegal drugs. Legal ones he carried all the time. One of his main money cargoes, matter of fact.

"So maybe I gotta crack the chickens, seeing as it's not a good manifest."

"You try Information?"

"I did indeed. No cigar."

She hit an intercom button on her desk. "Marty, Julio? Captain Freighter needs to crack his chickens."

He could hear her words echoing in the hangar, could hear, also, the snickers of the jet pilots.

He went back out on the apron, looked sadly at his beautifully loaded baby. She was all ready to go, looking like she was born for the sky.

The two mechanics came across from the hangar, moving slow. Who wanted to manhandle cargo? Not their jobs.

"Sorry about this, guys," he said. "I got a sour manifest."

Then Lucy came out. She had a weather fax in her hand. "I got a line moving in," she said. He looked northward and saw it, the flickering of lightning just below the horizon. Ahead of it would be winds, strong ones. He knew his front-range flying. He had about twenty minutes to get in the air and get out of here, or he wasn't going upstairs for hours.

"Well, fellas," he said, "looks like you're gonna get to earn your money another way." He took the FBO's copy of the manifest. "Oops," he said, jotting down a phone number beside Mr. Gorling's name. "Bastard gave us a dud contact number. How were we to know?"

He got in his plane and pulled the door closed.

Ten minutes later he was rotating. Ahead, as he rose, he saw the squall line racing down the range, alive with lightning.

He banked west, and flew off into the stars.

A thousand feet below him a man watched Todd's plane rising into the sky. The man had been trained, and carefully, to recognize the silhouette of the Cheyenne. He got into his car and drew his cell phone from his pocket.

For some moments, he studied his watch. Then he made a call. "Mother," he said, in his soft, calm voice, the voice of the dutiful son, "I am nearly home."

4

THE BRASADA

Jim had quickly found the spot where the kids had been dropped, but then he'd lost the trail. They had been radioactive because they were near something radioactive, but it wasn't leaking particles, and frankly, that made it look more and more like an X-ray isotope. It could have been that illegals had been concealed behind a shipment of perfectly legal isotopes and the children, with their small bodies, had been sickened by the radiation and tossed off the truck to die.

However, he had been to all local public transportation hubs, which consisted exclusively of bus stops. There was an airport but no regular flights. Conceivably, the bomb could have been shipped as air cargo, but he had found a faint radiation signature at the Kerrville Bus Company station on Jefferson, in the cargo-holding area. The bus company had no record of any isotopes or X-ray equipment being moved, so he had logged this as evidence to be followed up.

He couldn't personally track down every bus that had left the station in the past two weeks. It could be done by the FBI, but it was a dangerously slow way of working, no matter how efficient they might be. What they would most need to know was exactly when the device had arrived at the bus depot. That would narrow the search to just a few busses, and enable them to catch up with the bomb . . . if there was a bomb.

To find this out, he needed to investigate the two bridges that crossed the Rio Grande in Eagle Pass. If X-ray isotopes had been brought in, they would have been logged. Both bridges had advanced spectroscopic portal radiation monitors, ASPs, installed on them. This was state-of-the-art equipment, and after some false starts in the early going the system was testing to a high degree of reliability. In any case, if the plutonium was not detectable because of shielding, the presence of an unusual mass such as a lead container in any crossing vehicle would have triggered an immediate alert and a search of the vehicle.

He hoped that his visit to the bridges wouldn't make the Customs and Border boys uneasy, wondering who the hell he was and tripping him up every way they could. You think ordinary people don't like bureaucrats. Bureaucrats *really* don't like bureaucrats. As he drove, he opened his briefcase and fished out another set of creds, one of the many that he had developed for work along the Texas-Mexico border. Strictly speaking, identifying himself to a federal officer with a false credential was illegal, but his ambiguous status enabled him to get away with a lot. Annoying, but also useful at a moment like this.

He turned into the station parking area, which was full. He pulled up behind a couple of dusty official Blazers and cut his engine.

"Excuse me, no parking; you'll have to get that vehicle in motion."

Jim showed him his Customs and Border inspector credential. "What's your name, Officer?"

The guy looked over the cred. Then he looked up at Jim. The eyes of this very large young man were nasty little pins, full of hostile suspicion. "Arthur Kenneally," he said at last.

Kenneally was maybe twenty-two, spit and polish all the way, although heavy. And sad, Jim thought, and wondered if that meant something. "I need to take a quick look at your ASP," he said.

Arthur stared at him.

"You have an advanced spectroscopic portal radiation monitor on this bridge. An ASP. I need to check it out."

"There's no ASP on this bridge."

Jim was practiced at concealing surprise, but not this time, and he hoped that the flush he felt surging up his neck would not be visible in the parking-lot lights. "Are you sure?" It was all he could think to ask.

"I work here."

"What about the Camino Bridge?"

"Mister, there's nothin' like that on either bridge."

"Are they out for maintenance?"

"Look, there are no ASPs here. None whatsoever. Do you get that? The number is zero. And you're double-parked, Sir. If we need to go hunting, we gotta scramble these vehicles."

Jim watched him. Why was he so defensive?

"Sir?"

"That's okay, Kenneally. I'm moving out." A tingling crept through his body, his muscles tensed. He returned to his car, backed out, turned around, and drove into town. It was hard to stay on the road, hard even to think clearly. He recognized that he was panicking. But he had a major problem here, no question.

Homeland Security had placed ASPs on every bridge that crossed the Rio Grande. They had been problematic at first, but as improved devices became available, the bridges had been high priority. He'd been shown the deployment records by Cynthia Spears. But the records were wrong, which meant only one thing—at some level, there had been sabotage. Either the devices had never actually been deployed or they had been removed.

Was it local? Did that account for Officer Kenneally's manner—he knew that the monitors had been ditched, and therefore was part of some sort of illegal group, probably accepting bribes to allow trucks to pass without proper search? Or was the problem farther up the line, in Dallas, where the deployment of the ASPs had been managed, or even in Washington, where the whole national program was directed?

This felt an awful lot like what had happened in southern Russia, when Jim discovered that facilities listed as secured by the National Nuclear Security Administration were, in fact, not secure at all. And then—because of what was going on with Brewster Jennings and possibly the NNSA itself—his reports would sink into the system and die.

This had to be reported, of course, and maybe with the same lack of effect, but his mission wasn't to fix the problem on the bridge or even investigate it. It was his job to find what had already been brought in, and he needed to remain focused on that, because lack of information about when the truck had crossed was going to be a serious challenge.

The mere fact that this had been done to these bridges increased his conviction that this was not about X-ray isotopes.

Time was the enemy now, and he drove harder even than he had coming down. He would return not to Dallas but to San Antonio, where he would engage the FBI as fully as he could manage. He didn't have proof, but he certainly had evidence enough to justify an investigation of what was going on at those crossings and an extensive search for any possible nuclear devices that may have been allowed into the country.

In addition to the FBI's Weapons of Mass Destruction Directorate, the National Nuclear Security Administration's Office of Emergency Operations needed to be informed, and OEO needed to deploy all thirty-six of their teams to this region, armed with all possible radiation-detection and explosive-suppression equipment. The two FBI teams that specialized in disabling firing systems would need to be put on full alert. The staff at G-Tunnel, the five-thousand-foot-deep shaft where the device might need to be detonated, had to be warned that they were liable to receive a hot nuke within hours.

He was out on the highway now, driving into the dark, heading for San Antonio as fast as he could go, and it was here that the car took the first blow.

For an instant it shot forward; then there was another crash from behind as he instinctively hit the brakes. Struggling for control, he gripped the wheel. What was this, a shredded tire? A glance in the rearview mirror revealed only blackness.

A third crash knocked his head forward and back, and he understood that this was not about the tires. Somebody was ramming him from behind.

He switched on his high beams and accelerated, drawing away from the other vehicle, feeling his heart match the drumming of the engine.

So it was Customs and Borders, had to be. That bastard hadn't been a pissed-off bureaucrat, he'd been a scared-shitless crook. That would be a Customs and Border Protection truck back there, most likely, with Kenneally in it.

He smashed the accelerator to the floor, drawing farther away from his pursuer.

Long experience told him not to think more about who was back there. Speculations like that only slowed you down.

Given the fact that he might not get out of this, he needed to report at once. He flipped open his cell phone—and froze, horrified, when he saw that there were no signal bars.

His pursuers had known to wait for the dead spot, of course.

He had to get this report moving!

Wham! This time the car swerved, went up on two wheels, and almost left the road. As he fought the steering, something in the rear began clattering. Flashes in the mirror told him that his bumper was dragging, making sparks. Another blow might split the gas tank, and then this little game would be over.

His mouth was dry now, his palms sweating enough to add to the danger of losing control.

Wham!

The car shuddered; he felt the wheels slewing, regained control, but barely. No smell of gas, and—at least at the moment—no flames.

Then the rear window flew to pieces, spraying him with tiny bullets of glass. The flashes that accompanied it told him that he was being fired on with an automatic weapon.

Back to the drawing boards on the identity of his pursuers, because he'd seen that particular spray of light before, and that was a Kalashnikov, not exactly the kind of weapon used by Customs and Borders. There were incidents of ranchers reporting men with these weapons moving up the coyote trails, but they were drug runners, not U.S. officers.

He felt that coldness along the neck that comes with being profoundly exposed to a gun. Too familiar.

It chattered again, its rasp now clearer and closer.

He took the only choice left to him, and veered off the road into what Texans called the *brasada,* the brush country. Behind him, he heard the squeal of tires, then the roar of the truck's engine as the driver geared down to go off-road. Jim could feel his car wallowing in the soft soil.

The Kalashnikov rattled again—and suddenly there was light behind him, a lot of light, flickering. They'd gotten his tank and he was on fire. Now he had only the gas left in the line, maybe a couple of miles, maybe less, and if that fire ran up the line, he would need to get out of here fast.

As he continued on, he began to hear the fire, a sound like a fluttering flag, and smell it, too, the sweetness of burning gas, the nasty sharpness of the carpet in the trunk.

He had to keep maneuvering to avoid contorted mesquite trees and that was slowing him down and he thought that there was a significant risk of an explosion, so he opened the door and rolled out of the car and kept rolling, and the truck passed him at a distance of six inches.

He scrambled to his feet and blundered off into the tangle of thorny mesquite branches, cacti, and, he had no doubt, snakes. Both his training and experience made it clear that he was in an endgame situation. His pursuers were heavily armed. Already they were off the truck and he could hear them moving in the brush, speaking quick, quiet Spanish: "Over there, Raul. Three meters, that's it. Forward."

He had the uneasy thought that these were military personnel. Mexico was a complex society, the evolution of half a millennium of exquisite corruption. Certainly the military could be involved in something like this. That would be an important route of investigation, assuming that he survived.

But he had to survive—*had to.* If they broke this one little link in the chain, the bomb would be free and clear. He cursed himself for hitting the road before making his emergency calls.

He smelled the sourness of new sweat, the sharp sweetness of old, some sort of liquor, and many cigarettes. There was a human being within feet of his position, and upwind of him. He could taste this man, and the fear that would make him an animal in an instant.

If the man had professional experience, Jim was about to be caught. He'd seen it many times, the way a pro would just know his adversary was there and fire into him, and the guy had better have good cover. This man, however, blundered past his quarry. But then he stopped. Took a step back. Now he was two feet to Jim's right, facing in this direction.

Jim listened to the man's breathing. It was soft, meaning a relatively light individual. Then there was a rustle, and the sound of the breath ended.

The man had turned away.

Jim did not like to use his killing skills, but this was a situation that demanded every resource at his disposal. In this incredible situation, millions of lives might depend on his life.

He didn't even have his pistol, because he had stashed it in the glove compartment to avoid any metal detectors in the hospital. It was still there.

He deserved to be put up on charges. And now, maybe, they would need to include murder.

He stood up and was behind the man in a step, and grasped his head between the flats of his hands, and did something that he had done just twice before in his life, and detested. He snapped the man's neck, using the hard sideways motion he'd practiced on dummies and used in Iran when a camp he had established to take readings near an underground nuclear facility's venting system had been spotted by a couple of poor damn shepherds.

The body went instantly limp, but he wasn't dead yet, Jim knew. There was still air in the man's lungs that could possibly be used to make a sound. Jim had heard that sighing croak before. It wasn't a loud noise, but it would be audible in this silence.

As soon as Jim lowered him to the ground, he stepped on the man's back hard, pressing until he heard the air hiss out of his nose. He would smother now, as he slid into death, and Jim would add that last bubbling hiss to his own nightmares.

To his left, more breath. Another man, a larger one. Now to Jim's right, the rustle of a shoe pressing something dry.

And then the sun, so bright it seemed to roar, and he knew that he had been pinioned by a searchlight. "Now," a voice said in English with a Mexican accent, "now come."

For an instant, shock froze him—and not only the shock of being hit by the light but the fact that the voice had a Mexican accent. But no, he'd heard it on the bridge, all right. It was Kenneally. Scratch the accent. The kid was no actor.

Jim threw himself to the left, to the ground, then pushed himself with his feet. As he reversed course, the light wove about. He took off as fast as he could, because he knew that these seconds were his life.

The searchlight lost him, then came racing back. He dropped down; it passed him, returned . . . then went on.

He had been able to use its beam to see ahead, and now twisted and turned among the trees for a hundred feet, moving silently away while it sought him in other directions.

Abruptly he burst into clear land, felt the give of softness under his feet, saw the dark building more clearly now. His heart thundered; his breath roared.

There was a house, but he also knew that the three hundred open feet stretching before it could be where his career ended.

He sprinted ahead, pushing himself as hard as he could, hunched low, legs churning. But still it seemed slow, a kind of drifting dance, and from behind him there came the unmistakable, resounding crash of a .45 automatic.

Stumbling onto the porch, he shouted, "Federal officer; I need help!"

5

THE DOGS OF NIGHT

The house was small, it was dark, and it was silent. Jim hammered on the door. "Federal officer!" He prepared to break it down.

Lights came on inside, then on poles in the pasture that surrounded the house. In those lights he saw figures. Simple uniforms, perhaps official Mexican, perhaps not. Frozen now, calculating the changed odds.

Then the voice of the man in the house, a gravelly shout: "Awright, boys, time to go on home. My dogs is hungry tonight."

The man connected to the voice then came onto the porch, and Jim recognized him. He'd been riding horseback down the highway near here as Jim had driven past. It was the same tattered, ropelike old man, unmistakable. With him came a pack of dogs as lean and ornery looking as their master.

At the far edge of the light, a gun chinked. The Kalashnikov had been reloaded, was now being cocked.

"Watch out."

"Boys—*take 'em*!"

A dozen snarling, eager dogs swarmed off into the dark. The Kalashnikov chattered wildly, the flashes arcing in a crazy motion. Then there was a shattering blast beside Jim's head and he thought he'd been hit—but a fountain of sparks spewed away into the night. What had happened was that the old man had fired a shotgun, a big one. Then again, *whoom*!

The old man turned to him, gave him the meanest, most toothless, most dangerous-looking grin he'd seen since Afghanistan. "Jus' tryin' to warn 'em off 'fore they get et."

From off in the dark came the barking of the dogs, faint screams, growling, then louder screams that grew quickly frantic.

"Well, they gettin' et," the old man said. "Them dogs is gonna go blood on me, Vas-kez don't stop his invadin'." He dropped down into an ancient steel lawn chair that guarded the porch. "Gawddamn ticker, it gets goin', it don't stop. Gonna be the death'a me, of course. Now, what we got here?"

"I'm a federal officer—"

"Oh, how surprising. I'd never have thought that of a feller in a Sunday go-to-meetin' suit, getting chased through the damn *brasada* in the middle of the night."

"Who is Vasquez?"

"Emilio Vas-kez, local border control officer, Mex side. Moves flesh. He works closely with our border boys. Money changes hands."

"Where can I find this man?"

"In his office in Piedras Negras, be my guess. Me, I never cross. Be a one-way trip."

Piedras Negras, the Place of Black Stones, the Mexican city across the Rio Grande from Eagle Pass.

"You say that Customs and Borders know Mr. Vasquez?"

The old guy gave Jim a look that was a lot more careful than he had expected to see. "Now, you listen up, Mr. Federal Officer. This is Texas, here. It's another country, see. You got your border cops and whatnot, but that's only in the towns. Out here, there's another law, old-time Texas law." He rose from the chair, cupped his hands over his mouth, and called, "Boy-eees! C'mon, you devils! *Boy-eeees!*" Then he looked at Jim, eyes twinkling. "Won't need to feed 'em for a week, best guess." He stared off into the dark. "Might be one or two of those fellers still out there though. They must want you bad, Federal Officer."

"Let's go inside," Jim said. "I need to make a call."

As they entered the dark house, the old man turned on a floor lamp.

"Kill that!"

"Vas-kez ain't gonna come up here, not when the dogs're out."

"For my sake." He picked up the phone—and got silence. "Does this need to be turned on?"

"It's a phone." The old man took it, listened. Cursing under his breath, he returned to the porch. "Vas-kez, you damn cur, you cut my line again! I'm comin' over there, fella, and I'm goin' huntin! I know where you live, goddamn you!"

The dogs returned, quick shapes speeding under the thin light from the light poles. Jim stood in the shadows alongside the house, holding his cell phone at arm's length. Still no signal. He closed the phone. The dogs, he noticed, looked more like hyenas. "What are those, anyway?"

"Dingoes," the old man said, "smarties. I feed cattle, and these dogs are my caballeros. A man and twelve of these fellas can handle a herd of three hundred head very easily."

Kenneally had been working with what looked like the Mexican military. But it could be anybody, even other Customs and Borders officers in disguise, who knew? The kid was in it, though, in deep, and somebody was going to want to talk to him, for sure. Not Jim, though. All Jim wanted was to track down the bomb, if there was one.

"I need to get back to my office," he said. "I'll pay you to drive me, or I'll buy your vehicle."

"Where's your office?"

Was it dangerous to reveal that information? He wished he knew more about what he was dealing with. What if they came up out of the brush later and worked this man over? What might he reveal when his eyeballs were being washed with acid? "El Paso," Jim lied.

The old man was silent so long that Jim thought he hadn't heard. "Problem is," he finally said, "if I sell you the truck for what it's worth, which is about fifteen dollars, how am I gonna get another truck? And I can't go to El Paso; I got three hundred head on feed; they need papa."

Legally, Jim could not commandeer the truck. "How much do you need, then?"

"Ten thousand is gonna do me a decent replacement."

He couldn't write the man a personal check for that amount, because the expenditure wouldn't get approved and money transferred to his account before the check bounced. "Mister, I want to appeal to your patriotism."

"I am sorry to tell you, but I am faithful to an America that has been gone so long you never had the good fortune to know it. That makes me a real patriot, fella."

"I hear you and I understand and I agree."

"You only think you do, and that's the problem with all'a you people."

Jim had no choice. He would lie again. "Sir, I am going to commandeer the truck. I have the legal right to do this. I will leave you a receipt, and I will have it returned to you as soon as possible."

"Billions of dollars thrown down the drain every day, and all you can do is steal one old man's old truck. You oughtta be ashamed, Federal Officer. Course you're not, 'cause you're the same as the rest of 'em, just somehow lost the thread of freedom. I shoulda let 'em pop you, see how my dogs do on white meat."

Jim respected this man's suspicion of government, but what could he do? "The vehicle will be returned by six o'clock tomorrow night, and you'll be compensated fairly." He held out his hand. "I am taking the keys."

That brought a moment between the two of them, not pleasant. Jim could see the old man considering what to do—shoot him, set his dogs on him, or give him the truck.

He waited for the decision. The old man took in a breath, let it out as a sigh. "There goes one perfectly good truck," he said, "Federal Officer."

As Jim went to the truck, he watched the dogs carefully. They were no longer in the slightest interested in the night out beyond the house pasture, but they were tracking him with their eyes. A snap of the old man's fingers and he'd be torn apart.

The truck was ancient, its radio torn out, its cab dusty with old feed. He felt rotten taking it, even for a day. Worse, he'd have to rely on what was going to be a very busy San Antonio FBI to return it.

He opened his wallet and counted out as much as he dared to go light, a hundred dollars. "I'm sorry I'm not good for more. But I might need my cash."

The old man took the money. "My tax refund?" he asked with bitter irony.

"Is there any way out of here that doesn't involve Fifty-seven?"

"Well, you can use my track over to Eighty-three, then head down to Crystal City, then over toward Big Wells on Eighty-five. That'll get you to the interstate."

He went as fast as he could, listening to the brush scrape the truck, glimpsing a snake rushing in its headlights. As he drove, he pulled the battery out of his cell phone. He didn't know exactly what sort of detection equipment his pursuers might possess, and he didn't intend to experiment.

The truck was gasping by the time he reached Highway 83, another empty strip disappearing into the dark. His situation was extremely serious. With so few roads in the area, he understood that he was still in extraordinary danger. He'd been in similar situations before, though, and he knew from experience that the keys were misdirection and speed.

But they knew the area; he didn't. So much for misdirection. And as far as speed was concerned, as he accelerated onto the highway he found that the old F-150 topped out at under fifty. He kept the lights off, navigating by the faint glow of the road between the dark masses of brush that choked both sides. When he needed to slow down, he downshifted to avoid flashing the brake lights.

The highway made a sharp curve, and he found himself in a small community called Carrizo Springs. As soon as he could, he left the main road, pulling into a closed gas station and around the side of the building. He sure as hell needed a weapon. Maybe the thing to do was roust out the local cops. There had to be a sheriff's station here, maybe even a local police force. He needed to get that report called in, and fast. He must not be the only person alive with this information.

There was a pay phone out near the station's air stop, but it was out of order, long since shut down. Beside it, though, there still hung a badly weathered phone book. He found an address for the Dimmit County constable's office and headed for it. The streets of the small community were empty at eleven, and when he found it the police station was closed. There was an emergency number, but that meant using the cell phone. Probably safe, probably it would work, but what if these things weren't true and they caught up with him and killed him? You didn't take a job like this unless you were willing to die for your duty, and he had no problem with that. But he did have a problem with not getting that information through.

The problem was easily solved, though. On his way here, he had seen a motel with a lit sign, and he returned there now.

He drove past the motel, then turned a corner and cut his lights. Nobody appeared, so he went back and pulled up in front. Inside the lobby, he could see an empty clerk's counter. Hopefully there'd be somebody back in there somewhere.

As he prepared to enter the dimly lit lobby, the great cities of the American West surged and crackled with the energy of life. Las Vegas, Los Angeles, San Francisco—they were all gigantic jewel boxes packed with innocent humanity. In Las Vegas the Strip glowed and hummed with late-night excitement, but in the little community of Pahrump a few miles away all was quiet. Ressman had landed, delivered his cargo, and flown on. The crate had now been in the cage at the Pahrump Valley Airport for two hours. It was all alone, just a large, black box with a bill of lading taped to it indicating that it contained frozen chickens. The airport was dark, and the road leading up to it was even darker, the silence absolute.

After a time, though, a truck appeared on that road. It moved so slowly and quietly that not even an armadillo scuffling along in the nearby brush was disturbed by its passing. In the truck were two young men, their faces vague in the faint light from the dashboard.

The truck parked for a time. There were flashlights, and careful shadows as the two men entered the cargo cage and brought out the box. A moment later the truck left, its gears grinding. The cargo cage was now empty, the moon low in the western sky. The armadillo crossed the road, snuffling busily for beetles.

The Las Vegas metro area is home to over 4 million people, Los Angeles to more than 13 million. Denver, San Francisco, and Phoenix also are not far from Pahrump.

Las Vegas was a glittering target, as was San Francisco. But 43 percent of all goods that enter the United States come in through the port of Los Angeles. Destroy it, and the United States of America is plunged into chaos.

6

VIRTUAL NATION

Nabila al-Rahbi found the new website so easily that it crossed her mind that it might have been pushed just to her. The enemy knew, perhaps, not exactly who she was but certainly that she was here. Her work was to find terrorist websites—real ones—and determine who ran them and who visited them and uncover the links from one person to the next across the web. Unlike National Security Agency units trolling for e-mails, text messages, and such, her work was much more focused and personal. She was one of a tiny number of people in the intelligence community who could read Arabic, Farsi, and the other essential languages of terrorism. Her security clearance, however, was so narrowly focused that she couldn't even enter most of the offices on her floor, let alone talk shop with anybody. She came to work, reported upchannel, and went home.

She looked at the new page, comparing the simple Arabic to the English translation that had been provided by whoever had created it: "This from the Mahdi: Women of the West, you must assume the *hijab* or there will be a serious consequence." The translation was accurate enough.

According to Shia tradition, also endorsed in this case by many Sufis, the Mahdi was the Muslim savior. Most Shia were "twelvers," who believed that the Twelfth Imam, who went into hiding in the year 940, was the Mahdi. He was expected to return at the end of time, to join with Jesus and unite the world in peace. Sunni, far more numerous than Shia, did not have any specific doctrine about the Mahdi, but the idea had appeal. So whoever might be claiming to be the Mahdi was not being stupid. He could expect the support of Shia, and would appeal to the hopes of all Muslims, including the Sunni.

She worked with the site a bit, but this was all it contained, just the words printed against a beige background. It demanded that every woman in the West, presumably, take the veil. Well, the hell with that. She was a Muslim woman herself and she wore the veil when she chose to wear the veil, and that was what was right. Some stupid idiot had posted this, but the world was full of them, wasn't it, Muslim and otherwise?

She considered herself devout but also an American patriot, loyal to the country where she had been born, proud to be spending her life fighting for the ideals it represented, and very much a part of American culture. There wasn't the slightest reason that a Muslim couldn't embrace the modern world and modern law. Those who said otherwise were, quite simply, heretics. In fact, as far as she was concerned, Salafism, the reform doctrine developed in the eighteenth century by Muhammad ibn Abd-al-Wahhab, had been distorted into heresy, and that failing had started with ibn Abd-al-Wahhab himself. There was nothing wrong with Tawid—the Salafi doctrine of the oneness of God—but much of the rest of the teaching was like the Book of Leviticus in the Jewish Bible. Leviticus had been written while the Jews were captive in Babylon, and was designed to give them special rules so that they wouldn't forget their identity. Ibn Abd-al-Wahhab had been the first to sense the lure of the West, and had created his reform movement to ensure that Muslims would not be absorbed into the new and seductive culture that was emerging in Europe. In her not-so-humble opinion.

When she jogged through the park with the wind in her flowing black hair, feeling her limbs naked, she was proud of her womanhood and her government for respecting it, and when she bent to prayer she was filled with the joy that she liked to believe drew so many to the Muslim faith. Allah was there, part of you, part of your heart. You had only to listen and let yourself be loved, and never mind the cruel heresies that were currently afflicting the faith like a nasty virus.

Stupid though the little site was, because of the threat it contained her standing orders required her to identify it by server and, if possible, owner and report it upchannel.

She did a quick WHOIS, knowing in advance that it would lead nowhere. Next, a traceroute went to a server in Russia, but there was a masking attempt, so she would look a little further. First she downloaded and saved the site, then continued her analysis. The real server was not in Russia, which was a plus. Soon, she found herself in the GÉANT2 topology. The server was in Finland. A university, she saw.

And then the website was down. They'd seen her looking at them, and pulled it. This was unusual. Generally, they left sites up longer, so that more than one intelligence and media group would find them. Whoever had put this up had not wanted to stay around for long. Taking no chances, then, which could mean that this actually mattered in some way.

She saved the traceroute, knowing that she would be questioned about it by people who knew essentially nothing about what she did or how she did it but thought they did because they had learned a few terms. They could not even begin to understand the ever-changing complexity of the Internet, certainly not its delicious symmetry and chaotic beauty, or the organic way that it grew.

With the site down, she entered the traceroute itself into Grabber, a program developed by In-Q-Tel that would do far more than any ordinary tracing effort. In moments, she knew that the hosting server was on the campus of the Finnish State University of Technology, an institution about 160 miles from Helsinki that offered degrees in technology and economics.

A few keystrokes got her to the identity of the server itself, and she found that it—not very surprisingly—supported an on-campus Internet cafe. The place was called Origo. There were a hundred workstations there. The site had been created on station 13 at 1406 local time yesterday. She went to Google Maps and was soon looking at the university. But where was Origo? Ah, in the library. Good enough.

She would search the student body and faculty against all databases, of course. She stared at her screen. If they were just kids fooling around, why had they taken it down the moment they saw her? She was herself spoofed to a server at Keele University in Staffordshire, so her hit would have appeared completely innocuous . . . unless somebody really good was watching. Could that Russian connection mean the FSB was involved? Russian intelligence had superb hackers, for sure.

So maybe this was a Russian attempt to see how good their American counterparts were, akin to Russian bombers approaching U.S. airspace.

That would explain why the site was simple but contained a clear threat. They'd want to watch her investigate.

She recognized, at this point, that she would probably never know, but then again, one learns early that intelligence work has little to do with complete sentences. Ellipses and question marks were in the nature of the product. There were no slam dunks, unfortunately, which was why people like directors brought in from outside the community so often made mistakes.

She pulled out of the Keene spoof and came back on from a Kinko's in Tallahassee, Florida. She reset Grabber and waited for results.

If she got anything substantial on anyone at the university, she would request that SUPO, the Finnish intelligence service, be informed of the website and asked for additional information about any possible persons of interest she might have turned up. If the CIA elected to act on its own, some operational type would probably drive up from the embassy in Helsinki, take a few pictures in Origo, then return with the inevitable "no result" report.

Nabila put the site together out of her download and looked again, seeking hidden codes. Was that why it was so simple? Was it actually a coded message, not intended to be found by her office, and had her snooping spooked them?

Her job was to assume that it was important. But even when she looked deep, it seemed entirely clean. Unless the message itself was the code.

What might "a serious consequence" mean? Could be anything. Probably had to do with women. Shoot the queen, maybe, or blow up some monument symbolic of women's freedom? Perhaps she should feed it to the Brits. They'd be all over any suggestion of danger to the queen. She was surrounded by clever depth, as it was called, not just muscle but really smart security management, like the president. Nabila supposed that was why the old lady had once woken up in Buckingham Palace to find an intruder sitting on her bed.

The site, if you could call it that, was just one page, very rudimentary.

Had it been created, perhaps, by a child? Maybe, but not an Arab child, who would have covered it with Saudi flags and jihadist rhetoric. Perhaps it had been made by some little Finnish boy playing at terrorist. Did any Finnish schools teach Arabic? God knew, not many American schools did. Nabila's comfort level with it was probably the only reason she even had a job in the intelligence community. She'd never believed that Daddy's pull would have been all that was needed. Some pull; he'd been little more than a glorified lobbyist.

She stared longer at her copy of the page. Beige background, a few words in the Verdana typeface, a few more in a Kufi-style Arabic typeface.

What was troubling her, she decided, was the directness of that threat. There were no quotations from the Quran, none of the usual justifications and other bunk that, as what she considered to be a sane and truly devout Muslim, she found so deeply offensive.

She considered carefully. First, the site was rudimentary, but whoever had created it had been sophisticated enough to spoof its server address, then to pull it down the moment Nabila got past the spoof. So this was the work of an individual or group with at least a moderate amount of sophistication. The second thing that contributed to her uneasiness was more serious. It was that no Arab would state a threat so bluntly unless he was absolutely certain of both his ability to carry it out and his intention to do so.

She had a lot of resources. Every day she gathered hits on the many false flag websites the CIA owned, looking for patterns of interest that might lead back to identifiable individuals who were just beginning to explore terrorism. And that was just a small part of her work. She knew all of the serious terror sites, of course, everything that could be known about them. She knew, also, that she was a target, certainly of the Base, Al Qaeda, and of the Iranians, probably also of the Saudi intelligence service, the Istakhbarat, and Mossad.

She did not rate a full security detail, but she was driven everywhere and watched, always.

She sat back in her chair and went through the cigarette motions, folding a stick of sugarless gum into her mouth instead.

When it came to Internet terror sites, nothing was as it seemed. Many an apparent terrorist website was anything but. Pretending to be a terrorist group could be very financially rewarding to con men, and very productive of useful intelligence to organizations like the CIA, Mossad, the FSB, and, as always, the Istakhbarat. Many sites were run by con artists who cared nothing about Islam. Others were Mossad and CIA false flag operations—fake terrorist groups, basically—which gleefully took contributions from the very same Saudis who collected American oil revenue.

She loved her work here. Fundamentalism was going to destroy Islam, which she regarded as an act of sacred communion between man and God. Truth to tell, although she loved being of Saudi extraction, she was soured by the fact that it put such a limit on her advancement. Would a Muslim woman, a daughter of Arabia, ever become anything more than what she was? A department head, for example? No.

Because of the concerns that would arise, she did not dare to go to the native country of her parents, and had not done so since she was taken there as a child. One day, she would do hajj, of course, but she kept putting it off. After the promotion.

She picked up the phone, spoke to her supervisor. "Marge, Nabila. I've got one that's bothering me a little. I'm shipping you the download now. The site itself was taken offline less than a minute after Referer dropped the link in my lap." Referer was a system of 'bots that ceaselessly searched the Web looking for new sites that fulfilled a broad range of criteria having to do with terrorism, including threats, money transfer, indications of personnel movement, and a myriad of other factors. It was an excellent system. Gone were the days when the CIA was a technological fool.

"Have you translated it?"

"It's bilingual, and the English is correct."

"I'm waiting."

"Sent from this end."

Marge Pearson had been in the Soviet Russia Division back in the Stone Age. With thirty years in the CIA, she had not the slightest intention of retiring, and praise Allah for that. She was a company legend, and Nabila counted herself extremely lucky to have such an influential and respected boss. A recommendation from Marge meant automatic advancement, and she was generous to her kids, Marge was. So, maybe even Nabby had a shot.

"I'm looking at it. I see; that's a very direct threat."

"That's what's bothering me."

"We'll move this one along."

Nabila could almost hear Marge thinking. She decided to help a little. "An Arab would not make a threat this direct unless he could carry it out, and intended to do so."

"This could cause a run on scarves."

"That'll be the day." She cherished the safety of the West. The idea of Šarī'ah being imposed here was too horrifying to contemplate. Šarī'ah was an ancient and imperfect system that had only one place in the world of modern jurisprudence: it should be considered suggestive where appropriate, advisory and nothing more. Western law was one of the greatest of all human inventions, and the more it spread the better the world would become. It was that simple. Šarī'ah was from a time before human rights were really understood, and therefore it should be considered a historical artifact, not a living system of laws.

"Nabila, I want this to go to the prelim, but I'll need more if it's going to make the final."

Nabila swallowed her surprise. Marge was referring to nothing less than the Presidential Daily Brief.

But this—how could this go so far so fast? Further up the ladder, maybe they knew something Nabila didn't. Even the mention of getting near the briefer excited her. Getting in the briefer—in her world, that was game, set, and match.

She thought for a moment. How could she advance this? "Let me take a look around," she said. "I'll see if I can get anything more."

She could put in a request to the National Geospatial-Intelligence Agency to do a backward lookdown for identifiables on the ground at the Finnish university, but that would be futile. Such requests had to be vetted on both sides of the fence. The CIA might not let it go out. The NGIA might not let it come in. In any case, it would take the request hours to move between stovepipes, if it ever did.

No, the only way to get anything done was to jump the fence—that is to say, call somebody over there directly. That meant dealing with her brother, which was not a pleasant thought. They shared the house, at this point, in silence. Still, she dialed his number.

Day by day, his disapproval of her was growing. She'd seen by the way he prayed, the extra hand movements, that he was becoming Salafi. At home, she wore the veil. Increasingly, though, he spoke of purdah. *Hijab* for him, okay. Draping herself in a damned shroud, no way.

The phone rang. She did not want to despise her brother, but she did despise the strictures on women—the rejection of half the human species—that had grown up in Islam over the years, spreading like some sort of soul cancer.

It rang again. Her heart began beating harder. It was almost sickening to ask him for help—but she loved him; she did. He was her little brother, who had clung to her in fear when they went to the seaside and he saw the waves.

The female members of Mohammed's family had never been in purdah. If Mohammed and Jesus were to return and see what had become of their faiths, she thought—no, knew—that they would be sickened.

Rashid picked up.

"Rashid," she said, "good afternoon."

"Hello," he answered, sounding as if he had forced the word out through a sphincter.

"Brother, I need a lookdown-backed-up twenty-four hours of all the physicals at a Finnish university. I need it, specifically, around a coffee bar called Origo, which is on the top floor of the library. You'll see the building on your map. Entries and exits."

People in intelligence knew not to ask why. But that was not what mattered. "Who wants this?"

"It's for the briefer," she said smoothly.

Now the silence became as sharp as a blade. But facts were facts: he was male but not as senior, largely because his language skills weren't as important in the technical post he held. So his advancement was even more constrained than hers. He did not report to somebody who could propose for the briefer. Rashid's work might end up there on occasion, but it would be background.

"I am looking at the location," he said. "I'll do a run now."

"I'll find comparables." She then went into the university's database, which proved to be a relatively easy process, and found three names that matched the CIA's internal watchlists. She e-mailed him the photos off their dossiers.

"One," he said.

She was so stunned she could hardly speak.

"Which?"

"The Indonesian."

"Thank you, Rashid."

"Your husband also telephoned."

"I thought he was in Afghanistan."

"Where he called from is not known to me. But I provided him, also."

"With related information? Why are you telling me?"

"Because he is your husband. I am telling you to let you know he is alive."

She could think of nothing more than to thank him and hang up. Jim was not her husband; Rashid had to face that. They had divorced in American law. But Jim had not divorced her in Šarī'ah, because, as he put it, "I'm not Muslim." Anyway, she didn't want it, either.

She looked at this Indonesian. He had entered the coffee bar six days ago, at three in the afternoon, local time. The site had gone up six minutes later. With only the single page, that would have been easy even for a complete amateur. Because it was so small, it had taken the 'bots all this time to find it. It had not been pushed to her, after all.

She telephoned Marge. "I have an Indonesian male, Wijaya, means 'victorious.' Patronymic is Setiawan. Thus, Sumatran. And matronymic Padang. Thus, also, a Minangkabau. This group is a center of Islamist reaction. He has been at university for two years. His police record is clean. Driving violation, wrong side of road, forgiven due to recent arrival. Bank account in order, no strange activity. He has traveled a lot. His results at the university in civil engineering are average."

"So, why is he on our list?"

"There is an access level on the file. You'll need to run it by Counterterrorism."

"Thank you, Nabila."

Nabila hung up. For a moment, she rested her head against the edge of the desk. This man was a known terrorist; she was certain of it. That would be what was behind the "no access" part of the file.

She had gone deep, and found gold . . . perhaps.

7

INSHALLA

On the day that the Americans found the message, the wind boomed in the long tunnels of the old base in Pamir, but down here in the long-abandoned command center the air was always still and cool, smelling of tobacco and people and the cook fires of the women.

Aziz had been designated the receptacle of the hidden Imam, the Mahdi, two years ago. Although Sunni, he had accepted the ancient title, and with it the belief that the Imam had actually entered his body and become him. The brotherhood of Inshalla intended that both Sunni and Shia would accept the Mahdi as savior. They were relying on the Arab love of legend to overcome the antipathy between the sects, and the idea that he had at last come out of his long ages of hiding by entering the body of a believer would inspire them.

Before this, Aziz had been a very Westernized Arab, had shaved himself and kept a closet full of fine English suits in his villa in Peshawar. All this he had given up to follow the law to the letter. The villa was behind him now, to be used only in case of emergency. He'd lived too many places to have a home anymore. The world was his home.

"Oko is up," his assistant said softly.

"Ah." He glanced up from the writing he was doing, a poem to commemorate the coming day, which would be first day of the new world.

October 10 had been chosen because it was the anniversary of the Battle of Tours, which had driven the Children of God from Europe and condemned the poor Europeans to live now for more than a thousand years in misery, separated from God.

Tomorrow, there would be a little moment of suffering among the worst sinners, but then Islam and happiness would come at last.

Emir Abdul Rahman al-Ghafiqi, chosen of God, blessed of name, had seen defeat on October 10, in the year 117 Hirja, the Christian year of 732. Charles Martel—the Hammer—had shattered the emir's faithful soldiers on that day, God have mercy on their souls.

So tomorrow, all these years later, came another October 10, and this time the victory would go to God.

Inshalla, God's Will, was the name of the organization that was doing this work, of which he was now, as Mahdi, the head. Before Al Qaeda, there had been Inshalla. Al Qaeda had been born out of rage, after the Saudi king brutally murdered people of faith who had entered the Grand Mosque. Their holy mission had been to correct the apostasy of the king's stooge of an imam.

Inshalla had been created in an apartment in Brooklyn in 1981, long before the present troubles had begun. It had been created not in reaction to a crime but out of the simple joy that comes from being close to God and the desire that this joy creates in the heart to bring it to others.

Even though Inshalla was a small group, for further security it was divided into cells of no more than four. Although it was unknown to most intelligence services, it was one of the most powerful entities on earth, behind only the Western nuclear powers, in terms of its weaponry. It also had two gigantic advantages over them, which Aziz believed would enable it to rule the world. First, it was invisible. Second, its nuclear weapons were already sited in their target countries and could be detonated quickly.

Even as the fires of Islam resurgent rose all over the world, Inshalla had remained hidden, doing its patient work. They moved small things—a bolt here, a casing there, a bit of radioactive material to another place. It was all in the good cause of freeing mankind to taste the joy of Šarī'ah and indulge in the sweetness of Islam.

Now all preparations were done. When it had been founded, Aziz had been twenty years old. Now, at forty, he had been named Mahdi, not because he was of the Ahul al-Bayt, the House of Mohammed, in blood, but because, he had been assured, he was of the house in piety. However, everyone knew perfectly well that this was not true. God forgive him, he was a worldly man. He wanted to believe that he had been chosen by Allah's mysterious hand, but Aziz thought there were other reasons. First, he was rich and could afford to keep everybody in this place supplied. Also, he was not important to the brotherhood. He was not a member of the council. In all truth, his death would be no loss. The title of Mahdi would then be passed to some other equally expendable man.

Eshan reminded him, "Oko is up." Eshan, faithful clerk, Inshalla's eyes and ears.

Aziz sighed. He was watched, always. He turned on the shortwave radio, tuned to the correct frequency, and listened to the numbers. Oko was a Russian number station broadcasting to the Kremlin's spies in China, Afghanistan, and Japan.

From Inshalla's contacts in Russia they had acquired the one-time letter pads necessary to decode the Oko ciphers. Because each cipher was used only once, breaking the code was essentially impossible. But the use of the system was difficult, especially because the same set of numbers meant different things on different pads, and the Russians were not aware that anybody was piggybacking messages onto their system.

The result of this was that decoded messages were often ambiguous and subject to interpretation. As he was the only person outside of the council who knew the whole structure of the plan, he was generally also the only one who could resolve these ambiguities.

As he worked, Eshan copied the numbers coming from the station, handing another tissue to him whenever he was ready for a new page.

A fly came and went, buzzing into his luncheon dish. He let it feast on his *palaw.*

Here in the Pamir Panhandle, the Russians had dug deep enough to defeat the American missiles of the day, and they had built to last. They had never expected that they would lose this base. How could they lose? They were the Soviet Union. The mujahideen were the mujahideen, ragged, reeking, and armed with little more than Chinese-made Kalashnikovs that would melt after a few rounds. Nobody with weapons you could bend across your knee was going to beat the Red Army. Unless, of course, they were also armed by the United States, which provided weapons that did not break, most certainly not. Terrible weapons, the Americans made. They were a clever people.

The Russian intention in Pamir had been to construct missile installations that could threaten China and, potentially, other Asian states and deepen Russia's relations with India by giving the Indians some tangible support . . . and also something to think about, should they become too interested in turning toward America.

There was space for fifty large missiles in the tunnels, as well as control facilities and personnel housing. Immediately after 9/11, Osama bin Laden had used them—to hide not from the Americans but from the far more dangerous Afghans, both the Taliban, who wanted more money to leave him alone than he could raise, and the Northern Alliance, who wanted to collect the American reward that was on his head.

Aziz said to his clerk, "It is done," and Eshan withdrew. Aziz put the thin tissue of the one-time pad into his rice and ate it, then burned his thicker worksheet in the little brazier that kept his food warm.

He listened to the number station droning on, moving agents, he supposed, issuing requests for information, whatever else the nursemaids of spies did. His part of it had come today for four minutes between 1306 and 1310. Tomorrow, there would be a general call at 0600, which would tell him when later to listen for his messages.

Now tea was being served by the Persian boy who had been left here to be Aziz's student. The boy's father was a powerful Iranian politician, a man of the holiest aspirations. Aziz, in his new role as Mahdi, had said on first seeing the boy's deep, soft eyes and the glow of his smooth skin, "His name is Wasim, the handsome." And so it was.

This place was ten meters below the surface, under steel-reinforced concrete. There were no telephones allowed here, no radio transmitters of any kind. Al Qaeda had learned an almost fatal lesson in the months after God's glorious gift on September 11, 2001, when it was discovered that even the briefest transmission would immediately be detected and tracked by the Americans. Lives had been squandered, because it had been so hard to believe that they could do this. But it was true: after a call or even a burst transmission on the radio, the cruise missiles would come, or the planes, the monstrous planes full of Crusader lackeys and carrying bombs that could dig deep and tear men to pieces.

But Inshalla had endured, and had never been identified. Al Qaeda had been forced into the backs of caves and mountain fastness. Eight out of ten of them had died. That many. But Inshalla had not been so much as scratched. Always, they had been able to continue the great work, assembling, gram by radioactive gram, the triumph of God.

Aziz had read the report of the Crusaders: "It is now believed with confidence that Al Qaeda has been reduced to a small headquarters and a few scattered sympathizers who have no contact with central command. This command unit is in North Africa, and is itself dispersed. The individuals involved, bin Laden and four associates, rarely meet, and move each night from one house to the next."

Only the Russians knew of the existence of Inshalla, and then only a bit, and not the true name. They were a mercenary people, the Russians, always willing to trade what they did not want for what they did not deserve. So they were willing to sell bits and pieces, no single one of which revealed the truth of what was actually being acquired. The plutonium had gone out from so many different places and in such small quantities that it looked like loss, not theft. The same with the parts.

Finally, the complex sequence that would lead, at last, to the imposition of true happiness across the world was in place. This small, invisible nation, this joyousness, this God's Will, like the United States, like Britain and India and Russia and Israel and the apostate country Pakistan, was an atomic power. It had the weapons, and it had the means of delivery.

This made Aziz, as Mahdi, a great world leader . . . and yet his existence, let alone his name, was known only to perhaps a hundred people.

Sometimes he had the urge to tell others who he was, that the most pious men on earth, the truest friends of God, had declared him Mahdi. But as he now was hidden by the cleverness of Allah himself, the temptation of the old Aziz to indulge in his braggart ways had always to be overcome.

Mohammed had said, "During the end of days, my beloveds will suffer great calamities and torment from their kings. Persecution will engulf them. The people of God will be tortured and suffer injustice. God will raise from my progeny a man who will establish his peace on earth and justice for the faithful."

This headquarters had both radio receivers and a reliable means of sending messages, if an old one. Aziz's messages out went by camel or mule, not by electronic means. Only idiots would use mules, the Crusaders would think, even in this place, where they had been used since before the time of Iskander. So their animals were laughed at. And as far as his men were concerned, what proud NATO officer would think a rag-head could accomplish anything, one of the stupid rag-heads who carried orders all the way from this place down to Peshawar, orders that were not written but woven into the hems of the *chapans* that the rag-heads wore on their foolish backs?

The Crusaders wore steel helmets and were encased in armor. These arrogant ones treasured life more than they treasured God. Their white faces were burned by the sun, their voices quick in the way of Western languages, chopping out their brute words.

Aziz spoke Arabic and Dari and Persian, all ancient languages full of history and nuance, languages of the deep mind. He and the men and women who were here read only the song of God, the Holy Quran. None of them ever ventured to the surface of the old installation. Nothing crossed there but dust, not by night or day.

The other benefactor of this place, the Persian Sayyad, whose son now served Aziz under his new name of Wasim, purchased their stores for them in a hundred villages in Khyber, in Malakand, in Kohat. From here came gourds, from there potatoes, from another place rutabagas. Water came from the wells within the fortress, dug by Russian engineers to provide for a force of a thousand men.

Only after the Crusaders came here in 2006 and mined the place and blew down the entrances with artillery shells had Inshalla ventured to occupy it. The Crusaders would not carry their own mines into the deep tunnels. Too dangerous for these precious sons of Europe and America. But rag-heads were another matter, so rag-heads had done the dangerous work. Rag-heads could lose their limbs or be killed. That was delightful to the Crusaders.

However, these workers, in the pay of the Crusaders but loyal only to Allah, had kept careful records. So each mine they had laid was now marked by a small fence, to keep the beloved of God from being injured.

Aziz preferred his tea sweet, and there was sugar enough for it today, for which he was glad.

He still indulged himself, but only a little—a bit of sugar here, some music there. He had no need to use the gadgets of the West, the GPS devices and iPods, the glittering cell phones, the CD players and televisions. None of them had need of these things. What they did need was the food of Islam, the food of prayer. They could live forever on prayer, he thought. They were that far from the material world. Although, of course, he did miss his iPod.

Now, though, he only listened to the radio station Burak Mardan, FM 104. And, at the moment, there was a song of Abu Shaar Thayir. Then came Hadiqua, singing of lost love.

"You enjoy Hadiqua," he said to the young Wasim, who lingered nearby, waiting to take away the tea things.

"I thought I was here as a student. But you are not a teacher."

"I am the Mahdi. Watch my life. My life is your teacher."

"You don't really know the Quran."

"I love the Quran."

"You teach me nothing."

"Do you fear me?"

"I fear only God, *the* God, the one God."

The Mahdi nodded. "See, you have been taught. That is a lesson important to learn." He would not ask of the boy whether he was Sunni or Shia? Aziz knew that Wasim was Sunni. This eternal war between the Sunni and the Shia was certain to become history in a few weeks.

Aziz did keep one Western bangle, a watch, and he glanced at it now. Just after eleven, the Duhur Salat. In the Pacific time zone, just after 2100. The time was not far, now. Not far.

He motioned to Wasim, who at once brought him pitcher and towel. He performed *wadu*. "O you who believe, when you rise for prayer, wash your faces and your hands up to the elbows and lightly rub your heads and your feet up to the ankles."

The boy also.

Then they turned to Mecca and performed the *salat* in the silence demanded of the noon prayer. How Aziz's heart filled with love now as he began Al-Fatiha: *In the name of God the merciful and compassionate, praise to God the Lord of the Universe, master of the day of judgment. Thee alone we so worship; thee alone we turn to for help.* And then he drew himself deep into his heart, for he was a leader of men, hiding here in the kind earth, and needed God's help always, could do nothing without it. *Show us the straight path,* he said in his mind, in his soul. *Show us the path of those whom you have guided to Islam, not the path of those who earn your anger or go astray.*

Over a thousand years since Charles the Hammer had led the children of Europe—God's beloved children also—astray, Aziz was going to bring them at last into Islam. Now they held drunken sway, protected by their tanks and their knights. They were eating the world, gobbling its gold and its oil and its precious water, spitting out bangles and baubles and sweets, and suffering meaningless desires and fornicating, then drowning it all in a soul-rotting slurry of alcohol and drugs. He'd had a blue Mercedes CLS in Peshawar, and the women who had come to him—what a life!

No, to be forgotten. He turned his mind back to the Crusaders. Filthy! Curse that CLS and the temptations it brought!

He felt something on his neck, and knew, then, that it was the boy's hand. Wasim had laid a kindly hand on Aziz's neck. He felt the light child's touch, and the heart of the child also.

Wasim held him, then looked at his face. Solemnly Wasim lifted a corner of his thin coat and wiped Aziz's cheeks, drying the tears that he had known would be there, that were always there after prayer.

Aziz smiled. "May Allah be with you, Wasim," he said.

The boy muttered something.

"What is it you say, Wasim?"

"That's not my name!"

The boy went away then, to the far side of the room. He worked a moment, then returned with a pomegranate sliced on a little tray.

Aziz took the food, and ate. "I have a message," he said. He had thought long on this message. It must be one of two randomly chosen words, "purple" or "green."

He would try now to find God in his mind. Would he see a horseman, a wandering beggar, an eagle rising in dawn light? There were many images of God in his mind, secret, impious things that had been there since he was a small boy and first praying and then wondering how this God who so dominated their lives must appear.

When he had said, "God is an eagle in dawn light," his father had given him a shaking. When he had asked his father, "Is God like a horseman on a fine mare?" his father had slapped him and said, "God would not ride a mare." He had asked his father later if God was like a beggar on the road, and his father had gone to the kitchen and returned to their schoolroom with a broom, and beaten his back with its long wooden handle.

He had not asked again what God looked like, but the images still danced in his mind when he prayed.

Then he saw God the eagle with his dark wings, God crying rage into the dawn.

"The word is 'purple,' boy. The English word 'purple.' Tell Eshan now."

Wasim hurried from the room.

Aziz felt the Mahdi within him, and the Mahdi's heart seemed to swell with joy. All would be well, now. Happiness was at hand.

8

ESCALATION

Jim Deutsch's world had ended. He'd been in plenty of trouble in his life, but not like this. No matter how bad it had gotten—running from one bunch of semi-official thugs into the arms of another, you name it—somebody had always had his back.

No more, not after the fantastic escalation that had taken place at the motel in Carrizo Springs. In that dingy room, his world had collapsed around him. The Brewster Jennings problem was one issue that he was aware of but was obviously not the end of the compromise of American counterprolif-eration. The system was deeply penetrated, and at high levels. It had to be.

What had happened had placed him in the worst position an agent could find himself. He dared not expose what he had discovered to the very system that was designed to support him in his work, because he would be revealing it to the enemy.

So he had continued on his own, and now an exhausted, scared man moved through the Colorado Springs Greyhound station listening to his Geiger counter tick over and trying desperately to guess where they would have taken the plutonium from here.

He needed the WMD interdiction infrastructure; he needed satellite look-downs and the support of CIA analysts; he needed the FBI's investigatory skills and powers; he needed the local and state police and the entire national enforcement and detection apparatus.

He'd assumed that the assassination attempt had been a local thing—Kenneally and his buddies trying to protect themselves.

This was why when an FBI arrest team had appeared at the door of Jim's room at the little motel he had known instantly that he was facing a far larger problem than he had imagined—than he could have imagined. Local guys on the take couldn't cut orders that would send the FBI after somebody. That would have to be done from above.

It had been eleven thirty at night when he'd entered the lobby of the little motel and called out, "Excuse me," in the gentled voice of a tired salesman. The clerk had appeared. Jim had shown his driver's license—*a* driver's license, not his own—paid his forty dollars in cash, and left the lobby. The whole transaction had taken under five minutes.

Always careful, always overdoing it, he'd parked the old truck some distance from his room and gone through the interior of the motel to reach it. He hadn't used the radio or the television, or even turned on the lights.

He had been in the process of making his emergency call when he had noticed a change in the pattern of light under his door. He'd looked at it. Only one possibility—somebody was out there. He'd thought it might be the clerk, suspicious of so late an arrival. Then Jim had seen the knob move. He'd gone into the bathroom but found it to be windowless. There was a double door that communicated with the next room down the line, and he'd used that. He had no bag with him, no luggage. But he did have some skill with locks.

The mechanism had clicked, but it had not disturbed the snoring, scrofulous drunk in the cigar-choked room Jim had entered. He'd stepped quickly to the exit door, cracked it, and seen a sight that had, quite simply, stunned him almost to paralysis.

There were FBI agents there, four of them, an arrest team.

As he had ducked back out of sight, they had broken down his door. They hadn't been wearing assault gear, just those inevitable business suits of theirs, muscle-packed worsteds, a cut below the sharkskins the Russian FSB cats wore.

He'd stepped into his neighbor's bathroom and stood there for half an hour. Aside from that first crack of the breaking door, there had not been another sound. Given the absence of luggage and the fact that Jim had been in the room no more than five minutes, he allowed himself to hope that they would conclude that they had been misdirected.

High-end tracking was the only way he could have been found. To gain access to the kind of satellite data needed to track somebody, you needed high clearances. You needed power.

The FBI team might have been following orders, just executing a warrant. But who could generate that warrant? Certainly not Arthur Kenneally. Jim had to assume that he was facing an organization of unknown dimensions that was embedded in the American enforcement and intelligence communities.

He'd faced it, he thought, in 2002, when he had first suspected that the U.S. system in the Middle East was compromised. It was big, powerful, and damned effective. It had not taken them long to get on his tail.

It was the most dangerous penetration of American security in the history of the country, and he couldn't even begin to think how extensive it was, or who was behind it, or where it went. He couldn't afford to worry about it, not now, not yet, not with work like this to do.

Arthur Kenneally's attack had made it clear that the bridges were a problem, but the appearance of the FBI at Jim's door told him that he was right about this bomb. It was real, it was here, and somebody very far up the ladder was protecting it, and God help the American people.

He had waited in what turned out to be the bathroom of a guest called Charles E. Madison, and fortunately the agents had made no effort to extend their search into Mr. Madison's room.

An hour later, Jim had taken Madison's driver's license and a couple of his credit cards, then opened the door and observed a clear hallway.

In the parking lot, Jim had spotted a stakeout car. So he was being advertised internally as a pretty big fish. He wondered what the FBI officers' arrest warrant said. Above all, where it had originated.

He had left the motel by a rear exit. Even though following a man on foot in a city by satellite was damn hard, he did not choose to underestimate the skills of his enemy again, and he walked under trees and along the very nicely turned-out local riverfront, keeping hidden from above as much as possible.

As there was no way for him to tell what was wrong, his professional responsibility was to assume that everything was wrong—which was not far from the truth, given that whoever was pulling the strings could control FBI arrest teams.

Experience had taught him that the only chance of survival under official pressure of any kind was to be very fast indeed, so he had stolen a car he'd found parked in a driveway and driven north on 83 until it hit Interstate 10. Then he'd headed west.

He was now thrust into a situation that was totally new to him. His information was crucial, but how could he communicate it when he no longer trusted the system? Obviously, orders no longer applied. Not only that, he feared that it was only a question of time before they found him again. His car had been almost the only vehicle on 83, and still virtually alone traveling into the dawn on I-10. Someone like Nabby's brother, Rashid, would make quick work of locating Jim.

He had one objective now: stop that bomb. He must take no risks except those that related directly to gaining control over the weapon.

He'd driven hard, ditched the car in Fort Stockton, and taken a bus to El Paso—from which he'd gone from stop to stop along the Greyhound route westward, finally picking up the trail of the bomb in Roswell, New Mexico, in the form of an increase in the clicking of a Geiger counter he'd bought from a hardware store that stocked mining supplies. From Roswell he'd followed it to Colorado Springs, and here the trail had stopped.

He decided that the only person he could now safely inform of his activities would be the president of the United States, but the president was far away and unreachable, hidden behind a wall of officials and guards. Jim's CIA creds—the real ones—might get him as far as the chief of staff, Thomas Logan. Might. But could he get past Logan, a lowly contract employee like him, working outside the chain of command?

He even wondered about the Office of the President. The Plame affair had led back to Lewis Libby, who was just one tier below Tom Logan's level. Jim knew little beyond the press reports, but he had to wonder, now, just how high up this thing went.

A lot of individuals and countries had motive to harm America's ability to track illicit nuclear materials abroad—arms dealers, smugglers, nations, and groups hoping to acquire nuclear weapons.

But this—it was way larger than any of that. The conclusion was hard to escape: somebody was trying to suppress interdiction of an actual bomb in this country, and, incredibly, they could call on the power of the FBI to do their dirty work.

There seemed to be only one choice open to him—move fast and interdict the weapon himself, then find somebody he could trust with his discovery.

The bomb had been removed from a bus's cargo bay here, he was sure, and probably within the last day or so. So, was it still in Colorado Springs? No, they would keep it running toward its target, and now that they knew he was on their trail, they would be doing that as quickly as they could.

They would want to get the bomb in the air, and maybe that's what was happening right now . . . or had already happened. They wouldn't take it near Colorado Springs Muni, too much danger of detection. So they'd fly out of a smaller field. If they were going to hit Denver, he could be seeing a flash on the northern horizon at any second. But there were bigger prizes farther west.

The bus station phone book revealed a general aviation airport outside of town and a couple of air cargo operations with the same address. Would he find the bomb there? If so, he was liable to end up in one hell of a firefight over its possession—which would be interesting, given that he had no gun.

A lone cab stood on the rank outside the bus station. At this hour, the driver was asleep. Jim approached the vehicle, looking first at the tires. Mismatched, worn. That worked. And the paint was old, the cab scraped and dented. No question this was a real cab, but was that a real driver? He was Mexican, looked about sixty. Peering down, Jim could see that a small billy club protruded from the door bucket. Was that the driver's only weapon?

Jim tapped on the window until the driver opened his eyes.

"Kreist Air Charter," Jim said as he got in. "2121 Burlywood."

The driver started up. As they moved through the empty late-night streets, Jim watched the man's reflection in the rearview mirror. The guy kept to his business, driving efficiently. Jim let his eyes stray to an ad for *Fiddler on the Roof* playing at the Paramount Theater. He didn't do amusement. When he was a kid, he'd enjoyed things like daring onrushing trains to smash him to bits. Down behind the family farm, there was a quarter-mile trestle. When he heard the first blare of the Amtrak diesel's horn, he'd start running ties. It was a near thing, always, and if you didn't make it, you had to climb down the pilings and hold on for dear life as the train highballed past a few feet over your head. It beat everything except sex.

"Know anything about this place?" he asked the driver.

"Don't get much custom. Looks like a dump, far as I can tell."

Their kind of place, then.

As the field was open twenty-four hours, there would likely be somebody on duty in the FBO.

The cabbie pulled up to the front, stopped.

"I'll be a few minutes," Jim said. He didn't want to lose the cab.

"How many minutes?"

"Give it fifteen."

He pushed the worn glass door of the FBO open and went into the lobby. There were a couple of black sofas, some old magazines, and one of those vending machines that sold dead sandwiches. A guy with a white ghost of a beard and deep, vague eyes sat behind a counter fingering his way along the lines of a Bible.

"Excuse me."

He almost threw the Bible into the ceiling. Then he unfolded himself. Six feet two of angles and elbows, a laugh like an engine dying. "Well, hell, I thought you were a ghost." He looked Jim up and down, his face registering curiosity, then confusion. Then the eyes glanced away. He'd grown suspicious of this past-midnight stranger. "Got nothin' due in, mister," he said, "and nobody's goin' out until tomorrow. No plans on file, and it's too late to put in a new one."

"Nobody's ready to fly?"

"Not a soul. And nobody's prepping. It's just me and the cat. We got a airport cat."

Three possibilities: He was early. He was late. The bomb was not being moved through this airport. "Any traffic out of here earlier?"

"Tonight? We had a couple of landings. No takeoffs."

"I'd like to take a look around, if you don't mind."

"Well, you can sure look around here in the lobby, but not out on the apron or in the hangar. Them new regs. What're you lookin' for?"

Jim drew out his DEA identity card. Silently he showed it to the guy.

"Oh, for the love'a—we got nothin' like that here. No suspicious traffic."

"I'd like to just walk through the hangar, if you don't mind."

"Hell no, I don't mind. We're clean as a whistle." He became confidential: "Lemme tell you, but I guess you guys already know this. Them Mex cartel boys're goin' direct in DIA now. Private jets, don'tcha know. Nobody touches them boys."

"You have many of 'em come through here?"

"Private jets? Sure. Every day. Hunters, you name it, goin' back in the mountains." He stepped over to an elderly computer. "You want me to bring up the log? Whatever you want, I'll do."

"Well then, I just need two things. First, don't log my visit."

"Oh, nossir, I understand. I understand that."

"Then I'll need to go out to the hangar on my own."

"The door's rolled down, but it's not locked. Plus, we got twelve tie-downs on the apron. There are two working charters, both of 'em hangared. Ressman Air Service has a Cheyenne, shit plane, always givin' him problems, gonna look at the fuel system in the morning. Kreist has his Baron in for cleanup; he had a passenger do a toss."

Jim walked out onto the tarmac, in the sharp air of night. The stars always made him think of the truly dark places he had been. Siberia, the taiga, where the forest echoed with the cries of animals and the stars were so bright you could believe that it was the first night of the world. He looked east across the faint glow of the apron and the runway with its green guide lights. Beyond it was the glow of a back porch light, maybe a house, maybe a convenience store along the road.

He remembered seeing that porch light down in the *brasada,* and knew that he would take the memory of it with him forever, adding it to the moment he'd found the car—strangely, a Buick—that had gotten him out of Russia, and the first time he had known that Nabila was naked in the dark, from the way her breathing became shallow and sharp.

He went into the hangar. Under the dim, high lights were three planes—the Baron, the Cheyenne, and a trim Citation with an opened-wing access. Hydraulics.

He removed his Geiger counter from its small carrying case and turned it on, then waved the paddle around the hangar. *Tick. Ticktick . . . tick.* Nothing. He looked toward the equipment bays, went closer. If the thing had been repackaged, maybe it wouldn't be emitting much radiation anymore. Previously, it had been dropping dust, which was what had enabled him to track it. Now, maybe not.

So maybe they'd show up later. Or maybe they weren't going to Denver at all but moving the bomb farther west. There was one hell of a plum out there, after all. If they hit LA, the radioactive dust clouds would be contained by the mountains and turn into the most poisonous damn smog in history. Nearly half of U.S. import-export went through the LA Long Beach port complex. Plus, people couldn't get out of the LA basin, not when they were all going at once. No, a nuke, even a small one, would turn Los Angeles into hell on earth.

THE SUN RISES AT MIDNIGHT

Jim paused to examine the planes. One of these charter guys could've unwittingly flown the bomb west a couple hundred miles, then come back here, no problem. Could've done it last night.

Jim approached the old Cheyenne. It was one tired airplane, with cracked paint and slick tires and what could be metal fatigue crazing one of the landing gear. This plane was going to take somebody to heaven, and soon.

Again, the faint, empty ticking from the Geiger counter.

Jim did a walk around the Baron, with the same result.

He was so tired now that he was worrying about his ability to notice details and make judgments. He had caught not so much as a catnap since his predawn escape in Texas, and it was past eleven now. He was beyond exhaustion, and it looked like he was coming up against another blank wall here, and it was just so damn dangerous to do this alone.

The Citation and the Baron were both passenger carriers. The Citation could probably lift the bomb as well as a pilot, but the Baron couldn't, so it was out. Unless, of course, this was one of those legendary suitcase nukes. But such things were science fiction. Nuclear materials don't work like that. You might be looking at only a few pounds of plutonium, but the rest of the bomb was going to be a good three or four hundred pounds, possibly more.

The Cheynne could take a decent payload and it was configured for cargo. It would belong to some air tramp, probably. Guy who might do a fair amount for money.

Jim got up on the wing and unlatched the door. He leaned down into the warmer air in the plane, scented with leather and machine oil.

Tick. Tick.

Shit.

He pulled his head out of the confined space and returned to the FBO. To help him keep his eyes open, the old man had turned on the radio. "Oil prices are going through the roof, the dollar is in free fall, and gold is predicted to be at fifteen hundred dollars an ounce by year end. . . ."

"Could I see the filed manifest and logs on the cargo guy?"

The old man unfolded himself, got a large logbook, and brought it over to the counter. Jim turned to the section tabbed "Ressman" and looked through it. One flight earlier today, up to DIA to pick up a load of antibiotics and move them to Telluride. Guys like this did a lot of medical supplies, no doubt.

Jim turned the page. Last night, it had been machine tools and chicken to Pahrump, Nevada. "Chicken to the Chicken Ranch," he muttered.

The old man chuckled. "Ressman didn't get a lick of it, I don't think."

Jim copied down the recipient's phone number. But where was the 707 area code? In fact, was 707-747-7727 even a phone number? Maybe Boeing?

"I need to make a call."

The old man pushed a telephone across on a long cord. He dialed. "The number you have called is not a working number. . . ."

The phone number was handwritten, the rest of the manifest typed. This number had been jotted down by a pilot in a hurry, and the numbers of Boeing jets had just slipped into his head.

Jim made a second call, this one to Mr. Ressman's emergency number, noted on his particulars form.

A ring. Another. "Hey, Barker, whassa matter?"

"This is not Mr. Barker. I am Agent Edward Ford, Mr. Ressman. I need to talk to you about a load you moved last night."

"I knew it! Damn it, I *knew* it!"

"You knew what?"

"It was drugs; damn it, I shoulda cracked that damn crate!"

"You had evidence to suggest you weren't carrying a properly manifested load?"

"Officer, I had no such evidence. Which is why I carried it. Goddamn it, stay right there. I'm just across the highway, I'll be right over."

In a normal situation, Jim would have had Ressman controlled immediately. Because this was a national security emergency, he would have been taken to a safe house for interrogation, and no lawyers need apply. Not tonight, though. Jim needed help immediately, and this man, he felt sure, was able to provide it.

He went outside and watched, and soon lights were coming along the road, then turning into the airport's drive. He paid off his cabbie and let him go. Jim would be a while with Ressman; he knew that.

A man in a soiled mechanics coverall got out of a tiny rental car and strode up to Jim. "Todd Ressman," he said, putting out a big hand.

Jim took his hand, shook it. "Mr. Ressman, tell me about the load with the manifest error."

"I'm fucked. Goddamn it, I am fucked! Look, I'm not into any illegal activity, and there was no reason to doubt the load. It was—"

Jim still wasn't sure what he was dealing with here. The plane had shown no evidence of a radiation signature. Maybe it had indeed been a load of chickens, or, more likely, coke. "What made you think you might be carrying drugs?"

"Nothing. Nothing at all. It all seemed completely normal. Just a guy left a phone number off the manifest, and I was looking at weather on the way and—"

"Where did you take the load?"

"I left it in the cargo cage in a little airport in Nevada."

"Mr. Ressman, you are going to take me to this airport."

"I—"

"Let's go; we need to be in the air right now."

"Uh . . . I—"

"I'll pay for your fuel used at the end of the trip. If you don't cooperate, you're going to go down right here, right now."

How far down, Mr. Ressman could not begin to imagine, but it looked bad for him. This man was facing life in a supermax if the bomb didn't detonate. If it did, he was headed for the needle.

"Going down?"

"You filed a counterfeit cargo manifest, Mr. Ressman. If the cargo was illegal, then you are going to need a lawyer. As it is, you're facing a significant fine. So I expect your full cooperation."

Ressman strode into the FBO. "I'm taking a passenger to Pahrump, Nevada," he told the operator. "File it for us, please. I'm gonna go over at ten on heavy mixture, full cruise. Got that?"

"Got it."

As they entered the hangar, the operator pushed the big doors open.

Jim settled into his seat, watching the plane come to life as Ressman threw switches. In minutes the engines were roaring and the plane was rolling out toward the night. "How long?"

"At full power, a couple of hours."

"Fast as you can."

The old plane clattered down the runway, then seemed to leap off and just slide into the air. She didn't look like much, but she wanted to fly. At least, as long as the engines kept running and the tail didn't fall off, or a wing.

"We've got seven hundred miles to cover, and I'm good for three hundred and eight miles an hour," Ressman said. "There's a headwind, so I think we're looking at about two-seventy. That's gonna get us in just past midnight, Pacific time."

"Just don't blow the damn thing up."

"Oh, she'll make it. She's too mean an old cuss to quit."

Which is what they all said before they went in. Jim closed his eyes. Pahrump. The airport had to be tiny, without a doubt completely unguarded, probably totally abandoned after dark. You could fly out of there and stay under FAA radars all the way into the LA basin. Then you just pulled up to about three thousand feet, and the rest was going to be history.

"You want to set that radio on the NOAA emergency channel for me, please?"

Ressman set the radio. Jim saw Ressman's eye shift in his direction, then return to his work. Ressman's mind was probably a hive of questions right about now. What would NOAA Emergency have to do with a drug bust? Why was it so urgent they chase down the cargo right this instant, instead of, for example, bringing in the feds in Las Vegas?

Well, let him be suspicious. He'd learn nothing, not from Jim Deutsch.

The plane bounded along as it crossed the silent Rockies, invisible in the darkness below. They were probably far too close to the peaks for comfort, so Jim was just as glad that the instrument lights, dim as they were, still made it almost impossible to see out. He'd flown one too many missions over trackless mountains in dog-tired planes. His number had to have been up a long time ago.

For what seemed like hours, the plane bucked and pitched.

"Lotta turbulence," Jim commented.

"Mountains make the air restless at night."

On and on it went, the pitching, the wallowing—until, suddenly, everything changed. Now, a sense of stillness settled in, as if the plane weren't moving at all. So they were over the desert at last. Here and there below, Jim could make out a faint light. He'd always wondered what kind of lives unfolded in places that lonely, in a country like this. In Iran or Afghanistan, he knew, the lives were terrible. But here you probably had satellite television, some kind of ranching to do, farming, maybe, if there was water. A peaceful life.

He squirmed in his seat. The bomb had now been at large for at least three days, maybe four. He watched his own reflection in the window. Tired man, eyes shadowed with fear.

As a child, he'd always protected the younger kids. He'd been good to his little sister, to Mary the angel, as he now thought of her. Mary. How strange the world was; how odd that death even existed. He forced the thought away, of what it must have been like on the night she died, the party, all the kids, the lights of Cancún. She'd gone swimming drunk at four in the morning. His last relative, Mary. He'd gone halfway across the world to bury her.

Only when the drumming tempo of the engines rose an octave did he realize that he had been napping.

The plane hummed; the night flowed past outside. "How far out are we?"

"Ninety-six miles. Twenty minutes, we're on the ground, assuming I can find the damn ground."

"No lights?"

"You can turn 'em on as you come in. Assuming you've guessed right and you're in range."

He stared into the darkness ahead. Vegas would be at about two o'clock, still below the horizon. LA would be at eleven o'clock, and well below it.

Out the windshield, he could see the cowling of the plane, ahead of it a faint glow, rising steadily as they came closer. "Vegas is out there," he said.

"Yeah. Gonna be pretty, when we pass south."

Then he saw the cowling as if it were lit by the midday sun, a black, nonreflective surface covered with chipped paint. Then the glare faded and winked out.

"Jesus," Ressman said, shaking his head. "What in hell was *that*?"

As Jim's eyes recovered, the instrument lights flickered and turned off.

"Shit! Battery!"

Red running lights soon illuminated a cockpit full of dead electronics.

"What the fuck? What *was* that?" Ressman's voice was high.

As Jim's vision returned, it brought with it a depth of anguish that was unlike anything he had ever felt before. This was not grief or shock. It was anger—rage. At whoever had done this stupid, stupid thing, but more at himself. He should have found a way to make his report. Maybe if he'd just flown to Washington—but no, he didn't see how he could have done it differently, not without compromising security.

The pilot was struggling, the plane wallowing and pitching, barely under control.

Jim had failed as profoundly as a professional in his position could fail. The system had failed, too, but he didn't count that. He was ninety miles from the bomb and the bomb had gone off. That close!

It was deep failure, profound, in-the-bones failure, of the kind that weaves the darkest strands of history and leads to the ruin of nations. He said, "Are you in control of this thing?"

"I've got no instruments and it's dark out there! What happened to my instruments?"

"Can you get me to the closest airport?"

"Las Vegas?"

"There is no Las Vegas."

10

THE SONG IN THE DESERT

One could say that a man in a certain hotel room picked up a stub pencil and marked the number 2 beside the word "croissant" on a narrow yellow menu, then saw silver light. Or one could say that a girl called Sally Glass feigned a moan of pleasure in the bed of a man whose soul was tired and found that the man's face spattered her like hot grease. Or one could say that the light that came like a hammer set everything from one end of the Strip to the other on fire and scraped the surfaces off all the buildings and smashed them like crushed hats.

In that moment there were chips being exchanged and sports books in action and Ethel Rhodes in the buffet at the Flamingo walking among the diners saying, "Keno, keno," with her cards and her entire history from birth to this instant, she who had once caught a twinkling glance from Frankie Laine, and who had a daughter, Crystal, making a good dollar in Nye County.

In that moment, the temperature rose from seventy-three degrees Fahrenheit in the Baccarat Room at the Bellagio to thirty-eight hundred degrees. To those who happened to look up at the instant of death, it appeared as a smooth, glaring surface, silver-white. To those who heard something, it was a sound like a lonely whistle on a late-night street, as gamma rays destroyed their auditory nerves. In the split paroxysm of death, they felt not pain but a perverse euphoria as the atomic particles shot electricity into their pleasure centers.

All became steam, then fire, then vapor, the transformation in under a millisecond.

Did they ascend, or was Jim Deutsch's view the truth, that we have this life alone?

Still, death in that place was in the details, the sewage that was set afire in the drains, a deck of cards, fused into a brick, that would be found the next morning in the garden of a house in a suburb twelve miles from ground zero, and the head of Linda Petrie from Grand Coteau, Louisiana, the eyes wide, a little sad.

Body parts, whole bodies, shoes, clothing, furniture, sheets, forks and knives, cars, trucks, beds, window frames, groceries, roofing, rugs, dogs and cats, within two miles of ground zero, were swept up and hurled three more miles, dropping—many of them in flames—over the more distant suburbs.

In the desert night, ten minutes ago: Jim Deutsch is ninety-three miles away at an altitude of eight thousand feet. Delta 424 is on final at McCarran, Northwest 908 behind it just rolling into approach. Claire Nester on 424 is waiting for her baby to wake up and howl from the pain in his ears, and she remembers a time just a few weeks ago when there was no Georgie. Her eyes of love regard the man sleeping beside her, her Tom, in amazement and gratitude. *He loves* me. *He wants* me. *He loves the baby. Our baby. My son from my belly.*

And then the red light streaming in the windows like sunrise, and the tremendous jerk, and her last thought, *hurts*—

To go from being to nonbeing in a millisecond—is that death?

Is not death details, the laying down of hands, the sliding away of breaths, the light going from the eyes?

There are prayers being said at St. James's Catholic Church. After a long struggle, twenty-four-hour adoration of the Blessed Sacrament is now a reality here, and Mrs. Alfonso DeLaGarza kneels in the chapel. In her left hand, she has a missal open to next Sunday's liturgy. She glances down, and the little book disappears from between her fingers and that is the last thing she knows.

The gray bricks of the building turn to vapor as hot as the surface of the sun.

In Hari Sushi, Joe Manila pretends to be a Japanese sushi master, but he is not like the sushi chefs of Tokyo, who might spend years learning. He has a good knife and a lot of jokes and sees the fish turn black before his eyes, the chunk of tuna, then sees no more.

Fire in splendor.

In Chippendales at the Rio, the France, Texas, Red Hat Club is clapping in unison as "Derek"—actually Harry—Fisher dances and plays with his G-string.

Then there is air there, white air.

The stage on which he stood will be found by an urban archaeologist. It will be part of a larger chunk of fused black glass. In it will be the shadow of a male torso, and some sequins. This discovery will be made in seventy-three years.

Within half a second of the detonation, the ceiling of Nine Fine Fishermen in New York–New York implodes, and everybody looks up toward the popping sound, and sees it coming at them, a forest of tiny cracks squirting fire.

The plane that brought the fire had bounced along the desert floor, and its pilot had thought that it would not rise. The name of the man who flew it isn't important. He had been born in Indonesia in 1988 and had little experience of life. He had flown to Mexico from Finland under one name, then crossed to California under another, a careful, narrow young man who looked Asian, not Arab, but whose abiding passion was his faith, and who found it fantastic that others, on hearing of Islam, were not inspired to accept this truth.

Outside the Hilton, Eddie Timmons was raising a match to Jenny Hilly's cigarette, wishing she did not smoke, fascinated with her fingers and her lips, and thinking, *She will see me naked; she will know my passion.*

Mort Carmody lost eight thousand dollars on a single throw of the dice, and cursed craps patterning, and the first syllable of the word "bullshit" became his eternity.

As it took off, the little plane had wallowed from the weight that it carried, had fallen back, had struck its landing gear against a fence and caused the pilot to jam the throttle. There had been a moment when the ground raced up. Then had come the rattling sound of brush striking the fuselage, and the desperate kid had closed his eyes and pulled his stick into his gut.

He did not know that he had missed crashing by the width of a child's finger.

So it is that the vastness of history rests in the details. A crewman fails to tighten a screw, the antenna of a reconnaissance plane blows loose, a signal revealing the position of Bull Halsey's carriers fails to reach Admiral Yamamoto, the Japanese lose the Battle of Midway and therefore World War II. On the turn of a single screw. And why? Because the cry of a seagull made a homesick boy dream, for just a moment, of his childhood.

So it is here, on this night. Had another boy drawn the stick into his gut just an eighth of a second more slowly, a city would not have died.

History trembled with the shuddering of that airframe, sighed as the plane rose free and sailed off into the night.

Its course had been carefully calculated. It would approach Las Vegas from north-northwest at an altitude of five hundred feet, not running any lights. Until the pilot popped the nimble little craft up to nine hundred feet, it would not be detected by FAA radars at McCarran.

Military radars at Nellis did detect it, though, and Airman First Class John William Carr said into a microphone, "Bogey incoming altitude zero four hundred, speed one-thirty knots, proceeding west-southwest toward LV Strip."

Ahead, the pilot could see his target, which was the Bellagio Hotel.

As he flew over the houses, the roofs, the pools, some lit and some not, he thought not at all of the lives within, not of the children with their toys and night-lights and unlived lives, nor of the happiness that was general in the place, like a song in the desert. He thought of the harlots in the evil towers and the alcoholic drinks that stupefied a man's moral sense, and of the cruelty of the lies in the gaudy gambling halls, and saw steeples here and there. But his mind clung to his own home, to the sweet tropical evenings, when he had swung in the tamarind tree, and smelled the toasty smoke of his father's water pipe coming up from below. He thought of the madrassa where he had been taught the Five Pillars and had memorized enough of the Quran to receive an honors. But he did not think of the moonglow that had illuminated Damascus a thousand years ago, in the innocence of Islam, nor of the softness of his mother's hands. He did not think of Chrissie Powell, who stood now at her sleepless window, and heard the small plane come and pass, and thought it was some high roller coming into McCarran, and envied him the plane and the night.

He leaned out his mixture and increased throttle, then drew the stick back and began to gain altitude.

At Nellis, J. W. Carr instantly recognized this as what it was: this pilot was about to execute an attack in the form of an airburst at altitude. Carr hit the scramble horn, and Captain Michael Waldron leaped to his feet in the ready room, shouted, "Shee-*ut,*" and ran for the flight line.

The pilot in the small plane watched the Bellagio, tan in its lights, disappear as his nose went up. Dirty people were inside the hotel; he had walked through it and seen the strutting whores, listened to their filthy songs, watched the gamblers in the ringing dens.

All Las Vegas was dirty people in filthy dens. He stared through the windscreen now at the stars. Heaven above, dirty people below. A sacred moment.

Among the dirty people were Bruce and Caitlin Moore, who lived on West Katie Avenue—and her nickname was Katie; that was funny—who at this moment were making love. Their infant, Tara, slept in the co-sleeper beside them, the immeasurable sleep of the very young. Tara with her dusting of red hair and the infinity of love in her eyes had inspired them to make another child, and pleasure wracked them as a single wriggling spark of Bruce and all that he was found its way into Caitlin's wet folds.

There was laughter, then, and the unnoticed hum of a plane passing low overhead, then disappearing.

Mike Waldron leaped into the cockpit of his F-15. Jimmy and Tuck were already running it up.

In among the folded limbs and warmth of the Moores, the new electricity stopped. Death came to the new person three seconds after life began.

From Nellis Boulevard to Rainbow Boulevard, Las Vegas was now burning. The Bellagio, at ground zero, had been transformed into a heap of lava gushing smoke. The rest of the Strip was an inferno—and, in fact, a firestorm like this had not been seen on earth. Not even Hiroshima and Nagasaki had known such destruction.

This was the most malicious single act in human history. One instant, life. The next, fire.

Most who died from the blast had no awareness. They were alive, then not. Many would remain entirely unrecorded. Some would be left as shadows in the ruins, on walls here and there that remained. Shadows raising their arms, shadows not.

All who had awareness saw the same thing: a sheet of white fire, like a gigantic lightning bolt slamming directly into your face. There was sometimes pain, but mostly not. Death came in the form of details: "my dinner is on fire"; "the slot has a short"; "the curtains are burning"; "my skin is gone"; "my throat, face, eyes, tongue hurts." Only the first hundredth of a second of death would be recorded. Across the second hundredth of a second, the temperature of the body would rise from ninety-eight degrees to more than two thousand degrees. Destruction that violent carries with it no sensation at all.

Las Vegas is a busy city, busy at night, and there was traffic on all the highways, some leaving, some entering. Vehicles within the blast area were thrown like toys, some of them to altitudes of a hundred feet, their occupants screaming, confused, mostly blinded by the furious light, their eardrums shattered, feeling extreme, incomprehensible lurches, hearing nothing, their feet jamming their brakes.

From afar, the front wave of the blast appeared to be filled with sparks, each of which was a dying, confused person.

Beyond the blast zone, on all the highways coming into Las Vegas, on Interstate 15, on 95, on 595, there were long lines of stopped cars, and in the roads and on the roadsides, wandering in the fields, stumbling, falling, were the occupants. All who had been facing toward the city had been permanently flash-blinded. Many of them were on fire. Around them and onto them there fell more fire, in the form of burning ceilings, bodies, clothes, carpets, vehicles, sheets and mattresses, chairs, slot machines, tables, telephones, fans, bricks, roller-coaster rails and a train like a great smoking centipede full of strange, insectoid figures: the skeletons of the riders.

Hearing the tremendous noise of the disintegrating city, the blind uttered high, singing wails such as one hears when a forest in Java or Borneo is set alight and the apes catch fire.

They were not human now, not in the intricate depths of this much terror. The blind did not understand why they were blind. They did not understand their pain, did not know why they had been driving one moment and now were wandering in a field or along a roadside, some of them crawling now, feeling along, crying names: "Jenna! Jenna!" "Bill, where are you, Bill?" "God help me! God help me!" Their voices joined to the great roar of the collapsing buildings, the only sound that remained after the cracking blast had died away.

Half the city still lived, the half that had not been vaporized.

Wind blew toward the fire from all directions, setting up a banging of shutters, a hiss of trees, and the wail of eaves. A terrier called Mr. Pip was the first creature to be lifted by this new wind and carried toward the red center. Mr. Pip writhed and yapped, hit a roof and bounced in gravel, then went rolling on, limp and sleek and silent.

The blast-effect cloud rose into the sky, lazy, flickering with internal disruptions, supported by a roiling column of deep red. The flash that had blinded eighteen thousand and the gigantic *crack* that had deafened a hundred thousand more had left the city in darkness. Toward downtown, all that was visible was blackness—a huge, starless darkness shot through with suggestions of flame. All was chaos and surprise. There had been not the slightest warning. One second, one life, the next—this.

Captain Mike Waldron's neck and left arm and shoulder tumbled through clear air. His plane, just sixty-three feet into its roll down the runway at Nellis, was burning and exploding, the rest of Mike Waldron stewing in the cockpit.

From out beyond Buffalo Drive and from the direction of Nellis, when you looked toward downtown you would see the shape of the blast-effect cloud, and you might understand that this was an atomic aftermath, that a nuclear bomb, and a substantial one, had been detonated here.

Farther away, fifteen or twenty miles, it was entirely obvious. From here, the cloud was clearly defined, a weltering horror in the light of the moon.

At Nellis, the flight line was on fire. The USAF Warfare Center struggled to get its communications back on track, but the building was burning and would need to be abandoned if fire crews did not come within minutes. They would not come, though, not within minutes or even hours, or at all. They would never come.

Just two emergency vehicles were operating, one with a full crew of six, the other with two. They worked the flight line, foaming burning airplanes. Inside Nellis's hangars, most planes remained intact. The four training missions that had been under way when the detonation took place had all crashed in the desert, victims of failure due to the bomb's electromagnetic pulse, which had destroyed even hardened electronic circuits over a 180-square-mile area centered on the blast, and damaged many more, much farther out, especially those of planes at higher altitudes.

At this hour, there had only been the two commercials incoming to McCarran, and none of the distant fliers were fatally damaged.

Aboard United 221 out of Seattle for Denver, the copilot was slowly recovering his vision. He did not know what he had seen—it had not appeared to be on the ground, though. He had perceived it as a flashbulb going off in his face. It had seemed as if it was inside the cockpit, and his initial reaction had been to declare an emergency.

Seven minutes later, there had been significant buffeting. The plane's radios now crackled with pilot chatter, as everybody tried to figure out what it had been. There was amusement in some voices: "Looks like they've landed," "I'm not reporting any UFO. . . ."

But then, on 221 and American 806 and Alaska 43, silence fell. There was too much light down there. Captain Baker of 221, who had been looking down when the flash took place and had not been affected by it, said into his radio, "Las Vegas is burning."

In the parts of the Las Vegas metropolitan area that had not been destroyed, there were 73,000 private homes on fire and 2,613 businesses. There were 381,000 people with third-degree burns outside of the blast area itself. At that moment, sixteen thousand more of them were actively on fire, frantic beyond words, screaming, staggering down streets or running, torches all.

Inside the blast area, the outright death rate was 87 percent. The unfortunate few who remained alive were for the most part maintenance personnel in basement areas. They were either trapped in absolute darkness, screaming, feeling along the floors of rooms now tangled with broken machinery, or struggling to find their way using flashlights or emergency lighting. Many had received fatal radiation doses. Many were bleeding from cuts, had broken bones, burns, bruises, or were injured in other ways. None would survive.

Not even specialists who had thought carefully about the consequences of an atomic explosion in a modern city had understood what the vast amount of combustible material in such a place would mean.

The Dresden fire in 1945 had dragged people into it from five hundred yards away. But here, even fifteen minutes after the blast, the wind was rising to a howl in the eaves of houses outside of the blast zone, picking up larger and larger objects. Along streets and roads, struggling people, most of them already weak from shock and injuries, began tumbling toward the flames, in the dust, in the chaos.

All communications with the city had ended in an instant. Four thousand, three hundred, and eight telephone calls of various kinds were disconnected. All local radio and TV stations were instantly killed.

However, ham operators in outlying areas—such as Pahrump—were not thrown off the air. A ham, Gene Lerma, was operating his powerful station sixty miles from ground zero when the detonation occurred.

His wife and child were asleep, but Lerma's wife leaped out of bed when she heard the great roar that filled the house, shattering windows and causing curtains and blinds to whip into the rooms. He, in his windowless studio, had been talking to a ham operator at McMurdo Station in the Antarctic when there was a voltage surge that popped Lerma's circuit breakers and the whole building was shaken to its foundations.

"I think we just had an earthquake," he said into the lifeless microphone. Then he was plunged into darkness. A moment later, his generator cut in and the emergency lights came back. His next thought was for his wife and baby, and Lerma jumped up and ran out of the studio.

His wife said, "What is happening?" She had their still-sleeping little girl in her arms.

"Stay here." He moved out onto the front porch and down into the stony garden. There were great booms echoing from somewhere and he thought it was the sound of the earthquake spreading through the land. As he turned to go inside, though, he happened to glance in the direction of Las Vegas.

For a moment, he was confused. What was that thing, that great, glowing *thing* just rising above the flat line of the eastern horizon? He stared, trying to understand. Was it smoke? No, it was glowing internally. There were periodic flashes of lightning, too, forks of it dancing across the face of the monster. But it wasn't a thunderstorm, not so close to the ground.

Then it rose up still higher. It took form. A jolt as if of electricity shot through him from head to toe, because he had just recognized that he was seeing the mushroom cloud of an atomic explosion in the process of forming.

For a moment, he thought, *Dirty bomb,* but as the gigantic cloud billowed into the sky, towering, huge, and so horribly fast, he knew that there was only one thing that could do this. An atomic weapon had been detonated over Vegas.

His baby, his wife—he thought to get them into the RV and head west. But no, that was a mistake; if Vegas had been hit, LA might be a mess, too. Angie came out onto the porch, still with the baby in her arms.

"Go back," he said, then hurried up to her and put his arm around her waist, and drew her back into the house.

They'd lost windows in the living room and the bedroom. They would need to shelter in the studio. But he didn't think that fallout would be a problem, because the prevailing winds would carry the cloud east. And any cloud from LA would be funneled out across the desert well south of here.

Their problem was not going to be fallout. It was going to be food and water and security. An atomic war had started, he thought, unless this was a terrorist incident.

He went into the bedroom and dragged the mattress off the bed and into the studio.

"What are you doing?"

He had to tell her. He sat her down and said gently, "There's been a very large explosion in Vegas—"

"Atomic bomb?"

"I think so."

"Radiation?"

"Not here, not yet. But we're going to stay in the studio. The generators have gas for thirty days, so we're safe enough."

It was then that he returned to his radio station. He'd lost a number of his electronic systems but not his tough old radios. He powered up and was soon looking at 150 watts output. A few adjustments enabled him to crank it up to the max the station allowed, 300 watts.

He began broadcasting in the 40 meter band and was soon talking to a ham operating out of Salt Lake City. He worked for news station KSL, and when they'd lost all contact with the West Coast he had gone to his nearby apartment and powered up.

Thus it was that an amateur operator made the broadcast that rocked the world: "I am talking to you from a town sixty miles west of Las Vegas. We are looking directly at what can only be described as a mushroom cloud. I cannot prove it, but it is my belief that Las Vegas has sustained a nuclear attack. I repeat, Las Vegas, Nevada, has been hit by an atomic or possibly hydrogen bomb. A large bomb. As I speak, I can see the cloud literally covering the whole western horizon."

Then he wept.

11

RETREAT

Seventy-five miles east of Las Vegas, Ressman still struggled with his control problem. He called out over the blare of his engines, "I have to land this thing wherever it happens to be!"

Jim Deutsch said nothing. His misery was so great that he halfway hoped that the bastard would crash and kill them both. All Jim cared about now was getting to a phone. Any damn phone!

Then Ressman made a turn. "I see a light," he shouted. "I see a light!"

Ahead, Jim saw it, too, the faint but unmistakable outline of a runway.

They came rocking and bouncing in on the strip of the Grand Canyon National Park Airport. Ressman laughed with relief; he threw his head back; he sucked great gulps of air. He said, "What happened to my plane?"

Jim heard him but didn't bother to explain what the electromagnetic pulse that emanates from an atomic explosion does to electronic circuits. The hell with Ressman and his plane.

The Grand Canyon airport was quiet and dark, with a strong night wind coming in across the desert from the west.

"Is that the moon?" Ressman asked.

Deep in the western sky there was a curious light, a crescent. It was dim purple. "It must be," Jim said.

"What happened out there?"

Too many years doing what he did had made Jim react automatically to questions with silence. Nabila had hated that about him, because habit had extended it far beyond the necessities of the job.

He could have told Ressman that his greedy stupidity had killed a great American city. He could have slugged the bastard, but he knew that would drop Ressman, and if he dropped this man, he was going to go further; he was going to kill him. His hands itched with the death in them. To be sure he wouldn't use them, he jammed them into his pockets.

He could not yet see the cloud from here, but the color of that crescent moon told him that it was just below the horizon. They had about four hours before the prevailing winds brought its deadly radiation over this airport, not to mention all the people living in the region.

He had no iodine pills. He had nothing to save himself or anybody, nothing except his mind and what was in it: the knowledge of what had just happened, of the fact that it had been accomplished because crucial security forces were penetrated.

But the top level didn't know this. The White House would call on every asset the country possessed, and some of those assets were going to be doing the wrong damn job. How deep was the penetration? How much more damage could it do? And worse, the biggest question of all: were there more bombs?

"Get a plane ready," Jim told Ressman.

"Excuse me?"

Jim gestured toward the three light aircraft that were visible on the hangar apron. "Those guys are ready to roll, and they won't have damaged electronics because they were below the horizon."

"What?"

"Find the one with the best range. We're going to take it."

"But—they're locked! I don't have keys."

Jim went to him, took him by the throat. "Be ready to fly in ten minutes."

"It's theft."

"I'm commandeering the aircraft due to the fact that this is a national emergency." He released Ressman. "Do it now."

Jim went to the small, locked waiting area. He sprang the lock with a credit card. Inside, he found a phone. He lifted the receiver. If it didn't work . . . but it did. He dialed CIA Operations in Washington, waited for the computer, and input his personal code. A moment later, a young man's voice said, "May I help you?"

"I have observed an atomic weapon detonate over Las Vegas, Nevada. The time was twenty-four zero one. That is midnight plus one minute local time."

There was a silence. When the voice returned, it belonged to a scared boy. "We don't have that."

One of the many problems the intelligence community had was that its members were now younger than they had ever been. Due to cannibalization from outside employers, and the fast-growing contractor business, the median age of CIA officers had been dropping for years. Thus the young man's crisis experience would be limited.

"I want you to tell me the procedures you will now carry out."

"This is a drill?"

Jim remained silent. He didn't care how agitated the kid became or what he thought he was involved in, as long as he did his duty correctly.

Jim was not surprised that the CIA didn't have the information yet. One of the things that characterizes extraordinary destruction like this is that it conceals itself inside a circle of ruined communications systems. McCarran Airport would be off-line, probably permanently, Nellis AFB would be in chaos, and the local Homeland Security office would obviously be down. Probably there were no radio transmissions, no phones or cell phones, nothing at all getting out. Hams in outlying areas, maybe.

"A ten- to thirty-megaton atomic explosion has taken place above Las Vegas, Nevada. The probable agent is a plutonium bomb detonated at an altitude of five to seven hundred meters. It has caused extreme damage. They city is nonviable at this time. It is burning."

"Please confirm your identity."

Jim went through the classified identity routine. Then he added, "This needs to go upstairs right now, do you understand that, with my identity tagged intact all the way to the White House and the NSC. Do you know how to write up those tags?"

"Sir, I do not."

Since the 1990s and the various failures that had resulted in the CIA blowing three capture and two assassination opportunities on Osama bin Laden, it had been possible for certain officers in sensitive situations that might require extremely fast response to move information on an expedited basis—that is, if the lines of communication weren't compromised, which this one certainly could be. Jim had to assume that whoever had been able to use the FBI to try to arrest him would also have made sure they had access to communications like this one. What he had to say, though, was beyond the need for secrecy.

"I want you to patch me in to the White House. Can you do that?"

"Yes, Sir. But, Sir, excuse me, shouldn't you be reporting in the chain?"

Now it was time to play his ace, the new card that the disaster had put in his hand. "It could be that the president has only minutes to live unless he takes shelter, so do as you are told and do it now!"

A silence followed. Then clicking, a ring, and a voice: "Security."

"I need to speak to Tom Logan. It's a matter of critical national urgency. There is a time problem. I need immediate access."

"Who's speaking, please?"

Unbelievable. He contained himself. "I am a CIA officer. My name must be on your monitor."

"I need to confirm your credentials, Sir."

He had the chilling thought that he might be talking to a conspirator. They would want to get as close to the president as they could. Nevertheless, he repeated his identifiers. He waited. There was another click.

"Hello?" God, had they hung up? *Don't do this, for the love of all that's holy!*

"Logan."

The chief of staff, and thank you, God. "Mr. Logan, my name is James Deutsch. I am a Clandestine Operations contract officer operating under extreme deep cover within CONUS."

"Excuse me?"

"Sir, this is the greatest national emergency in U.S. history. Within minutes, you will receive word that Las Vegas, Nevada, has taken a nuclear hit."

There was a choked sound.

"You need to get POTUS in motion at once, but know this: there has been betrayal, probably for years, probably since Brewster Jennings in 2001. You are aware of that?"

"Of course I'm aware of it! But that's—it's solved. That was Ahmad Khan. State was ordered to leak Brewster Jennings to Pakistani intelligence, and Khan used the information so that he could smuggle nukes around Brewster's operatives. It's old news. Contained. Done with."

"Okay, leave it. I know that our problem is in Customs and Borders at least, and I can identify one person of interest. There is also FBI involvement, but they may be acting on information with all good intentions. There must also be traitors, further up the chain of command, close to you guys. Understand that. *Must be*."

"What are you saying here? Las Vegas—"

"Listen to me, God damn you!"

"All right! All right! It's three in the morning; I had—I had an embassy staffer . . . uh, here. I have to get POTUS moving?"

"Las Vegas has sustained a gigantic nuclear strike. Largest bomb ever detonated over a city. You must move the president to safety, but you must know—*are you registering this now*?"

"I am!"

"All right. The bomb was transported in country due to sabotage of the border detection system and a penetration of our security apparatus."

"How bad? How bad?"

"I have no way of knowing, but they were able to generate an arrest warrant that nearly got me taken out of the picture. It's up to you guys to figure out who could have done that. Find the warrant and work from there."

"My God. And you're saying—what? How serious is this explosion again?"

"Las Vegas is on fire from one end to the other. And, Mr. Logan, *there are probably other bombs*."

"You have knowledge of this detonation?"

"I'm here, on the scene! I saw the blast!"

"What I need to know is why this happened. Where was our interdiction program?"

Jim could only hope that the man was not actually this stupid. He was in shock and half-asleep and maybe on pills or drunk or whatever. It must take a lot to enable a man in his position to sleep. Jim tried to inject more control into his voice. Sound calm, authoritative. Seconds counted. "Get POTUS in motion. Activate the Emergency Response System. Federalize the National Guard and put it under the Continental Army Command."

"Who are you, again?"

"My name is James Deutsch, and I am on my way to D.C. because I cannot communicate everything I know over phone lines. Not *any* lines anywhere in the federal system, especially yours."

"This is the White House!"

"When I get there, I will contact you again and you will conduct me to the president. Do you understand?"

"No."

"If we are penetrated, there could be hostiles anywhere along the chain of command. I know the DCIA will back me on this. So will the DD. The deputy director knows me by name. Jim Deutsch. Tell the CIA to isolate information flow—oh, shit, I'm overcontrolling. I'm scared, buddy. Obviously, you need to communicate with the director level across the whole security system. Warn them. Tell them that this could have grown out of the Brewster Jennings problem. That'll get their attention."

Jim hung up. He leaned his head against the wall of the old-fashioned telephone booth for a moment, and breathed deeply.

He returned to the flight line to find Ressman sitting in an ancient V-tailed Beechcraft Bonanza.

"Let's fly."

"I've got the guy's info right here," Ressman said, "but you need to give him a call. I don't know where they keep the keys."

Jim took the pilot's logbook from Ressman and returned to the little lobby. He dialed the number in the logbook but got an answering machine. "You have reached the home of—" Then a click. A concerned, older voice: "Hello?"

"Mr. Timothy Whitehead?"

"Yes?"

"My name is Agent James Deutsch. I'm calling on a matter of national importance. I am at the Grand Canyon airport with a pilot. I need to use your airplane."

"What the hell?"

"It's a national emergency, Mr. Whitehead. An atomic weapon has been detonated over Las Vegas and—"

"What?"

"Sir, please listen to me. I am at the airport. I need your plane." He thought of the old man in Texas, now without a truck, struggling to survive. At least the owner of a plane wasn't going to be hurting that bad. "I need to know which keys are yours." There would be a set at the airport, of course.

"They're on hook twenty-two in the safe. What's happening? Are we in any danger?"

"Sir, are you in the Grand Canyon area?"

"We're in Flagstaff."

Jim made a mental calculation. That was far enough away to survive the worst of the radiation. "Keep your doors and windows closed. Turn on the radio and follow the alerts. You'll start to hear them in about ten minutes."

He hung up the phone. The "safe" was not a safe at all but a lockbox. He'd sprung many heavier-duty setups, and doing this one was no more difficult than rolling down a widow.

Perhaps Nabila could help. She was need-to-know on a thing like this. In fact, his guess was that she'd be getting a call-in within fifteen minutes.

He phoned. It rang. Rang again. "Nabila?"

"Jimmy!"

"The news is bad. Las Vegas was just nuked."

She did not gasp; she did not cry out. In the background, he heard a male voice.

"Get Rashid on, too."

"Jim?" His voice was tightly controlled.

"Rashid. Hi. Listen. I'm in Nevada. Las Vegas just took a multikiloton nuke. Plutonium, I think about thirty k's. Three times the size of the Hiroshima bomb."

Nabila choked out a cry.

"Nabila?"

"I have a warning! I have a warning that Maggie wouldn't put in the briefer because we couldn't confirm!"

"What warning?"

"Women in the West must put on the *hijab* or there will be a serious consequence. It was deployed out of Finland a few days ago."

"Deployed out of Finland but originating in Russia?"

She was silent. They were violating the law, talking like this to each other and on a clear line and with another party with yet a different set of clearances on the call as well.

"Nabila, I have a need to know."

"But I have no authority."

"Where in Russia, Nabila?"

Rashid's voice interrupted. "She asked me for lookdowns in Helsinki, then St. Pete, then—"

"Jim, is there a Russian connection?" Nabila asked.

"Listen to what I'm going to tell you. There is a penetration of U.S. security forces involved and it is extremely serious. Very high level. Obviously, a Russian connection is possible."

"The Muslims are surrogates, then?" Rashid asked.

"They were, but they're in control now, because nobody running them would have a motive to actually detonate a nuke like this, least of all Putin. But the internal system that's protecting them—it's still in place and it's active, because they're trying to kill me. Probably, whoever's involved inside is doing it to save their own skin, at this point."

"These terrorists are insane," Rashid said. "Not all of us are like this. It's heresy and it's madness."

"I know how painful it is for you guys. All the more motive to do what you can to help, am I right?"

"We will do anything!"

"Okay, here's what I need. I am under threat pressure and I am moving east in a small plane with about a five-hundred-mile range. I'm going to take it down to Phoenix and I need you to wrangle me a jet out of Deer Valley Airport. I need clearances in order by the time I get there."

"Consider it done!"

"Rashid, *how*?" Nabila asked.

"Nabby, I don't know, but we will do this!"

"Travel me as someone too important to divert. The deputy director, say. And this is important—make sure the plane moves, even if nobody's on it."

"But . . . why?"

"Just do it. Make certain."

"How can we even get a plane, let alone convince them to fly it with no passenger?" Nabila asked. "It's all crazy."

"We will! Now stop; this is enough. Jim, it will be as you say."

"Thanks, both of you."

"Rashid—"

"Enough, sister! Jim, it is done."

He could imagine Nabby's eyes, the widening at the edges that came when she felt insecure, or when she was being taken to bed. He could almost feel her body against him. When he was under fire or running hard, she would float into his mind like this, what guys called a battlefield angel. He wanted to say that he still loved her, but he feared that he might insult her, and he would certainly offend Rashid.

Rashid said, "Assalmu Alaykum."

Jim replied, "Ma'a Salama."

"Ma'a Salama," Nabila said. Good-bye, in their formal Arab way, a convention full of the fatalism desert life induces.

Jim went to the little Beechcraft. He gazed into the pure air of the late night, staring for a moment back toward the huge flickers, red and orange and pink, that swept the western horizon. He climbed into the seat. "We good to go?"

"Checks out."

He pulled down his door, made sure it was latched. The field around them was dark and silent. Or was it? Now, he had to assume the worst. Always. When he spoke, he made sure it was loud enough to be heard from the edge of the apron: "Take me to Deer Valley Airport near Phoenix. Do you know it?"

"I've flown in there."

Ressman started the tiny plane's engine. It darted down the runway, and rose into the night. For a few moments, Jim let its running lights remain visible; then he told Ressman to cut them. The plane was lost to view.

Jim sat listening to the drumming of the old engine, scanning the meager instruments, watching the altimeter rise. When it reached nine hundred feet he said, "That's enough."

Ressman trimmed, throttled back, and dropped the nose. "We got mountains ahead," he said.

"Not really. I want you to reset the course. We're not going to Phoenix at all. I'm going down to Piedras Negras. So what I think we need to do here is refuel in Nogales, then take me to P.N. and we're done."

His call had been a diversion. He didn't know who might be listening and he didn't even know for certain if Nabby and Rashid could be trusted. If by some miracle they actually got an empty plane to fly to Anderson, he might achieve a major misdirection. If not, his pursuers would at least be a little confused for a while.

"I don't know if I can find Nogales."

"Out in that desert, it'll be the only lights."

"You're running. Staying below radars."

"I am running, Mr. Ressman. You got that right."

When Ressman didn't respond, Jim allowed himself to close his eyes. If Nabila had understood the silences between his words, a specially cleared jet would take off from Deer Valley in about two hours and head for Washington. It would be empty, except for the pilots, but hopefully nobody would realize that until it landed. He would be far away by then, on a different route and mission entirely.

12

EMERGENCY RESPONSE SYSTEM

Among the first things a president learns is that when his bedside telephone rings after midnight, the news is never good. He threw back the quilt and sat up. He picked up the receiver. "Yes?"

"Sir?"

"Hit me, Logan."

"We need to get you in motion; a nuke's gone off in Vegas."

The world shuddered; the room swayed. He sucked breath, sucked more. His heart started in, bad. His mouth went so dry he could hardly form words. He grabbed the glass of water on the bedside table and drank it down.

"Sir?"

The president of the United States sat on his bed, a phone clutched in his hand, dying and dying, a million deaths. "Oh, God, God, God."

He was no kid; he had his share of health problems; his heart wasn't invulnerable. He took deep breaths until the sensation passed. Then another sensation came—that same heart almost broke with sorrow. His administration was ruined. This was the worst disaster in the history of the United States and it was his watch. He had a place in history and it was a hell of a bad one and—"Those poor people! Are we doing what we should? Where's FEMA? Where's the Guard? Where's the National Emergency Response System?"

"We need to move you, Sir."

"Where's my wife?"

"She's in Newfoundland, Sir," Logan said. "They landed as soon as they got the emergency signal."

He forced himself to think. This place could go up any second. He could be about to die—God, in seconds! "Okay. Okay. I'm calm. Is the government disbursing?"

"Across the board. The Emergency Response System is active; the whole country's being warned—"

The president grabbed the remote off the bedside table and jabbed at it. The television turned on. He tuned to CNN.

At first, the screen appeared black. Then there were stars on it. "We're eight miles west-southwest of the Strip, Charlie," a voice said. Then more silence. "I don't know if I can be heard. We're eight miles west-southwest of the Strip, Charlie. Are we on the air?"

The stars bulged into blurs, then resolved.

Tom Logan came into the room.

"Oh my God," President William Johnson Fitzgerald said. "God help us all."

Hundreds and hundreds of fires turned the screen into a weltering orange glow. Buildings, homes, whole neighborhoods, all were burning. There were dark figures visible here and there in nearby streets. And in the center of it, like some sort of monstrous autumn bonfire, the Strip was sending a tower of fire into the sky.

"Sir, we need to get rolling."

"I hear you. Get me the governor of Nevada."

"Sir, we're under imminent threat!"

"Do it!"

Logan made a call. "Governor Searles, please, this is the president calling." He gave the phone to the president.

"Mike? . . . Look, I want to know what you need. I'm federalizing the Guard, but not there. You keep them. And if you need any military. Any military. Or planes. Nellis—excuse me? . . . Oh, God. Of course Nellis is gone. All right. Look, I'm going to give you my direct line, but I've got to get in motion. They're afraid we could be about to take a hit. Washington." He gave Logan the phone.

"Sir, I need to tell you something—"

"Talk to him!"

"Oh yes, Governor, it goes without saying. It's a disaster area. We'll make certain that all possible fire equipment, Phoenix, Salt Lake, LA—everything that can be deployed—"

The president grabbed Logan's arm. "Go slow on that. This could be one of many. They might need their own services."

"We'll make sure everything's moving toward you as soon as possible."

Two Secret Service men had come in with the coat and shoes that were kept ready for a sudden move in the night. The president put the coat on over his pajamas and put the shoes on and followed them.

Logan said, "Sir, Mr. President—"

From outside, the president heard the helicopter landing. "I don't want that," he said. "We're too vulnerable in that."

"It's the protocol we're using—"

"No. No. We're going down." Few people realized just how extensive the tunnel system under Washington actually was. There was not a single embassy without an FBI listening post under it. In fact, the first tunnel had been constructed by L'Enfant during the building of the city. It led from the White House to the Potomac, and was intended as an escape route for the president. During World War II, it had been widened and an electric railroad installed for the use of FDR. Until the advent of presidential helicopter travel in the sixties, it had been the primary escape route. It was why presidential yachts had been so important for so long, and why they had been anchored where they had. Every president from Washington to Kennedy had kept a yacht at the ready.

With the advent of missiles that could reach the city from Siberia in twenty minutes, though, other means had to be found. Thus the current system of moving the president to the National Redoubt by helicopter.

As they hurried down from the residence, the president could see one of the young men speaking into his radio.

At the bottom of the stairs, they were met by an ashen Milton Dean, head of the president's security detail. "Sir, excuse me, but the tunnels are not safe in this circumstance; you have to understand—"

Among the agreements that a president made was to abide by the orders of his security personnel during times of danger. Was the chopper really safer? Certainly it was fast. They would be in the bunker in twenty minutes.

But that wasn't enough, and he knew it. "Where's the Continuity of

Government Act?" he asked Logan. The president had introduced it earlier in the year, but it wasn't a legislative priority.

"Stuck in committee, Sir."

"Goddamn it." The act would provide a structure for the governors to reconstruct the federal government, in the event that Washington was destroyed before the federal emergency dispersal program could be enacted. He took a deep breath. *Okay, fella, this is why they elected you. Good in a pinch.* "Where's Matt?"

"The vice president is moving."

The president headed out toward the Rose Garden and the waiting helicopter. He stepped into its plush, nearly silent interior, followed by a running Logan. But the Marines closed the door and took off. Their orders were clear: during an imminent peril emergency, move the moment POTUS is aboard.

Because there was only the dispersal program and no continuity act, if a nuclear weapon was detonated in Washington without warning the U.S. government would collapse. Why such an act had not been passed years ago was beyond President Fitzgerald's comprehension. And yet he'd let it get stuck in committee, hadn't he? You didn't like to think about things like that. You didn't want to believe it could really happen—which was your weakness, the enemy's strength. As things stood, the government had to survive or the country was ruined.

"Get this thing moving," he shouted into the intercom. "Flat out, boys!"

He closed his eyes. At least Linda and Polly and Dan were all right, for the moment. But God help the American people. And . . . oh, God, Las Vegas. "Damn those bastards; *damn them*!" Fitzgerald would not stoop to hating all Muslims. No, not this president. But he was tempted, because there was an incredible weapon being constructed that he could potentially use to entirely change the face of human society. Dream Angel offered him that much power. To order it activated, though . . . it would be the most monstrous, most terrible thing ever undertaken by any human power. What was worse, it was still unfinished. Parts of it were just theoretical. More terrifyingly, nobody really knew what it would do—except for the fact that it would kill millions.

He was going to be asked to make the decision about whether or not to attempt Dream Angel. If he lived. "Where are we?"

"Eight miles out."

"Put on the goddamn gas!"

13

A WORLD AT BAY

It was now one ten in the morning in Las Vegas, four ten in Washington, and eleven ten in England. A benign sun shone on the spires of London and the new skyscrapers that increasingly defined the skyline, and flashed against the wings of the pigeons wheeling above Trafalgar Square. In Regent's Park, the roses were lingering in the long, warm autumn, and Queen Mary's Garden was filled with noonish strollers. One by one, they took out their cell phones and one and then another stopped and concentrated on what their friends were telling them. Then they noticed bells beginning to ring, everywhere, bells.

In seventeen languages around the world, the BBC's announcers read the same main story: "Bulletin from America: The U.S. city of Las Vegas, Nevada, has sustained a large explosion and has fallen out of communication. There are reports of extensive damage and fires in outlying areas. Area witnesses report a blinding flash followed by a series of severe explosive shocks. A fiery cloud hangs over the city at this time. Many are believed dead, and there has been much property damage. Owing to the darkness there, a full assessment of the damage, and an official announcement about the nature of the explosion, will not be forthcoming until the predawn light in approximately an hour and a half."

Radio 4 went back to the reading of the letters of Sir Arthur Conan

Doyle to his mother, Mary Doyle, and the prime minister, who was watching a live video feed from Las Vegas being provided him by MI6, became sick in the toilet of his office at 10 Downing Street. Then his security personnel came and soon he, also, was in motion. Like the United States and every other Western country at risk of nuclear terrorism, the United Kingdom lacked a definite continuity-of-government process. If London was destroyed this moment, the British people would not only be without a government; they would also be without the slightest means to reconstruct one.

In Dharmsala, India, Tenzin Gyatso, the Fourteenth Dalai Lama, considered the dark event. He made an unprecedented decision to telephone His Holiness the Pope, who came to the instrument from his luncheon. The Dalai Lama stepped into his small garden, where the sun was setting over the wide-leafed trees. The pope listened with shock and concern to the old man. He did not consider that there was any doctrinal validity to the Dalai Lama's beliefs, but the pope certainly respected the man's sincerity. As the pope listened to the description of the catastrophe, he knew precisely why this other religious leader had called him. This was the beginning of an attack on religion; that was clear. And, more specifically, an attack on Christianity.

The pope next telephoned the prime minister of Italy and asked that he send troops to seal off the Vatican immediately. Then the pope ordered the Swiss Guards into action, and they began moving through St. Peter's and the Sistine, quietly but persistently directing the tourists to leave. In the crypt beneath the great church, other men moved among the tombs with powerful flashlights, finding here and there lovers, and once a priest on some nameless mission, who hurried away. Along with the interlopers, the tourists at the tomb of Saint Peter were returned to the surface.

In Paris, police surrounded important public buildings and the Louvre, the Eiffel Tower, and the Musée d'Orsay were closed, as were the Uffizi in Florence and the Prado in Madrid. All European governments made similarly frantic efforts to escape their capitals, and all faced the same danger—total lack of continuity in the event of sudden catastrophe.

The United States, Canada, the European Union, Mexico, Japan, India, Saudi Arabia, China, Russia, and many other countries grounded all flights immediately. Most countries issued grounding directives, but many did not have sufficient control over their own airspace for this to be effective.

Flights over most of Africa and various Asian countries continued, at least until planes made scheduled landings. All flights incoming to the United States, the European Union, and Canada were either turned back or landed under fighter escort.

The news reached the Middle East at approximately ten thirty in the morning local time, when Al Jazeera carried a grim bulletin: "The U.S. city of Las Vegas is in flames after the detonation of a nuclear bomb. There is no communication with the city, but news helicopters just arriving on the scene report that the entire metropolis is burning. The famous gambling strip is no more."

For a few moments, the channel went back to its regularly scheduled program, *The Fabulous Picture Show,* featuring an interview with Sudanese film director Lina Makboul about her latest project, called *Water.* A moment later, the channel returned to the news and the same feed of the city burning, now in the pink light of the predawn, that was being broadcast worldwide.

Cairo, Baghdad, New Delhi, Rawalpindi, Kabul, Tehran, Tel Aviv, Jerusalem—all the great cities of the Middle East—simply stopped. Cars stopped in the streets; people stopped on the sidewalks.

As soon as it had received the alert from Mossad, the Israeli government had put its military on immediate alert. Across Jerusalem, across Tel Aviv, in the streets of London, of Paris, of Berlin, of New York, of Houston, of Mexico City, a great silence descended. But that was not true in Cairo, it was not true in Tehran, in Riyadh, in Damascus, in Gaza, where people rushed cheering into the streets, leaping, dancing, and soon the news crews were there, too, taping the sweating men, the dark rush of women.

After ten minutes of this in Cairo, the Egyptian government, desperate not to offend the Americans, sounded the air-raid sirens, with the result being panic and confusion, then a stampede to evacuate the city. In Iran, a frantic military went into defensive posture but was careful not to put more than a few aircraft in the air. President Ahmadinejad issued an announcement on state television that any attempt to attack Iran would be met with "fierce resistance." Immediately thereafter, along with the rest of the government, he left for a mountain retreat north of Tehran. Privately, he was furious. Who had done this? He sent a message of condolence to the U.S. president, assuring the Americans that Tehran was not responsible. But would they believe it?

Similar messages were sent by Syria, Pakistan, Sudan, North Korea, and every other country that worried that it might be held responsible.

In the Pamir Panhandle in Afghanistan, a clear, quiet noontime arrived and people took their lunches of olives and cheese, of lamb and tomatoes, eating quietly in the profound silence of the place, while the grasses bowed in the noon wind and a truck passed on the road, its gears grinding as it began working its way up a hill.

In London and Paris, New York and Los Angeles, and most especially in Washington, it crossed many a mind that they might be in trouble, too, and quietly, in twos and threes, in family groups, among friends, they got in their cars or on trains, or on planes or busses, and left, and the roads at first whispered with their passage, then hummed, then roared, and finally the highways thundered and the terminals howled with terrified hordes, and the employees left and the security officers, and riots spread through shattered streets, and children fell first.

As the sun rose over Las Vegas, a sight never seen before presented itself, for Hiroshima and Nagasaki had been lightly constructed, while Las Vegas was huge and complicated and packed with the complex wealth of material objects that defined the modern world—and people, of course, such a vastness of human detail.

The great cloud that was moving east with the prevailing winds turned rose red on its western flank, black in the east, for no light could pass through its density. Its leading edge was filled with glittering dots that appeared from afar like sequins or snowflakes. Some of them probably were sequins from Cirque du Soleil or one of the more traditional floor shows, but the cloud had lifted brassieres, glasses, seat cushions, chair legs, legs, hands, heads with dead eyes, bits of cars, sheet music, CDs, DVDs, watches, some on arms and some not, toilet paper in grand streamers, jewels driven to an altitude of thirty thousand feet and dropped in the endless sky, and all of this came with the fallout, dropping in gardens, on roofs, on speeding cars, on the runners and the dead alike, festooning trees with plastic toys and skirts and diapers and meat, diaries, stuffed animals in bits, wallets, money, chips like rain, some of them covered with ice and become hail.

So it is: when a giant place is exploded the center of it is vaporized, but then the blast sweeps out, snatching all and tearing all from its moorings, spreading tornadic, unexpected chaos far and wide. For the first time humankind knew the truth that had occupied the sweated nights of two generations of statesmen and generals: what a modern atomic bomb does, even one of moderate size, is even more unimaginably ghastly than the public has been allowed to know.

Terror rode on the shoulders of the world.

14

THE FIVE PILLARS OF ISLAM

Nabila was at her home workstation trying to find anything, anything at all that might help, all the while imagining Jim out there in the night, imagining his peril, when the phone rang. She snatched it up. It was Operations, telling her that the deputy director had not appeared at Deer Valley Airport.

She forced her heart down out of her throat. "Move the plane anyway," she said, obedient to Jim's instructions.

Had she just lost the husband whose love she had so unexpectedly rediscovered on this terrible night? She might never know.

She wanted coffee and, even more, a cigarette, but no more of that. But the fragrance was so comforting, the tobacco scent of memory.

She found Rashid standing silently in the kitchen, staring at the television that stood on the counter. She could not offer him the comfort she had given him when he was little and afraid. She held her own tears in, her anguish—no, despair—for her husband, her life, her poor, misconstrued faith, and the people who were suffering and dying now in Nevada.

"I feel so responsible," she whispered. "If only we'd been better!"

He turned to face her. "We must respect God's will."

"This isn't God's will. Evil is *never* God's will!"

"All is God's will."

She stopped her angry reply in her throat. This was no time for a religious argument. Like him, she'd read every word of the Quran. But she had approached it with a Western eye to the text, and had come to believe that Mohammed alone had not written the whole book. The reason was that the writing style changed so much. She saw that there were three Qurans. One of them soared above the mind of man, another was practical and wise in the way God must be wise, and a third, very different document was about brutality and power and the ruin of all who did not embrace the faith. She thought that the Muslims needed to reform their approach to the Book. As the Christians had gradually abandoned Deuteronomy 13, with its admonition to kill all nonbelievers, the Muslims must accept that the violent suras were a corruption inserted by human beings and not the word of God.

The clock on the stove ticked its frantic ticking. Outside the open window, the lower branches of the oak stirred with a predawn breeze. How was it, when she looked back across her life in the Company, that it always seemed to be night? The sky was deep blue, dawn just visible now at the top of the window.

She and Rashid were both waiting for their pagers. All across the planet, military and intelligence operations were going into action, as the vast, immensely complex protective infrastructure of the world raced to crisis mode.

Certain countries, she knew, would be preparing for the worst: Iran would fear attack, and Syria. North Korea would not, because they had dismantled their nuclear program in 2007. But, of course, everyone in the community suspected that they had actually sold the highly enriched uranium that they had produced, probably to Hezbollah. In fact, the nuclear material that the Israelis had destroyed in Syria in 2007 was believed to have come from North Korea. Damascus hadn't protested the incursion because the central government had not known that the shipment of highly enriched uranium was even present in the country. It did, know, however, that the detonation of a nuclear weapon in Israel would not only decimate the Jewish population, it would kill millions of Palestinians, too, and lead to the immediate destruction of Damascus.

Had the North Koreans been somehow responsible for what had just happened to Las Vegas? Her mind flashed with an image of Pyongyang in the springtime, the streets empty, flower boxes everywhere blooming with pink Kimjongilias, the begonia variant cultivated to honor Kim Jong Il's birthday in 1988. She had never been there physically, but she had traveled those streets in real time, when she'd worked on a photomapping program that was designed to map every important place in the world.

"I'm not getting a call yet," Rashid said.

"Me, neither."

"Suppose they don't call us because we're Muslim."

"We're cleared. They have to call us. Especially—"

Her pager beeped—screamed, it seemed to her.

"—especially you."

It was not a call to go on dispersal. It was her emergency code requiring immediate action. "I have to go on the secure network here, right now," she said.

His beeper warbled. He looked at it. "I'm on dispersal."

The reality of what the two messages meant was immediately clear to both of them.

She looked into his eyes. Saw the shock there, in their wideness, their liquid glassiness. His tongue touched suddenly dry lips.

What had just happened was that he had been ordered to go to dispersal and live, she to stay in Washington and probably die.

They embraced. If his unit was on dispersal and she wasn't even being given time to drive to Langley, it could mean only one thing: her services were needed immediately because Washington itself was under threat and the Internet might help them deal with it in some way right now. His work did not require him to be in harm's way. He would therefore come under provisions of National Security Presidential Directive 51, which required him to go immediately to a secondary location outside of the metro area.

Without speaking, he turned and went into his bedroom. She heard him pulling out his emergency case and then went back to her own office, closed and locked the door, and drew the curtains. She turned on the green gooseneck lamp on her desk, then pulled the radio-frequency shield out of its hiding place in her bottom drawer. It was designed to absorb any radio frequencies emanating from her laptop—frequencies that could be picked up by ultrasensitive satellites. Her every keystroke could potentially be logged and transmitted to any location in the world.

The shield was green plastic embedded with copper screen. She fitted the laptop into it, then opened it and turned the computer on. This was not a home computer. It was a highly sophisticated instrument in a smallish box. It flashed on at once. She saw the seal of the secure network, and waited as a link was established. Saw Marge come up. She was in her home office also. They could communicate verbally, but it was less secure. Marge's message box said: "We've got orders to do a selective shutdown of the Internet. Isolate the U.S. west of the Rockies, no I/O. Thoughts?"

"BI." Meant "bad idea," which it was.

"?"

"They need information. Take it from them, you spread panic."

"WTU." Meant: Will Transmit your opinion Upstairs.

One of Nabila's 'bots began flashing. She double-clicked it.

And there was the most stunning, the most monstrous thing she had ever seen in her life.

It was a Web site coming out of Japan. In an instant she saw that it had originated at the Toyama Campus of Waseda University in Tokyo. She grabbed the site, just glancing at the first few words.

The site wasn't intended just for her, not this time. It was in the open.

She saw that it must not be allowed to reach the media, not in this form, not at any cost. Her fingers flew as she plunged into the Japanese Internet backbone, racing after Waseda's server farm.

She found it, shot Marge an instant message: "Doing a DSA Waseda University. MTC."

She set a million calls a second on Waseda's servers. That would freeze them. She could only hope that nobody else had seen this, because it was the most incendiary single document ever written by the hand of man, and it almost made her literally scream aloud, howling her terror into the dawn light that was beginning to stream in the windows.

She ported her copy of the website over to Marge, then watched her 'bots. They weren't finding anything else like it. No, this had been done the same way as the *hijab* document—a single website, probably put up for just a short time. But she couldn't risk that. As far as she was concerned, Waseda would remain off-grid forever.

They could have posted the site in a million different places, public as all hell, but they had not done that, and she now realized why. It was the humiliation factor. World leaders—the president first—were going to have to tell their people about this.

COMMUNICATION FROM THE MAHDI OF THE EARTH OF MUSLIM PEOPLE
GLORY TO GOD, THE CALIPHATE OF ETERNAL PEACE IS COME.
THE END OF TIME IS HERE.

Because the Crusader harlots, fallen daughters of God all, did not bow their heads beneath the veil, there was a serious consequence.

Now, bowing before God, all must pray. The Five Pillars of Islam are established for all, and all must now join themselves to the joy of prayer as established in the Law.

All law, and the only law, is now the law of Šarī'ah. Immediately, all must perform *sadaha* in accordance with the Law.

The Crusader King, William Johnson Fitzgerald, must perform *sadaha* before all mankind at once. He must say before all the world, "Ašhadu 'al-lā ilāha illā-llāhu wa 'ašhadu 'anna muñammadan rasūlu-llāh," in a clear voice. He must then say in his uncivilized tongue, that the ignorant may understand, "I testify that there is no God but Allah, and Mohammed is his prophet," and must say, then, that he is humble to the Faith. He must open the vaults of his weapons and cause his soldiers to lay down their guns in all the world. The minions and viziers and soldiers of the Crusader King must all perform *sadaha* at once and be seen to face Mecca in prayer, in accordance with the Law. They must remain in the dirty city of Washington. They may not leave.

All lairs of apostasy are closed and may not be entered. Anyone entering a Christian church is apostate and subject to the Law. Anyone entering a Jewish synagogue is apostate and subject to the Law. All worship in the names of false gods and statues now ends, and the Hindu, the Christian, the Jew, and all others proclaim *sadaha* in accordance with Law.

From the high places all around, henceforth this is ordered: that the prayers be proclaimed in loud voice at the appointed times, in performance of the *salah,* the five prayers of each day.

This must be done at once, or there will be a serious consequence. Your savior loves you, and will be pleased to communicate further with God's people, when God wills.

15

A LOST WORLD

The president was still in his helicopter when news of the latest Mahdi communi-cation came in the form of an urgent bulletin from the Director of National Intelligence. The president took one look at it and picked up the phone. "Logan?"

"Yes, Sir."

"Is Matt safe?"

"They're in their bunker."

"Thank God." So the vice president could reconstruct the government if he had to. Or rather, when. "I'm coming back."

"Sir, you can't—"

He hung up, then communicated with the flight deck. "Take us back," he said.

Immediately the chopper banked and began its churning return to the White House. A headwind made it bounce. Outside, dawn burst forth in shades of pink and red. They flew low over the glowing trees of Bethesda, so low that he could see autumn leaves running along the streets.

His secure phone rang. Webb Morgath, Director of National Intelligence. The president snatched it up. "Webb?"

"This document *requires* the entire U.S. government to remain undispersed."

"Make sure that no media says anything about the Fifty-one activation. And nobody—I repeat, *nobody*—is to know that I left the White House at all. If there's any media awareness, invoke national security and suppress it. It can't look like we came back with our tail between our legs."

The chopper circled and came in for a landing on the lawn. He saw that the entire damn press corps was swarming outside the closed gates, waiting to be let in.

As he stepped out, Tom Logan met him. "Sir, we have evidence of deep penetration of the FBI and probably the operational infrastructure of the CIA. There is an agent coming in with more detail."

"Reliable?"

"You're never sure, are you?"

"What's his résumé?"

"He's a counterproliferation expert. The deputy director says he's the best there is."

"Is he reliable or not? Come on, goddamn it, evaluate the man!"

"Reliable!"

"Okay, hit me."

"He won't disclose anything over the phone."

"Crap!"

"What else can he do?"

"Yeah, if they're out there, they're gonna be after White House communications, for sure."

The president's thoughts went to Leandro Aragoncillo, living proof of White House vulnerability. He'd been in the Office of the Vice President for years. Because of that case, an effort was being made to establish an effective internal security program that would cover all sensitive services.

Two months ago, in response to Fitz's request, the inspector general of the Justice Department had reported that their efforts were "progressing," which he knew was bureaucratese for "nothing doing."

Aragoncillo, a Secret Service agent, had worked in the offices of Al Gore and Dick Cheney, and had been reporting to the Philippines, for the love of God. And who the hell had those bastards been selling the information to?

That, plus Brewster Jennings and other situations—who knew how deep the problem might be? One thing was very clear: Fitz was master of a ship with a broken rudder, and they were in shoal waters.

As he walked toward the White House, breathing the cool, tart air of a smoggy morning, Tom continued, "The pope and the prime minister are both holding. France is scheduled in twenty minutes, then Germany, Japan, and Italy. Russia—"

"No Russia."

"Israel?"

"I want Webb Morgath, Wally Benton, and the generals on a conference call in my office in fifteen minutes." That would be the Director of National Intelligence, the CIA director, and the Joint Chiefs. "I want the statutories on call." That was the National Security Council and its statutory advisers. "I want *no* support personnel on the line whatsoever. I want a Marine guard around the White House and around my person. The Secret Service is going to have to withdraw."

"Sir?"

"You heard me. Do it, Tommy."

"Sir, the Secret Service?"

"If we are looking at a penetration, we have to assume that they would try hard to compromise my personal detail." He stopped, looked at Tommy's ashen face. "Your eye is twitching."

"I know it."

"This, too, shall pass. Maybe. Now get things in motion for me, please."

"Sir, everybody's here."

"*Here?* My God, they belong on dispersal!"

"Sir, when you came back, so did they."

"But not Matt?"

"No, he's still secured."

Had he returned, Fitz would have had him arrested, returned to his bunker, and imprisoned there.

Still striding, Fitz shook his head. The others were still fools to come back. Without them, rebuilding the government would just be that much more difficult. So he'd do this as fast as possible and get them the hell out. He reached the Rose Garden and went inside. And there stood Dan, his son. Gone was the nose piercing. His hair was cut—roughly, but in a conventional cut. The media's beloved Goth had disappeared, transformed into the kind of kid this president had hoped to show the world.

"What in hell, Danny, get out of here!"

"Dad—no."

Sudden anger flared in him. How could Dan be so dense? "This is a death trap, for God's sake! We're in our grave, all of us who are in this place."

"Dad—"

"You're young; you have no business taking a risk like this. Look, your mom's in Newfoundland, and I'm ordering you to join her. You go out to Andrews. There'll be a plane. You and your sister be on it."

"Mom is here."

"That can't be true."

"She landed at Andrews twenty minutes ago. And Polly's on her way."

"This place could go, Son. Any minute. You need to leave."

"Dad, your family is here, and we're *gonna* be here."

Then it would be all of them, all of the Fitzgeralds, vaporized together in this lethal place. He didn't want it, but he accepted it because he had no time to argue. He embraced his son and felt his arms around him, felt his hand patting his back, a gesture of gentle support, simple, telling of the bond between them.

He took a deep breath, then gave his son's elbow a squeeze and went past him into the Oval. He'd do it all from the ceremonial office, because today was history—probably the last day of history as the world knew it—and he was damned if he would do it anywhere except in the center of power and authority. The Oval.

16

EXCELLENT PLANS

Fitz supposed he was nothing but a sentimental fool, but he never entered the Oval without feeling the presence of all the great men who had worked here before him. He thought of decisions that had been made here, and what might have gone through the minds of the men making them. From here, Truman had dropped the bomb on Japan. From here, Kennedy had sent men to the moon. From here, Johnson had ended segregation. And from here—in here—Fitz would do what he could to repair the most horrendous breach of American security in history.

On his desk, the classified briefer lay open and ready to read. Fitz glanced down at it. A probability study analyzing who might be responsible, based on that idiotic concept of "chatter." Why would chatter be so important, for the love of God? It was chatter, wasn't it?

The Iranians were chattering the most, it seemed. Of course they were; they probably expected a bomb down their throat at any moment. The Syrians were chattering, the Israelis, the Egyptians, the Afghans, Pakistanis, Indians, Chinese, Kazakhstanis, Ukranians, Russians—along with, he supposed, the rest of the world. Who wouldn't be chattering right now? Even the Vatican was on the list.

There was, in short, nothing of value in the briefer.

Billions of dollars a year, a decade of reorganization, thousands of brilliant and courageous people, superb equipment—and *Las damn VEGAS was murdered*!

Shame. Shame on them. Shame, above all, on William Fitzgerald, who had believed in a system that was rotten, broken, shattered—*penetrated.*

The thing was, and he could not deny this, he had known. Why else had he been after the Justice Department to plug the holes? *Face it, Mr. President, you knew damn well.* Not specifically, of course. But he had known that somewhere in a system this large and this porous there had to be water gushing in, bulkheads collapsing, watertight doors that should be closed being left wide open.

You knew, Fitz. Their souls are on your conscience. You're the president and the buck just stopped. Their blood is your responsibility.

He hit the intercom. "Millie, is it still burning?"

"Sir, you can see. It's morning there now. It's all smoke."

They seemed to come to the door of his soul, the ocean of the dead, holding out their children's smoking bodies, calling to him, asking him why he hadn't protected them.

He wanted to cry, but he was too mad to cry.

He looked down not at the briefer but at the hands that held it. His hands. Mottled, a bit thick, a broken nail, his gold wedding band the only decoration. They were the hands of a man who, before this day was out, might order retaliation for this terrible, evil act.

Dream Angel would take hundreds of millions of lives. What was worse, Dream Angel was one of those absurdly theoretical plans that never worked the way they were supposed to work. All he knew about it for certain was that it was going to cause untold human suffering.

He pressed the intercom again. "When the Joint Chiefs arrive, I'll expect to discuss Dream Angel."

"Yes, Sir," Millie replied.

Quickly he considered the protocol of his telephone calls. The PM first, then the pope. The United States was a secular state, after all, and in any case, what could the pope offer but prayers?

Fitz picked up the phone. "Good morning, Cameron, sorry for the delay. I'm in my pajamas and an overcoat."

"Fitz, first, of course, there are no words—"

"Can you help me?" Four simple words, from one man to another and from his American people to their ancient British source.

"I've asked MI6 to review everything. Literally, everything, for any shred, any scrap—"

"What about London?"

"We're on crisis dispersal now. And coping with the civilian traffic moderately badly, I'm afraid. I think every hotel in the countryside has been booked by Londoners."

"You need a continuity-of-government plan."

"We're behind on that."

"You're not alone. I just hope it's not too late. Where are the French, the Italians, the Germans?"

"Nobody has a continuity plan, not that contemplates decapitation."

"We've been fools, all of us."

There was a pause, as if to absorb the enormity of that statement. "I'm not at Number Ten, in any event," Cameron finally said.

"I'm in the White House."

"Fitz, I just wish to God that there was something I could do!"

"You have this so-called Mahdi's little missive?"

"Oh yes."

"It came from Japan. The one before that—so innocuous they didn't tell me about it—from Finland."

"It was designed to create discord, that first one."

"In what sense?"

"Too small to matter. Therefore, the people who didn't recognize its seriousness will be blamed."

"No witch hunts. No time."

"They will be demoralized."

"Cameron, we have a security problem on this end. Is there any knowledge of it over there?"

No response. The silence extended. Then, "Truthfully, how can I know? Certainly I haven't been told."

"Ask MI6, if you don't mind. If they know anything, any hint, let me know. Or Matt, if I'm no longer involved."

"Fitz, you're a great man."

"Too scared for that, Cameron."

"We'll raise a glass together, in victory."

That sounded about as hollow as anything Fitz had ever heard in his life. "We will," he said, trying to force something like optimism into his voice.

He hung up and said to Millie, "I'm going to do the press conference at nine sharp. Let them know."

"You have an urgent from Mr. Hanlon."

The director of the Secret Service. Fitz picked up the phone. "Charlie, don't talk; just listen. I have credible evidence that there is a penetration of our security services, which made this whole catastrophe possible. I cannot know who we can trust."

"Sir, we are absolutely clean. You know how carefully we vet our people."

Except for spies from the Philippines, of course. "Thank you, Charlie."

"Sir, we're clean!"

He just could not take the risk. "I'm using War Powers to remove you. Stand the presidential party down now." He glanced toward the door. "Where are my Marines, Millie?"

Logan had come in. "Company A is deploying now."

"Okay." Fitz went back to the phone. "Charlie, I don't want war to break out between the Secret Service and the Marines. You stand down."

Charlie did not reply.

"Charlie, that's a direct presidential order issued during a national emergency." He fought to recall the exact terms of the act. What did he need to say to get this to happen?

"Yes," Charlie said at last. "Yes, Sir."

Fitz hung up. Logan said, "The pope is waiting."

"The pope, Millie." A click. "Your Holiness."

"I speak on most urgent matter," the old man said, his English lightly accented. "I have received a threat from an Islamic fanatic that calls himself the Mahdi. He says we must close all churches or there will be a serious consequence. Mr. President, I must know if this threat is with substance."

He considered, then threw the question back: "Do you have any indication from your own sources?" Contrary to popular belief, the Vatican didn't have an official intelligence service, but it was the world's best listener.

"We believe that the threat in this document has substance. If we do not close our churches, there will be a further bomb. What I want to know is if this is what you call a credible threat?"

The president did what presidents must do, but only good ones do well. He made an educated guess. "Holiness, I can confirm that the document you have is authentic, and is almost certainly linked to the group that has detonated this weapon."

When the pope's voice returned, it was low, and now so thickly accented that Fitz could hardly understand. "We cannot close all churches."

"It's not in your power, anyway."

"No, only the Catholic." He paused. "Is there anything to be done?"

The president considered his answer. He had to communicate force and caution both. "We're evaluating the situation. World leaders will be notified first, including Your Holiness."

"God be with you, then."

He hung up the phone. Millie came in and laid a color printout of the Mahdi's Web page on Fitz's desk. He fingered it, read it, read it again.

He went to the window, and watched the shafts of morning sun, gold and soft, spreading across the lawn. He wondered if he would be alive in fifteen minutes, or in ten . . . or one?

"Fitzie!"

Joy possessed him, followed immediately by as cold a dread as he had ever known, because his wife should not be here. Then the sound of her voice shot a bolt of memory straight into the depths of his mind. He saw her in girlhood, when they had been kids together, saw her in the tree house with little boxes of cereal and milk she had brought for a picnic, holding them while he kissed her and she turned away from him, her eyes as sharp as crystal, her cheeks red. She had a dusting of freckles then.

Tall, proud, her blond hair swinging, she strode to him. But her eyes did not have that crystal sharpness in them now. Her eyes were terrible. She had been crying, and doing it a lot.

He opened his arms and she flew in, and he said, with all the determination he could force into his voice, "Get out of here."

She looked up at him. Briefly there was the old twinkle there. Then it was gone. "Not gonna happen, buddy."

He kissed her.

Logan hovered. "Sir?"

Fitz drew back, taking her taste with him.

"Sir, your meeting's here."

"Let's roll."

The Joint Chiefs came trooping in, and the intelligence chiefs, the secretary of defense, the secretary of state, and the military secretaries.

"Gentlemen," Fitz asked, "can we carry out Dream Angel?"

Air Force Secretary Hobbes said, "The planes are already in the air, Sir."

Fitz looked at the faces of the assembled men, and of his wife and now also, he saw, his son and daughter, who stood in the back of the crowded room.

Dream Angel was the most fearsome military operation ever conceived. Over a thirty-hour period, it would deliver 1,750 W101 neutron bombs across all areas on the planet controlled by Muslim fundamentalists. At least, this was the theory. But Fitz knew military planning and its accuracy. He'd been a young congressman when a U.S. smart bomb had blown up the Chinese embassy in Belgrade. One thing was certain—wherever the bombs actually exploded, they would certainly kill an almost inconceivable number of human beings.

"Very well," he said.

Planes and cruise missiles would deliver the ordnance. From Saudi Arabia to Indonesia, the affected areas of the world would literally be depopulated. The expected death rate was so high that there was an environmental impact assessment that discussed the climatic effects of the huge amount of methane that would be released by the decaying corpses.

"Do we go?"

The question, raised by Air Force General Alfred Mandell, hung in the silence.

Fitz wished that he could raise the question of the penetration. But how could he? Once he reaches office, a president learns very quickly why such a massive intelligence organization is needed. Presidential power extends only as far as presidential knowledge. For example, they were helpless right now because they didn't know anything about this so-called Mahdi, and even more helpless because of this catastrophic security issue.

"What fools we mortals be," Fitz said. He looked at Webb Morgath, who literally twisted in his seat on the uneasy end of a couch. "Webb, can we narrow this thing down? Who's the Mahdi?"

"Sir, I don't have that information."

"Do you know why?"

"We have the website—we know that it was set up on a server at a Japanese university, but that's all we know."

"Japan," Fitz said softly, tasting the history in the word: Tōjō ruining the country, then people bowing to MacArthur's car as it passed, now Toyota and Honda standing astride the industrial economy of the planet.

The world, as it existed now, was an outcome of American victories in

World War II and over the Soviet Union, and American foreign policy since.

But all policy is based on knowledge, and Fitz's knowledge right now was compromised. He knew that Las Vegas had been nuked. He knew that this had happened, almost certainly, because U.S. security assets were being used or neutralized by the enemy. He knew that somebody who called himself the Mahdi had taken responsibility for the bombing. But he did not know if Dream Angel would work, and for a very specific reason. "So what happens if this attack isn't coordinated from within the target areas? We execute Dream Angel and it doesn't help?"

"Sir," Secretary of Defense Mike Ryland said, "with all due respect, that isn't the issue. The issue is spreading terror a thousandfold greater among the Muslims than they can deliver to us. Break their will."

Fitz's phone rang. Every eye turned toward it. All knew the same thing—Millie would never put through a call at a time like this unless it was terribly, terribly urgent.

He picked it up. "Yes?" He listened, then put it down. "Mosques are being set fire to all over the world. The UK, Germany, France, Italy, Japan, India—a huge backlash." Then he added, "It's working both ways. In Cairo and Beirut, they're driving through the streets of Christian neighborhoods, machine-gunning people at random. In St. Louis and Atlanta and Mobile, mosques are burning. A man walked down a street in Seattle, shooting men with moustaches. A Sikh was strangled with his turban in a Dallas shopping mall while a crowd applauded and cheered."

"We need to deploy the Guard," Ryland said.

"Let it run," Webb countered. "Let the energy dissipate now or it'll be worse later."

"No." A voice from the back, tiny with unease. Polly. Fitz sought his daughter with his eyes. She looked back at him from as if from another dimension, her gaze resplendent with the unquenchable hope of youth, her mother's proud lips, determined, supremely confident that her dad was the great man she believed him to be.

"Here are my decisions," he said. "I am federalizing the National Guard in every state except Nevada, under provisions of the National Defense Authorization Act of 2007. I am declaring that a state of martial law exists in the United States, and I am ordering the armed forces to DEFCON 1, with the specification that nuclear weapons must be mounted and armed at once.

I am further commanding that any aircraft without specific military authorization found in flight in the United States, day or night, are to be shot down without warning. I am closing the borders, and please inform the Mexican and Canadian embassies that anyone crossing will be shot on sight until further notice, with regrets; I'm sure they'll understand." He stopped.

There was silence. He knew why. All of the above was expected. It was another order that they were waiting to hear.

He looked again from face to face. Briefly his wife's eyes touched his. He went on. His daughter's pleaded. Brave girl—until a month ago she'd been working at an AIDS mission in Botswana. She knew all too well the suffering of the third world and therefore the agony that Dream Angel would cause.

"Very well," he said. "Now listen. I am going to communicate to the vice president that it is my recommendation that Dream Angel be enacted if Washington, D.C., is destroyed. Is that understood?"

Polly shook her head back and forth, back and forth, so hard that the only sound in the room was that of her hair swishing. Her face had gone bright red. He could see tears flying.

Then they all erupted. "Mr. President!" "Fitz!" "Sir!" All of them, their voices furious.

"What do you want me to do?"

"Not be a damn coward!" General Mandell blurted.

"That's out of line, General." Fitz knew that there could be a coup. He knew that the entire government could fly apart on this morning like an overwound spring.

Mandell saluted him. "Sorry, Sir."

"What I am looking at is threats that originated in Finland and Japan. Not in Iran, not in Saudi Arabia, not in Pakistan." He took a deep breath. "And I am looking at something else." He glanced toward Logan. "That I cannot discuss, even in this room.

"What I can say is this. Power—world power—is gone from our hands. While we've been listening in on the pillow talk of the princes, the little guy has come up from the kitchen and stolen the damn silverware."

"Mr. President, that's defeatism."

"Shut your mouth, Ryland. You're a damn fool! Fifty years ago, we had divisions to fight against. Waves of Chinese soldiers to cut down in Korea, columns of tanks to blow up. Then came Vietnam, and that was a little different. A sort of army that came and went in the shadows. Then 9/11 and Iraq, and we were fighting ragtag Bedouins, disorganized and sparse on the ground, but far more effective than the Vietcong. But now where are we? Warfare has gone from divisions to individuals to . . . nobody. The virtual state. So you expect me to kill ten percent of the world's population—just to be sure we *don't miss*?"

Now the chorus of complaints rose to a roar, and there was menace in it. He saw bulging eyes. He saw spit in the shouting throats.

"Hear me out!"

They fell silent.

"If we carry out Dream Angel, and afterward we are still under nuclear threat, as I am sure we will be, we might have to surrender—"

There was an explosion of voices. He held up his hands. Sought them with his eyes. He regained control of the room . . . barely.

"Face this. It's reality. What if they do another city, and then tell us they have more, and will do worse? What we do then is surrender. And that can happen *after* we execute Dream Angel."

"You're talking about Western civilization," Polly said, the youth in her voice almost taking Fitz's breath away. "We can't surrender."

But they could, if they were beaten, and he knew it. They would have to. "If we execute Dream Angel and we destroy all those countries, and we miss the leaders of this thing, then they could end up in control anyway. They will punish our people terribly for our actions. We'll be marked as a nation of war criminals, cursed for a thousand years."

Fitz had seen many men break, and they broke all in the same way. There was a stillness; then the shoulders dropped, then the head. He saw his secretary of defense break. "Trust my decision, Mike."

Ryland looked at him. Looked him up and down. Fitz had brought him in because he was hard. A tough, brilliant man with a history in the military, in business.

"You are saying that we've lost."

"Is that what you think?"

"Fitz, we need to retaliate."

Fitz put his hand on Ryland's shoulder. "I want you to say to me, 'We need to kill two hundred million people.' You say that."

"We need to kill these terrorists!"

"*Who?* Who in hell do you mean?" He glared toward the intelligence chiefs, who stood together near the door, as if they wanted to escape. "With all your equipment, all those damned listening devices, all those brilliant agents, you can't tell me a thing. You know when Assad jacks off or Putin blows his nose, *so who is this Mahdi? Where is he*?"

"Sir—"

"We've thrown away billions watching the embassies and the palaces. And what do we have? Not one damn thing!"

Millie gestured from the doorway to her office. The media was ready.

"We're done here," he said.

Logan said, "Your speechwriters—"

Fitz turned to his loyal chief of staff. Tried a smile. Didn't work. "They can't help me," he said. "I'm alone now."

As he left the room, he felt as if he carried a weight of stones. Polly came to him. "Daddy, we're so proud of you."

Anger suddenly came up in him, deep, raw, helpless. "Get out of Washington," he rasped.

She stepped back, her face flushing, her dry lips opening with surprise.

He turned, took her in his arms. "You're so young," he said. "So very young."

As he passed along the corridor, flanked by Marines in full battle dress, preceded by two and followed by three, he gave the order to release the communication that had been received from the so-called Mahdi. In five minutes, Fitz would speak. Now, however, on TV screens, on websites, read over the radio, slapped into newspaper extras, the words of the only man who had ever come close to conquering the world were seen for the first time.

And not one intelligence service anywhere on the planet knew his true identity.

Or no, that wasn't quite true. One knew. It knew him well.

17

BLUE SKIES OF HELL

Ressman had successfully landed Jim in Piedras Negras. Jim had done what he had to do there, then crossed the Rio Grande in some shallows and made his way to Kenneally's little love nest. Jim had been watching the mobile home for an hour. From inside he could hear the president's voice on the television, could catch a few words. It was seven twenty in the morning now, full light. He hung back in a grove of twisted mesquite trees, moving as little as possible in order to take advantage of the dark trunks as camouflage.

He knew the contents of the terrorist website. He'd heard it read on the car radio. Everybody on the planet, he assumed, was aware of it by now. Whether the president embraced Islam or not, Jim thought that Washington would be destroyed, probably at midnight tonight. He knew all too well how hard it was to prevent such an attack once the bomb was in place.

They would try to interdict this, of course—even now, Homeland Security operatives were doubtless moving through the city with radiation detectors, filling its streets and skies with surveillance mechanisms, watching every detail of desperate life as the place unraveled. God help Nabby. He could only hope she had made it to her dispersal point.

He moved closer to the double-wide. Thankfully, there were no children. He didn't know if he could do this with children present. It was now seven thirty. His target was moving about inside, so he was probably on an eight-to-four. He would leave in about ten minutes.

Carefully Jim pressed his ear against the wall of the trailer. A female voice, high, quick, full of sobs. Him then, lower, quieter, an edge of tension that suggested a possible vulnerability to Jim.

He went along the gray wall, staying below the line of the windows. He reached the screened back door, grasped the handle. He saw that the door was spring-loaded and would make a distinctive creaking sound as it was opened. There was no way to surprise them; they were going to know that he was coming in.

He took a breath, deep. He was going to have to face a gun. He was going to have to terrorize people and hurt them, maybe kill them. He thought of the towering cloud and the dead, and pulled the door open.

The moment the springs creaked, there came a challenging male voice: "Hey!"

Jim stepped in, finding himself in a kitchen—green linoleum, a countertop range crowded with four small burners, a narrow fridge. The window above the sink looked out on a black Tahoe. The room, the whole trailer, was thick with cigarette smoke. From the living room a parrot chattered above the droning, mournful voice of Anderson Cooper on CNN.

"Who are you?"

Jim smiled at Kenneally. "A ghost. That's why you couldn't kill me. Who's your contact?"

"Get out."

"No can do. Who paid you?"

The wife called out, "Arthur, who is that?"

Arthur Kenneally was big, hulking even. Like some big men, he could move quickly—too quickly. But Jim was also quick. He stepped past Arthur and into the living room, where a handsome woman of perhaps twenty-eight sat in the dark watching the television. She had a large cross in her hands.

He reached down and closed his fist around the lace collar of her nightgown and dragged her to her feet.

Her eyes widened; her body flopped, a fish dragged to the surface. She would scream, but not just yet. He swung her around and slammed her against the fake wood wall beside the door. The whole trailer shook; the wall snapped; she cried out.

"Who paid you, Arthur?"

"Freeze!" He pointed a pistol at Jim.

Foolish move. Jim needed a gun. He wheeled, putting Mrs. Arthur between himself and his adversary. "She can die; it's okay by me."

"Arthur!"

"Who paid him, love?" Jim threw her against Arthur, who stumbled back into the kitchen, his gun flailing.

It was a Colt .45, U.S. Army issue, heavy and hard to handle. Probably Arthur's daddy's gun. Customs and Borders weren't issued weapons like this. Jim saw the two pounds of pistol shaking, its muzzle wobbly. Using a quick, accurate step, he raised his foot and connected with the man's wrist. The pistol hopped, then flew from the man's flopping hand.

With a crash, it slammed into the ceiling. Jim hurled Arthur's woman into his face and caught the weapon as it fell. "New rules," Jim said.

They lay in a heap, both now in shock, Arthur still believing that he was going to be able to control a situation that was far from his ability to handle.

Jim grabbed a fistful of collar and dragged Arthur to his feet. "Who paid you?"

"*What?*"

Carefully restraining himself, Jim pistol-whipped him.

Arthur slammed into the wall. In the living room, the parrot began screaming.

Now Jim got the woman to her knees. So pretty, the face tiny and delicate, the skin almost translucent.

He jammed the gun into her mouth, shoving hard enough to make her gag, jerking it so that there would be blood for Arthur to see. Then Jim pulled it out and threw her on top of Arthur. "Who paid you, Art?"

"Get out," the woman shrieked, blood flying from her mouth. "Get out!"

Jim took her by the hair and dragged her into the living room. As Arthur came to his feet, Jim waved the gun at him. "I excite easily," Jim said. "It's a fault." He pressed her face against the television. "Arthur did this. Las Vegas is burning and Arthur is personally responsible. Arthur will be executed, and if you don't tell me everything you know right now, you'll take a needle, too."

Jim drew her away from the television and threw her onto the couch. When she hit, she cried out.

"I had nothing to do with this!"

"Don't even try, Arthur."

"But—what? What did I do?"

"Removed the ASPs from Bridge One. Who was out there in the *brasada* with you, Arthur? Who was in command?"

"Arthur, what is this? What is this man saying?"

"What I am saying is that your husband took out a major U.S. city, goddamn it! He killed a million people!"

"Arthur?"

"Shut up!"

Jim felt a fiery pain in his back, and realized that she had pulled a knob off a cabinet and gouged him with the screw in its base.

Roaring, Arthur pushed toward Jim. His aggression told Jim that he understood that something was wanted from him and therefore that the gun was only a prop.

Jim stepped aside with a dancer's ease, and Arthur crashed into the kitchen table, bending its aluminum legs and causing it to slide to the floor.

Now the woman leaped on Jim's back. He ducked forward, twisted his arms behind him until he could find purchase in her clothing, then hurled her forward and out into the living room, where she fell hard against the birdcage, releasing the terrified parrot, which flew out screaming, his green plumage gay in the clutter of the wrecked space. As he fluttered around and around the swaying ceiling light, his shadow made the walls dance and the woman screamed and screamed, cringing on the floor.

Arthur came back and found out that the gun was not quite a prop when it slammed into the side of his head, knocking him into the stove.

Jim leaped on Arthur and pinned him. "You tell me or I will turn on this burner in three seconds." An otherworldly calm had descended on Jim, as it always did in these situations. Afterward, he knew, he would turn into a knotted mass of agony, his throat burning with acid, his guts sour with bile. But now, he was moving in his zone of balance.

He turned on the burner, which was under the back of Arthur's neck. As Jim expected, the whole body lurched, the face turned purple, the eyes bulged, and spitting, orange flames came out around Arthur's head, making him look for a moment like a crazed saint.

In Arthur's howl Jim heard the tone of assent, and he turned off the burner. As Arthur chewed, his face bright with grimace, Jim drew well back. Arthur's vomit was white froth. "Egg Beaters for breakfast," Jim said. "Good idea. You oughtta stop smoking, too."

Jim yanked Arthur up off the range. His burnt hair added a nauseating stench to the fetor that already filled the house. Now a new smell—piss. Arthur's sphincter was releasing. "Now, Arthur, tell me."

"It was an order!"

"From?"

"Channels. An ordinary order. And we'd gotten them before, when that system was first being deployed, and it turned out not to work."

"The order is filed?"

His wife began screaming again. Jim turned toward her. "Shut up," he said. She didn't. "What's her name, Arthur?"

"Gloria!"

"Gloria, if you don't settle down, I have to kill Arthur."

As Jim dragged Arthur back into the living room, she gobbled the next scream. Jim tossed the big man onto the couch, then picked Gloria up and threw her down beside him.

"Now, let's all understand each other. I am here for two reasons. First, Arthur destroyed or disabled the advanced spectroscopic portal radiation monitors on Bridge One, which enabled Mr. Emilio Vasquez to smuggle at least one atomic bomb into this country, which was detonated at midnight over Las Vegas. And Arthur tried to kill me when I found out." He smiled at Arthur. "So let's see if we can get past that bullshit about you following orders. Unless somebody ordered you to come after me. Who might that have been?"

Gloria's face contorted so much she took on the appearance, almost, of something not human. Jim was reminded of ancient busts of Medusa. It was terror so great it appeared as rage. He knew it, he'd seen it before, and it shamed him to know that he was responsible for such suffering—but not enough to make him stop.

"Tell him," Gloria said.

"Shut up!"

"You tell me if you know, Gloria, and you'll be spared the needle."

Her eyes were furtive now, stopping at the door, stopping at the window. The parrot flew round and round, his cries as precise as a metronome.

She lifted a hand, as if to capture the bird. "He'll fly into the window!"

Jim braced the pistol in her face. "Last night, Arthur burned sixty thousand or so children to death." He had made up the number. "So you can understand why I don't give a shit about the damn bird."

"Don't tell him anything," Arthur snarled.

Jim put the muzzle of the gun against Arthur's knee. "This will blow your leg in two."

"I'll go into shock."

"She knows, Arthur. And I know she knows. So your life no longer matters."

Arthur closed his eyes. "We had an ONI officer come down here. He met with me and we went over to Piedras Negras together and had dinner with Vasquez. That night, I was ordered to stand the bridge detail down for twenty-five minutes between four and five in the morning, which I did. I saw men in the river; then I heard noises under the structure. That was it."

"The ONI officer showed a badge?"

"He sure did, and it checked out."

"You did a GSA secure database run? You personally compared the officer to the photograph?"

"It was the same guy."

"Name?"

"His name is Franklin Isbard Matthews. He's in ONI security, works out of Washington."

Probably a real person who had no idea that he was following orders generated by the enemy. In other words, a dead end, not even worth following.

The parrot flew past screaming and Jim reached up and caught the little green guy, and carefully returned him to its cage.

"God, you're fast."

"Fast," Jim responded without interest. He pushed the gun into his belt. "Thanks for the piece." He would not leave them bound. They were useless now, and nothing they could do would change anything.

As he left, though, he went along the side of the building until he found their phone line. He ripped it out and shattered the switch box with his heel. Then he stepped into the yard, backed up until he could see their satellite dish. He drew the gun from his waist, aimed it, and fired. This produced a deafening roar and the predictable hard kick. But he was practiced with many pistols, and he loved a .45 automatic, and one of the reasons was what happened on the roof, as the dish and its box of electronics shattered into dozens of pieces, accompanied by another scream from Gloria and the cries of grackles that rose from the mesquite trees surrounding the house.

He went to the Kenneallys' car, opened the hood, and pulled off the distributor cap. Taking it with him, he faded back into the brush, moving as if he was angling toward the road their property fronted on. He passed mesquites and cacti, inhaling the dry air, faintly sweet with autumn rot, the smell of the ripe mesquite beans the grackles were eating.

When he was invisible from the house, he shifted direction, and headed for the actual location of his car, a little-used fence road two miles back on a neighboring ranch. On the way, he tossed the distributor cap aside.

When he got to his car, he opened the bottle of water he'd left on the seat and drank it down, then ate the power bar he'd bought after he'd crossed the river. His first stop had been Piedras Negras, where Mr. Vasquez and his entire family now lay dead in their house. Unpleasant task. Horrible, even. But Jim was past caring about small deaths.

He pushed away the memory of their struggles, the plump wife, the twenty-year-old son with the eyes of a rodent, and Vasquez himself, flapping his hands as if Jim were an annoying fly.

He went onto the roof of the car and looked across the low, brushy land. He'd chosen his position carefully, because from here he could see Arthur's little homestead. The trailer was a white gleam in the sea of yellow-green mesquite. Nothing moving. The truck was still there. Arthur would be wanting medical attention, so he'd probably already be on the hoof. If he got lucky and a car stopped, he might be in Eagle Pass in an hour.

Just to check, Jim opened his cell phone, put the battery back in, and watched as it powered up. A moment passed. Another. Nothing. He didn't want the phone's carrier signal to be available for more than a few seconds, so he removed the battery as soon as he was certain that there was no incoming service. Then he got back into the car, started it, and pulled out onto the fence road. The Global Positioning System came up, but the screen was simply white. No detail. He zoomed out all the way to fifty miles, but still nothing. It didn't matter, he knew where he was going, but still, it was impressive that the 50th Space Wing had shut down NAVSTAR. Made sense, though. A lot of it.

He had one objective, now: Get what he had learned to the president. To Logan. Jim had no intention of giving any names to security at any level, not FBI, CIA, ONI, none of them. If he could get hold of Logan, that would be it.

How far the country had slid, that ordinary civil service types like

Arthur Kenneally and Franklin Matthews would do what they had done, probably for a couple of grand.

Jim arrived at the ranch compound he'd passed, lights out, at four thirty this morning. The ranch had just been getting up, and nobody had noticed the silent, dark car that had moved along the fence line.

They noticed now, though. The rancher, a short, portly man in a weathered straw Stetson, came marching over, waving at Jim to stop. "Yessir," the rancher said as he hurried along, "yessir." As he got closer, he added, "I ain't gonna see none'a my game in your trunk, I hope."

Jim waited for him with his creds in hand. He showed the best he could, which was his real credential. It was not a wallet he often opened, but this was getting actionable on a whole lot of different levels, and if the country survived this crisis, there was going to be an inquiry into every move he made from the moment he discovered the missing detectors on that bridge.

"Well, Sir," the rancher said. "I'm Tom Folbre; you're on the Cut Four Ranch."

"I need the use of a phone and I need it to be private."

"Sir, I can't do that—"

"This is—"

"Sir, they shut down all the phone lines along the whole border. All we have is the TV and radio. No way to call out until further notice. Plus, it's martial law, on-site curfew from Brownsville to El Paso. Nobody leaves home except in an emergency. They got the Army on its way down from San Antonio."

Jim left the man standing there, whipping with the Stetson at the dust Jim's car kicked up. At least the rancher hadn't been as ornery as that old and pitiful guy with the dogs.

Now, what could Jim do? There was another bomb. In fact, there were probably many other bombs.

He wished that he could throw himself on them, become a human shield. He could not have felt more alone.

18

THE FIELDS OF HOME

Jim turned west on Highway 277 and headed for Laughlin Air Force Base near Del Rio. It was a training facility, but a major one, and if there was no C-37 on station, Colonel Adams was going to be able to get Jim to Lackland in San Antonio, where he could pick one up, this time to fly to Washington for real. His call to Nabila had told whoever must certainly be watching him that he was on his way from Deer Valley. That little misdirection was over, though, because that plane had landed empty. He could assume that locating and killing him was once again a number one priority of the people who were enabling this horror to happen.

He turned on the radio. All the stations were broadcasting news. He listened to a border blaster rebroadcasting WFED, Federal News Radio, out of Mexico City. The Hipódromo de las Américas had been closed. The Federal Security Police Service was claiming that the bomb had not entered the United States through Mexico, and the president was protesting the militarization of the border. All flights of any kind had been grounded. Citizens of the Federal District were urged not to buy gasoline unless needed, and a general traffic curfew was in effect.

The chaos and suffering that must be behind these reports infuriated Jim. This was what the bastards had done—not only murdered a great city but also sent all the rest of them, worldwide, into turmoil. How many would be trampled in frightened mobs, how many fail to receive essential drugs, how many go without water or food? And the economic costs were incalculable. Even as things stood now, it would take the world years to recover and there would be blood and sorrow.

His jaw clenched so hard it cracked. He fought back a surge of self-hate that was itself a kind of black internal tidal wave, a rage against his own failure so great that he would have jumped out of this car if he weren't needed to repair the damage.

"Don't," he said aloud. His work depended on self-confidence. He had to push his despair back down into the pit for now.

With an angry stab of his finger, he hit the radio's scan button. Here was WOAI in San Antonio, the voice grimly announcing that all military reserves must report to their units. CONUS was no doubt scrambling for bodies. Jim's guess was that there were under a hundred thousand military personnel available for deployment in the United States.

World stock markets were closed, but the price of gold had gone up eight hundred dollars and oil was pushing through three hundred dollars a barrel. Ships at sea had been ordered to stop, all of them, and the U.S., British, Japanese, and European navies would sink any vessel that entered their territorial waters. Europe had also stopped any nonessential road traffic.

The litany went on and on and on. Jim saw a picture of a world that had been frozen in place as it fell into chaos. How long would it last, though? What of the massive traffic jams, the people fleeing the great cities? Where were they in this? Who was enforcing the various curfews? The answer was clear: nobody.

He moved on along the dial, this time picking up something called KGOD-FM. A Reverend James Haggerty was telling his congregation that God had used the heathens to destroy a place of sin and evil and good Christians must rejoice and fill the churches and prepare to meet God, for the rapture was at hand.

The clash between Muslim fundamentalism and Christian fundamentalism was a battle between two grotesque distortions of religion. The mad battling the mad over, in Jim's opinion, nothing. God's silence was God's truth, and that was what they could not bear to face. Somewhere, there had to be a heaven, justice, and a better life.

Life may or may not be preparation for heaven; Jim didn't know. What he did know was that a hungry kid or a ruined businessman or a worker on a breadline was real, now. And all those burnt bodies, and all this suffering, this was what was real. *And it was his.*

The car's tires whined. He was doing an eighty-eight, and this vehicle, older than the one he'd had on his way to Eagle Pass, had no more in her. He really didn't care to be out here when Army regulars started their deployment. They would be scared, confused, and armed to the teeth. Getting past them was going to be real hard.

He passed Laughlin's auxiliary base and radar station, then shot through the tiny towns of Normandy and Quenado, glimpses of rural poverty and rural peace. He saw chickens in a yard, a little stone house. The lights you saw from the sky at night, in the lonely places—these little towns were such places. He wished he could stop, go into one of those houses, and that would be it.

But his mind returned to Washington. Even if the president and the world did all that the document demanded, Jim thought that the terrorists would destroy Washington if they could, and other American cities. The gauntlet was down. They had to break America now, or they would gain nothing.

He pressed the gas pedal until his foot tingled, but the car would not pass ninety.

He began to watch on his right, waiting for the big, friendly sign that generally announced a U.S. Air Force base. The car seemed to be drifting, the highway gliding past like a slow, old river.

Whereupon he saw the sign and also a dark blue Air Force bus and what looked like a squad of APs in full battle dress. As he dropped his speed, he surveyed the men—kids, actually. They were armed, for sure, but did they have a laptop? If so, they would run whatever ID he gave them, and he didn't trust anything to pass at a time like this except his real cred. If they got a bad answer, he had no idea what they might do. Problem was, his real cred was going to be flagged by the folks who were after him.

No choice, though. As he slowed, they turned toward him, stirring nervously, their hands clutching their weapons. Pulling off the side of the road under the eyes of kids this scared and this well armed was not a pleasant experience. Their lieutenant's lips were dry, his eyes staring. Jim knew how dangerous the stillness of these young men was. If they so much as glimpsed his pistol, they would kill him.

"Sir, get out of the car."

He moved to conceal the gun.

"Get out of the car!"

"Coming out! Coming out slow!" He pulled the door handle. "I want to warn you, there is a weapon on my person."

One of the squaddies rushed the car like a charging lion. *"Get out of the car; get on the ground!"* He threw the door open.

"Okay! Take it easy!" Jim hit the deck, digging into the hot tarmac and the dusty hardscrabble beside it. He could hear insects buzzing, smell dry autumn grass and the sweet, hot odor of his engine, could hear the overstrained block tinkling as it cooled. "I'm a CIA officer. My name is James Deutsch."

"No CIA around here," a piping young voice screeched.

"I am going to move. I am going to get my credential."

A gun barrel thrust into his back. "Where is it?"

"Left side." He hesitated. "When you get it, you will feel the pistol in my belt."

They backed away, then consulted together in hurried voices. Arguing. Then the lieutenant got on his radio.

"No!"

The kid froze. Stared at him.

"Do not put this on a radio. If you've got a gate phone, fine, but if you broadcast this, you are murdering me."

Now they argued again, and this time it was furious. The lieutenant sounded outnumbered. These kids were certainly not prepared to face a situation like this. Their experience probably ran to extracting drunk pilots from beer joints and manning guard stations where they knew everybody who came and went by name.

While they were busy, he pulled out the .45 and slid it toward them.

All the weapons came up. *"Stay on the ground."*

Next, he pushed out his cred. "That's my credential. You read it now, Lieutenant, and then take me to Colonel Adams." Nobody moved. *"Do it now!"*

The lieutenant kicked the pistol away and picked up the cred. Looked at it. "I don't know what one of these things is supposed to look like."

Those words told Jim that this boy knew he needed help. Jim was good at projecting authority. "The credential is fine," he said.

The kid looked down at him. "Where are you from? Why are you here?"

Jim took a calculated risk and got up. Nobody threatened him. "I could tell you, but then I'd have to shoot you."

"You don't have a weapon."

"Okay, let's go," Jim replied, "and leave that radio turned off."

He walked over and got into the car, passenger side. "You need to post a guard on me. That's what your colonel's gonna expect—what's your name?"

"Rawson, Sir."

"Okay, Lieutenant Rawson, you drive and post your guard in the backseat."

With one of the airman sitting behind them, they drove onto the base—which, on first viewing, appeared to be abandoned. Jim knew that this was because it was in its highest alert state, which meant that personnel did not move unless ordered and all aircraft were under cover. The sky would normally have been full of trainers and the streets full of vehicles and airmen. But the only things flying there now were buzzards, wheeling with dark grace.

As they entered the base proper, they passed a golf links. "Decent course, Lieutenant?"

"It's okay."

"Where am I going, son?" As long as it wasn't the guardhouse, these two boys were going to be able to keep their weapons and preserve the fiction that they were in control of this vehicle, which they were not. If he had to, Jim could disarm both of them in five seconds. In another five, their necks would be broken . . . if he had to.

"You're going to HQ. We called it in on the guardhouse phone."

That was acceptable. "Can you tell me if there's a thirty-seven on base?"

"Nothing's flying, sir."

Jim did not reply. When they pulled up to the curb in front of base HQ, an AP in fatigues opened the door. "Come with me, please, Sir."

As Jim walked with him, the rest of the escort fell in behind. They went down a long, polished hallway and entered Colonel Adams's office suite.

The colonel's compact, powerful build told Jim that he'd flown fighters. He stood up without smiling and took Jim's credential. Examined it. "How can I help you, Mr. Deutsch?"

"I need a ride to Andrews. Now."

"That is hard."

"Is there a thirty-seven available? Anything that can get me there?"

"Oh yeah. It's just clearances."

Jim took a chance here. He said, "The White House will take care of that. I need to make a call. I need the most secure line you possess. And I'm also going to need a uniform and the name I'm flying under."

"Uh, wait—"

"You have AFOSI staff here, I'm sure. I'll fly under the credentials of the senior officer."

"That would be Major Carstairs."

"Very well, Colonel. Major Carstairs is going to Washington to an OSI emergency meeting involving border-related issues too sensitive to transmit. He is leaving as soon as clearances are in place." Now came the big one. "Let me make that call."

The colonel took him down the hall to the AFOSI station, where he was able to use an encrypted line. He called the number Logan had given him. It rang. Again. A third time. "Logan."

"Secure on your end?"

"Go ahead."

"Deutsch. I need clearance to fly Laughlin AFB, Texas, to Andrews immediate."

"Done."

"I'll come to you direct from Andrews."

"Is there anything you can say now that will help us?"

Jim glanced at the colonel, nodded toward the door. The colonel stepped out, closed it.

"I would take the ONI and FBI out of the loop immediately."

"I can't do that!"

"This is isolated. Small, but we have to assume that it's perfectly positioned. Normally, I'd say that it wasn't at the director level and that the overall organizations were secure. But under the circumstances—"

"He won't shut them down, not on information like this."

In other words, not on the recommendation of a field operative whom they'd never heard of before. "I can understand that. If he does nothing else, he needs to shut down their communications capabilities."

"Thank you."

Jim hung up. If it happened, it might buy some time. Then he thought, *Maybe it wouldn't do that. Maybe it would do the opposite and make them move faster.* He said to the colonel, "You got any Tums?"

"No, Sir."

"Send 'em to the plane. If they don't get there before we take off, I'll let my goddamn guts eat themselves. And minimize the number of people who see me, and see this plane take off."

"Sir, I—"

"Best effort."

"Yes, Sir."

While the plane was being made ready, Jim was taken to the quarters of a lieutenant who was allegedly his size. The kid was not all that big, though, and Jim had to cram into the uniform.

A silent AP drove him to the jet. The colonel was as good as his word. Aside from the plane's ground crew, there was not a soul to be seen.

"Sir," the AP asked as Jim got out of the car, "what do we do with your car?"

"It's not my car."

"Is it rented?"

"Stolen. There'll be a police report on it in Eagle Pass, be my guess. Tell them your lieutenant went joyriding."

"I'll be sure to do that, Sir."

Jim climbed the steps and pulled the door closed, then secured it. He called up to the flight deck that he was ready to go.

Exhaustion overcame him, and he closed his eyes. He didn't want to; he wanted to watch the route. What happened was not sleep, but it wasn't consciousness, either. The plane became a boat; the morning, night; the air, an ocean. Wind screamed in the rigging; phosphorescent spray flew across the tops of the waves.

The storm was so hellish that he opened his eyes. He looked out across the cold military luxury of the cabin. Outside, white, clean clouds, blue sky, green, sweet land far below. His beautiful homeland, concealing now behind the smiling face that it presented to the sky the darkness of hell.

19

THE NECK MAN

Nabila's familiar office felt unreal to her, as if her desk were a landscape from somebody else's life or the distant past. The leaves still clung to the trees outside her window and the morning garden was dappled with sunlight, all very pretty and peaceful, and for that reason the scene seemed more like a painting on a wall in hell than something real.

She looked at her personal cell phone. This was the number Jim used. If he could call her, it would come in on this line. And how strange that was also, the flush of longing she had felt when she'd heard that careful voice, low and precise and so maddeningly arid, telling of this terrible event, and drawing her into his needs. Later, they would investigate that call. They'd want to know what he had been doing ordering the plane and why she had violated so many rules to help him. There were lying phone calls to explain, forged orders.

She realized that she had not started loving Jim again. She had never stopped. Her heart was tortured with love for him and fear for him—above all, that. To bear her fear, she had suppressed her love. She had not been able to live with the endless worry, the long, dark nights, the cold bed, nor with that sense of being shut out of so much of his life and his thoughts. She recognized that he could share nothing with her of his life. She could share little of her own. But her heart—it recognized only the loneliness.

To stop caring about him, she had divorced him.

She looked at the cell phone, all but willing it to ring again.

Wives of lost intelligence officers waited in sweated anguish, often for years, often forever.

"Jimmy, where are you?" she whispered to the sun of midmorning.

Somehow, she would do her work, continuing to search the ugly backside of the web, the deadly electronic landscape of religious sociopaths and their ugly blogs, spitting hate and, sometimes, clues.

The television spoke of Muslims being killed in London, in Berlin, in Amsterdam, in Paris, even in Mexico City, being shot by truckloads of marauders ranging the streets, the sodden, ruined neighborhoods where the Libyans and Syrians and Iraqis and Palestinians and Algerians fried their little food and muttered over their sweet tea, the Egyptians with their careful, disrespected ways.

They were killing Muslims in their private ghettos, she thought, the lands of the sad.

The heretics—for that's what the fundamentalists were—would not win this. Of course not. Nature and destiny did not work that way. The Arab world had made itself into a dead end. They were like a nation of men somehow washed through time from the distant past, muttering by their fires while the West soared overhead in gleaming planes.

They would not win, but Washington also would not win. Today, Washington would die. She knew this. She had read it certainly in the Mahdi's message. The Mahdi, king of the end-times. What arrogant, stupid nonsense. There was no Mahdi, no more than there was a Wizard of Oz. And that idea of this being the end-times—she refused to consider it. Every woman had a right to experience being the wife of a good man and mother of children.

Washington would not win, because it had already lost. The mere fact that this could happen had ruined it. Now, the breathtaking vulnerability of the West was known.

Suddenly she wanted Rashid to hold her. She wanted to be the dutiful sister she had not been. She wanted not to loathe his effort to restore Šarī'ah in their lives.

She laughed a little. How self-serving was that thought? *Now that Šarī'ah might become the law of the world, you're already seeking to surrender to its bondage. Fear corrodes.*

She closed out her work, isolated herself from the network, then turned the computer off. She went to the door and confronted the large regulation security lock that was required to protect any computer as classified as hers. This room was well sealed, even its windows and the door. When she opened it, she could hear the church bells that had started in the midnight still ringing—she'd never known that there were so many bells in Washington, D.C.—and also sirens, wailing police cars, and the busy, frantic fire horns. There were other sounds, perhaps shots; she couldn't be sure.

Then she heard clattering. She realized that Rashid was still here. She was astonished to find him working on his laptop.

To avoid seeing his screen, she stood in the doorway. "Rashid?"

"What?"

"Shouldn't you be on dispersal?"

"I'm selling that rug."

She almost cried out, she was so astonished. He'd received an emergency call, the country was at war with an enemy he was uniquely positioned to find, and here he was, selling the Sarouk he'd put on craigslist. "You are selling the rug? Now?"

"I have a bite."

"There are people on craigslist today?"

"The offer came in last night."

He was in denial. There could be no other explanation. You did not sell rugs in a city that probably had only hours to live. Or maybe you did. There had been that famous tobacco auction going on in Krakow when the Germans marched in, and in Baghdad the shops had stayed open as the Americans took the city. And wasn't it Boethius who had commented on the barbarians traipsing through his garden while he wrote *The Consolation of Philosophy*?

She heard herself say, idiotically, "I wouldn't have minded if it was the green." The purple Sarouk had been in their mother's bedroom.

"The dyes are bad."

"The dyes are fine. The rug is precious."

She could see his back stiffen. In Šarī'ah law, he was the one with authority to do this. "Would you beat me, then, if I disagree?"

He turned off his computer, got up, and came toward her, two steps. His face, the eyes so large, looked as it had when he was a child, so unsure. "You have a gun," he said, laughing a little.

"I do have." They'd issued it to her and made her learn its secrets. She could fire her AMT Backup with proficiency, difficult as it was to aim the little pistol. "It's in my drawer."

"Right now, it should be with you."

She bowed her head. "You're right, of course." She did not add that he was in violation of Directive 51, still being here. Even craigslist didn't explain it. It was two hours since he'd gotten his orders.

He slid his laptop into his backpack.

She wanted to say something about what was happening to them. "If we—" She stopped. She could not utter the truth. Her blood seemed to moan in her veins.

He looked her up and down.

"Cape May," she said. "Do you remember?"

He nodded. "Blue sky, hot sand, running after the sandpipers."

"Are you afraid, Rashid?"

"I am afraid."

"Me, too. More than I thought I would be. Why didn't they disperse me? If I were you, I'd have gone the second I got my order!"

"It's all God's will. If we live or die. It's just—surrender. Surrender."

"We are responsible for our lives."

"That isn't the story we've been told, Nabby. It isn't faith, to put our own will in front of Allah's."

"Faith is deeper than doctrine. There is only one faith, beneath all the stories."

He gave her a sidelong look. "If I tell you why am I selling rugs, will you tell me why you are spouting philosophy?"

"I'm trying to reach the brother I once had. I believe you're still there, Rashid. I believe in you."

He threw his arms around her. "Come with me, Nabila! Forget your orders and come!"

She shook her head, she fought her tears, but they came anyway, great, wracking sobs that brought with them a thousand memories, so many happy days. She and Rashid had been happy, before Mom and Dad died, and actually for a long time after. So happy!

She held him back away from her. "You go now."

"Nabby—"

"Now, Rashid. God go with you!"

He held her to him, kissed her hair. "God go with you, Sister."

Then Rashid drew back, stepped to one side, and went off toward the garage. She heard the kitchen door slam. Then came the silence of the house.

She went along the worn runner that Daddy had put down in this hall when she'd been ten. It was a lovely Kerman, only now, twenty years on, looking as if it had just discovered it was being trod upon. She jabbed her combination in the lock and went back into her own office, still with the angels on the walls from when it was their childhood playroom, the angels that Rashid was planning to have removed in favor of a geometric pattern.

The bells outside made the familiar space seem desperately silent, and she turned the radio on. "God will not allow these evil monsters to destroy America! I tell you, crowd the churches, jam them, let this monster know what we're made of! Don't tread on me, you Islamofascist bastards! *Don't tread on me!*"

As she listened, she came to realize that this shrieking voice was old Rush Limbaugh, the right-wing talk-show host. For a moment, she was transfixed by the fear in his desperate howl. Then she twisted the dial to the local National Public Radio station and, in the excessive calm of the voice there, heard a different version of the same terror: "Authorities worldwide are canvassing for more bombs, and federal officials now admit what has been an open secret for some time, that in January of 2006 nuclear materials were located in Las Vegas and destroyed. Why the public was not informed at that time will be the subject of a question to be posed to Homeland Security Chief Random Wilkes."

Random Wilkes, another empty suit, as far as she could tell. The expansion of the director level in the intelligence community had done nothing but increase the amount of bureaucracy. Information had to get through so many levels nowadays, it was a miracle that the president ever found anything out. Had the old system still been in place, she had no doubt that he would have seen the threat in the first website. Probably it would have made no difference. But what if it had?

She tuned to the all-news station, where she learned that violence against Muslims was worsening throughout the United States, that Muslims were rioting in Paris, and that the Russian air force was bombing Chechnya.

So far, nothing about U.S. retaliation. Over the course of her career, she'd heard whispers that that there was a scorched-earth scenario available to the United States that involved the destruction of half the population of the Muslim world. It was a hateful, horrible notion, and when Rashid had first thrown it in her face she had agreed with him that it was monstrous . . . and reminded him that it was, also, a rumor.

She hoped that, if it was real, using it would indeed save the West. She had serious doubts, though. Where would the leaders of a program like this be? Not in Karachi or Riyadh, certainly. Far more likely their headquarters would be in some out-of-the-way location too sparsely populated for a program like that to cover, or, more likely, in some middle-level Western city like Barcelona or Columbus that would not be on the nuclear list.

Feeling a congealing, twisted hatred for her own kind—for herself—she forced herself to concentrate on her work. She should never have left this desk, let alone gone off-line. But regs required her to shut down when she left the office.

The ceiling seemed to be getting lower. When the bomb went off, the ceiling would slam into her, she thought, crush her before she could perceive a thing. One instant, she would be this richly alive human being. The next, nothing.

She gave her thumbprint to her laptop, then input her latest password sequence. Her personal seal appeared, confirming that she was back on the secure network. How secure, though, given what Jimmy had said?

The CIA's networks were supposedly secure, but not if there were spies inside the system. Because of her particularly sensitive work, she'd be a very specific target. They would be watching her right now. So here she was, forced to trust something that she did not trust. She opened the small program that told her if anybody was on this node with her. The space remained white, so she continued on, opening her browser and lining up her 'bots.

They were finding hundreds of new sites. Of course, every lunatic on the Internet had something to say, every terrorist group something to claim. Stupid people. Worthless.

She knew she shouldn't do it, but she found herself navigating to craigslist. What was Rashid really doing, anyway, worrying about such a thing as a time like this, to the point of violating orders?

She went to the D.C. section, then to collectibles. She searched on "rug," and there it was, the only one. She opened the page. Stared, confused. How could you sell anything with this sparse offering? There was no picture. There were only four words of description: "Antique Sarouk carpet, purple." Not even the size. And yet he said he had a bite? Impossible, he was a complete idiot.

She knew that she shouldn't use her skills for this, but nevertheless she hacked into their civilian Internet service provider, Washington Cable, and was soon looking at the server space allocated to Rashid's account. She opened his e-mail.

Nothing there except spam, some from as long as six days ago. So if he had read his e-mail as he said he had done last night, why was his spam still on the server? It would have been downloaded with the rest of the e-mail.

She looked in the record of items he had recently sent. There was an e-mail there, its subject heading "Sarouk Carpet." She opened it. There was only one word in the body of the text: "Purple."

Odd and odder. She saw the address of the recipient, a Gmail account. If she wanted to go any further, she would need to contact Google Security. It wasn't difficult. Her program automatically secured the legal permissions necessary.

She wouldn't be alone, though. Every keystroke would be recorded, and Legal might have questions later. If she couldn't answer them, she'd end up under investigation.

She couldn't honestly check the box that said it was a national security matter, not quite. It was just—well, it was odd, that was all.

But this was Rashid, her brother, perhaps too intense about his religion, but certainly a patriot! She was going paranoid. Because this was an insane thing to do, an abuse of power, probably a criminal act.

Instead of checking the box, she did something that was far less illegal, and replied to the buyer as Rashid. She could see that the buyer wasn't in his e-mail account—probably still in his car, in fact—so she spoofed him: "This is Rashid. I am sorry, I have decided not to sell my rug. The offer is withdrawn." She hit send—and immediately the message returned. She checked the network, the servers. The backbone was intact. The route was clear. The problem was quite simple: the address no longer existed in Gmail.

In other words, the recipient had closed the account as soon as Rashid had sent his strange, single-word e-mail.

She sat, staring at her screen, thinking. Her heart was blasting; sweat was running along her underarms.

Now she returned to Google's security sign-in area. She certainly had justifiable suspicion this time. "Rashid," she whispered, her voice miserable.

She checked the boxes, checked that this was a national security matter, and that she had probable cause.

From behind a veil of tears, she sent her request to Google. Sometimes there was a delay. They had their legal issues, too, their oversight protocols. But not today. Today, the reply came back in just seconds. The Gmail account had been opened this morning from a T-Mobile HotSpot in Alexandria. It had been open for just six minutes. Of course, the account's information still remained, but all it did was direct her to that particular Starbucks. She noted the address, though, because she knew now that this was important. Her heart was breaking, but her mind was clear.

"Purple" was a coded message, and therefore her brother was involved in something. What if it had to do with the nuclear attack? Oh, but God, no, that was impossible. Rashid might be tangled up in some silly extremism, but not that. Or there might even be some innocent explanation—a secret society, perhaps. Wahabis in the United States were secretive, and for a member of this community to be flirting with them—he would be very careful.

Still, he had violated the most important order he had probably ever received in order to transmit a code word on a morning when he should have been racing to his dispersal point.

She threw her head back; she clenched her jaw; the tears rushed from her eyes; her nails dug into her palms. Then she drew breath, and a choked cry came out of her, instantly silenced.

Again, she heaved, fighting herself, clapping her hands over her own mouth. She forced herself to stop shaking, to swallow the next scream.

Their father would weep with rage to know that the effort he'd made to get his kids around the prohibition against Muslims in intelligence work had led to this: "Senator, you know Rashid and Nabila from their babyhoods! You know what kind of kids they are!"

She told herself that it wasn't just them, not just the Muslims. After all, had divisions between families like this not happened here before, in the Civil War? But this was her brother's betrayal of her and of their country, not the betrayal of some other brother from long ago.

Jim had warned of a penetration and a serious security problem. She had known at once that her work would be of intense interest to anybody wanting to follow the CIA's efforts to contain this problem. She was an important link in that chain.

So they were almost certainly watching her online activities. Of course they were. But this also meant that they had seen what she had just discovered about her brother.

They would have to act, and at once.

She picked up her cell phone—and then turned it off. She took the battery out and laid it on her desk. She closed her laptop, unplugged it, then removed the battery. She dropped the computer and the battery into her backpack.

How long might she have? Not long. They might be on station somewhere in the neighborhood. Probably were.

Rashid had left her here not to die but to be killed.

She left her office. She knew she had no time to waste, but the weight of the lost past, as she went through the house, slowed her movements. Leaving here was pushing against the strength of a river that was made up of the pictures on the walls, the carpet that had pleased Daddy so much, the couch Mother had loved. Nabila could hear the happy voices still, her mother calling her from the kitchen, her dad—well, she had felt herself a royal child once, simply to be his daughter.

Feeling now like a refugee from some sort of hurricane, she bowed her head and left the house. Rather than taking her car, she walked down to the coffee shop on the corner. She had no intention of using the WiFi node there—or of using the computer again, not until it had been completely examined by digital security, in the unlikely event that she managed to reach Langley.

She walked past the silent houses and the houses where people were leaving, filling their cars, calling to their children, throwing their luggage in, their clothes in piles. An SUV raced away, followed by a dog running hard. The vehicle rounded a corner, the dog still behind it, his big ears flapping as he ran with all his might.

She found the old pay phone in the cul-de-sac beside the coffee bar and dug into her purse, praying that she had change.

She put in two quarters. Dialed. She scrambled for more money. Paid more. And heard ringing. Again. Again. "Please, Jim, oh, *please*!"

"Please leave a message." His voice, at least.

"Jim, it's Nabby. I think Rashid is in it! Oh, God, Jim, help me! There is a word, I think a signal. 'Purple.' That is, the word 'purple.' Jim, where are you? Am I talking to a dead man?"

Unwilling to hold the line open longer, Nabila hung up and walked quickly away. She wasn't sure where to go. The Metro? That might help. Take a few stops, then phone Marge, see if she could be picked up.

But how could she know that whoever showed up could be trusted? She could not know.

She turned a corner, and saw coming this way a car that was too careful to be anything but a spotter. She stepped back into an alley. The car went past.

Her heart hammered. The car was looking for her and therefore the car was proof. Somebody had indeed been watching her every online move, and had seen her make her discovery about the carpet sale.

She watched the car stop at the far end of the alley. There was no time now; whoever was surrounding her would have her in their gun sights in minutes.

They were probably a detail from some agency or other that had been ordered to bring her in or kill her or whatever. They themselves wouldn't even know why—or, ultimately, where—the order had originated.

She went down the alley and into the tangle of bushes behind a row of houses, and used the crackling shrubs for what cover they offered.

Then she saw a man watching her from the tall back window of one of the houses. He wore a T-shirt and had a rifle ported across his chest. She had never felt so acutely aware of her black hair and enormous brown eyes. All she lacked to make her identity certain was a burka. He stared with the steadiness of a practiced hunter. She smiled at him and went on along the alley. Ahead was 9th Street, and just down the block Eastern Market and its Metro stop. But was the Metro still running?

Just as she exited the alley, another suspicious vehicle, this one a white Jeep Cherokee with tinted windows, came around the corner and passed her going north on 9th Street. She tried to duck back, but it stopped. It sat, motionless, engine running. Coming through the alley from the other direction were two men, moving fast. They had pistols in their hands.

She looked again toward the man in the house. Was he a civilian, or another pursuer? No way to know, and no way to know if he would help her or hand her over.

She opened the gate to his back garden and went in. Motionless, he watched her come. Behind her, the men moved more quickly. She reached the house. He opened the door.

"I need your help."

He drew her in.

20

YOU HAVE NEVER MATTERED

Alexei offered Vladimir a Sobrainie. Vladimir looked hungrily at the black tube. "Not smoking," he said. "It is your last lung," Dr. Abramov had told him. "Respect it."

The two men watched the valley, waiting for the last pink echoes of sunlight to disappear. Birds, screaming faintly, sailed in the high light.

"You do it," Alexei said.

All the way from Tashkent, they had carried on a desultory argument, drinking and watching the bleak landscape pass by. "It's for you to do."

"It's loathsome."

Vladimir made scrambling motions with his fingers. "They're going to run all about screeching, 'Don't, mister, don't.' " He chuckled. "You will do it because you are an exceptional man."

When Alexei started with his knife, he couldn't stop. He terrified even himself, the way he killed.

Far below, a truck wound its way along the road. From the installation there was not the slightest sign of activity. "Such peace," Alexei said.

"You're a superman, Alexei."

"Let's go, then."

They were in Afghan dress. Vladimir wore a *pakol,* the favored hat of the mujahideen who had destroyed the Soviet armies. Alexei was in a dark *lungee*, clumsily arranged, which the meddlesome desert wind threatened at all times to unwind. He felt the wind, cooling quickly now, as it insinuated itself under the folds of his *chapan*. He would have preferred the sand-mottled uniform of Russian desert forces, but the American, British, and French satellites could all see two people moving in terrain this sparse, and would immediately notice them. Soon, the drones would arrive, and then God knew what might happen.

Alexei stopped. "Now, what is that spit of land? Is that it?"

Vladimir unfolded the oilcloth map, which whipped in the rising wind. "God, I hate deserts," he muttered. The damned Americans had turned off their Global Positioning System, so the Garmin that Mother Russia had bought for them was now nothing more than baggage. But it had an MP3 player in it, so they could listen to music, anyway. "This is it," he said. "Down there, we find the air shaft."

"Why not just let the Americans complete their fez-boil? We could go back to Tashkent now and drink."

"I have plenty yet." He produced a flask.

"How many of those did you bring?"

"You've stolen everything else of value in my pack. You should know."

"I only steal what others don't need." Alexei took a swallow from the flask. "Jubilee, no less."

"Don't be ridiculous. That's Hennessy X.O."

"I only drink patriotically."

"Then I will be drunk while you kill the children." He pointed. "That's the right ground formation; the entry is there." As he moved ahead, he heard Alexei scrambling along behind him.

"Do we know why we're doing this?" the young man asked.

"Do we care? Without Las Vegas, my hopes for a better future are lost."

"Your sense of humor is too French, dear Vladimir. There was a time when a statement like that would have sent you to the gulag."

"True enough, under Stalin you would be Beria and I would be dead. Now, it's the time of the thinking men, so I lead and you do the bloodletting. It suits you, anyway. Your butcher's hands."

"I have the hands of a pianist."

"Same difference. Did you ever see Denis Naumov perform? His hands look like roasts, but his Debussy—amazing."

"Naumov. Debussy. When I hear the word 'intellectual,' I go for my gun."

They came to the entry port. It was a kilometer from where the fezzes were living, and nobody but a Russian with a proper schematic could possibly get through to the personnel deck. Vladimir had never been inside the installation. They'd been shown photographs, though, so they would be able to comb through it until they reached the flesh. Then their orders were to kill everybody, no exceptions, no mercy, no bribes. If they did not do this correctly, they would, themselves, probably be killed.

Often Vladimir wondered if he actually cared for his own life. He had when he was young, certainly. Had loved it, loved just to breathe. They don't say it in the movies, but when you kill for a living, gradually you also die. Then you are like he was now—dead and alive at the same time.

He had a condo in the South of France, in the development of La Californie. He was happy there, happy to watch the French with their snails for luncheon and their wonderful legs. He would get drunk there, good and drunk, and recite Lermontov, who had been his father's favorite and was therefore also his favorite. "I love you, my friendly dagger, dear friend forged of Damascus steel."

"You're mad as a Chechen, Vladimir."

"Mad and sad, which is to say, Russian. Come now, roast-paws, let's do this work that is ours to do."

"You call it work?"

"What else is it?"

They entered the air shaft, bending low and moving fast, their way lit by their powerful German-made flashlights. The deeper they went, the louder the intake fans became. Soon they were churning and wind was whipping past the men's heads. "Don't let that idiotic turban get into that thing," Vladimir said. "I don't need your head torn off."

"I was issued this turban."

"I was issued a turban also. Do you see me wearing one?"

"I see you wearing the uniform of the bastards who wrecked our army."

"Let me ask you this, Alexei. What is one mujahid with a cigarette lighter responsible for?"

"I have no idea."

"Six Soviet tanks."

"Traitor."

"Just getting your blood up. Here's the hatch." He opened his general-purpose tool and loosened the old bolts, probably last tightened thirty and more years ago, by some sweating Soviet technician who was now an old man with a nicotine-stained moustache—or, more likely, dead.

They had to heave the heavy hatch back together. "The USSR built to last."

"But not my flat."

"Worthless roast-hands, what are you doing in our glorious FSB? Ah, the quarry is heard. Listen."

Wailing Arab music echoed from beyond the end of the tunnel.

"Do they have happiness? Humor? All of that wailing . . ."

"A love song. Her man is a shit."

"All fezzes are shits, in my experience."

"You fuck their sisters in Tashkent."

"I have to. They demand it. Anyway, they're not Arabs. Just with the mullah shit."

They went out into the broad personnel tunnel, carefully closing the inner access hatch behind them. Silent now, each intent on his work, the two men moved off to their respective areas of responsibility.

Vladimir had to kill his old friend Aziz, who used to masturbate in his bedroom, leaping like a great frog while he did it, no idea he was on video in ten different departments of the FSB, let alone the iPods of many of the department heads' teenagers.

Vladimir went into the old communications shack, with its walls lined with ancient, useless radio equipment. To evade American detection, Aziz's operation used manually delivered messages now. The mules were their shortwave radios, and piggybacked number stations. The fezzes actually believed that the Russian operators knew nothing of the fact that they were using the number stations. Absurd, of course.

"Hello, Vladimir."

The prick against the back of his neck told him everything he needed to know. "I hope it's sharp," he said to Aziz.

"It's dull as stone, Vladi. Your sort of a knife."

"I was afraid of that."

Then there came a sharp, echoing cry. The surprise—no, astonishment—in Alexei's voice was unmistakable.

There was movement behind Vladimir, and then he was shoved into the small communications room by two figures in full purdah. Women? No way to tell. One of them had what looked like an antique Arab dagger, curved to tear out guts. The other had Alexei's pistol. They were followed by a boy with a meat cleaver. Aziz stood in the concrete hallway behind them.

"We've been waiting for you," a familiar voice said.

"A double agent, then, Eshan?"

"You always underestimate us, you Russians. You cannot accept our abilities."

Aziz came in. He nodded toward Alexei. "That man was here to cut your head off, boy. Kneel down, Alexei; young Wasim here is going to cut your head off instead."

Alexei cried out, then stifled it.

"What? You were going to cut his head off? But he can't do the same? Why, because he's only a stupid fez?" Aziz took a step toward Alexei. "You helped us. Useful Russians. But it's finished, the bombs are there, so you don't matter anymore."

Alexei grinned—a thin, pitiful attempt. "I can pay." He shook like a palsy victim, and Vladimir was embarrassed for him, and for Russia.

"Alexei, face it. We've been betrayed and we're dead," Vladimir said. "You might as well do as he says." Himself, he felt only a dull, empty hopelessness. He'd been at this most of his career, assembling and transmitting the thousands of tiny packages that had been sent to the hidden stations around the world. It had taken eleven years of work to get the bombs in place, moving them bit by bit, then getting the Islamist fools to assemble them correctly, these men who did not know a motor from an engine.

"Wait," Alexei yammered. "Eshan, Wasim, and you women—listen to this! Yes, listen! There's a reward—many rewards—for him! Yes, for Aziz! The Americans, ten million, the Syrians, two million—dollars, yes, listen! The Pakis, two million—oh, a long list! You can betray him and be rich. Rich!"

One of the women knocked Alexei in the shoulder with an empty butane tank she had been carrying as a weapon. Squalling, he lurched away from the figure, whereupon Eshan tripped him, and he went down groveling like a whipped cur.

Vladimir simply waited to die. He didn't care anymore. This operation had gone out of control. It would not be recovered. The group grabbed Alexei's arms. They pushed him to his knees.

Aziz said to the boy, "Chop at it, at the back of it. Let him scream; they're holding him."

While Alexei screamed and twisted his head, the little fellow took a gingerly chop at his neck. The touch of the blade caused Alexei to bob his head almost comically. Vladimir was reminded of a chicken. How banal, for this to be among his last thoughts, Alexei the pecking hen. Shouldn't he contemplate Pushkin or "O God, our help and aid in distress . . ."? But it was a long prayer; he'd best come up with a shorter one. The Dinner Prayer, perhaps. Could he recall the damned thing?

Again the boy hacked and Alexei squalled. How afraid he was, old roast-hands, who would have strangled this pretty boy slowly, just to watch his eyes fade.

Aziz shouted, "This is a Crusader devil; do it!"

The boy, weeping, muttered something in Persian. Aziz snapped at him, and the boy hacked at Alexei harder, the cleaver now making a sound like a butcher's off-center chop. Blood spurted and Alexei stomped and babbled some sort of slurred plea. He was losing blood fast. Consciousness was going.

But that poor child, dear heaven, what a thing to make an innocent kid do! "The boy will not forget this," Vladimir shouted. "Never! Aziz, it's wrong to do this to him!"

"To the Muslims, execution is not extraordinary."

"There soon will be no Muslims."

"The Muslims have won the world."

"Have you any knowledge of Dream Angel?"

"They will not execute Dream Angel, Vladimir. They will choose to live as slaves."

The boy stood trembling.

"Do it, boy! Do it!"

The kid's big eyes bulged, his face shone with sweat, and he chopped and chopped. Like great, swaying birds, the women in their black burkas hovered nearby, their arms sweeping in their distress like impotent wings.

Alexei's screams became sucking hisses, and then the boy lifted his head by the hair. "It's heavy," the boy cried.

"Then put it down," Aziz replied mildly.

"This is not a lesson I was sent to learn!"

"'As for those who disbelieve, we enter them into the fire and often, so that their skins are terrible with fire. Then we will change them for other skins, that they may taste the pain of it again.'" He took the boy by his collar and raised him eye to eye. "Which sura, boy?"

The boy stared right back at him. "Four. Fifty-six."

He threw the boy to the floor. "Now, Vladimir, you have some work to do for me. There must be a signal, to be sent when you succeed. I want you to send that signal."

"Fine. I don't care." He gave no sign to Aziz that he was mistaken. No signal was to be sent. The least flicker of radio transmission out of this place and the Americans would be here within the hour. So, let them come.

"What is it, then? Not a radio signal, surely."

"Of course it is."

There was a flash in Vladimir's face, and a terrific blast of pain. For a moment, he was confused, his mind questing for some understanding. Then he realized that he'd been slapped with a gun butt. He had not the slightest intention of being tortured. "Here's the truth: If I don't return to the forward base at the appointed time, then a radio signal is sent. It will appear to be from you. It is intended to draw the Americans. There are rangers waiting on top of this structure. They have a transmitter."

Aziz had known Vladimir for eleven years. He had first met with Vladimir when he was a spy in Chechnya, had lived with him in Moscow, had slept with him on drunken nights when they were hunting bear in Siberia and the two of them were in a tent in the depths of the taiga, and—it had simply happened. It was nothing, a matter between men. Nothing sinful.

Well, never mind. Vladimir must now die.

It was also necessary to abandon this place, given that the Americans might indeed be somehow alerted. Very well, they would return to Peshawar. It was past time, for there was political work necessary. Hezbollah had condemned him. Syria, Iran, even the Taliban were uniform in rejecting this messiah of whom they knew nothing. Hamas, of course, those running dogs of the Jewish state.

"Do you know, Vladimir, that we have a weapon in Moscow?"

"You do not."

"Do you want to find out?"

"What code are you using?"

"Purple."

"You're lying!"

"Why should I be lying when the president, in his very office not three hours ago, said to launch Dream Angel. But wait, he said."

"Dream Angel is going to its fail-safe points?"

"So I have been told by a simple man with a very bad truck, who drove along your terrible Soviet road with a certain message. Here, I have a photo." He showed Vladimir a picture of the Kama 3 of old Hassan, with the names of certain djinn written on the door. It was the order of the names that revealed the information.

"I can't read that. Is it Pashto?"

"Dari, Pashto? What does it matter, some stupid writing of us fezzes?"

"You've conquered the world, haven't you?"

"Allah has." Then he took the knife from Wasim, and raised it to Vladimir's throat.

Vladimir looked into Aziz's eyes. "Old times," Vladimir said.

Around them, the women, Eshan, Wasim, all became still. "There is no God but Allah, and Mohammed is his prophet," said Aziz. "You know, the Americans are on their way to this place already, aren't they?" He smiled a little. "They have followed him. He has let them."

"Aziz, no, I despise the Americans! Despise them!"

"You were in the pay of the CIA."

"As were you!"

Aziz laughed at him. "But I ate the money."

"Please, I can be of use. Yes, I'm a whore. But of course! Yours, now, Aziz."

"Putin's, the CIA's, mine. Who knows who would be next? Nasrallah, perhaps? With Hezbollah singing the song of the Crusaders, why not?"

"The world hates you. The Muslims are all against you. Al-Zawahiri has condemned you!"

"Certainly. Al-Zawahiri is like Nasrallah. His whereabouts are known to the Crusaders. So he is nothing but their slave."

"I can be of use!"

Aziz gave the knife to Eshan and turned away. "The Americans will be here soon," Aziz told him. "This man works for them. We must go at once." He hurried off down the low concrete corridor.

Behind him, there was the sound of the throat being expertly slit, a noise like water spattering. Aziz hesitated for a moment but did not turn back. He heard the thud of Vladimir's collapse, and the drumming of his feet. When the bubbling of the breath faded, Aziz walked on. He had work to do, and very quickly.

His first wife, Zaaria, threw the gas cylinder she had carried off to one side. "Why are the Muslims against you?"

"No Muslims are against me. Only apostates."

"And all these millions on your head, Aziz? What is this?"

"A Russian lie."

She looked at him, her eyes dark in her concealing *hijab*.

"We leave at first light! Prepare everybody!"

"We go to Peshawar?"

"We go where God sends us."

She hurried off toward the women's chamber.

21

ONLY A DREAM

In Alexandria, Virginia, "Ronald Alfred Mullins" and his younger brother worked in their garage. Ronald, whose real name was Bilal Aboud, had the plan in his hands. "The circular valve is to be turned twice," he said to Hani.

"And then does it explode?"

"It does not explode. Turn the valve, Hani." During the night, Bilal had heard Hani weeping. He had seen Hani go to the kitchen and eat peanut butter from the jar, and had heard his smacking. He must not weigh more than 128 pounds or the plane could not fly, and for that he had needed to starve himself for nearly a month. His Ramadan fast had never ended.

Of the two of them, only Bilal knew what the word "purple" that had appeared in the craigslist advert meant. When he had been counseled by the psychiatrist about how to ensure that Hani would indeed carry out his mission, it had been explained to Bilal that anticipation was the worst thing. So he had not told Hani when the flight would take place. However, they had to be in readiness, and so had to install the bomb into the airframe.

Hani had also been carefully trained. He knew not to ask, knew that he did not want to know: "The only thing that matters, Hani, is what you are doing right now." So Hani had trained like that, concentrating only on the momentary activity. He would think of getting the plane off the ground, then of the four-minute flight to his ascension point, then of pulling back the stick. He would not think of his death, never that, never at all. He was not a simple creature; he had his own ideas of heaven and afterlife. In truth, he did not think he had an afterlife. Hoped he didn't, because what he was going to do was so extremely evil. But he had his brothers' and sisters' lives to consider, and the honor of his family. Their father, he believed, had been shot dead by Blackwaters in Baghdad. He had been an electrical engineer driving to his work. He was not a fighter of any kind at all. He had been shot, Hani had been told, for sport. People said that he had pleaded, but the Blackwaters had shot him, then shared cigarettes among themselves. Perhaps he had been killed by American mercenaries . . . or perhaps by somebody seeking to radicalize the two English-speaking brothers. In any case, Hani fought for honor, not for access to a heaven he did not believe was even there. For him, America was Blackwater.

"Now, this is the bomb?"

"This is the bomb."

"There's a lot of wiring. It looks delicate."

"It only needs to work once."

"Will the radiation kill us?"

"Not as long as the plutonium is properly contained."

Hani laid a hand on it. "Cold," he said.

"You can't feel the power of it."

The two of them lifted the black melon by its handles, moving it into the flimsy aircraft.

"It's not easy! Careful!"

It was not supposed to exist, this bomb weighing only two hundred pounds. But it did, did it not, and there were many more of them, Bilal hoped. The new land mines was how Bilal thought of them.

It dropped down into the compartment they had welded together with such effort, struggling with modifications to the kit. But this was satisfying. It was stable in its position now.

"Now, the wings," Hani said.

They had to fix the wings to the body of the aircraft, which must be done in the street. It could not be done here; there wasn't enough space. "It is not time," Bilal said.

Hani smiled. "Time is only a dream. As is this life, also nothing but a dream."

Bilal laid a hand on his brother's shoulder. "Allah has no need of time. In heaven eternal, there is no time."

"Do you believe it, Bilal?"

Bilal did not like this question. He himself couldn't fly the plane; he was too heavy. In the training camp in Texas, he had been taught that when a pilot asked when he must fly that was a danger sign. "I believe that the world the Crusaders have made is evil," Bilal said. "The nation that murdered Dad for sport is evil."

Hani nodded. "We've never been able to train with the wings. Do you think we'll get them to work?"

"If God wills." The wings had been modified to fold back, and would need to be carefully opened and locked, once the plane was out in the street. That would be the most dangerous moment.

"Bilal, I'm—"

"We are all afraid. It's natural."

Hani smiled again. In it Bilal saw a new fragility, and he thought that Hani was failing in his resolve.

"I was going to say I'm hungry. I want some lunch."

Bilal put his hand on his brother's narrow shoulder. They went to the kitchen together.

22

A ROOM OF ONE'S OWN

Rashid's space was tiny and stuffy and deep, so crammed with equipment that it was almost impossible for him to move from his chair. Rashid hated the claustrophobic hole. He had not even wanted to come in during drills. But now he must live here, in a tiny two-man bunk with another controller. He was the only Muslim among them, of course. The token.

He did not dislike his coworkers. In fact, very much the opposite. Their dedication to the service was admirable. They were not Muslim because they did not understand, not because they had rejected the faith. They were not like his sister, foolish creature, with her apostasies. Why not bow before the word of God, proud woman?

Even though she had accepted the faith and prayed—actually prayed—she had her demonic justifications for not even so much as wearing the veil, except when she pleased. Immodest creature, self-willed sinner!

Her arrogance was why he had suggested that the first demand be the veil. She had ignored it. Had she not, perhaps he would have also suggested that the bomb be detonated in the wilderness, not over Las Vegas. He would have accepted the danger of making such a suggestion to the powers. So it was her, Nabila. She had killed Las Vegas, and before he was through with her he would make certain she understood that the bombing there was on her head. Once this was over and power properly consolidated, it would be his faithful pleasure to execute her with his own hands.

Before him was an array of screens, each one providing a different view of his surveillance sector. It was normally a high-interest area, but at present management was concentrating on the continental United States, not on Afghanistan and Pakistan.

His mission was to co-analyze production from the new Rugby Altair class Synthetic Aperture Radar satellites, and the Echo 12 systems in higher Molniya, invaluable for his current effort, because of their dwell capability. It was a piece of luck that the Echo 12s were at a high fuel level, having been refueled by Shuttle Mission STS-201 last month.

He had all manner of software assistance and his computers were essential to his work, but he had intentionally developed a reputation for liking to look at his imagery at once, rather than waiting for it to process. He was extremely careful and, he thought, extremely good. Never, at any time, did he do anything that might suggest that he had another agenda. Of course, they watched the Muslim with a special eye. Of course, they secretly despised him. It wasn't their fault; it was the evil in them. Evil comes to us all. We must actively go to the good, and Crusader lies made it hard for these poor people to do that. Greed, the dark master of the West, had locked their hearts, and a good Muslim addressed their tragic state with compassion. This was what Nabila didn't understand. When they were unpleasant to her in the shops or whatever, she cursed and spat and stomped out her rage. She should thank God for the blessing they gave her, which was a chance to give her suffering to Allah.

Rashid's teacher at the mosque, who had brought him out of the folly of moderation and into the light of the truth, had said to him, "Evil exploits human weakness. The men of the West are not to blame any more than locusts are to blame. But we must still kill the locusts, or the field will be ruined."

That was true, and look why—even now, there was blue water at the north pole in the summertime, the glaciers of Greenland were sliding into the sea, the oil of his homeland was being devoured by the Great Satan and his minions, and God's beautiful earth was dying beneath an avalanche of plastic bags, discarded buttons, bottles, toys, and who knew what else—a mess being made by humankind, in defiance of the will of God.

Rashid never did anything to compromise his mission, but he also served his real master, and as he watched his screens he saw that this service was going to once again be needed.

His protocols dictated which sectors he was to observe most carefully, and the Pamir Panhandle was not one of them. This was why, when the clear outline of a Fennek reconnaissance vehicle appeared during a look-down, he had to fight his rising heartbeat. This was important, because everybody knew that inappropriate indications of stress could bring on an incident-targeted lie detector test—and not with a polygraph, not anymore. The much more effective No Lie fMRI was now in use, and like all of his colleagues, he'd had a baseline exam that made it essentially impossible for him to conceal a falsehood. He must never forget, not now: all they had to do was ask the right question and he was finished.

He queried ISAF HQ, Afghanistan, for their deployments in or near 37°19'43"N, 70°44'35"E. What a Fennek might be doing in an area he secretly knew to be enormously sensitive he did not know, but it was very worrisome, and he had no choice but to take the risk of asking.

ISAF came back: "No deployment coordinates req." So it wasn't a Fennek but rather a vehicle disguised to appear to be a Fennek. This meant only one thing: Russians. Russians were within a few kilometers of their old installation. From its size and shape, he thought they must be in an old BRDM reconnaissance vehicle, fitted with plywood panels to make it appear from above to be modern NATO equipment.

Of course, they would have blueprints of the Pamir installation. They would know all the old trip wires, all the mantraps, and, above all, the secret ways in through the ventilation system, pathways that NATO would not have mined. They would be able to penetrate right to the heart of the place without detection. Would Russians understand what was being done there?

He could not even ask that question. The fact was that they were penetrating the place, so of course they knew something, possibly everything.

They must have come in through Tajikistan, a team of specialists. Putin must have realized his mistake in letting Inshalla have this base in the first place, and the Russians were there to clean house. They would kill Aziz and his entourage, and clean up the entire base to a forensic level of thoroughness. Inshalla had done Russia's secret work in throwing America into chaos, and now it was time for it to stop.

It must not stop.

Perhaps he could suggest an attack on the Russian target. There were

SiMiCon Rotor Craft available in Afghanistan, armed with Hellfire missiles. But no, that would look like he was reaching above his level of authority, perhaps attempting to bypass his superiors, and that would cause suspicion.

He composed an instant message: "Poss. Russian BRDM-2U camoed as German-marking Fennek observed scout mode coordinates near 37°19'43"N, 70°44'35"E. Unknown mission. Lookback shows route out of Tajikistan. Recommend immediate site investigation Sov era installations region."

He could not warn anybody in Pamir. He knew this: if the martyrdom of Aziz as Mahdi was meant to be, it would be. God forgot nothing, knew everything. However, it was hard for Rashid as a technician in command of these powerful resources not to try to help Allah decide what his will was going to be.

"Allahu akbar, Allahu akbar. . . ."

The words had come as if from the interior of his own soul. They shocked him so badly that he almost lost his balance in his seat. Instinct caused him to pull down the cover that concealed his controls. And then he saw a face peering at him over the cubicle partition. His neighbor, Carol Wilkie.

"Hello, Carol."

"God is a woman."

"He will be surprised to hear that."

"Saint Teresa of Avila went bald. Would she still have to wear a veil?"

"Why wouldn't she want to?"

"It's time for Asr," Carol said, "by my reckoning."

"Ah, thank you, my *adan*. I was far away."

"Your keys told me that. Anything up?"

"It's nothing. . . ." She was not need-to-know for his area, and compartmentalization here was extremely strict, especially now. "Actually, even this peering over the divider is illegal."

She gave him a questioning frown.

"To look in here. You're not cleared to see what I am doing."

She sighed. "They should've put the walls all the way to the ceiling. Damn congressional cheapskates." She laughed a little, and it was very pleasant to see and hear. She wore a black veil, out of respect for her coworker's sense of modesty. It was a fine thing, and he was very appreciative of her for this act of respect for him—and, for that matter, for herself.

He was tempted by Carol of the long, soft hands and the wide eyes that so deliciously pretended innocence. But not now; she was not part of his mission and she had to go away.

"Want to meet for tea?" she asked.

"No tea today. Just work."

"Understood." She snapped him a salute and disappeared.

He unrolled his carpet and used a moist towelette to make quick *wadu,* then went down to his prayers, imagining his soul flowing across the world to Mecca, and coming as a supplicant to the feet of God. How he longed to be with God! How he loved God!

During the prayer, though, Rashid's computer beeped the alarm of an incoming urgent message. One of the satellites had detected movement on the ground. He had consulted his mullah about moments like this, and it had been decided that Rashid could compress the prayer. Pilots did it, surgeons, soldiers in the heat of battle. You wrapped the whole prayer up into a single word, and sent it off to Allah with praise and thanks. Allah understood these things. Rashid had been instructed, "You must obey Allah and follow Allah's laws to the letter, but you must also love Allah and enjoy Allah. Allah is the vengeful lion, but Allah is also the pomegranate in the summer garden, ripe for plucking."

It smacked of Sufism, but Rashid had accepted it, for this man who instructed him had himself an excellent reputation among Saudis in America, and had been the choice of Rashid's father. He had known little of Salafism. He had not understood the beauty of its purity, or the power of its message of reform. He had not understood how it felt to belong to the deep truth of the faith, which was only available through total acceptance of the precepts of the Kita at-Tawib, and a return to the ways of the first and best generation, the generation of Mohammed.

Another beep came, and Rashid sent his prayer off on its voyage, and returned to his console, where he saw that a passing Rugby had detected movement along the river, seven figures moving south and west. They had sheep. Rugby satellites had almost no dwell time—a little more than the Lacrosse series they had replaced—but it had been enough to project the probable route the figures were taking.

He knew that this was the Mahdi Aziz and his entourage, escaping into Pakistan. Nobody would drive sheep in that hostile region, a freezing desert without sufficient grass to sustain them, let alone fatten them for market. So this meant only one thing: the Mahdi and his followers had escaped from the Russians in the BRDM.

Rashid saw a chance to end this threat. His supervisors would not know that there were no shepherds in that region. He could safely peg the alarm: "Shepherds seeking lowland pasture due to seasonal weather changes." It was October, so of course they would be going to lower pastures, and nobody would ever know that he had saved the Mahdi, the very man who was delivering the human species from its long age of darkness into the light of Islam.

Rashid looked at the perfect image, the little band struggling along in what appeared to be a nasty wind. A glance at weather conditions told him that it was minus 8 degrees Celsius there, wind at twenty-two klicks out of the north. Winter was coming to the Kush, even though the Crusader billions were doing the work of Satan and destroying Allah's beautiful world. They had no respect for the Tawid, the unity of God with his creation: "And it is He who spread the earth, and set the firm mountains upon it, and the rivers; and all manner of fruit." So it was law that man respect the world, and not eat it with the jaws of a hungry caterpillar.

Then a hand came down on Rashid's shoulder. His cubicle was locked; only his supervisor could enter. "Hello, Mark," he said without looking.

"What is it?"

"Shepherds, I think. Have a look."

"Running from whoever was in that BRDM?"

"With their sheep? I doubt it. Unless the Russkis are out for mutton."

"Could be, could be. I see you called for a closer look from ISAF."

"Something seems off. Why are the Russians there?"

"Those old installations are listed as destroyed, not useable."

"So they say, Mark. But what's on the books and what's real—" He shrugged.

"Well, we'll soon find out. They've got a chopper going in. Live bait." That was the term around here for manned reconnaissance aircraft. The best possible information, but—well, there were many people in that area who might shoot at a NATO helicopter. Even children, just for a little excitement.

Rashid thought of the men in the chopper, churning through the cold dawn, being buffeted by the winds, watching for the wink of rifle fire, or the swift white arrow that marked a speeding rocket.

Mark shook his shoulder. "Good work, Rashid. If anything comes of it, I'll buy you supper."

"If anything comes of it, I'll eat my hat."

They laughed together. It was a close comradeship, here in this office. So very close.

SNIPER COUNTRY

As Jim's plane landed at Andrews, he watched two dark blue jeeps loaded with air police pace it, then maneuver onto the apron that stood in front of the VIP receiving area. Of course they would assume that anybody flying in under current circumstances would be important. It went against Jim's instincts, this. He preferred to be the same color as the walls he passed.

In the plane, he'd slept, but badly. Every time he began to go under, he'd see that terrible light blooming across the cowling of that bastard Ressman's plane.

When they banked on their way to their landing approach, Jim had seen Washington in the distance, white structures afloat in the colors of autumn. He had come here to track backward through ONI records, trying to determine if Franklin Isbard Matthews, who had supposedly duped Arthur Kenneally into pulling the detector off Bridge 1 in Eagle Pass, was a real person. If he was, Jim was going to force information out of him.

That was the way it worked in this business. You swung on vines of information through a jungle of lies. Eventually, either you reached a dead end or you didn't.

It was seven hours and forty-five minutes from now that frightened Jim. Given that they hadn't already detonated the bomb that was certainly hidden here, they were going to do it at the most dramatic moment, which he thought would be the same as at Las Vegas: midnight. This would show their power, their absolute control of the situation. They could blow up cities on schedule, no matter how hard anyone tried to stop them.

As the plane's engines wound down, he stepped to the rear and cracked the door. "Thanks, gentlemen," he called up to the cockpit. "You got the fuel, I'd turn this lady around pronto."

The pilot came into the cabin. "Yessir, we're ready to roll."

"Then go. Right now. Don't even stop for a drink of water."

The young man nodded and disappeared into the cockpit.

As Jim went quickly down the worn aluminum steps, the engines began gaining power. He heard the faint thump of the door closing but did not look back toward the departing plane.

He hardly saw the APs, either. He couldn't bear looking at their young faces flickering with hope that this might be the man who *does* something. The weight of history oppressed Jim acutely. He crossed the tarmac, his worn sneakers whispering on the asphalt, a strange contrast with the uniform. As he moved toward the glass doors, the details of the moment crowded him, the faint rustling of his trousers, the slight movement of an awning, the smell of burning jet fuel lingering in the air, and the sweet, infinitely sad scent of—of all things—some sort of late-season flower. Where was it growing, he wondered, in this ocean of concrete?

A Sufi he had known and had sat with in a stifling tiny room in—God, was it Kabul, was it Herat?—had said to him, "The world is memory." He had reacted in the way a young man does when facing the profound, with nervous, uncomprehending affection. He remembered that old, weathered man now, with his water pipe and his tea and the laugh lines around his eyes.

Jim pushed through the glass doors into the freezing, over-air-conditioned lobby. It was empty, utterly silent, a wide expanse of Air Force blue carpet, rows of plush leather seats, a large color photo of Secretary Robertson on the wall, beside him the smiling face of President Fitzgerald. Jim knew that Fitz was canny, but was he smart? There was a difference, and it could be huge. Jim needed Fitz to grasp things fast, above all to understand why an out-of-place operative was bucking the chain of command and agree to see him.

When he'd been in training, they had been given a lecture by old Gus

McCall, a legendary guy, a very bright man, who had done hard things for his country. He had said something Jim had never been able to forget: "Presidents are scared. Not sometimes. All the time. And scared men can be dangerous. You are the messenger, remember, and the news you bring is always bad. If you do your job right or if you don't, in the end he will want your head."

How a man dealt with this fear was the measure of his success in that monstrously difficult office. Jimmy Carter had been frozen by it, Richard Nixon driven mad. Eisenhower had overcome it, Lincoln been made great by it, Johnson victimized by it. Fear—relentless, open-ended, cruelly distorting of everybody and everything—drove all presidents. So the question was, what was it doing to Fitz right now?

Out the far side of the building, Jim found a courtesy car waiting, a sedan that he knew at once would not survive a chase. But he wouldn't be in it long. He knew that every intelligence service in the world had been interested in who was on the plane that flew from Texas to Washington during the tightest lockdown in history. He knew that AFOSI, the Air Force Office of Special Investigations, had this car bugged and fitted with tracking devices.

He drove quickly off the base, heading along the Capital Beltway into the city. His plan was to ditch the car as soon as possible and take the Metro to the Mt. Vernon Square stop and from there walk to the ONI offices. There he hoped to talk his way onto a secure line to the White House and an invitation to meet with Fitzgerald.

As he drove up the entrance to the Beltway, however, he found that the outbound lanes were in gridlock. He could see people out of their cars, some fighting, others trying to push stalled and wrecked cars off the roadway. It was hell, he thought, with children peering out the windows.

Then he realized that he was looking at an SUV coming straight at him. He swerved—only to see another big grill as the cab of an eighteen-wheeler bore down on him, horns screaming. In the windshield, he could see a girl driving. The cab was full of kids.

He ripped the ungainly car's steering wheel and missed the truck cab by inches. The entire road was crowded with traffic leaving. The only way he could make progress was to drive next to the inner barrier, flashing his lights and hitting his horn continuously.

As a car with cardboard boxes badly lashed to its top passed him, a guy in the passenger seat showed a silver Magnum. His grimacing, teeth-bared face said, *Try me, Uniform.*

No, thank you.

Then there came a fight across the anarchy of lanes. Jim slid between two cars, then went around a pickup that was on its side and burning. When he slowed, people on foot began beating on his windows, one woman making spiderwebs on the windshield with a spike heel. There was a sickening crunch when he sped up to get past them, and the kind of lurch that meant only one thing: he'd driven over a body. "God," he whispered, "God help him."

There was no way to stay up here, so Jim pulled off on the D Street exit and went down into the streets. Despite the alleged twenty-four-hour curfew, he had not so far seen a single police vehicle. No doubt, the cops had stopped reporting to work or even had been themselves dispersed. One thing was clear: public order was nonexistent.

There was a man lying on the sidewalk, his face so flat against it that Jim knew that he was dead. Jim also knew how he'd been killed—he had been clubbed in the face, then, as he pitched back, pulled to his feet and clubbed again, then knocked over with a body blow from behind. You saw bodies like this in alleys, in the world's hard places.

A hurrying crowd moved around the dead man, their feet grinding his blood into the sidewalk in long, red smears. There were people with backpacks, pulling children's wagons full of clothes, cases of bottled water, boxes of cornflakes, you name it. Down the street, a gutted convenience store burned.

Once again, the car attracted attention. Here came a woman festooned with kids, her face soaked with tears and blood, her clothes torn. From another direction, a man with a deer rifle at port arms approached, trotting as if he'd spent time in the military. He probably knew how to use that weapon, too. It was clear that if Jim was going to keep this vehicle, he was going to need to kill to do it, but doing that was going to slow down his progress toward his objective, so it wasn't a necessary option for him to take, thank God.

The moment he stepped away from the car, a crowd leaped on it.

Walking to the ONI offices from here was too dangerous, but he was only a few blocks from Nabila's place. Given that his mobility was so limited, he would risk using her secure equipment to connect with the White House. She'd be on dispersal, of course, but he might be able to get to it.

By the time he had reached the end of the block, he saw that there were probably a hundred people fighting over the car. Ahead, a man sat on the curb laughing and firing a shotgun into the air, the booms creating a permanent swooping riot of pigeons, some of which lay in the street, ruined puffs of feathers. The detonations snapped off the buildings, the explosions coming as regularly as metronome ticks. Two women passed, leading six children linked together with a clothesline. Another body, this one burnt and smoking, was curled up under the stoop of a brownstone.

The beauty of Nabila's neighborhood was wildly out-of-focus with the mayhem unfolding in it. Percy's, a restaurant they had loved, stood open. For an instant, it seemed to be untouched; then he saw a cardboard barrel of sugar burst just inside the doorway and a tattered Irish setter frantically gobbling the spilled contents, its russet dewlaps touched as if with snow.

He would not see Nabby, of course, but he wanted to as badly as he had ever wanted anything. Not only was she beautiful, but she also had a gorgeous, supple mind, which had made their love affair also an ongoing conversation, at least at first, when they were both stationed here and their marriage had flourished. True, they had lost that when he'd moved to Operations and become involved in counterproliferation and ended up halfway around the world and in situations where he couldn't communicate with her.

Then even the trips home had stopped working. They'd slipped into being strangers, and he knew from her dutiful tension that even lovemaking had come to seem to her like an affair with a stranger.

Until Las Vegas, he had not wanted to see her, not because he didn't love her but because he did. In the field, he'd become a sort of addict. He needed the tension of lonely places now, the sense of being a player in a dangerous game. He was able to kill, and although it was a huge issue, it was also a source of pride. The warrior's way. In a job where a second's hesitation could mean your life, you had to be able to do violence with ease, and he could do that, and it excited him and made him feel fantastically capable.

He was a form of wildlife that had thought itself domesticated—like those dogs of the old rancher down in Texas, being transformed into killers by the taste of blood.

She had said, before they were married, that she wanted a quiet life. Deep inside this fiercely independent woman, he had come to understand, were expectations born out of her upbringing and her culture. Home was sacred to her in a way that could feel confining to a Westerner. He loved her so damn much, and knew now that she still loved him—and knew that she was probably suffering agonies right now, wondering about his safety.

But they were back to the old problem—no communication. As things were now, calling her and telling her he was all right might be the exact thing that destroyed him. From the moment he did it, he would no longer know whether or not his presence in Washington had been detected.

God, he had never thought to see this city like this. Washington had warts, for sure, but this scramble—it was grotesque. Ancient Rome must have been like this when it was being sacked. Except for one huge difference—technology had enabled the barbarians to become invisible men. They were here, all right, just as they had been in Rome . . . but here, in the magical modern world, you couldn't see them but only feel the effects of their savagery.

As he approached Pennsy Avenue, though, he was surprised to find that the atmosphere was beginning to change. Now, closer to Eastern Market, people were walking, not running. There were fewer guns, and he hadn't seen a body in a block.

Ahead, to his amazement, he heard singing. He knew the music. It was "Amazing Grace," and the voices were ragged at first, then richer and bigger, and when he turned the corner and had the whole Eastern Market plaza before him, he saw that it was an assembly point for some sort of rally or perhaps even a march. Children held their parents' hands; there were baby strollers everywhere, people in turbans and djellabas, people in Western street clothes.

Few of the Muslim women wore the *hijab,* but the Westerners were getting blue veils out of cardboard boxes. He saw Muslim women dropping their head scarves as they joined the group.

Dogs jumped and capered, and the song rose, grew stronger, then tailed away. Somebody spoke through an electronic bullhorn in a Middle Eastern accent, a portly man with a dark moustache. From his demeanor and his accent Jim thought he was Lebanese. He stood in a sea of video cameras, some of them professional, most amateur.

The man had an iPhone and a BlackBerry and was reading text messages. Then he looked up. "We are with more cities! Six in this country, and London joins us and Cairo. Cairo joins us! Mexico, we are in Mexico; we are in Peshawar. We are in Peshawar, too, it's true!" He held up his BlackBerry. "It is here; I see the video; it's true! Peace, peace is coming!"

So the Mahdi wasn't the only one who could use the Internet.

"We start to move, start to move! Everybody join us, chant it, let's go, hey, TV—" He waved at the cameras. "We do it! Here we go!" He turned and strode off up the broad avenue, bellowing "Amazing Grace" through the bullhorn in his dense Middle Eastern accent. Then, "We are all together, all together!" The crowd shouted back, "All together." Various hymns came and went, ragged, brief. Snatches of "Nearer, My God, to Thee," "Happy Land," and others.

People raised placards, "Sura 2:125/Genesis 17:9," "God is God," "Islam is Holy is Christianity is Holy." A tiny, gray-haired Asian woman threw back her head and shouted at the sky, "All we are asking is give peace a chance." The voice, though small, brought a silence. This was a woman these people wanted to hear. Then the leader was standing, waving the crowd past him. Jim recognized senators, congressmen, and a cardinal. He saw familiar faces—was that Meryl Streep, and the little, intense woman beside her Ellen Page? Was the tiny old lady actually Yoko Ono? In a wheelchair, a man who looked like Jimmy Carter was being pushed by a woman Jim thought might be Shirley MacLaine. All of these people must have been in Washington making movies or doing benefits or for other reasons. Certainly they had not arrived after Las Vegas. Or had they? It was always a mistake, he thought, to underestimate the power of the people. Somehow, they would find a way.

Then the leader had connected with the small gray-haired lady, who took the bullhorn and shouted again, "All we are asking is give peace a chance!"

Jim had to fight back tears, just to see this enormous crowd, every one of them certainly aware that they could be vaporized at any moment, but still here, still trying.

The voices rose, the chant spread, and blue veils became a sea, and turbaned men and hatless men, a smattering of black fedoras, even. The voice of the crowd deepened. The milling mass swirled, took form, and the march magically organized itself, heading off toward the center of the city.

A girl carrying a newborn in a sling came trotting up to him. Her eyes were as blue as her scarf, her face so pure that it seemed as if it had been brushed by a shaft of light. She reached out and before he could stop her took his hand. "Come on," she said. "Don't be scared." Then he saw her baby sleeping in her innocence, and a great, choked sound gushed out of him. She squeezed his hand. "I know it's hard, but you can do it." She met his eyes with her own, and the courage seared him.

He said, "I'm on a mission."

"There's only one mission now," she said. "Come on. Come with us. This is Madison. I'm Senna." Her smile, it seemed to him, contained within its glow some sort of proof of what he had always denied, that there was such a thing as the human soul. He thought he was being touched not just by this young woman but also by the God who had willed her—and him, and all—to be.

Only sentiment, no doubt, but there was certainly something here that the barbarians did not have. They owned only the shadows. These people owned the light.

He went with her, and she smiled up at him but then was off, trotting to a group who had come out of a house. "Come join us," she shouted as she ran to them. She would carry her baby for all the miles. She would go to everybody she saw with her message. She would not stop.

He saw skeletons, hers wrapped around her baby's, skeletons and flies. *If only he'd been a little faster, a little less rule bound.* Had she known that she was talking to the man whose failure had let this happen, what would she have said then?

He reached the far side of the march and suddenly was on a street sacred to his heart, the short block of D Street, SW, where Nabila had her house. Every inch of this sidewalk had meaning. Here she had taught him "In Doha Ya Doha," when they had been planning to have children. She had sung it on a raw winter night, when they walked on crunching snow and the moon glared through the naked trees. "In doha ya doha, wa al-ka'aba banooha . . ." for a child who now never would be born.

That was the truth of Jim Deutsch, right here in this street, his barren truth.

He faced the house itself, looked up to the bedroom where they had made their happiness. He climbed the short steps to the front door and started to ring the bell. He stopped, though, because his instincts told him instantly that the house was empty. Buildings do not lie, and this one was saying two things. First, there were no living creatures within. Second, something was wrong.

He pulled out his picklock, worked it for a moment, and was in. He closed the door behind him, being careful to reset the lock. Here was the familiar coatrack, Rashid's blue pea jacket hanging there . . . and his own old corduroy with the weathered leather elbows and the pocket she had mended for him in another life, long ago.

He threw off the uniform tunic and went deeper into the house. "Rashid? Nabby?"

Jim knew that silence would be the only answer, but he called them anyway. He went upstairs and turned down the hallway that led to her office and the bedroom he had once shared with her.

When he saw that the office door was open, he knew instantly that she was in terrible trouble. There was no way she would leave this house on her own initiative without locking and alarming that door. Just no way. The office had been secured by the Company. Its door moved on quiet hinges, the steel of the thing concealed by veneer that matched the other mahogany doors of the old house. Inside the wall there was a copper grid to keep prying electronics at bay and on the desk another to further secure her computer.

Had it been locked, this door would not have been passable, not even by a well-equipped professional. Because Jim had seen her coming and going, he was aware of the combination. He'd memorized it; he hadn't been able to help himself.

He stepped into the office and had another shock: her computer was on. Incredibly, the secure network was wide open from this terminal. Anyone could come in here, sit down, and enter a deep tier of classification.

So he wouldn't be risking the use of this terminal; that was crystal clear.

He looked around for some clue as to what had happened. Taking the steps four at a time, he went down to the kitchen and yanked open the garage door. Both cars were gone.

Back up he went, back to their bedroom. What he saw there stopped him, but not because of danger. It was because nothing had changed. She had told him she had redecorated, had said it with a sneer of anger in her voice, but it wasn't true. He was everywhere in the room, his books, his Bose radio, his bedside CD collection—even the novel he had been reading on the last night, when their battle had stirred the neighbors and he had left and hadn't come back, even that lay undisturbed on the bedside table where he had left it.

He stood silent, bowing his head to the sacredness of the love he saw here. He sucked air through his teeth—*he had to fix this*. Fix it all. Find the murderous bastards who had wrecked Vegas and put the noose around Washington's neck, find Nabila, find what he had lost of himself and his marriage.

A glance at his watch revealed what he most did not want to face: if he was right about the way the enemy thought, he and his world and the woman he loved—if she was still in Washington—had just five hours to live.

Forcing himself, he went methodically through the rooms, looking for some clue, some indication of what had happened to her.

There was nothing. Again, forcing himself, he went back upstairs, and took advantage of the presence of his clothes to shed the uniform.

As he was leaving, he noticed that the back door was not completely shut. Without going too close, he looked out into the garden. To find out more, he needed to go out there.

That could be death.

24

THE CARD OF THE LOVERS

He stepped out quickly, moving toward the nearest shrubs as fast as possible. Every visible window—and there was an entire row of brownstones across the alley, all of them looking straight into this garden—potentially concealed a sniper. He looked for slightly open windows, because he'd never encountered a sniper who would shoot through glass and risk deflection of the bullet.

As Jim approached the end of the garden, he saw breaks in the shrubbery, twigs that had been snapped. He'd tracked in places a lot more challenging than a Washington back alley, so he knew at once that she had pushed through the shrubs to the alley gate. There were a couple of partial prints on the ground—sneakers, woman's size. Nobody following, so whatever had happened to drive her from the house, it had not been somebody behind her.

She had been using her computer when she left—so quickly that she'd violated every regulation in the book.

He went through the overgrowth to the back fence, and opened the gate. A quick glance told him that she'd taken a left. He followed, and soon saw that she'd turned and moved into the yard of a nearby house, one that fronted on South Carolina, the street opposite hers.

He entered its back garden. A hundred and fifty feet away stood the brownstone, with black wrought-iron steps leading up to its rear door. There was a tiny patio with an expensive-looking barbecue grill to one side, and a table and chairs, also wrought iron.

He could see from the way the dry grass was bent here that Nabby had headed directly for the steps. As she'd entered the yard, she'd been moving fast. Running from somebody who her computer had told her was coming after her.

He opened the gate, following the dry, bent grass. A glance at the house revealed only locked windows. No sign of movement along the roofline, either, so no sniper taking aim at him.

Looking down, he followed the track a few more feet. Here she had stopped, and suddenly. When he raised his eyes, he saw why—there was a figure in there, first visible from this point. It was a male, wearing a white shirt, standing back from the window. He carried a rifle across his chest. Jim remained motionless, evaluating the gun by its outline. There was a thick barrel, a gas canister below it. It was only an air rifle, but the guy probably felt protected by it. This was useful, because when people felt protected they were vulnerable.

Jim waved, to indicate to the man that he was seen, then mounted the steps and twisted the ancient spring bell that was affixed to the doorjamb. Almost at once, the inner door opened. The screen was still locked.

"May I help you?"

"Actually, I'm from over there—" He pointed toward Nabila's own back garden. "I'm trying to find my wife."

He did not respond.

"Dark hair, five three. She's an Arab and I'm worried . . . you know, given the situation."

"Not here."

"Has she been here, then?"

He shook his head. So Jim grasped the handle of the screen and gave it a couple of the quick, twisting shakes that would spring the lock, and barged right into the guy's face.

The man fell back against his kitchen table, then recovered himself. Jim stepped up to him, turning to one side to deflect the aim of the air rifle. Then he grasped it with both hands and plunged the stock into the man's stomach.

The power of the blow made him cry out as he flew backward across the table and crashed into the swinging door on the far side of the kitchen. He hit the floor with a thud, and the door banged back against him. He lay between the kitchen and the dining room, making little gasping sounds, "oh . . . oh."

"Nice kitchen," Jim said, "love your granite." He went over to the prone figure. "You're looking pretty peaked, fella." He put his foot down on the man's face. "Crush a guy's jaw, it kills him if he can't get treatment. Windpipe swells closed, but it's slow as hell. Tell me where my wife is."

"F-f-f-f—"

"Fuck me? Wrong answer." He pressed down until he felt the nose bend. Now the hands came up and grappled with Jim's ankle. "You don't tell me the truth, it gets worse right now. Where is she?"

"I am Undersecretary of Defense Charles Walters, and I don't know where in hell your wife is!"

"DoD Comptroller Walters. I thought all of you guys were Georgetown clowns. What're you doing over here on Capitol Hill?"

"Get off me!"

Jim pressed down harder. "Nonessential personnel, so no dispersal. They left you behind without even a Secret Service party. Shame on them."

Walters growled—or perhaps groaned—through his shoe-stifled mouth.

"Now, I know she was here because I tracked her here. So you're lying and if you lie again, right now, you will be demolished, Sir. Understand this clearly: as far as your god-for-damned title is concerned, *I do not care*. So, let's start again."

The shoe-stifled voice became complex enough to convince Jim to remove his foot.

Walters leaped to his feet. "How dare you!"

"Your face has a footprint on it. Where's my wife?"

"Let me see your cred!"

"You got *cojones,* I'll give you that. Sure, I'll let you see my cred." Jim pulled out his real credential.

Walters opened it, read it. Then looked up at Jim. Then down again. "You really are Jim Deutsch."

"I really am."

Walters went into the dining room and sat down at the gleaming mahogany table. It was a splendid big room, with gorgeously detailed moldings and a fine, glittering chandelier. *What would blast effect do to it?* Jim wondered.

"She was here. She established her bona fides and I confirmed her clearance with ONI."

"That was stupid."

"I know the whole story and I know that now, too! But they were already on to her. A whole capture and suppression team, with shoot-to-kill orders."

"You're certain of this?"

He nodded. "Five minutes after she left, they appeared. Wanting to know if I'd seen her. It was a full-bore security detail. I contacted ONI again, and they couldn't confirm anything. The office was in chaos by then, so who knows? By the time I'd returned to the door, the team was gone."

"The front door, since she's the only person who came in the back. Did she also leave by the front?"

"You're good. I bet you earn your money."

"So, what you're saying is, she had a five-minute lead on them."

"The Metro was still running then, so she might have done a little better."

"You know it was running? How do you know?"

"You feel it. The line's under this street and you feel it."

"She mentioned me. Did she have any message for me?"

"The cred looks real. I wish I could confirm that."

"So, she had a message. What was the message?"

Walters slumped, a man filled with defeat. "The phones are dead. The computer is off-line."

"You aren't on a secure network?"

"DoD shut down everything except intelligence traffic. I'm out in the cold."

"I'd hate to be an accountant."

Walters sniffed a laugh out of his swelling nose.

"You've gotta trust my cred," Jim added.

From his office in the Pentagon this man must see a lot of craziness, disappointment, and culpability. The money men always know the skeletons personally.

"Mr. Walters, I need any information you have *now*."

"She said, 'Rashid knows. Tell Jim that Rashid knows.' "

The cold of absolute zero. The explosion of an electric shock. Then heat rushing into his face, his hands going tight, needing to kill.

No wonder the divorce had made Rashid so furious. No more production to be derived from Jim's comings and goings. However infrequent, they must have been incredibly useful.

He told Walters, who was rubbing his face, "You treat that with ice."

"I know how to treat it!"

He had to control Rashid, but that involved determining his dispersal location, then getting there. Only the White House might be able to help. "Do you have a car?"

Then it hit him. So obvious. "Never mind." He went out the back again, thundered down the steps, and ran across the yard. He threw open the gate and in moments he was in Nabila's back garden. Then he was in the house. He went upstairs, went to her office—and found the door closed.

He stood there, for a moment too stunned to move. But—when he'd seen that her network was live, he must have instinctively pulled the door closed. Not a problem, though. He never forgot a number. He input the combination. Waited. Nothing happened. He did it again. "Shit!" She'd changed the damn thing.

He gave the door a kick so ferocious that he heard things falling off shelves downstairs, but he didn't even leave a dent. Of course not. It would take a shoulder-launched rocket to knock this thing down. He ran his fingers across the lock. There was no way around it, not without the combination or explosives.

Even so, he shouldered the door and got a sharp, cracking pain for his trouble. "Goddamn it!"

He'd seen the room being installed. He knew there was no point in trying the attic or coming in through the wall or the windows.

Despair settled into him at last. Resourceful though he was, he now felt sure that midnight was going to arrive and Washington was going to find its fatal end. He would not be able to communicate with the White House in time for there to be any chance at all of locating the bomb.

His jaw clenched, his teeth bared. What a useless gesture, keeping the White House open. Noble today, but what about the leaderless country tomorrow? "Sure, there's the veep," he muttered. "But it's the symbol, you moron! The civilization rides on the *symbol*!"

A three-thousand-year journey toward human freedom was ending. He had no illusions: when Washington went, and Fitz with it, the Western world would bow to its new conqueror. Then, gradually and over time, Russia would emerge as the new superpower, as the one source of relief from the Mahdi's awful rule. Oh, that was the plan. He knew it. He knew those old KGB types, understood the way they thought. *We play poker with foreign policy; they play chess.* For them, the end of the Cold War was only a setback, strictly temporary.

Then he was aware that the movement of air around him had just changed. Something was moving in the house, he thought, and at the same instant was aware that the quality of light around him had altered as well. Without looking, he knew that her office door had been opened from inside, and very quietly.

The next moment, he smelled a woman—woman's sweat, edged with soap and scent.

"Come into the doorway where I can see you, please. I have a gun."

"Nabila!"

"Jim?"

Then she was there. Before him. So small; he had remembered her as formidable, but she was only this little slip. She raised eyes that were red from crying but shimmering with joy.

In that instant, he recognized that the power of love becomes overwhelming when it touches souls together and that this had never happened between them before, but it was happening now, and he threw open his arms and she rushed into them, and they covered each other with kisses and whispered names, and he felt himself stirring—no, exploding—and she threw back her head and laughed but also pushed away from him.

They stood like two duelists now, suddenly wary, expecting anything. "Rashid," she said, "my brother—"

"Walters told me."

"I tried to get out there, to get to him." She showed Jim her AMT Backup. "I would have killed him."

Jim took her face and kissed her. "You don't want to go down that road, Nabby."

Here came that delicious small smile of hers, touching the edges of her full lips, the sides of her dark eyes. And he thought, *O Arabia,* and cared nothing but for the beauties and magic. A strange, forbidding, and gorgeous place, a fragile, artful civilization . . . and the darkness invested there, its parasitic talons sunken into the same holy book that gave the Arabs the poetry in their souls and, he was beginning to admit to himself, their connection to the God whose silent reality defines us all.

What people did not understand was that his reality makes true every name he has ever been given. God is Allah, Yahweh, Ahura Mazda, Athene, Zeus, Ra, on and on, each name representing another human convergence with the mystery.

All of this passed in just an instant, in the compression of a man's intimate, inner shorthand, and in the next instant Jim said, "He's on dispersal. Where?"

"Maryland 28. Westmond. In a building there. But I had problems—there's a shooter team after me. I nearly got killed!"

"I know."

"I saw I had to do this at any cost, shooters or no shooters. But I didn't even get to the Beltway. The car was attacked, Jim! Time and again! And my face—I look too Arab; I just about got shot! I was lucky to get back here at all. Did you get my message?"

He shook his head.

"On your cell."

"I haven't had it on. Danger of detection."

"I found a code Rashid sent. The word 'purple.' "

"To whom?"

"Somebody in Alexandria. It went to the cable company's servers there. Then I lost it."

"Purple" would be a case identifier. When they got that word, they would know which case was being activated. "Alexandria," he said. You thought of it as a D.C. suburb, but it was a big city. You could easily hide a nuke in Alexandria, and if you could somehow get it on a plane, you'd be not five minutes from an airburst over the White House. Even if you didn't have a plane, a nuclear detonation there that was the size of the Vegas one would devastate the whole region.

"I've got all the ASP readouts from there, but nothing shows up," Nabby said.

He considered that piece of information. It would be easy to conclude that the bomb wasn't there, but his sense of it was that this would be wrong. The location was too perfect. "It's there," he said.

"I concur. But it's a big place."

"Nabila, we have one card left to play."

"But—what? How?"

"Call it the Card of the Lovers. Low card, odds always against it. But if you trust it, it's a powerful card."

"In Islam, trust is surrender."

He wanted to kiss her, to somehow melt away the scars. But there was no time.

She followed him downstairs and outside, into the dangerous streets.

25

SOME SORT OF LIFE

As midnight swept westward, city after city rose from cringing desperation, and knew that life—some sort of life—would continue there at least for a little more time. Because Las Vegas had been destroyed at midnight, the world had become focused on that as the hour of lightning. But why must it be midnight? The truth was far more bleak, and was reflected in the offices of intelligence chiefs and their screaming prime ministers, presidents, dictators, and kings across the whole planet. With the exception of a few professionals like Jim Deutsch, who understood something of the mind they were dealing with, nobody knew if midnight actually mattered. The inner circles of the world feared that another bomb could go off at any moment, and that made them panicky, and their panic played right into the hands of the Mahdi. The more chaos, the better. Chaos, for Inshalla, was safety.

In the Muslim world, the stunned jubilation—the joy riots of Cairo and Tehran, Karachi and Baghdad and Gaza, and a thousand other places—faded as the images from Las Vegas began to march across TV screens. Initially, the scenes had been of burning buildings and lines of cars on highways, all taken from helicopters miles away. Now, though, video shot on the streets was appearing, and the horror was beyond imagination, even to people who lived in a world of street-corner bombings and public executions. One image, of a little girl being sucked toward the firestorm, followed by her shrieking parents, broke hearts across the planet. All three had died. The man with the camera had died. A reporter had found the camera. Thousands of burnt bodies littered the streets in gutted neighborhoods, and now great clouds of buzzards and gulls descended on the city, circling in swarms, spreading their wings over the corpses like feathery shrouds.

Nobody could see images like this and not be affected, and Muslims, inside themselves, found themselves saying, *This was done by people who pray as I do, who worship in the same mosques, who believe as I do.*

The reality of the crime, there for everybody to see, was, across the Muslim world, transforming jubilation into shame.

Women went about silently if at all, heads covered, eyes down. Men sat in tea and coffee shops, smoking and staring. If anybody played music, somebody would stop it with a curse. Men were angry and argued, but never about the pictures from Las Vegas. The images evoked a shame similar to that which attaches to pornography, because of the intimate connection between pleasure and violence, and they came to taste obscene.

The princes of Riyadh quietly dispersed, aware that their city was at once the capital of extremism and of moderation and that none knew where that left it, as an enemy of this mythical Mahdi or as his ally. Who knew, maybe he was even harbored here.

Certain Muslim leaders knew of Dream Angel, and there were anguished meetings taking place in various capitals. Some years ago, the Fitzgerald administration had intentionally leaked an outline of the plan to Tehran, and the government was well aware that while substantial areas of the city would be spared, an intricate pattern of bombing would so decimate the believers that the faith might collapse here and the country be given over to the powerful Western leanings that were its suppressed truth.

Riyadh did not know of Dream Angel but would have been appalled at the extent of the targeting in Saudi Arabia, where individual towns and specific neighborhoods in every city were marked for death. In all, Dream Angel would cut the population of the Kingdom by a third, and destroy the religious police utterly.

Even though elements within certain Muslim national intelligence agencies were aware that the Pentagon was creating an ultradetailed map of the Muslim world, and that it had military significance, they had been unable to obtain details.

So they inquired of the social sciences community, and found that something called a social-associative network could be involved.

Some of these states had constructed their own versions of the American map, using their own social scientists, so they knew roughly where the targets were.

They also knew that innocent people would die, and in staggering millions, something the West once would never have contemplated doing. It was genocide on a scale that made Hitler look like an amateur.

But these people were not innocent, not according to the new definition of guilt that the West, under increasing pressure and without consciously realizing what it was doing, had adopted. Guilt no longer attached only to action. Guilty wishes, guilty dreams, the inability to expel terrorists from your community—these were the new crimes.

But what was the sentence for committing them?

The Syrian and Iranian intelligence services both hit on the same answer: the target areas would be annihilated by small nuclear weapons delivered to their targets with great precision.

There could be only one type of bomb that would do this—a neutron weapon. It would deal death in the form of sheets of high-energy particles that would slaughter microscopically, instantaneously boiling the victims to death, cell by cell.

The mathematics of such bombs could be made as exact as the map of the targets, and only if they got very lucky indeed would any national air defense manage to shoot down a plane or two. None of the cruise missiles would be destroyed. Except for the West and Israel, there were no powers on earth that could intercept a cruise missile.

So, in conference rooms and offices across the whole of the Muslim world, the same question was asked: will they now kill us all?

What a few of the leaders knew, the whole population of the Muslim world suspected: there would be retribution, and it would be terrible. So the cities of the Muslim world were soon just as convulsed as the cities of the West, and even more so, because they were more densely populated and less well organized.

The old part of Jakarta was soon burning, the streets so packed with vehicles that dogs were jumping from car roof to car roof amid running crowds. Rumors were everywhere, and whenever a plane was heard overhead, thousands died, trampled.

Despite all this chaos, Washington was not the only place where people were struggling to find reconciliation, and the vast majority of Christians and Muslims saw themselves as being joined together on the same side in a desperate struggle against an evil so great that they had not been able to imagine that it could exist—until it emerged in the form of the fiery sun that had murdered Las Vegas.

At the moment of the explosion, it had been eight in the morning in Rome and the pope was in the dental chair in the small medical facility in his Vatican apartments. Guillermo Cardinal Mosconi, his secretary of state, approached. It was quite a surprise to the pope, because the formal nature of Vatican life meant that an unannounced visit like this was extremely unusual.

Mosconi, a short, quick man currently dressed in a business suit, made a sharp motion at the dentist as he approached the pontiff. "Holiness," Mosconi said, "I am bringing news of the most critical nature."

The pope got out of the chair and went straight into his private office, clearing his mouth of cotton as he walked, dropping it behind him. Mosconi was not given to outbursts. Whatever this was, it was extremely serious.

They sat across from each other. Behind Mosconi were many of the pope's collection of twenty thousand books, which had been provided for when the apartments were remodeled after his election to the Throne of Saint Peter. Pope John Paul II had lived like a monk, but that discipline had died with him, and the apartments, therefore, were pleasant, this room decorated in deep, dignified reds and excellent woods. The desk was an antique that had been with the pope since he had been elevated to archbishop, a gift from the faithful of his home diocese.

Pulling off the dental apron, he sat heavily. The papacy was, in truth, a wearisome trial for him. He did it for love of the church, for love of Jesus and the great power of the sacraments. In his privacy, he longed for the rambles of his boyhood and the solitary evenings of his childhood summers.

He raised his eyebrows to Mosconi. "Cardinal?"

"There has been an atomic explosion in the United States."

"God preserve them."

"It has destroyed the city of Las Vegas. One million are dead. The churches all are burning. All."

The pope had closed his eyes and turned his inner being toward the Lord. Surrendered himself, mind and heart. He had asked the question he dreaded to hear answered: "An accident?"

"Deliberate."

Then he knew. It was the Muslims.

"Yes," Mosconi said, reading the very familiar face of this man he had known for forty years. "An unknown Muslim organization. Unknown to the Americans, they say. It has demanded, also, that you order all churches to be closed. They are using the atomic threat to force the entire world to embrace Islam."

The pope gave Mosconi a careful look. "So," he said, "you are saying that we know more?"

"We have, as you know, a connection within the Belorussian exarchate—"

"Yes, Mosconi!" Of course he knew. "Go on."

"There is indication that a plutonium bomb of Russian manufacture was used."

If Mosconi said it, there was no question of any indication. It was certain. "And do the Americans know this?"

"I have no belief that they do."

The pope realized immediately that he held the fate of nations in his hands. If he directed this information to the American president, the third world war that the church had fought so hard for so long to prevent would then unfold. Both the Americans and the Russians would fire their missiles at each other. Each side would be afraid not to, lest the other side fire first and destroy their ability to retaliate.

The key would be to reveal those directly responsible, the Muslim group that, the pope had immediately concluded, was the out-of-control tool of the Russians. They wanted the West on the defensive, not destroyed.

The people directly responsible could be punished, and nobody ever need know where the bomb had come from. "Are we aware of directly responsible parties?"

"There is this 'Mahdi,' so he calls himself."

"Then he's the one to drag into the light."

"We don't have the reach to do this."

Inside himself, the pope begged the Lord for guidance. Perhaps the answer came in the cardinal's next suggestion, which was to call the president.

The pope did this, offering his condolences. Then he asked if the Americans had any specific expectation that there was another bomb. Fitzgerald said little, but the grave tone of his voice caused the pope to end the call in a mood of deepest foreboding.

"We have here a possible Antichrist," he told Mosconi.

Both of them knew, of course, of the prophecy of Saint Malachy, and the fact that it had been written not by that twelfth-century holy man but by the odd and dangerous Michel de Nostredame, popularly known as Nostradamus, in the sixteenth century. There was something horrible about it, something profoundly unholy, that made the pope almost queasy when he so much as thought of it.

He thought of it now, though, in particular of the prophecy of the next pope, Peter the Roman, who was to be the last. He quoted, " 'In persecutione extrema sedebit Petrus Romanus.' "

As if to shield himself from the words, Mosconi raised his hands, brushed them across his face as if warding off an insect. "During the final persecution, the seat will be occupied by Peter of Rome. Yes, Holiness."

The pope reached across the desk, and took Guillermo's hand. " 'Qui pascet oves in multis tribulationibus: quibus transactis civitas septicollis diruetur, et Iudex tremêndus iudicabit populum suum.' "

"He will feed his sheep amid many trials, and when these things are finished, the city of the seven hills will be destroyed, and the great Judge will judge his people."

The pope and the cardinal looked into each other's eyes. " 'Finis,' " the pope said. The last word of the prophecy. "Is it happening, Willy?"

"This you must give to God."

In the silence that followed, they heard voices coming from the square.

The pope stood up. "Dress me," he called, and his dresser came quickly with the cassock and mantilla. The pope dressed, then went to the window in which popes customarily appeared.

Below, in the light of a gray morning, there had been perhaps a thousand souls, looking in the great square almost like none at all. But when they saw him, the cheer was so robust that it raised the pigeons, who flew in graceful arcs, their wings flashing when they swept into the sky.

By noon of that day, St. Peter's Square was half-full. The pope was making preparations to speak to them from the balcony of the basilica. He would come at just before six in the evening, the hour of midnight in Washington, when it was expected by all the world that the American capital would be destroyed.

He had telephoned President Fitzgerald again, urging him to leave the city. The president would not leave. "Continuity of government has been assured," the president had said.

Was the man committing suicide? The pope was not sure that he understood the president's motive. A sort of desperate defiance, he thought. In his most private mind, the part of it he shared with no living man, he was coming to the conclusion that America was finished. For a long time now, they had been caught in a situation where their power was decompressing. Their inability to find an effective way to control Muslim guerillas and their failure to understand that what seemed like Muslim terror was often a projection of state power had brought them, inevitably, to this execution ground. The tool of Islamic terrorism was used by many hands.

"Holiness, Signore Manconi has arrived."

He had asked earlier that Hilario Manconi, the president of the Vatican Bank, brief him on the world financial situation. "Very well."

Manconi, whose dreary, equine face made his first name seem like a sardonic joke, proceeded into the presence. At a gesture from the pope, Manconi sat beside the desk and, with an officious snapping of latches, opened his briefcase and drew out a sheaf of papers. "It's a catastrophe," he said.

The pope was so tired, so emotionally stripped, that he almost blurted out a bark of laughter at the sight of the woebegone Hilario announcing disaster. "Go on," he said.

"The dollar has collapsed. It is at this moment fifty-three dollars in the euro, and none can know where it will end. The U.S. central bank has exhausted its foreign currency reserve and nobody will buy treasury notes at this time. Gold is to four thousand, one hundred euros, tripling from the open. Bourses are closed, but not commodity exchanges, and everything—" He stopped. His throat worked.

"Continue."

"I am continuing! Oh—sorry. Holiness!" He drew out another sheaf of papers. "The bank's position is very sound. We have not much in dollar holdings. And our gold—" He shrugged. "The wealth we command is almost beyond calculation, Holiness."

"My concern is the welfare of the people of the world. Are they starving, signore?"

"It's chaos. Transport disrupted. All shipping lanes shut down. No flights. In Europe, not even road traffic, nor in America, but the U.S. authority is collapsing. There are all sorts of presidential orders going out. Nobody obeys. They all run from the cities."

"And here?"

"In Roma? Some, certainly." He blinked, looked up sharply.

"Not here," the pope said. "God willing."

"No, Holiness!"

The pope waved him to silence. "If it is God's will that this test be given us, then we are grateful for his faith, for God does not give unfair tests. So if the Mahdi succeeds, I have no doubt that St. Peter's will become a great mosque, in the same manner as Holy Wisdom." He referred to the Hagia Sophia in Istanbul, which had been the greatest center of worship in Christendom for a thousand years, before being converted by the force of Islamic arms into a mosque.

"But, Holiness—"

"You know, a few years ago the Royal Aal al-Bayt Institute for Islamic Thought—do you know of this?"

"No, Holiness."

"A Muslim institute published a letter of peace between the faiths that also contained an admonition against Christians' waging war against Muslims on account of religion. And yet, there is no place on earth that has ever been forcibly converted from Islam to Christianity. Have you ever been to the Hagia Sophia?"

"Of course."

"The Quran says they should conquer." He thought back across his life, his mind touching a memory of the long-ago afternoon he had spent wandering the halls of the Alhambra in Granada, among the most beautiful buildings in the world—a Muslim building. "The conqueror of Spain was also called the Mahdi. His prophecies are in a work called the Hadith, and it is their fervor for conquest that has always animated the Muslim spirit. These terrorists are part of a deep tradition of Islam. They are not separate from it. I will tell you this: after the conquest is finished, this time, I will be knocked dead with stones."

He knew that his feelings should be more balanced, his mind concerned only with being shepherd to the faithful. But he was so very, very angry. He thought of those poor people of Las Vegas, all burned and their homes ruined, and the gigantic suffering that this economic collapse would visit on mankind.

The knowledge came to him—perhaps, he thought, from God—that this invisible Mahdi was not a creature suffused with spiritual power, an Antichrist. Rather, he was like Hitler, an ordinary but ambitious man whose arrogance, aggression, and refusal to humble himself in prayer had opened the door of his soul to evil. "So," the pope said, his voice low, "he is only a man."

"Holiness?"

"Thank you, Hilario."

The banker stood and stepped back, then turned and hurried away. Looking after him, the pope reflected that he was probably in the middle of the most frantic day of his life, poor man.

Alone now, the pope went across the apartment and entered his chapel. As always, he knelt in the back of the ornate little room. He heard an increasing great roar from the square. The faithful were gathering in the arms of the church. Closing his eyes, he prayed. Had he publicly called this foolish little creature the Antichrist, he might have set the whole world on fire. "Jesus, I hear your voice within," he said. "Thank you, my beloved master, for this guidance. I give you my weakness, my anger, my senseless hatred. I give it to your compassion, oh my friend." He followed this with a fervent Pater Noster, then raised his eyes to the blue-veiled virgin John Paul had installed here. "Thank you, Mother, for your intercession for me. I will not speak my anger, Mother." Quickly he prayed a decade of his rosary.

When he turned from the chapel, he was not surprised to see that Mosconi was back.

"The Grand Mufti has come."

"What is this?"

"The Grand Mufti of Saudi Arabia is here."

But how could this be? "There was no such meeting arranged."

"There was nothing. He has come on the king's plane." Mosconi shrugged. "He simply arrived."

After the pope had publicly told the truth about Islam, that it was a religion of violence, there had been that letter signed by a number of high Muslim authorities saying that they had no argument with Christians, as long as these Christians did not seek to invade Islam. Then the Saudi king had come to Rome and said essentially the same thing. The pope had refrained from speaking of the Islamic invasion of Christian Spain and the Christian Middle East. But, in his mind, he had not forgotten the truth of history, and he did not forget it now. Islam had invaded the Christian world then and was doing it again now.

So this—a meeting between the church and Islam, at this moment? "Mosconi, I'm at a loss."

Mosconi bowed his head in assent. "In the private audience chamber?" He offered the pope no choice as to whether or not he would receive the Mufti. But the private audience chamber was a state room, private or not.

"No, no, it's not a state visit. It can't be official. Bring him here."

"Will you take the throne, then?"

The pope considered this. If he sat in the symbolic chair that stood in this room, gilded and red, before the wall bearing his portrait, the meeting would take on a symbolic meaning that neither man wanted to cope with. But at his desk perhaps the Mufti would feel an unpleasant sense of being a supplicant.

"Mosconi, I have no private places! I cannot take him back to the dentist with me."

Mosconi smiled slightly. The pope's sense of humor was well known behind these walls. "Where, then, Holiness?"

"Let's go to my books."

He crossed the room, his feet whispering on the carpet—an Arabian design, he recalled, a gift from the king of Jordan—and went to the little nook of chairs that was his private lair, where he indulged himself in history, poetry, and thought. He sat beneath the tall shelves of volumes, every one of which had been read. It was like an extension of his mind, his library. The treasure of his life. "I will receive him now."

Mosconi turned toward the desk, reaching to press the intercom button.

"Wait. What do I call him? A name? What is his name?"

"You call him Sheikh. He will call you Pastor." Mosconi picked up the telephone, and in a moment the outer door opened.

The Mufti was tall and very straight, and came striding forward, his spotless white robe whipping behind him. The pope could see a hint of a dark cuff under its hem, and a gleaming shoe peeking out as the Mufti walked. Beneath his robe of ancient design, there was a business suit, no doubt from Savile Row.

As he came closer, the pope rose. This was something the outside world would never see, but he realized that this man could possibly know a great deal about what was happening. He could be a key.

"Pastor, I bring you greetings from the king, as custodian of the Holy Sites of Islam and leader of the Islamic Kingdom, and I greet you from my sad heart and the hearts of all good Muslim people." He spoke a densely accented but understandable English, and his face—the expression—caused the pope to at once cease to be wary of him. The man was exhausted. His eyes were desperate. Many tears had been there. The pope could imagine this man on the king's palatial plane, sitting alone, weeping in the privacy of the sky.

Suddenly, as if it was entirely natural, as if it had been meant from the beginning of the world, the two men embraced. The pope felt the trembling bones, then stepped back, holding the Mufti at arm's length. How fragile was this old man, beneath his robes.

They were silent, and the pope suddenly knew why. He knew that it was because God was there, directly there, speaking to both of them in the eternal language, the pope believed, of truth.

He told the Mufti, "We say that our God is not your God, but it isn't so. It isn't so."

"We have it, 'there is no God but God.' " Then his eyes pleaded. "These people are monsters. Heretics in our faith."

In English, also, the pope responded, but carefully, "Sheikh, it is a tragedy when holy faith is used as justification for violence."

"You and I have both been to the Alhambra," the sheikh said softly. "I know that you have."

"You and I have both been to the Hagia Sophia," the pope replied. "I know that you have."

Their eyes said the rest of this history, and their silence.

"The king has conveyed our sorrow to the president and the American people. I am here because I wish to appear with you before the multitude in the square and before the world."

The pope was affronted. This lost soul could not appear here, in God's church. The pope started to speak his refusal—but, again, he felt that presence. This time, there seemed to be a little girl here, she was all burnt, standing behind the Mufti, and with her was an angel of God. They were silent, watching the pope. Even so, he shook his head. A thing this great could not be done in a moment, no, not even for the angels.

Such an event would normally be years in the planning, perhaps decades. There were three congregations that should be involved, and many cardinals who would expect to be consulted, and rightly expect this. There were many orders, also, that would anticipate offering their opinions, not to mention Opus Dei and other powerful lay organizations.

But the child was still there, still watching him. He could hardly bear to look at her blackened flesh, but it would not leave his mind's eye. "Be as little children." He recalled his mother saying it to him, recalled her telling him that if he forgot this, he forgot Christ.

He knew what a child would do. He forced himself to smile. "Mufti," he said, "I sense that God is with us."

From outside, the roar of the crowd was now enormous, louder than he had ever known it. He thought of each of them, each an astonishing microcosm of the whole. "The Kingdom of God is within you." The Lord had said that not to kings but to simple folk just like the multitude whose hopeful faces were turned now toward that window over there.

His heart bowed, and he knew that when he and the Mufti went to the window Jesus would be with them.

"We will go before the world, then, you and I."

The Mufti closed his eyes for a moment. In the tightness of the lines around them, the sunken cheeks, the pope saw that he also was in deepest inner conflict. "There is only one God," he said. "I will say it."

"I also." It was now five fifteen. Less than an hour. He wanted to telephone the president again, to beg him to leave Washington. But the president, he knew, had ascended already into another state. He had observed it in John Paul, the sudden sense of distance that comes as death steals closer.

No, President Fitzgerald was beyond telephone calls now. He was busy, that poor man, with the waiting that comes before dying.

26

TWENTY MILLION DOLLARS

As the president danced on the end of his rope in Washington, in Peshawar birds were making riot in the high morning and it was pleasant in the gardens of the town. Later, it would grow warm, but the heat of summer was gone, and even here there was that sense of echo that haunts autumn days.

Aziz took his tea with careful design, for he knew that history would record his actions in every detail. There would be poetry and song and texts, and each gesture of his that Eshan and the Persian boy Wasim were observing now would become part of the eternal history of human freedom.

He must be seen as the confident servant of Allah, not the man he felt himself to be, full of flutters and fears.

It must be, this thing, for this was be the world's last chance to join itself to the love of God. In a very few moments now, the Great Satan would be finished.

Aziz wanted to look at his watch, but he would not show anything that might later be taken to mean that he was not entirely surrendered to Allah. He nodded to the Persian, who came forward, his enormous eyes, as always, full of wonder. Again, he nodded.

The tea gurgled into Aziz's glass. "Thank you, Wasim," he said, bringing the whisper of a smile to the face of a boy who was just beginning to understand his own role, that not only was he here as a student but also his duty was to serve the Mahdi and give him relaxation when his heart was heavy with cares.

There were sounds coming from outside, voices shouting. The Mahdi allowed himself to wonder if word had come to Peshawar that the Great Satan had been brought down.

"I am not here to give tea," Wasim said. "I want to return to Tehran. I don't want to wear this—" He gestured to his *djellaba*. He shook his head.

"Children are beaten for impertinence."

"I want my Xbox back! This is all crazy! You live like it was the Stone Age!" The beautiful eyes bored into him; the voice dropped, the lips barely moving. "You're ignorant and you care about nobody but yourself. You're a monster."

Aziz sucked breath. Every cell in his body wanted to strike this insolent boy. Even so, in Aziz's deepest heart he felt an abiding sorrow for the terrible thing that had been done, and the fact that it could never now be changed.

He shook it off. There could be no faltering now, no weakness.

Outside, more voices were rising.

The boy smiled at him. "When can I go? All Tehran is against you. All Muslims are against you. Even Hezbollah says you're evil!"

"They are cursed of God. Our Brotherhood is not evil!"

"The Muslim Brotherhood has also condemned you, whoever you are. Nobody knows! Are you some madman's stooges? Osama's? He's stupid enough to try this. Who are you?"

He would say nothing of Inshalla to this boy. He would not say the name to this rebellious child. "I will ignore your insults now, but later I will beat you."

The boy looked straight at him, his eyes glinting with accusation. "I hate you," he spoke with a mildness that was chilling to Aziz. He reflected that this boy had killed, and so become a man. A man could kill again.

"Your father paid a great deal to put you with me."

"My father is a fool."

The voices outside had become a roar, and Aziz was beginning to be curious about what might be happening. Surely if the bomb had detonated, Eshan would come and tell him.

Then the boy spoke again. "You lied; you're not a teacher. You teach nothing. I want to call my father! Why is there no telephone?"

Eshan appeared. His face was impassive. "It is three minutes past the hour now," Eshan said.

Perhaps Eshan had not heard what the crowd had heard. "History is three minutes long now," Aziz said to Eshan. "In the first minute Mohammed is born; in the second the Quran is finished. In the third all the world rejoices at the death of the Great Satan."

Eshan did not respond but only lowered his eyes. Aziz wanted to savor this event, as the people of Peshawar, so used to the oppressive faithlessness of the apostate government and its Crusader-financed police, realized that the Crusader king had been killed.

Aziz got up from the chair where he had been taking his tea, and moved across to the heavy door that sealed the garden off from the outside world.

"Mahdi, perhaps, have a care."

"Why is that? Do they suddenly know me in Peshawar? Am I not hidden by God himself?" The Twelfth Imam had been rendered occult by Allah. He would not be discovered, could not be, until the time was right.

"I don't know, Mahdi."

"I do know, and I tell you that I'm in no danger here."

"Yes, Mahdi."

He enjoyed Eshan calling him by his title. Glorious title. Eshan had seen the way his hell-raising boss had changed once the great office was conferred on him, had seen him literally transform into a new man, as the Mahdi's ancient spirit filled his own young and brash one.

The door in the thick garden wall was kept locked. Aziz approached it, took down the big key, and fitted into the lock. "Are you afraid, Eshan?"

"Yes, Mahdi."

When he opened the garden gate, he saw a woman rush past with her hair flying, then another in Western dress, who was wearing a blue veil. There were men, too, and he saw a great column of smoke behind the roofs of the houses.

Eshan came behind him. "Master, don't go far."

"What is this, Eshan? What's burning over there?"

"Sethi Mohalla."

"A mosque is burning?"

"The mosques of the truly faithful are all burning."

"But—"

"You should look at the news!"

Eshan's tone astonished Aziz. "Where is your respect? Don't forget who I am."

"Then stop sitting around drinking tea and pretending you're the Prophet's left foot. We're having a catastrophe! Anyway, we've known each other a long time, Aziz."

Aziz held in his surprise. First the boy goes mad, and now this. "We must trust in God. God does all." Some girls passed, again without veils. He gestured at them. "What is this? What is this business?"

"Our women are removing the *hijab* in protest against the bomb, and Christian women are wearing the blue veil to announce respect for Islam, the Veil of Mary, Mother of Jesus. Christians and Muslims are worshiping together, all over the world. They are praying together everywhere, hand in hand."

This could not be true. His clerk was overwrought. But the matter of the *hijab,* this Aziz could see with his own eyes. "This is illegal, to remove the *hijab.*"

"Not in Pakistan."

"They must be stoned, Eshan."

"Mahdi, there are not enough stones. Millions of Muslim women are doing it. The whole Muslim world is united as never before—against you, Mahdi."

Eshan quoted the great words of the Muslim Brotherhood. " 'Allah is our objective. The Prophet is our leader. Quran is our law. Jihad is our way. Dying in the way of Allah is our highest hope.' " He continued, "Conversion is violent, often. It has always been thus. But afterward—what happiness!"

"The Muslim Brotherhood denounces us."

"We are masters. Above the Brotherhood."

"We are denounced."

Anger raced the Mahdi's heart, but he strove to appear serene. He let the breath of rage slip from his body. "Very well," he said. He wanted to curse the arrogant devils, especially these females, but he turned, instead, and went back to his garden. He gave the outer door a good, hard slam. They would learn of the power of Islam, these women, all of them! Devils!

From deeper within the house, he heard the voice of Al Jazeera—another female, and she also was speaking of the "universal protest of the Muslims against the monsters who dropped this bomb."

"Zaaria and the others are watching television?"

"Yes, Mahdi."

Not even his three wives knew for certain who he was. This was a man's secret, this secret and sacred life of his. "Go and turn it off! Devils!"

There was movement from behind the black curtain that concealed the women's rooms. A small hand darted out; then the curtain parted. Slowly, his daughter Jamila came into the garden. At thirteen, she had a roselike purity about her, with flawless skin, her olive cheeks brushed pink, her lips just becoming sensual. It would not be long before she went into purdah, but not just yet. Every father longed to delay that moment, especially when he had such a beautiful child as Jamila.

Jamila wore a blue *hijab,* not a black one. Black for the heart of the female, black to prevent disturbance among men.

"What is this blue?"

"Oh, I don't know." She twirled around. "What if I take it off?"

"You will be stoned, Daughter."

"Oh, *stoned*! With little stones or big stones?"

Absently he gestured toward some cinder blocks that were stacked against the garden wall.

"Do only women get stoned, Father, dear Father?"

"Whoever disobeys a law that requires stoning is stoned. Now let's leave this subject."

"My mommas say you're the Dajjal. Are you the Dajjal, truly?"

"This is monstrous! A monstrous lie!" The Dajjal was the antithesis of the Mahdi, an evil being such as the Christians called the Antichrist.

Jamila twirled, and as she did, the blue scarf floated off her head. "Do you like me," she trilled in the music that was her voice, "or perhaps I'm not pretty to the eyes of a demon."

"This is madness." He took her wrist. "Stop this!"

"No! Don't you touch me!"

"Be silent! I am your father! Get that *hijab.*"

"Stone me; you'd love to even though it's not the law! I'm not in purdah yet, and I'll never go into purdah, not for you. You're a bloody, evil *monster*!"

It took all the strength he had in him not to slap her senseless. They had been infected by that accursed Al Jazeera with its rubbish nonsense!

"Wasim! Come stone me; my father commands it!"

Wasim came from inside the house, followed by a scent of cooking spices. "What is this?"

"I'm disobeying the law! I must be stoned!"

Wasim looked toward Aziz. "Mahdi?"

"She will not be stoned."

"What? But Wasim, you cut off heads! Surely you can stone, too!" She took his wrist. "Here, come to these blocks. Pick one up. I'll be a good girl; I'll kneel. You can crush me easily!"

"Mahdi?"

"Wasim, go back to your cooking."

But Jamila blocked his way. And then she did more; she did the unthinkable. "Ba-ba-*bang,*" she chanted as she tore off her blouse. "Ba-ba-biddy-*bang*!" She bent, then came up again. She stood naked. "Now, Father, I am obscene. The filthy female." She danced in front of Wasim. "Getting excited? How about you, Father? Is not your filthy daughter pretty? Will you not want me among your virgins in your heaven?"

"No! No, oh, God, what is this? This is madness!"

She went to the blocks and hefted one. The big, gray thing almost caused her to fall back, it was so heavy against her frail nakedness.

Certainly a woman going naked would be severely punished. But a child?

"Daughter, there is nothing in the law to require the punishment of a foolish girl." He went to her and lifted the great block out of her hands, and returned it to the stack.

Then Zaaria, who was Jamila's mother, came out of the curtained room. She came to the center of the garden. He knew her by her eyes. His wives obeyed the sura, and thus she was in full purdah.

"Zaaria, your child is misbehaving. Please take her away."

She reached up and unbuttoned her robe, her dexterous fingers working quickly.

"What are you doing?"

"You are not of the Ahul al-Bayt. You did not become known in Medina."

The robe opened, and in her hand he saw the knife used for the dressing of chickens.

"You are no Mahdi, but I will tell you who you are, because I know."

"I am Aziz, of course, only Aziz, son of the carpenter. The Mahdi is concealed within me. Only when the Caliphate is restored will you see my transfigured form."

" 'The Dajjal will bring hell to paradise, and what he will call paradise will be actually hell; so I warn you against him as Noah warned his nation against him.' "

"How dare you quote scripture to me! And stop this immodesty. Get the naked child and go away."

Then his other wives came into the garden, one of them wearing a Western bathing suit, little more than a gaudy yellow string. The other was in jeans and a sweater, and, like Jamila, wore the blue veil.

"Dajjal," Maya, his second wife, hissed. "You murdered a whole city!"

"I saved the whole world!"

Maya carried a big butcher's cleaver and Salwa an iron bar. Salwa hefted it and came forward. "You're the monster of the whole world!"

He knew what these weapons meant. He knew that he was being betrayed. Only one thing mattered now. "Eshan, is it completed?"

Zaaria said, "Tell him nothing."

"Tell me!"

Eshan saw what was happening. The Mahdi was leaving this man. "I must go, now, Aziz." Eshan had been told exactly what to do in this event. Should Aziz become too dangerous a receptacle, Allah would simply move the Mahdi to another.

"Help me! Get the gun, the gun, Eshan!"

Eshan left the garden and went into the house. Aziz shouted after him, "Is it completed, Eshan?" There was no response. *"ESHAN!"* But Eshan did not answer. He must go now to a certain madrassa.

The women came closer to Aziz.

"What are you doing?" He tried to smile. Their faces were awful.

"Do you know that Salwa lost toes?" Zaaria asked him.

"I don't understand."

"While you were warm on your djinn of a horse, do you remember the figures walking behind you? The *shadows*!"

"Of course I remember!"

"And no hospital, then. No hospital for her! She has gangrene, you *scum*."

He backed away, toward the outer door.

"Don't let him," Maya snarled.

Wasim took a few steps, until he was between Aziz and the door. He turned around and threw Wasim against the wall. "You're all apostate! I am the Mahdi!"

"Dajjal," Jamila sang, twirling with her hands over her head. She danced on her mother's discarded burka.

Outside, there were shots; there were screams. The sick-sharp odor of cordite sifted through the air.

"They are purging Pakistan of the ones like you, the followers of the Dajjal." Salwa raised her arms high. He watched the beautiful arms, watched the black bar in them. Above it, he saw the fading green of the trees that overhung the gardens and, higher, white clouds in the blue.

There was a pain, and then ringing silence. He knew, then, that he was on the ground. Salwa stood over him, the iron bar in her two hands.

As he was raising his arms, she hit him again, this time a blow that glanced off his shoulder, making him cry out as the bones separated. A rush of nausea swept him. He pushed himself away, and the third blow slammed into the ground with a sickening *thunk*.

"No! Please, I'm young; I deserve to live! I was forced. Yes! They told me if I did not obey, you would all die! Yes! They told me this!"

Maya came down to him, pressed her soft face into his. "You deserve hell! What of the children you burned? Have you seen that? The fields full of charred bodies? *What of them, Dajjal?*"

Then he felt a coldness on his neck, then searing heat, then an agonizing choking sensation. He reached up; he felt, his hands trembling, losing control—an effort now—he felt the handle of the cleaver. *It was in his neck!* He fought the growing weight of his own hands, fought to close his fingers—and then it was out; it was in his lap. There was a sound. Rain. No, his blood—*blood*—gushing out of his neck.

He managed to raise his head, and they were all there, Maya, Zaaria, Salwa, Jamila, and Wasim.

Aziz's throat had a torch in it. "Please, I can't breathe," he said.

Wasim barked out a laugh. "Kiss the feet of the dead, Mahdi."

"Don't call him that; it's impious," Zaaria said. She took out a pack of Marlboros and passed them to Salwa and Maya, and as his struggle turned slowly from agony to a sort of floating warmth, they stood smoking and watching him die.

"It . . ." He wanted to tell them that it changed nothing. But there was no strength.

Then it was dark; there was a child singing in perfect voice, like a distant lark.

They watched his head loll, his eyes roll back. Then his breath stopped.

"Well, it's done," Zaaria said.

"Are we rich, now?" Wasim asked. "I want to go to live in Paris!"

Zaaria went to Aziz's office. There was little here, just his mysterious codebooks and Eshan's laptop. She picked up the laptop and hid it under her burka.

"Let's go," she said. "To get this money, we need to start with the police."

They opened the garden door onto a street that was quiet again. A police truck stood at the nearby turning. Beyond it, fire equipment rumbled; and white steam rose where the firemen directed their streams into the ruins of the mosque.

It had come time for prayer, and muezzins raised their calls across the city—most of them, to be sure, electronically, but the age-old call of Islam nevertheless spread far and wide, echoing off the old stalls in the markets, off the walls of houses, floating through the gardens, the call to prayer.

Zaaria walked up to the police truck. From the back, uniformed men watched her, lazy with disinterest. "Nobody prays?" she asked.

One of them smiled a little; that was all.

She went around to the front of the vehicle where their officer was facing Mecca.

"The peace of God be with you," she said as he finished.

"And with you." He came to his feet. He was a prim man with a neatly trimmed moustache and an aroma of ginger and roses. His uniform was so bright and clean, it appeared to have been just made. "Have you trouble for me?"

"I have news that the man who is behind all these plots is dead."

"You can prove this? That it's him?"

"We have his codebooks, his radio equipment, a laptop, many things."

"So, you will have done Islam a great service."

"And the twenty million dollars the Americans are offering?" Salwa asked.

"Is it so much now?"

"I saw it on Al Jazeera. Last hour, they doubled."

"If this is true, you will have it."

"We can lead whoever you want into Pamir, and show them his hideaway. And his clerk is here in Peshawar. We can identify him."

So ended the life of the Mahdi Aziz, the son of a carpenter. His life ended, yes. But nothing else did.

27

THE LOST PLANE

At ten minutes to midnight, Bilal had embraced Hani. "Soon, you will know the joy of heaven! What happiness!"

Hani had not smiled, but Bilal had not seen the danger of this, fool that he was. Now he hurried through the streets, looking for his brother.

Bilal had thought that surely Hani was ready. He had prayed so earnestly, had worked so hard on the preparations. He would fly; it would be over in a minute; all would be well.

Didn't Hani realize that they were both dead anyway? The bomb had been removed from its shielded container. Nothing protected them from its radiation. They would both sicken and die in days. In any case, it didn't matter, because this house in Alexandria was only ten miles from the White House. This house would burn—and, in any case, Bilal planned to be on the roof, so that he would be killed immediately. Why wait and suffer?

The plane was stationed too near the point of detonation for it to be stopped in time. F-16s circled constantly, and an E-4B flew higher. It was officially a flying command post, but Bilal thought that this one must be modified to work like a very sophisticated AWACS, with the kind of downward-looking radar that would immediately guide the F-16s to a target.

Hani needed under four minutes in the air, but still it would be a near thing. At the first sign of a missile launch against him, he would detonate, no matter where he was.

It had all been so well planned. Their training had been so excellent, the aliases given, everything! And now look at this Hani; in the end he values his own life more highly than Allah's will!

Bilal thought of all the men and women who had so willingly given their lives in Palestine, in Iraq, all over the world, for love of God, and now this little fool, the most important of them all—here he was—he ran away.

The promise of heaven was true. How could he, a good Muslim, not know that? Bilal had to find him. But where? Aleph Street was empty and silent.

Bilal had kept Hani far from the Islamic Community of Northern Virginia, lest he be tainted by their apostate ways. They were worse than Shia.

Bilal wished that the Mahdi with all his knowledge of the universe, of the souls of the living and the dead, of heaven and hell, were here to offer the advice that Bilal needed, but that could not be, because the Mahdi was still hidden by Allah himself, and would remain so until the final triumph. Must be, or he would certainly be killed. The Americans had always in the past paid their great rewards to those devils who gave up holy warriors, and now the reward for the Mahdi was up to $20 million. Even with the dollar falling like a stone into a bottomless well, that was still much money. If the Mahdi was indeed proved to be dead, the Crusaders' wealth would rise again, along with their steel armies and their deadly, godless ways.

"Hani," Bilal called. His voice echoed. "Hani, I am weeping! Hani!" It was already twelve fifteen. *"Hani!"*

Most of the shops were dark, the Flair Cleaners, of course, but also the 7-Eleven on the corner—dark and the door chained closed. But then, at the far end of the street, Bilal saw a glow. That could be that little café, the place of the badly seared hamburgers. Those men in there were Muslim. They would do their business and trust to Allah's will. Or the Starbucks on Kingdom Street, perhaps, but the blacks in there, they were like all Americans; they would certainly run.

Bilal raced down Aleph, his legs pumping, hating to get away from the plane and the bomb. Crusader trucks bristling with antennae were ranging the streets, helicopters passing overhead. There was a reason that he and Hani had rented an apartment on a street directly behind a medical-imaging center, full of radioactive elements to throw off just such a search. And so far, it had worked, but it would not work much longer. With the bomb no longer shielded, it was only a matter of time before the searchers would see that the imaging center was emitting too much radiation, and would investigate.

There was no hiding an unshielded plutonium bomb, not for long. *"Hani!"*

"Can I help you?"

Bilal stopped, breathing hard. He tried to smile at the Crusader policeman, knew he had failed. "I am sorry. My brother, he is—" Bilal touched his head. "Beloved of God, we say, do you know?"

The cop nodded. "A little slow?"

"Yes, that's right. And he's afraid. He's wandered off."

A big hand came down on Bilal's shoulder. "He'll be all right." The policeman smiled, then, and his smile was strong, firm. "Look at your watch; what do you see?"

"Twelve twenty-two," Bilal said, trying to keep the despair out of his voice.

"So, they missed! Your brother's probably celebrating!"

Bilal raised his hands. "Oh, thank God," he intoned.

"Him and all the angels, buddy," the cop said. "We got a curfew, now, so you need to get back home. Has your brother got a cell? I might be able to reach it through the police net."

"No cell. Oh, look—the Starbucks—is that open?"

"Cops only."

Bilal hurried past him, but a moment later there was the squawk of a siren, then the flashing of the police car's lights. Bilal stopped, raised his hands. The cops, two of them, now both in their squad car, gave him genial looks. "Hop in. If he's not in the Starbucks, we'll cruise you for a while. We'll find him."

So Bilal got into the police car, sitting in the cage in the back. Had the devils captured him? They were clever, the Crusaders. He sat forward on the seat, trying to appear calm.

"Rough one, today," one of the cops said.

"Yes, Sir. Very definitely."

"You guys staying under cover?" asked the other cop. "Because there's a lotta folks—you know—well, it's a tough time for you now. You Arab?"

"We are Iraqi. I'm a procurement specialist. My brother—well, he keeps our house, God willing."

"What agency you with?"

"No. Iraqi government."

"Yeah. That must be interesting work."

"Very interesting!"

Then he saw Hani. He was sitting in the Starbucks, but what was worse, he was there among a dozen police and other helmets, sitting working on a laptop! What was he doing there with that computer? Was he giving them all away?

"Oh," Bilal said, "he's there. Stop. Stop now."

"Hey, we found 'im!"

Bilal pulled the handle, and found that the door had not been secretly locked, after all. These Crusader fools had helped their enemy.

He went into the Starbucks. There was music playing; was it Joni Mitchell? Sweet voice, anyway, some Crusader harlot or other, "Give Peace a Chance." Idiots. "Hello, Hani."

"Hello."

"Is this betrayal?"

"No. I'm only playing King Kong."

"King Kong?"

"That game. It was in the house when we rented it. It's good fun!"

"Hani, it's half past twelve."

"I know it."

"Are you not going?"

Hani played the game.

Bilal sat down across from him. "My brother, this is defamation for our family. Even in the eyes of God."

"It's fun, but hard to get the gorilla to leap. I think perhaps it's a little defective."

The first of the two policemen came in. A few of the others greeted him.

"Here we are in the den of the Crusaders! Hani, please come home."

"Hey there, guys, we gotta roll. You comin' or not?"

"We will come."

"He can use a computer?"

"All the time, he plays a gorilla game. We will walk home later."

"You better come with us. It just ain't safe for you folks."

Bilal looked up sharply.

The policeman smiled. "I'm embarrassed, but I think you understand that it's not safe for somebody who looks like you. Not safe tonight."

Bilal took Hani's arm, and gently brought him to his feet. "Come, my brother. You need never do that chore I asked of you. Come home with me."

Hani touched Bilal with his eyes. "There is no other way."

"Brother, there is. When we are home, I will show you this."

They were taken home by the police, back to the plane and the bomb, and as they went into the house an F-16 thundered low overhead, its fuselage glowing in the city lights.

Inside the house, Bilal said, "I have another way. I am too heavy now, but perhaps that can change."

Hani's eyes grew as quick as those of an uneasy sparrow. Flick, flick, they went, looking to the living room, to the kitchen, resting on the door into the garage.

"You must help me, Hani." Bilal tugged at his brother's shoulder. "Here, come to the garage; we have the saw."

Hani pulled away. He looked at the floor. Shook his head. "I will go," he said.

⊕ ⊕ ⊕

As midnight had approached, President Fitzgerald had ranged the White House like Banquo's ghost, followed and guarded at every turn by Marines.

At ten minutes to twelve, he had taken a call from the Pakistani leader: "Mr. President, I know that Dream Angel is off the deck. I am calling to beg you for our lives."

"I don't know what you're talking about," Fitz had said, and immediately felt weak for saying it. He sensed his power—American power—ebbing away, dying with the dollar and the terrible passage of this night. He'd hung up, not listening to the man's further protests.

There had been two calls from the pope, who was apparently with the Saudi Grand Mufti. The Saudi king had telephoned twice. More pleas, no doubt. There had been other calls from Syria, from Iran, from Indonesia, everybody knowing that Dream Angel had moved to its fail-safe points, everybody knowing that the moment Washington was destroyed, hundreds of millions of Muslims would also be destroyed.

At five minutes to the hour, the vice president had called. "Fitz, I want you to know that the Document of Transfer arrived safely. I have it here."

"Thanks for letting me know, Matt." The world was distant from Fitz now, full of details—the singing of the crowd out on Pennsylvania Avenue, the distant roar of a passing F-16, the tap of heels along a corridor he could not see.

"That's not why I called."

"I'm not leaving."

"Come on; I've got the chopper on the lawn!"

"America does not run."

"The death of the president will be looked on as proof of our weakness. It will be seen as a defeat!"

"The courage of the president will be seen as strength. Then the world will see a smooth transition of power. That's what history has to remember, not that I turned turtle and saved my own damn ass. There's a lot of movers and shakers out there, for God's sake."

"Who?"

"That crowd. Senator Martin is there, Cardinal O'Halloran, for God's sake. They've been singing for hours. Standing their ground because I am standing mine. This is the best way, bro. Take it from me."

"It's a waste of life! The kids, Fitz, Linda. Think of them!" Matt paused. When his voice came back, it was darker, and there was a lot there, Fitz knew, that was not being said. "You could have evacuated a lot of people from that city."

"And risk an immediate detonation? No. Listen to me: Dream Angel is approaching fail-safe. They can remain on station for four hours; then there's a refueling cycle."

"The moment Washington is destroyed, they're goin' in. Should've gone in hours ago."

"You don't think my decision was the right one, either."

"Fitz, there are no right decisions in this thing. I would have sent Dream Angel and gotten the hell out of D.C. You look at things differently."

One minute to twelve had come. "You wouldn't have. No way. Not if you were in this chair." The trouble with Dream Angel was that it was too big to use. You have an ant on a plate, you can't use a sledgehammer without smashing the plate you're trying to keep clean. But there was no use explaining any of this. One thing a president learns early—don't explain yourself, because you can't.

"Fitz?"

"Yeah?"

"It's twelve two."

"Well, hell, they're late, aren't they? Go with God, bro."

"You, too. My love to all."

"I have a cussed tough family."

They were both silent, then. Hanging up this phone, Fitz thought, was like an act at the end of the world. But he did it. He looked at the phone, on the old Roosevelt Desk. He was in the Oval again. He didn't give a damn who heard what. At last, the president of the United States had no secrets.

"Logan, we got anything from upstairs?"

"Nothing. There is not one bogey in the sky anywhere in the area. And every high point from Atlanta to Bangor has been searched at least twice. Plus the radiation detection teams are out in force. Fitz, there just isn't anything."

"I wish the damn detectors were better."

"The best technology in the world—"

"—just isn't good enough!"

He went to the window, looked out across the shadow-filled Rose Garden. Officially, he was a praying man. They liked that, the American people. Guy like them, grateful to his God. Fine.

He'd go to the National Cathedral on occasion, but it was more a time to turn over problems. He wasn't like those crazies who'd been around here before, with the gall to believe they were on some kind of special mission from God. He just hoped for the best. He knew what he was—as, he suspected, did most people—a little bit of nothing on a tiny dot of a planet in the middle of who knew where? Lost in the stars.

He bowed his head, and he prayed hard, not to some God who might be looking down on a president but to the God of his childhood, whose presence he had felt when, as an innocent boy, he had knelt and been grateful for his little days.

28

TWO STORIES

Twelve thirty came, and Rashid's stomach was in his throat, his heart racing, his blood boiling. He jumped up and went to the cooler and got a Coke, popped it, and chugged. Immediately, Mark was there.

"Are we looking at a coronary?"

They could see his medicals, of course. He was way off the charts; there was nothing for it. "I'm sorry. My sister wasn't dispersed. And the waiting—oh, God!"

Mark put his hand on Rashid's shoulder. "That's very understandable. If you're not mission capable, you just let me know, we'll have Horace add your con to his for a while."

"I'm not seeing anything. Bombers at their fail-safes. Pakistani military convoys heading out of target areas."

"They know the Dream Angel target areas?"

"The entire Pakistani establishment will be packed into Karachi. Wherever there are concentrations of moderates. You can be sure of that."

"What about those Russians?"

"They never reappeared. Only the shepherds, that's all that ever moved in the area."

"And low-level reconnaissance showed nothing. Dead, no activity."

"The vehicle remains parked where it was."

"Then the two Russians are still in there?"

He was going mad; he couldn't talk more about this; he was no actor! He had to get out of here somehow and get to Alexandria and find out what had gone wrong, and he had to fix it, God willing.

"They are in there. Perhaps it's some sort of—I don't know—bounty hunt. They thought perhaps this Mahdi nut was hiding there. They went in and now they're trapped in a cave-in or blown up by a mine. There is absolutely no sign of activity. Nothing. So that's what I think happened."

"Well, it bears watching. Why not send in some Dragonflies?"

These were small drones disguised to look like insects, which fooled nobody. "They haven't got the range. I can put in for conventional drones again, but it's going to mean diversion from targeting-related missions. I don't think we'll get them."

"Yeah, we don't want to rock that boat."

"Listen, Mark, do you think I could go outside and get some air? It's like hell in here for me. This place is so damn small!"

"That's totally against regs."

"Mark, I'm getting sick! My sister—it's driving me up a wall!"

"Yeah, your meds are spiking every alarm in the book. Look, I can't do a compassionate pass, not at this alert level. What I can offer is a tranquilizer and cot time."

"No tranquilizers. But I wouldn't mind if Horace took my con for half an hour. That would help. But if Washington . . . when—for God's sake, don't hold it back from me."

Mark went back to work, moving off through the door of the tiny canteen and down the narrow corridor, his bald head shining in the fluorescent glare. Rashid went to the rest area, closed the door, and looked around for some other means of escape. A grill in the wall, but he wasn't going to be able to make it through the ductwork. That was movie fantasy. The grill was small; you'd need to be a child to get through there. In any case, there were barriers back in the ductwork, he felt sure. This was a secure facility.

He lay on the cot considering his options.

His only means of departure was right through the front door, into the car park, down the twisting access road in his car, and out to the highway. This would mean breaking regs. It would mean a disciplinary hearing, maybe arrest, maybe even getting shot thanks to some trigger-happy cop with a rod up his ass over the curfew.

Given moderate traffic, Rashid was only twenty minutes from Alexandria. The traffic was almost gone, he knew, because he'd done lookdowns when he could. If he could get to the bomb, he was convinced that he could fix whatever had gone wrong.

As soon as he made his move, they were going to be after him. His car was loaded with tracking devices, of course, so they could afford to stand well off. They would be able to tail him from the very satellites that he himself used all the time. Even if he left the car, his implant would still be trackable. They all had them, in case they were kidnapped. So nobody would need to come near him, not until he made contact with whomever he was going to see.

If it was anyone other than Nabby, they would be all over him in minutes.

God, make the plane fly! Make it fly! Where was it? The stupid, evil betrayers, why weren't they doing their part? Did they despise God? What was wrong with them?

There were shouts. At first, he wasn't fully aware of them, so lost was he in his desperate thoughts. Then they turned to cheering and his throat closed; his head began to pound. He got up from the cot and went back to the work area, twisting through the maze of carrels. People were coming out, congregating, violating regs as if they no longer existed. They were pouring into Horace's cubicle, everybody.

"Hey, infidel," Carol Wilkie cried. She came up to him and embraced him. "Don't be modest!" She took her veil and drew it across her mouth. "The Paki cops got the Mahdi and a hard drive is on its way to the CIA station in Peshawar. They'll upload its contents to Langley in a few minutes."

"Oh! Oh, my God, how . . . wonderful! Wonderful! We are saved. Saved!"

"Not just yet," Mark said. "But we're going in a good direction."

Rashid forced his face into a smile. "But we still have our cons," he said. "This may make them act precipitately."

"It's being kept under a lid," Carol responded.

Suddenly Rashid saw what to do. "In Pakistan?" he said. "Don't make me laugh. Folks, listen up." He was proud of himself. This was hard, but he was doing it for Allah, this wonderful act. How had he come by it? God, only God, could have transformed him like this. They were all watching him now. He continued, "We need to go back to our cons. Let nothing past! Because, mark me, this will be known from Jakarta to Riyadh within the hour. Is already known. And it is going to make our enemies act."

Silence. Staring faces. "And I thought you were losing your gourd," Mark said.

"I was. Now I'm not." He went back to his own con. Washington had to wait, now. His work was here; God had just made that very clear. He had to do whatever he could to expand his operational area, to cover some more important regions.

He knew the cities that Case Purple covered. It was his job, now, to get his mission revised, so that he could do what he could to conceal suspicious activities in them. All one of these pigs needed would be to see airplane wings being unfolded on a street in Queens or Hammersmith or the Tiergarten and another nail would be driven into the coffin of mankind's future. Humanity could not survive much longer, if the Crusader world was allowed to continue to gobble resources. No, they needed balance. They needed the help of Allah, and so Rashid's job remained the same as always. He went to work.

From a window in the darkened residence President Fitzgerald stared down at the crowd. His lips moved to the rising chorus. Beside him, Linda stood resolute. Dan and Polly also.

"No indications, Sir," Logan said, his voice soft and admirably firm.

The second hand of Fitz's watch swept on. Overhead, the jets screamed back and forth, round and round. Higher, AWACS and the E-4B circled. "No joy, no joy," came the reports. The Air Defense Command was convinced that they could shoot down anything that entered Washington airspace within thirty seconds of its being observed.

"You can depend on us," the generals had told Fitz.

"Well overdue now," Logan said.

Linda's arm gripped Fitz's. "I love you," she said, then kept repeating it, a mantra, "I love you, I love you. . . ."

Freedom had to win, and death here was the greatest contribution that Fitz could now make to that cause. His anguish was that his family would not leave him . . . and his abiding joy. He was so angry at them and so proud of them.

Dan gasped, sobbed, choked it back.

"One thing I know I have. I have the bravest family in the world, and the most loyal damn chief of staff in the history of this office, and Logan, could you please get us that bottle that's in the drawer beside my bed?"

Logan disappeared.

"What bottle?" Linda asked.

"The one you don't know is there. You can't be president without hootch. It's never been done."

"Dad—"

"Dan, boy, we're not safe. They're just late. Could mean anything."

"It might still happen?"

"At any moment. But the longer we go past the hour, the more the odds drop."

Maxwell, the butler, appeared with the bottle of Blue Label. He brought it on a silver tray, with shot glasses.

"Max! I thought I told you to go back to Wheeling!"

"I lost my bus ticket, Sir."

"Well, I only see five shotters there, Max. You better get a sixth for yourself."

There, in the darkness, with the voices of the people singing and the autumn wind rattling the old eaves, the presidential party solemnly drank smooth whiskey. "History forgets moments like this," Fitz said. "But we must never forget."

Dan said, "You're a great president, Dad, and I didn't think you would be."

Now, that was a rock-back-on-your-heels stunner, coming from his hero-worshiping son. Who was Dan, really? He would have a hell of a time forging a life of his own. To its children, a presidency was a cursed shadow.

The crowd had stopped singing. All those faces were looking at something, some sort of movement close to the main gate. But what?

"What is it?" Linda asked.

"Somebody attempting entry," Logan said.

There was dripping, and a smell of urine, hot, intimate. Fitz did not ask who had let go. It wasn't him; he knew that. He wished he could spread his arms around his whole people, the whole world. " 'Yea, though we walk through the valley of the shadow of death,' " he said, and then, very suddenly, could speak no more without his voice revealing the terror that rode his soul like a mad horseman.

"We need to see the president," Jim shouted through the great iron gate. A Marine stared at him from fifty feet away, well into the White House grounds. Farther back, a Humvee stood, its engine grumbling, dim light within revealing more young faces. "Look, I know perimeter safety, too. I know you can't approach."

"Hurry, Jim!"

"I know—listen—I'm going to toss in my credential."

The Marine reacted immediately, snapping to a defensive posture, pointing his weapon at Jim.

"No!" Nabila cried.

"It's just a credential," Jim said. He dangled the small leather wallet. "Nothing else. You need to take it to your officer now."

The guard snapped his bolt. Other Marines came trotting closer. Around Jim and Nabby the crowd sighed and surged.

One of the officers in the Humvee said something into a microphone, and the guard pointed his gun into the air. Jim saw his finger close around the trigger. He had just been ordered to deliver warning shots.

"You're gonna have a bloodbath, you panic these people!"

"Jim, let's go! It's too dangerous!"

He turned on her, suddenly hot with rage. "Nabby, I don't think you understand. If I don't get in, then I have to die here. This is my mission, Nabby. I will carry it out *at any cost*."

"Jim, you're more valuable alive! Jim, *think*!"

He tossed in the credential. The guard took a step back. Another. He lowered his weapon.

"It's a quarter past," somebody shouted.

The old woman began crying out the words again: "Give peace a chance. . . ." She had come out of nowhere to this place; all of them had. Why had they thought to come here? What had moved them to risk their lives?

Jim found these thoughts moving him deeply. They were here to lend their memories to the same martyrdom old Fitz had accepted, in that solemn, silent mansion.

"You have to listen! I have essential information—"

Somebody grabbed his shoulder and roughly turned him around. He found himself looking into the face of a man in a suit, a hard, cold man with an earpiece. Secret Service, FBI, CIA—who knew? He was a man following orders, and it was clear from his eyes what he had been ordered to do.

Then Nabila cried out, and Jim saw that two other of these men were pulling her away. They would be fast, but he also was fast. He chopped the Adam's apple of the one confronting him, with a stiff, driving finger, then, as his head snapped downward, spun around him and got an arm around Nabby's waist.

Jim saw the black glint of a gun in one of the men's hands. "No," he cried, but it was too late. A woman saw it, too, then two other people, and they shrank away as she screamed, her voice rising to a trembling, penetrating wail, "*He has a gun!*"

The crowed seemed to sigh, an oddly soft, oddly gentle sound. Then the fool raised the gun, bringing it into the view of hundreds of people.

The entire crowd recoiled. The man struggling with his throat went down in the spreading rampage, followed by the one attempting to pull Nabila from Jim's grasp.

Jim hugged her to him. A shot rang out, followed by a roar of terrified voices. People ran, their eyes glazed, their faces twisted to animal forms. It was too much for them, all the hours of waiting, and despite the noble struggle and the ideals when they finally lost it, they lost it all, and in an instant the band of heroes became a mob of animals.

Then the gates swung open, and the Humvee came slowly forward. And, incredibly, Fitz was there. Fitz was standing in the damned thing and so was his wife and so was Logan.

Its horn blasting again and again, it moved out into the crowd, with Fitz standing there in his shirtsleeves, his arms raised in the air. Beside him, the First Lady was impassive, as motionless as a statue—and, somehow, the dignity of her pose combined with the passion in her husband's stance brought the couple so vividly to life that the energy of the riot was literally absorbed and people turned and they became silent.

Trotting along beside the Hummer, Nabila still cradled in his arm, Jim called up to Logan, "I'm the guy on the phone! I need to talk! We've got a target!"

The roaring of the Hummer, the clapping, chanting crowd—Logan couldn't hear him.

Then a Marine started working his way toward them. In the now-clear space before the gate, Jim saw the crumpled form of the man he had struck. The face was black. Jim had collapsed the poor guy's windpipe.

Then the Marine was on Jim, his big hand coming down, grasping his shoulder. He could waste the Marine—pop an eye or crush his windpipe, too. The kid could not survive a man so lethal as Jim Deutsch. But look at him; he probably hadn't been shaving for more than a year.

"Sir, the president wants to see you."

Jim looked into the tight young eyes, silent diamonds. "Let's go," he said.

Nabby climbed into the Hummer, too, and in another moment President Fitzgerald and Tom Logan had descended into the cramped crew compartment with them.

Nabby said, "A principal in the organization here in Washington is Rashid al-Rahbi. He knows crucial codes. He is an analyst with the National Geospatial-Intelligence Agency. I am ashamed to say that he is my brother."

"We've known that he was a traitor for about four hours," Jim added. "We've been trying to come in, but there's a lot of resistance. Whoever is working for the other side has the ability to order arrests and lethal actions. Attempts have been made on both of us."

The Hummer arrived at the side entrance to the White House, and Marines opened the doors as the presidential party emerged. They entered the White House reception area. Jim was surprised at how weathered it all looked, the tired glass doors, the steel desk where some of the world's most prominent people must stop to present their identification, the elaborate—but, he knew, quite ineffective—X-ray entry system. He could easily get a weapon through one of those things. It was like so much security hardware—great on paper.

As they walked down a dim corridor, Jim said, "This thing goes—"

The president turned on him, grabbed his shoulders. The great, leathery face—that Rushmore visage of his—glared, eyes dense with exhaustion, lips slack and dry. The president shook his head. "Not here," he said in a voice that seemed to rise from the tomb.

They went up a small elevator to the private suite. Here was a small foyer, on the far side a closed door. When Logan opened it for the First Family, Jim had enough of a shock to make him gasp audibly, and he was not a man who shocked easily.

The entire room had been stripped of its carpets, its furniture, even its flooring, even its plaster. He found himself looking at bare studs and framing, and walking across big hewn beams on a plywood path.

"They're everywhere," the president muttered.

"The bugs," his wife said in a chipper voice. Jim could hear something like despair there.

"I'm not wrong," the president said.

"No," Jim agreed.

"Are you implanted?" Logan asked.

"I am," Nabila said. "My brother may still be."

"Not folks in my line of work," Jim said. "We don't want the other side finding Uncle Sam under our skin. We go naked."

"You people are implanted?" the president asked. "With what?"

She held out her arm. "To track us if we're kidnapped," she said. There was a neat red scar an inch below her elbow, on her cloud-soft inner skin. "This is why I have had so much danger today," she said, her voice tight. "If the wrong people have your code, you cannot get away."

"Your brother has one of these, too?"

"Yes."

"Let's reach out for this guy," the president said to Logan.

"Consider it done," Logan replied. He opened a cell phone.

"Wait," Jim said.

Logan looked up sharply. The president half-turned. They weren't used to this sort of intervention. This was the president of the United States who had just given an order.

"We don't want to go through channels, Sir."

Logan looked to the president.

"We need to go directly to this man's personal supervisor," Jim added. "Bypass the entire system."

"Just how extensive is this conspiracy?" Logan asked.

"That's what we don't know," Jim said.

"You're right, Mr. . . . Deutsch," the president said. "But this presents a problem. I've got—God, how many levels between me and him? I have no idea." He shook his head. "Nothing this big works right," he muttered. "It just cannot work."

Jim could not agree more. Streamlining was what the federal services needed, not the additional layers of authority that had been imposed over the last few administrations.

"I can call him," Nabila said. "On his, um—well, there's back channels that we all use."

"His cell phone will be out," Logan said. "We've shut the entire system down."

"Call his supervisor." Jim said. "Not him. His direct, personal supervisor."

"And if he's part of it, too, Jim?"

"Nabila, would he be?"

"I have no way to know that!"

"Call him," the president said.

She took the military phone and dialed. Mark answered immediately.

"Mark, it's Nabby."

"Rashid is—"

"No, Mark, listen to me. Mark, are you near him?"

"I'm in my office."

"Good. Now, listen. This is life or death. Life-or-death telephone call."

"Yes."

She looked desperately at the president, who motioned to her to keep on.

"Mark, there has been a major security breach in your sector."

"How would you know?"

"I am going to put somebody on the line. This is going to be unusual."

She handed the phone to the president.

"This is President Fitzgerald. Do you recognize my voice? . . . Good. You are to get this man—"

"Sir," Jim said, "don't have him arrested. Get him to—uh, may I do this?"

"Mr. Chambers, this man speaks for me." He handed Jim the phone.

"Hello, Mark. Listen carefully. What I want you to do are two things. First, I want you to read back Rashid's entire con for the past hour. I want you to tell me every satellite he's used, everything he's flown, all of it. And I want you to send him a signal. Shut down his con. Close him down. Almost certainly he's already looking for some excuse to leave. Let him go."

"Yes, sir."

"Get back to us with every scrap of information you pull off his station." He hung up.

Rashid was surprised when he was messaged for an emergency conference. He stuck his head over the partition. "Hey, Carol, what's this conference?"

"What conference?"

When he turned back, he saw that his monitors all were plated. He knew instantly what those blank screens meant. Somebody had identified him.

As always, God had made his plans for him. In truth, he had been trained for this contingency by experts, Russian mercenaries working for the private army BlackWatch. They'd gotten twelve thousand dollars cash to put him through four days on the BlackWatch avoidance course in Georgia. He'd been CrackBerrying Nabila and Mark and whoever else he could think of from Bermuda that week when his real location had been Burge Island, where the accursed mosquitoes were the size of the ever-present and disgusting shrimp.

There was nothing for it now. He'd just been flushed, no question.

He hurried down the corridor to the front desk, passed the desk officer without a word, ignoring the, "Excuse me," that was called out behind him.

He got past the perimeter guards also, and he knew why. The NIO was watching him run, of course. They would want him to leave.

He reached his car, got in, and drove quickly away.

Mark Chambers was soon back on the line. "He's bolted all right."

"Okay, you keep on him," Jim said.

"He knows everything about this type of surveillance."

"And he will eventually evade us. But we will still learn something before that happens, and let's hope it's what we need."

For the first time, Linda Fitzgerald spoke. "Does this mean that Washington is out of danger?" In that trembling lilt Jim recognized hysteria. This woman was about to explode in their faces, and he did not blame her.

He answered carefully. "This man may lead us to the bomb. That's all I can say."

"But it could go off—"

"Linda, it could go off at any time," her husband said, his voice betraying a level of anger. "It hasn't happened yet, that's all."

For a moment, she was silent. Then she pitched forward as if struck a blow in the stomach. Fitz touched her, distantly, as he might a wounded soldier during a tour of Walter Reed. "Come on, gal," he said softly. "Let's pull together."

"Excuse me," Logan said. "How do we get a secure lookdown on this man? Where do we go for that? Not to his boss, for God's sake."

Given the need for speed, Rashid's own unit was the only place they could turn to. "We have no choice."

"What if they're all in it? Come on, man, think!"

"I've done that, obviously! And *we have no choice*."

"This is a big government. There's always a choice."

"Okay, first, how do you know we'll be secure someplace else? Second, it'll take time and we don't have that, do we?"

"We could engage the National Reconnaissance Office."

"The man is actually physically running right now, so can you manage that in twenty seconds?"

"Tom, goddamn it, will you stop this arguing?" the president said.

"Sir—"

"Mr. Deutsch, get on the horn and get us this man's location! Do it!"

Rashid stopped his car near some woods. On the other side was the Columbia Pike and, just north of here, a small neighborhood. He got out and moved in among the trees. A Rugby would be passing over now, and there were drones, he felt sure, running high and silent. Moving from trunk to trunk, he made his way beneath the thickest foliage he could find. If they were able to locate his implant without NAVSTAR online—and he assumed that they were—they probably didn't need a Rugby to find him now. But you never knew; he might get lucky.

He had to get to Alexandria and get that bomb detonated. Even if he needed to do it in the garage, that was fine. Just get the thing to go off, that was the key. If they'd turned coward or been killed—whatever—he would do it himself, never mind, and regard the task as what it was—a privilege. Death excited him, and the prospect of the wonderful heaven Allah had prepared was delicious. He'd wanted a boy first, then a girl. He'd wanted his own house, and the love of a wife. But those things were not to be, because Allah, it seemed, wanted him.

Walking out of the woods and into the little neighborhood, he wondered if he would have to kill now, which person, innocently living? It didn't matter. He would kill if he had to, but stealth was better.

The first house he came to was empty. Shortly he would need a car, but right now this was exactly right. He went to the garage, broke a pane in the door, and went in. As he did so, a small dog began barking frantically. It hopped up his leg, groveling and panting, absurdly grateful that he had come.

Of course, there was nothing absurd about its gratitude. The animal had been left in this garage with nothing but a bowl of water.

Well, good, in a moment he could make use of the dog.

How American this garage was, so tidy and yet so cluttered with possessions. Why would a man with a tiny property like this one require a chain saw? Or a collection of model ships, gathering dust on the workbench? It was all stupid, all this obsession they had with material. The Crusaders fed their hunger for God with rubbish like this. Television instead of prayer. That was no way to live.

He went into a splendidly appointed kitchen, where he found a good knife, small but with a blade of excellent quality. For some little time he sharpened it in the electric sharpener that stood on the gleaming granite counter. Then he went through the dining room with its silver-laden sideboard and glowing mahogany table, and into the bedroom wing. He found a bathroom, where he searched the cabinets for alcohol.

Because he had no choice but to do it this way, he took the knife in his clumsy left hand and sawed away at his right arm. Gritting his teeth, sucking back his screams, he cut deep, dissecting away fluffy folds of fat and lean strips of muscle, until he found the dull silver capsule he was seeking. Pushing at it, working the wound until it frothed and bubbled, he gradually got the thing between his fingers.

He looked at it. Featureless, dull silver. Inside, he knew, there was an intricate array of circuitry, a masterpiece of subminiaturization. The telemetry the thing generated could even be used to determine his state of consciousness, whether or not his eyes were open and functioning, his speed of movement, and, if he was wounded, how long he had to live.

All of that, and the only thing it would do now was feed a hopping, snorting little dog. Not much of a watchdog, this little thing. He opened the fridge and found a plastic container of turkey salami. Taking out a slice, he folded it around his implant, then gave it to the animal, which ate with the frantic gusto of the starving.

Taking it by the scruff of the neck, he put it out into the garden. It ran yapping to the back fence and began jumping at the gate. He followed it, remaining close to the few trees, then using a garden shed as cover.

When he opened the gate, the animal raced out, dashing off along the alley.

So now they had a dog to catch.

Rashid had no idea which Mahdi sympathizers in the FBI or the CIA cut orders to arrest or kill people like Jim Deutsch—or even if they were Mahdi sympathizers. Maybe they had other agendas. That was the nature of intelligence, now. There were too many players, too many agendas. The entire process was out of control. Unbeknownst even to most world leaders, the whole vast planetary community of spies had long since descended into anarchy.

Rashid reached the house, went through it onto the front porch, and walked quickly down its covered expanse. There was a little rail, a porch swing, some drying flowers on a white stand. This had once been somebody's refuge, their little nook where they had, perhaps, sat and read books. Filth. Western nonsense. He hated it all. The only book was the Quran. The rest was worthy only of the fire, all of it from Genesis to *The Great Gatsby* and beyond, without exception. He even favored burning the Islamic texts, the endless interpretations and such. Why did you need this when you had the original word of God?

Read the word, pray, do your work—this was the world that was being created, a happy world at last, freed of the vast burdens of the soul that the Crusaders had imposed, as part of their service to darkness.

He passed down off the porch, into the yellowing grass beside the house, and went into the next yard, where a red Dodge stood in the driveway. He looked in the window and saw no Global Positioning System in the dash. Good, the car could be used. But he needed a key. Perhaps it was in the owner's pocket, of course, but it could be in the house. He could get lucky. God could help him.

He went up the driveway, and stepped onto a porch similar to the one next door. There were shadings of difference, though—different plants, no swing. Also, the front door was solid, no windowpanes. So he kicked in one of the windows. Why not? What did the property of these faithless creatures matter? He reached in, opened the door, and entered.

"Excuse me!"

Rashid froze. A man stood back in the shadows of the room, a plump man of perhaps thirty-five, wearing shorts and a T-shirt. For a moment, he seemed like some sort of hallucination, his presence was so unexpected. But then he came forward, and in his hand Rashid saw a small vase. Then the man reached down and lifted a side chair by its leg and threw it.

As Rashid stepped aside to avoid the chair, he pulled out the knife he had used to cut the implant from his arm. He advanced on the man, who was fat and confused but still quick enough to slam the vase into the side of Rashid's head.

Just in time, Rashid turned, causing the blow to glance off behind his left ear. It hurt, but it did not stun him, and he slashed backward with the knife.

It connected; the man drew in breath; then Rashid thrust as hard as he could, digging and cutting, pistoning his fist as he had been taught.

The man gasped; his foot stomped so hard the whole house shook; then he drew back away from the knife, as Rashid had been trained that he would do. Rashid followed him, still cutting, feeling the resistance of cartilage and organs, feeling blood, hot, fast, gushing out around his plunging fist.

The man hit him with the flat of his hand, hit him hard enough to make his ear ring. Then the man came off the knife and fell against the wall. He made a noise, low, like he was gargling, as black blood gushed from his mouth. He slid down the wall, his eyes fixing on Rashid. "Hey, man," he said, then another word, a garbled mutter. His head slumped onto his chest.

Rashid found himself kicking the man, and when he did, there was an almost musical sigh, a poetic little sound.

He looked down at the figure. Was he only pretending? Or was this, truly, death? Rashid watched the chest. No breathing. The eyes were still open, also fixed, slightly misted over. Dead, then.

Gingerly Rashid pushed a hand into one pocket, then the other. He took the wallet, the keys. He went quickly through the house and out the side door that led to the driveway. There was a pot boiling on the stove, which he shut off. No reason to attract attention with a fire.

Then he saw, sitting in the sun in a tiny breakfast nook, an ancient woman. She was silent, staring, her face so deeply wrinkled that it looked false, like a caricature of great age. In front of her was an empty soup bowl. In her hand, in among knuckles like great stones, was a silver spoon.

He went back to the stove, got the pot, and went to her. He poured her some soup. Her mouth began to work—and then she turned with all the sudden intensity of a striking snake and said, "You're crazy; you killed my son. You're crazy."

He slammed the pot down on the top of her head with a huge clang. Soup splashed everywhere as her head snapped forward into the bowl.

He left, got in the car, grabbing the steering wheel as if it would somehow preserve his life.

At least the traffic was less daunting now, since the dispersal of the government was complete and most of the evacuees had left the area. He had no idea how long it would take him to get to Alexandria, but he had no doubt, now, that he was going to make it. His arm hurt. His heart was still pounding. The time for prayers had come, and he twisted his body so that it was indicating the east, Mecca, the true home of the human soul.

29

THE ITALIAN LESSON

For the pope, the day had been long and oppressively difficult, with numerous appearances, the reading of speeches, and the constant, vaguely disturbing presence of the Mufti. He had gone at last to the Domus Sanctae Marthae for the night. The pope could not house him in the Apostolic Palace itself, of course; that was not appropriate. Fortunately, he had not objected to the Domus. In fact, all day he had been faultlessly polite, even kneeling with the pope before the great altar in St. Peter's to pray through the six o'clock hour, as a terrified world waited for Washington to be destroyed.

He looked at the clock on the table beside his favorite chair. It was just going midnight now, so the danger was perhaps past in America, at least for the moment. He had telephoned two hours ago to offer his support to the president, whom he had met and found to be a man deserving of respect. Instead, the call had gone to the vice president, a clipped individual with a difficult name, who had thanked him politely and rung off.

For a moment, his eyes closed. When they opened again, they swam across the prayer he had been reading in his Breviary. The midnight nocturne, so familiar to a man who often did not sleep. Cares dragged at him late. He saw the ruin of the world coming, in the form of melting ice, storms, drought, starvation, and the end of oil. He saw it also in the strangeness of the violence that seemed these days to be everywhere. He felt his prayers as a drop of pure water in the dirty torrent of the demon. But here, now, in this silent room, with his beloved Breviary open in his hands, he felt close not only to God but also to the caressing arms of the Shepherd and his holy mother.

"Holiness!"

He looked up, startled at the sudden voice. Who would enter here without a knock?

A Swiss Guard was before him, and the expression on the man's face caused a horror of coldness to sweep the pope's whole body. "They have struck again?"

"Holiness, there is an airplane. An airplane in the night."

He did not understand, and his face must have communicated his confusion, because the man spoke again.

"Holiness, there is an airplane, a small airplane. From the cupola, we have a call to alarm. Holiness, please come."

He got up and followed the man. As they entered the corridor, other Swiss Guards came running, surrounding the pope.

"What is this airplane? Is the air force there?"

"The airplane is buzzing—we hear it. We can see nothing. And there are no jets."

"Has anyone called the Aeronautica?"

"There is alarm. There is alarm."

They went down the great staircase, now a whole phalanx of guards. "Where do we go?"

"Holiness, to the crypt."

And with those words, the great tide of history that was sweeping the world entered the Vatican, for they would be the last words spoken in that place for thirty-one years.

The next instant, the tall windows that the pope was passing belched fire like the maws of a row of monster blast furnaces. The pope and his guards instantly became blackened ash, their bodies flying with the molten glass into the grandeur of the hall they had been passing through, imprinting their shadows on the opposite wall, which, a fraction of a second later, became dust.

The first millisecond after the detonation slammed St. Peter's with an overpressure of 51 psi, the roof of the great church split with a massive crack. In the plaza, where many people were still praying, a sheet of light came that left them all reduced to ash. There was no attempt to escape; it happened too fast. Their prayers had prevented them from hearing the buzzing of the airplane.

On the plane, a young Albanian mother had struggled with the controls, shifting the tiny airframe clumsily around the sky, trying to position the aircraft directly above St. Peter's.

She had taken off from the Ippodromo delle Capannelle south of Rome. The plane had been hidden in a garage nearby, and brought there by her brother and her husband after dark. The Arabs had taken her children, Agim, Teuta, and tiny, dear Gezime, still nursing, poor little thing.

They would call on the cell phone and Gezime's wailing would be heard, only her wailing. But now she would never again get mother's milk! It was life, though, life for the children, if the woman did this. Otherwise, she was to be taken to them and watch as they were baked to death one by one in an oven. The Arabs has promised this, and she knew that they would keep their promise.

She had been taught to fly, but on the ground. This was her first experience actually in the air.

An hour ago, they had sent a video of Teuta with her hair burning, screaming, poor baby, her hair with smoke! So the woman and her husband and his brother had done as they had been told to do, had pulled the black plane onto the racetrack, and there a man had come, and instructed her. He had showed her how to make the plane rise only, not how to make it land.

Her body had grown sick very soon in the plane. The night was big, the city full of confusing lights. She had kept the thing straight, keeping the bubble in the right place on the faintly glowing dashboard. The thing belonged to the devil. It was a machine of the devil.

She had not seen her husband and her brother solemnly taking the money, the stack of euros, after she had flown into the night. She had not known that her children had been abandoned in the cellar where they had been taken, simply left there locked away to die on their own, and their father, who would soon be in Beirut with ten thousand euros, would never think of them again.

The two Arabs were now on a train that was sweeping down the coast to Naples, its windows lighting the dry farmland through which it passed. They sipped coffees.

Her brother and her husband, having been exposed to the naked bomb, were being sick in the dirt of the racecourse, their vomit black in the sand, euros blowing about on an easy little breeze.

Ahead, she saw the great church, the largest thing in the city, although she had for a moment been confused by the Vittorio Emmanuel monument. She knew nothing of any of these places. Her family worked in the fields. She and her husband sometimes made a baby of cardboard and cotton cloth for her to thrust at tourists, so that they would grab at it while her husband and her brother picked their pockets.

The men were not good pickpockets. They seldom succeeded.

The family was crushed together in a shack outside the A90 in Ciampino. Somehow, the Arabs had come into their lives. She did not know how. When the Arabs had taken the children, her husband had rolled on the ground and torn at his hair. How could so many misfortunes befall him? How could this be?

She could not fly this machine long. It swooped, it was buffeted by wind, it roared, and as she became more afraid, the instruments became harder to understand. Where was the bubble? Was she going right, left? Where was the compass?

Lights were rising to the north. She had been warned of this. Air fighters to shoot her down. Her mind fixed on her screaming daughter, on the smoking hair, the frantically bobbing head.

The machine hummed and vibrated. It reeked of petrol, and then something flew past outside—a roof! She had dropped almost to the ground: she pushed the rudder pedals, causing the whole contraption to shudder, and some sort of horn to start blatting in her ears.

There was pain all over her body. To the left, a great red wave that was not racing toward her but was the last electrical effect of an exploding brain.

Absolute fire in the sky. She, a vapor, not even that. Shattered atoms.

Rome was not expecting this at all. There had been no indication that the city was in any way a target. All eyes had been on places such as Washington, New York, and London. The theory was that Muslims would know, or would have strong suspicions, and would leave threatened cities.

They had not left Rome, nor Paris, nor Berlin, but the Muslims of Bay Ridge in Brooklyn and Finsbury Park in London had departed in large numbers, ignoring curfews, ignoring everything—which had, in turn, sparked mass evacuations from both cities.

In truth, these people had no special knowledge, but they also were well aware of the extremists among them, and the fact that America and England were considered the Crusader capitals of the world.

Not even these people, however, knew enough of history to make the obvious prediction, that after the great sin pot of Las Vegas the Crusaders' religious capital would certainly be the next target.

From Urban II in 1095 through Boniface VIII in 1271, all the popes had called for crusades. This had happened in response to Muslim invasion of various parts of the Eastern Roman Empire, which had, by 1095, been Christian for over seven hundred years, part of the Roman evolution from paganism to Christianity that had accompanied the slow decline of the old Western empire.

The fact that the only religious invaders in the area had been Muslim and they had taken Christian people by force did not matter to the Mahdi and his followers, for the Quran told them to "fight against those who have been given the scripture but do not believe in Allah." And again, "wage war on the idolaters, as they wage war on you."

So ancient prophecy came true on that night, when the Whore of Babylon at last was brought low, Rome, the treasure-house of the Western spirit.

The fire swept down, charging the roof of the Sistine Chapel with far more pressure than it could bear. Unseen by any man, a fissure appeared between the finger of Adam and the finger of God, snapped, and spread, and in the next instant the greatest artistic expression ever created by the human hand was atomized dust speeding and vaporizing in the searing heat.

The doors of the Vatican Library smashed inward, comets blazing fire, and librarians looked up and were made hollow, and papyrus and parchment began burning with a fury never known before. The Codex Vaticanus, with its careful script, leaped into flame and was gone in an instant. When this early Bible was transcribed, ancient Rome still ruled the world and the hand, neat and Greek, that had done the work had belonged to a human being who had looked upon the soaring marbles of the Temple of Jupiter, and heard the roar of the crowd in the Coliseum, and the thunder of horses in the Circus Maximus, and shopped in the ink-sour bookstores along the Argilitum in the jammed quarter called the Subura, to which the Roman poet Juvenal attributed "the thousand dangers of a savage city."

The library then imploded, and the Vatican Museum, and the great church itself, the skylights in its dome briefly spitting columns of fire into the interior, making it look as if the spokes of a great wheel of fire had invaded the space. In grand silence, as a young priest twisted toward the Blessed Sacrament that lay in the golden Tabernacle on the altar, the dome came down in great blocks, shattering the altar, the priest, the floor, and crashing with such force that parts of the nave collapsed into the crypt below, and in the tomb of Saint Peter there resounded a noise never heard there or anywhere else, the shrieking, weeping thunder of thousands of tons of concrete and art pulverizing.

The tombs of the popes were smashed, broken open, cracked, remains strewn and then set ablaze, ancient vestments and bones coming to lazy fire in the wrecked marble, fitful red pools flickering in the thick dark.

The great glass wall before the crypt of Saint Peter smashed into dust, and the lights there fluttered out. An instant later, debris from the floor of the church above smashed down, filling the space with stone that would not be removed again, not even in vast time.

The glare of the explosion lit the south side of the Piazza Navona, causing it to burst into flames. People thronging the north side were astonished by what they saw—awnings, cars, diners at their meals in the mild night—suddenly all was fire. Before the blast struck, two seconds passed, during which a woman started to raise her hands to the flaming skin of her face, a waiter threw a glass of Cinzano he was carrying, cats scurried in the alley, a Chinese woman, achingly lonely, realized that she would die in the kitchen that was bursting into raging, inexplicable fire around her. She had been dreaming, as she shook a skillet of mushrooms over the belching stove, of rain in May in the hills of home.

The ancient treasure-house that was Rome trembled as if being shaken by the fist of God. The Senate House of Diocletian in the Forum sank into itself, the oldest parliamentary structure in the world. The Pantheon, perhaps the finest piece of architecture on the planet, finally, after over two thousand years testifying to the orderly dignity of the human spirit, collapsed in on itself with a dusty sigh.

Dust and smoke rushed everywhere, gushing through narrow streets, howling in eaves, crashing through windows. By the millions, roof tiles swept into the air, shattered, and became a kind of red snow by which the disaster would long be remembered, after the helicopters came in the morning and the glittering camera eyes returned images of the ruined city dyed red.

The bomb was not as large as the one that had shattered Las Vegas. This one had been meant to destroy a symbol, not kill a community. But however carefully this evil act had been conceived, nuclear destruction remained something that was really beyond imagination, and its effects were far more terrible than its planners had anticipated.

They had probably imagined a neat decapitation of the Vatican, not what actually occurred. Of course, Vatican City was destroyed, with virtually all of its treasures, the accumulation of so many years and so much human genius that it was like killing a part of an eternal soul.

Not since the Arabs had attempted conquest of Italy in 846 had Muslim violence been directly enacted against Rome. In that year, the Saracens had robbed the Basilica of St. Peter, which was then outside the city walls.

But this was not robbery, it was devastation, and moments after the explosion the Vatican appeared as a sort of mountain wreathed in smoke. The great, welcoming arms of the basilica, designed by Bernini in the seventeenth century, were splayed outward, their colonnades tossed like matchsticks, the statues of the saints rendered into dust. The piazza itself was crushed down into its own foundations, becoming a blackened pit.

The Egyptian obelisk in the center had shattered. It had been moved there in 1586 from the nearby ruins of the Circus of Caligula, where it had been brought around the year 40. The absence of hieroglyphics on the obelisk had made its origin a mystery, but in any case, like so much that was destroyed on this night, it belonged to the depths of time and human consciousness. Its disappearance, although never remarked anywhere, left each human being less, as the loss of St. Peter's, the libraries, the Sistine Chapel, the museums, and also the people of the Vatican themselves, consecrated as they were to carrying on their shoulders one of the deepest of Western institutions, left all people immeasurably less.

In that instant of breathtaking cruelty and evil, the soul of man was made smaller, and a dark, brutal future seemed ready to spread in the hidden space within us all where the emblems that construct our civilizations are inscribed. Again, as in Las Vegas, it was the details—always the details—that were the places where the catastrophe was actually defined.

For example, the area around the obelisk was completely shattered but not completely lost, as some of the emblems of the winds—Ponente, the West Wind; Tramontana, the North Wind—that were embedded in the piazza there, were flung in the debris for kilometers and landed in the gardens of the Villa Borghese across the Tiber. These gardens, which were swept as if by a howling storm as the debris from the Vatican came pouring from the sky, had first been planted by old Roman republicans such as the populist ally of Julius Caesar, Sallust, and the libertine Lucullus, who used to organize torch races among the ancestors of some of the trees that were now burning down to the root, never to grow again. On this night, the trees themselves became the torches.

The baldachin that overhung the great altar of St. Peter's smashed down into it, followed by most of the dome above, which led to the collapse of the crypt and drove the fires deep, where they would burn on for nearly a year.

All the colleges, the abbeys, the institutes of the Vatican burst into flames. People who were not killed outright were set alight, and dashed burning against collapsing walls. In the end, nine out of every ten people in Vatican City were killed outright. The others, their bodies broken and burned, ruined by radiation, died within hours or days. Of the city's 820 permanent residents, only 11 were still alive twenty-four hours after the blast. Another 216 employees who were in the city at the time of the explosion were all killed.

Thus the entire central government of the Roman Catholic Church ceased in a moment to exist. But the damage did not end at the borders of Vatican City, which was, after all, a 108-acre enclave in the center of a dense metropolis.

The Mufti was an old man and sleeping heavily when he burst into flames. He awoke to red haze and pain and then was dead. So, ironically, perhaps, the second great sack of Rome by Muslims also took the life of one of the most radical of Muslim leaders, but not one so radical as to countenance open and frank evil.

At midnight, Rome was a sparkling, vividly alive city. Clubs were open, restaurants, theaters, bars, and coffee shops. People thronged the piazzas, the streets. On the sheltered side of the Navona, there was an eruption of complete panic, with people leaping sidewalk chairs and tables, dashing into the cover afforded by restaurant interiors, as the patrons inside rushed out.

As the enormous, killing flash struck, there were uncountable moments of horror and confusion. Nobody within two kilometers of the blast actually heard it. Instead, they lost their hearing, being left with ringing or silence or hammering sounds in their heads, their ears bleeding, some of them blinded, but fewer than in Las Vegas, where more open space had led to wider sight lines.

The whole center of Rome became a gigantic trap. Pushed down by the same overpressure that had crushed St. Peter's, buildings across the city collapsed into the streets, blocking all escape. People on lower floors mostly survived, rushing out to avoid the choking fire that gushed down from the upper levels of structures, poured along stairways, smashed ceilings, and brought with it a dense cloud of smoke and dust.

Four minutes after the blast, the power failed. That it had lasted so long was due only to the heroic efforts of station engineers in surrounding areas, none of whom knew exactly what had happened, but who flipped switches and turned knobs, moving loads in a flash around the country. But it was no use, the system had taken extraordinary damage, and no sooner had Rome gone down than the whole grid faltered and the entire southern half of the country was plunged into darkness.

For all of their years of training and preparation for even the worst catastrophe, across the entire center of the city the fire brigade was rendered helpless. This was not because of the power failure. They could operate without power, and even deliver substantial water using only their own generating equipment. They were prepared to draw huge quantities of water from the Tiber, but they could not reach the Tiber, not with so many streets hopelessly blocked. Indeed, the spectacle that Rome presented after the explosion was of a complicated mass of destroyed towers and roofs floating in a sea of burning rubble. Few streets were even visible.

Some of the Tiber bridges had been smashed, but not all, and one that remained was the Ponte Milvio, which was originally built over twenty-two hundred years ago by the Roman consul Gaius Claudius Nero. In 2006, Roman lovers had taken to commemorating the eternity of their vows by putting padlocks on one of the bridge's lampposts. When the lamppost had become so choked with locks that it had nearly collapsed, lovers had moved their vows instead to a website.

Now, both the lamppost and the servers containing the website were destroyed, and with them so many young lives, which had with hopeful fingers locked those locks.

As had happened in Las Vegas, communications initially failed completely. At the U.S. Air Force base at Aviano, there was an immediate alert. As was true the world over, there were patrols flying, here under overall command of NATO.

"We have a fireball—" came a transmission from an F-15 on patrol over the Tyrrhenian Sea.

"Say again?"

The plane was still on radar, but there were no further transmissions. Immediately a signal was sent to NATO Headquarters in Brussels: "Possible major explosion, Rome area."

The Aeronautica Militare, which had numerous bases in the area and was flying active patrols over the city, also experienced a regional communications failure due to the pulse of electromagnetic energy emitted by the bomb. But NATO's land-based communications infrastructure was left intact, and controllers who could not reach patrolling aircraft certainly could see, from bases around the city, that a mushroom cloud was rising over Rome. Second Air Region Command was instantly informed, but all attempts to reach the prime minister failed—as, indeed, all such efforts would continue to fail.

Parliament was in session, and most of the government was present in Rome. Prime Minister D'Agostini had made an appearance at six with the pope and the Mufti, praying with them as the hour passed and all the world waited for Washington to be destroyed.

When it was not, the mass in commemoration planned at seven became a mass in celebration. D'Agostini was one of hundreds of world leaders who had telephoned the president after it appeared that the danger had passed. He was one of many whom Fitzgerald, in the darkness where he dwelled, did not bother to answer.

D'Agostini awoke to a flash so terrific he leaped from the bed, crying out, "It's us, it's us." When his wife heard this, the perpetual fear that lives in the hearts of all world leaders and all who love them, instantly sped to the forefront of her mind. "A rocket," she screamed.

The prime minister did not know why the room was burning, but he thought perhaps the Islamists had indeed launched an attack against the residence. He had no chance to think more, though, as the blast followed almost instantly and the burning curtains, the window frame, the glass, and most of the wall around it exploded inward, tearing him and Mirania to pieces, burying the smoking chunks of their bodies in the fiery debris.

So each soul started with a question, entered a moment of horror, then knew death.

As in Las Vegas, the lucky died first. Because the bomb that had been detonated over Vegas was large, that had included most of the people exposed to its power. Not so here. Only the residents of the Vatican and those in taller structures or, like the prime minister, residing in a residence luxurious enough to be open to the sky were killed at once.

Like other world governments, the Italian government had no decapitation plan in place, and this instant was therefore the beginning of what would stretch into two generations of costly, sometimes violent and disappointing conflict over the reconstruction of the state.

Most Romans were trapped in what became a hell even more terrible than the hell of Las Vegas, as over a million separate fires commenced in ninety thousand structures and people with shattered limbs in apartments, in houses, in restaurants, busses, cars, everywhere they happened to be, soon saw flames and smoke, and began to burn in such numbers that the smoke drifting eastward with the prevailing wind smelled of cooking meat.

This was how Rome died, in a conflagration greater by far than the one that had consumed it in the year 64, and that fire had reached a heat so intense that it melted brick.

The true shock of what had happened almost at once began to be felt in the world. With the death of the Eternal City, a part of every decent human heart died, no matter if they were in Scotland or Syria, in China or Kansas.

In Beijing, the Central Committee called another emergency meeting. Previously, Chinese intelligence had viewed this as a problem involving only the Americans. Nevertheless, a report from the "Autumn Orchid" group that watched political activities in Hong Kong had indicated that an American retaliatory strike against targets in both Malaysia and Indonesia was possible, judging from rumors being traded among politicians there.

The primary concern of the Central Committee was not, however, the nuclear damage being done. It was the way that the upheaval would affect trade. Already, every cargo ship headed for the United States was stopped, on orders from the American authorities. The People's Bank of China had frozen all dollar-related monetary activities, but the breathtaking collapse of the American currency had rendered China startlingly illiquid, and forced movement of value to the euro, the only other currency with enough liquidity to provide a useful basis for trade.

Now, in a paroxysm of panic, the euro was also being sold in every bourse on the planet. In point of fact, value was being transferred by others to the yen and China's own yuan. The movement was of historic enormity, and could only lead to one conclusion: the collapse of value in the Western currencies and the subsequent inability of the West to continue trade.

Not since the fall of the Roman Empire had Western currency been so damaged, and the Chinese leadership, steeped in history in ways that Western leadership was not, remembered how profound the effects of that last unwinding of civil life in the West had been.

Marxist theory taught that capitalist systems were highly susceptible to destabilization, and the discussion touched on this. The West was falling. How far would it fall? Would governments and corporate entities embrace Šarī'ah law? If so, what of debt? Specifically, what of the gigantic debt that the West owed China, which was the world's true banker? China had poured out the sweat of its people and the wealth of its lands, in return for IOUs from the West, and now they were becoming worthless.

Outside of the theoretical value of currency and debt, there was not enough symbolic wealth to continue the functioning of the world economy. Not even with gold trading at present in London at six thousand euros an ounce was there enough of it to back a new world reserve currency. The only thing that could conceivably back such a currency might be the combined central banks of China, Taiwan, and Japan.

So China began discussions with both countries, and never mind the difficulties with the illegal government in Taiwan. While Rome burned, Asia struggled to save whatever shreds of economic civilization that it could.

And there were still bombs, more bombs, and waiting pilots, some eager, some too afraid to say no.

In the Kremlin, there was increasingly frantic activity, as the reality of the conspiracy involving former KGB officers became more and more evident. Terror literally gripped the Putin government. If these bombs were determined to be of Russian origin, there would almost certainly be another revolution, followed by massive, crippling reparations to the West, if not a nuclear attack.

Vladimir Putin had made a choice to isolate Russia and its client states from the West, so that he could manipulate world affairs in such a way that oil prices would stay high, but this was far more than he had bargained for, and he was, behind the scenes, a shattered, terrified man.

Without his direct knowledge, the old KGB had been working outside governmental authority to break the superpower of the United States in the same way that the Russian superpower had been broken by the Cold War. In the KGB's madness, they believed that this would leave Russia free to restore its ancient empire, because it was not thought that Europe, in the absence of organized American support, would stand against any Russian reoccupation of lost territories, such as Estonia, Latvia, Lithuania, and, the greatest prize, Poland.

In history, the independence of these states had never lasted long, and the secretive former KGB officers did not intend that it would last much longer now. Russia needed a territorial buffer to its west. Who knew when another Napoléon or Hitler would arise? Given the ferment in the ramshackle democracies that England and the United States had imposed on Europe after World War II, anything could happen.

Vladimir Putin paced his office. When FSB chief Alexandrov appeared, Putin looked at him, Alexandrov thought, with the same infamous beady-eyed fury that Stalin had, in legend, regarded his staff with.

"We're going to be held responsible," Putin said. "But we are not responsible."

"Now the Americans will release Dream Angel," Alexandrov said.

"That may happen," Putin replied.

"Do we open our silos? What do we do?"

"Do you think it matters?" Putin asked.

"Our missiles are the only real deterrent to theirs on the planet!"

Putin scoffed at him. How could the man be so naïve? "What the military conceals from us cannot be *capability,*" he said, trying to force a mildness into his voice that was at odds with the anger and panic he was trying to control. "The generals conceal only their inabilities. When have you received a readiness report that you could believe?"

"I . . . I'm—well, certainly there is a level of readiness." Both men knew that launch facilities that had been listed as fully operational had been found by the Kremlin's inspectors to be abandoned and in ruins.

"A level of readiness. I'm sure. God only knows what would happen if they tried to launch. The whole country would probably be blown up. Our country!"

The missiles were old and liquid fueled, and many of them were so unstable that they could not even be removed from their silos, let alone fired.

"Perhaps the Ameris don't know our situation," Alexandrov said.

"No? All the Kremlin is a stage." Putin chuckled. "We should dance and sing, provide some entertainment."

This had once been Lenin's office, bugged with radios disguised as filing cabinets. Now it was nanotechnology. Dust that communicated with satellites. You fight your way to the summit only to find that it is not power but the illusion of power that defines you.

"What is to be done?" Alexandrov asked.

Knowing all he knew, Putin could do nothing more than shrug.

"We can't have Dream Angel," Alexandrov said.

"Oh? Perhaps we want them to launch, but let's not speak further here, not on that."

"We must execute Case Forty," Alexandrov said. "Our friends must."

"It's finished," Putin said. Case Forty was the assassination of Aziz, the idiot who called himself Mahdi.

Alexandrov met his eyes.

"Yes, finished—as in, failed," Putin said bitterly. Then he shrugged, looked up at the ceiling. For all he knew, there could even be video cameras recording his every gesture for the Ameris right here in this room. The Kremlin was a theater. "Case Forty has failed and we will not be heroes to the world. Aziz is in Pakistan now."

"But how could he escape? Your man—"

"Dear Vladimir. Indeed, how could my man fail? Such a man? Aziz must have known that he was coming."

"So we have a traitor?"

"You know what Stalin used to say—everybody is a traitor. So, yes, we have a traitor. We need a general purge."

"Dare we do that?"

"To survive? Certainly. Kill them all. That way you can't miss. Another of Stalin's famous techniques."

"I don't have the apparatus to conduct a purge. I don't have the informants, the trained teams of officers. That's all gone now."

Putin shrugged. "Perhaps the Bible has it right. Perhaps we've come to the end of time."

"I can't believe that."

"Well then, you can believe this. Our intent was to unleash a nasty little cat to torment the Ameris. But that isn't what we have done. We opened the cage of the nasty little cat, but there was a lion in the damned thing, and now the lion is running free, my friend, and anything can happen. Even here. They could come to Moscow."

Alexandrov looked out the window, where the domes of St. Basil's glowed in the artificial light that flooded the old cathedral. "Here? It's unthinkable!"

Putin gazed also at the cathedral. " 'And he cried mightily with a strong voice, saying, Babylon the great is fallen, is fallen, and is become the habitation of devils, and the hold of every foul spirit, and a cage of every unclean and hateful bird.' " He smiled his small and careful smile.

"What is that from?"

"The Revelation of John. From the Roman Bible."

"Ah, yes. But still, it's about Rome, not Moscow."

"The world is Rome, you fool!" He laughed now, as cold a sound as Alexandrov had ever heard. "I don't know that Aziz will win. The Mahdi! And the Muslims believe him. They're rejoicing!"

"Carpet-bomb Chechnya."

"We've done enough suppression there. Anyway, we'd need our own version of Dream Angel." He considered for a moment. "I will tell you this, Alexandrov: we have lost a war nobody knew we were fighting." He raised his eyebrows, a smile touching his lips. "Including us."

Alexandrov knew when to leave him alone, and quietly withdrew.

COMMUNICATION FROM THE MAHDI OF THE EARTH OF MUSLIM PEOPLE
GLORY TO GOD, THE CALIPHATE OF ETERNAL PEACE IS COME.
THE END OF TIME IS HERE.

Because the Crusader King, William Johnson Fitzgerald, did not perform *sadaha*, and the Christian churches were not closed, and an apostate decadent and fallen Muslim danced on the balconies of the greatest of these palaces of sin and evildoing, there has been a serious consequence.

An attempt has been made, also, upon the life of your guide, but as he is held hidden yet in the folds of Allah's robe, he remains with you, and no amount of Crusader treachery can ever kill him or capture him.

Now, in view of the continuing Crusader apostasy, hear your Mahdi.

The law of Šarī'ah is enacted throughout the world, and replaces all other law.

You who suffer under the burden of debt, rejoice, for God has said it: your debt is canceled, and any trading in debt or with debt is liable under the Law. Further payment of debt will be punished under the Law. Extension of credit will be punished under the Law.

The existing authorities are ordered to arrest the money changers of the world, and the masters of debt, to wit, the chairmen of the leading banks, a list of whom will be sent to the kings and emperors of the world. And any citizen may also arrest them and bring them to prison, or imprison them himself, for the Glory of God and the Sanctity of His Word.

The use of intoxicants is forbidden now.

The apostate laws of marriage are ended, and now the only legal marriage is between professing Muslims. Divorced people may only marry other divorced people. The giving of proper bride wealth is obligatory for any wedding from today.

Women must strive to cease working at jobs outside of the home, driving automobiles, and going about uncovered. Gradually, the Law will be enforced, as women learn the happiness that it brings them. Adultery by man or woman, properly confessed or witnessed according to law, is punished by stoning until dead.

Sanctions against slavery are ended, and the holders of slaves may now go openly with their slaves.

All executions are now public. Crime is punished according to the Law. The thief must lose his hand, the murderer his head, and so on.

Criticism of Mohammed is no longer allowed, and to those who have the Crusader taste for satire and derogation, your Mahdi urges you: reflect carefully, for you are no longer free to curse God or his prophet.

We repeat, for the last time, that the Crusader King William Fitzgerald must at once perform *sadaha* before all mankind.

The Crusader King has an evil plan called the Dream Angel, which even at this moment is poised to visit death upon hundreds of millions of Muslim people. If the jets leave the fail-safe points where they are now cruising, fifty Crusader cities will be at once put to the atomic torch.

We have spared the Crusader capital, because the flagrant apostasy of the pope could not go unpunished. But unless *all* of the requirements listed here are met, the Crusader capital will be destroyed at midnight tonight, and it will then be known that the pure and noble forces of Allah cannot be stopped.

The glorious Day of Standing is upon us, and your Mahdi rejoices with you, in the name of Allah the Most Holy, and Mohammed who is his prophet.

LITTLE MARY SUNSHINE

The destruction of the Vatican and the burning of Rome brought silence to the world. The streets, which in some places had been full of protestors and in others revelers, now became empty. Most TV and Internet outlets simply posted a copy of the Mahdi's latest statement and left it there without comment. Radio stations recorded a reading of it, and repeated the recording over and over again, afraid to say anything else.

President Fitzgerald huddled with his family in the stripped wreck of the residence. He had not gone into the West Wing in days. When he spoke, it was in a whisper, to avoid being overheard by any listening devices that his attempt to sterilize the place had missed. He'd had the windows boarded up and covered with carpeting, to thwart laser-based listening, and with tinfoil, in a layman's attempt to scramble radar and microwave systems.

He feared that the penetration of the government might have turned the surveillance capabilities of the U.S. intelligence community against its master. Not because it was probable, but because he could no longer be sure.

Thus the place looked like the lair of a madman, Howard Hughes or some such. To an extent, it was probably useful if those who came here went away whispering about Fitzgerald's sanity. Let the new Mahdi hear rumors that he was unstable. Perhaps he would become overconfident, and be drawn into some sort of mistake.

Fitz stared at the latest pronouncement, delivered to him by his own son on a sheet of paper. Dan lingered near. Linda and Polly were in the president's bedroom, which he and Linda shared. That one room he had left untouched. They were under strict orders to speak of nothing important there. For his part, he stayed out. When he slept, in uneasy fits and starts that were more like falling than falling asleep, he did it on a cot brought in by his Marines. "Rome," he muttered.

"Dad?"

All the terror, all the rage, boiled up in him, blasting up from his deepest heart like bloodred lava. "*Rome! Rome Rome Rome*!"

Dan drew back. An uneasy Marine pushed open the door.

"I'm going to do it," Fitz said. Four words, softly uttered by a man who wished to the great God that he had never heard of politics.

"You mean . . . release Dream Angel?" Dan asked.

Fitz laughed in his son's face—barked it out, the bitter snap of it made harder by the flat echo off the stripped walls.

"I'm going to go out there"—he pointed vaguely toward the Rose Garden—"and I'm going to do *sadaha*." He felt himself crumpling, his heart echoing like an empty cave, and then Dan was trying to hold him, his good son, strong son. Fitz added, "We can't win. Not against this—this monstrosity. We need God and we ain't got God, have we?"

"Of course we do," Dan said.

Fitz advanced on the two young Marines in the room. "Out!"

They looked to Dan, young eyes darting under their helmets. Dan gave them a curt nod, and suddenly Fitz saw him as a sort of savior. Dan had the answers. Dan could retrieve this situation.

"What do you think I should do?"

"Dad, if we don't release Dream Angel, Polly and I are going to live under Šarī'ah law. That's going to be your legacy."

"They'll burn our heart out! Burn it out! Fifty cities!"

"Unless it's a bluff."

A rush of tingling raced up his arms, followed by swaying nausea. He moved quickly to a chair, immediately sank down in it. "Yeah," he said. "Kennedy played chicken. I guess I can." And then he saw it, saw it clear. "I will go down there and I will shout that *ula ula* shit for our little fucking unkillable Mahdi; then I will wait one hour." He went close to Dan, embraced him in a hug that made him stiffen. They were not a touchy-feely family. Fitz tried to stifle the loopy mirth that was coming up but couldn't. Looming like a great, mad golem over his son, he giggled. "Then," he managed to say, "I will release Dream Angel."

"Dad . . . it's a plan."

"A good plan!"

"Why wait, though?"

"Throw him off."

"The second those planes lock onto their courses and the cruise missiles are launched, he'll know."

"These are primitive people. They'll be celebrating. Rattling goddamn bones."

"They are not primitive. They're smart and effective. You can do *sadaha.* Who knows, maybe it will throw them off. But you better sure as hell move Dream Angel out at the same time." He seemed to swell before his father, and Fitz saw in him all the power, the pile-driver instinct, of their clan. "Break 'em, Dad. Break 'em! Because I don't want to live like that, and I'm telling you, nobody does, not even the Muslims—the normal ones, that is."

The moment Fitz had considered releasing Dream Angel, his next thought had been of the fire in the cities, London, Paris, Berlin, Madrid—who knew, perhaps Moscow and Beijing, too, and why not Tokyo, LA, Chicago, and, certainly, old New York? " 'What candles may be held to speed them all?' " he said. " 'Not in the hands of boys but in their eyes / Shall shine the holy glimmers of goodbyes.' "

" 'Anthem for Doomed Youth,' " Dan said. "Wilfred Owen. Verboten, now, under Šarī'ah."

Dan suddenly seemed like a comic figure, somebody from the Sunday funnies, a capering, grinning goon. Fitz had to literally fight the urge to slap him down, it was so strong. He compelled his fists to open, compelled his mind to push away the savagery that was a hair's breadth away from possessing him. "Okay," he said, "time to chop-chop. *Logan*!"

The outer door opened immediately, and his chief of staff came in.

"You sound like you're walking in socks even when you're not," Fitz commented. "That's a joke, Son." He turned to Logan. "Okay, my dear—" He went close to him, gazed into the eyes. Sad, *sad*! "We are going to do this so-called—what's it called, Son?"

"*Sadaha.*"

Logan took a deep breath. "Sir, the entire cabinet is downstairs, and I think you owe it to the system to at least enter the Cabinet Room."

"Ah, yes, of course I do. I owe them! I owe everybody! And hell, it's real convenient, because now that slavery's coming back, I can literally belong to everybody! Snap your fingers, here comes Fitz. The ultimate in public service. Cabinet Room, sure. Boots to lick, here I come!"

He saw Logan's eyes flicker toward Dan, then come back again, not reassured. Fitz continued, "You know, you two fellas know me by the moles on my damn butt. But lemme tell you. I am light-years away. I look like I'm here. Yeah. But I am not here. I am way out on the far edge, and the wind is blowing from behind and I am looking down, and sliding closer, and while you guys are in the White House, the truth is, I'm looking down from this terrible precipice. And I know what I am seeing. It is the abyss." He clapped his hands. "Dresser! Suit me!"

The bedroom door clicked. Cracked a little. Opened. Linda and Polly came out. "We released the staff," Linda said. "But I can straighten your tie."

Polly stood to one side, shoulders hunched. He knew her when she was like this, his pouty willow of a girl, her fifteen-year-old face capable of so easily breaking his heart or mending it, or sending it with her slightest smile into high orbit. "Hey, girl kid, you don't look so hot."

An eye rolled on the visible side of her face, rested on him for a moment, then looked away.

"You need makeup, too," Linda told him. "You look dead."

That made him smile, proving, he thought, that corpses can. "Just a little tired," he said.

"Daddy!" Polly's face was hard now, gray and gleaming, a wax effigy, or something left behind by a vampire.

"Honey?"

"You're going to surrender."

"I am going to try to buy us some time."

"If you surrender, and we have to go into purdah, Daddy, I am going to commit suicide, and I'm not the only one."

"Polly!" Linda said. "Don't pressure him like this!"

"Mother, he has to know that I won't be the only one! I am not going to go into this slavery that these crazy people have for women! What's wrong with being a woman? A woman is a beautiful thing, a woman is a gift from God, a woman is equal. *Equal,* Daddy!"

"I know it! And I am not going to surrender. Perhaps, create that appearance. But, darling, I swear this to you on my heart and on the blood of my mother, I will not let this nightmare come here. No matter what it takes, they will not succeed." Whereupon he heard, as distinctly as if he had been a comedian dying on a stage, a ripple of sinister laughter, and thought, immediately—no, knew—that this was a symptom. His first definite symptom of psychosis. He'd been expecting it, because his reading of history told him that one of the primary things that drove leaders mad was being trapped between two unbearable alternatives. Leaders who had infinite power but were imprisoned by profound vulnerability—Nero came to mind, who had been excellent, then gone mad—lost their hearts, their minds, their souls. Such leaders could kill a quarter of a billion people without a qualm. It was a road Fitz was going down, and he knew it, and every step he took he went a little faster.

Out there in the dark, across the whole world, the ships waited, the planes.

"Okay, Linda, tie's straight, suit's looking sharp. So, now, my lady, let's get the Nixon trenches out from under these old eyes." He followed her into the bedroom suite, crossed to her makeup table, and sat down. "Maybe some mortician's wax would be the ticket."

"It melts," Linda said, "on skin that's still warm."

"Oh, mine's not."

"Well, I have some concealer," she said.

When she began to brush it under his eyes, it felt as if the life were sifting out of him, sifting out into her fingers, drawn away by the tickle of the brush.

"Where's that paladin of yours?" Linda asked as they went downstairs.

"Yeah, Dad, that guy with the Muslim wife. Mr. and Mrs. Reliable."

"She's got a lot to prove. And he's effective."

"Which doesn't answer my question," Linda replied.

"I'm not going to answer it."

The familiar sharpness in his voice stopped their inquiry. They'd strayed into classified territory.

The doors opened. As they moved toward the Cabinet Room, he could see the press assembling in the Rose Garden, a huge throng of people and equipment. The demonstrators who had been on the front gate for so many hours had dwindled to a few. They had helped and inspired him more than they could know.

He stood before the door to the Cabinet Room. "Are the spiders in the web?" he asked Logan.

"The cabinet is waiting for you."

"Clear out the staffers."

"Sir?"

"We have no way of knowing who's loyal and who isn't. Lay on guards. Weapons at the ready."

Logan nodded. Fitz saw that he'd turned his retainer the color of wet chalk. Well, let him worry. Fitz wanted them to think he was crazy. Crazy was weak, and he felt reasonably sure that something said by somebody on the other side of that door would reach the enemy. Not that there was a traitor in his cabinet, of course not, but somewhere among their staffs, yes, and more than one.

And what of Linda's question? Should he trust Deutsch and that wife of his, Nabila of the endlessly twisting hands?

"These terrible hours," Fitz muttered.

Linda heard, put a hand on his shoulder.

He entered the Cabinet Room. "Good morning, ladies and gentlemen," he said. They all rose. He noticed that both Lucinda Goodavage and Marion Murphy wore discreet blue head scarves. "Courage," he said, looking into Lucinda's stricken face. "I want to thank you all for coming here. It took guts, and I know that."

Absolute silence. Time to deliver the bombshell. He took a deep breath. The curtains, he noticed, were green. First time he'd ever looked at the curtains. "I'm going to go out to the Rose in a moment, and I want to tell you why." He looked around at all their faces. Did they all think him insane? No? Well, they would. "I'm going to do *sahada.*"

"You can't," Homeland Security Chief Wilkes blurted.

"Since when do you give the orders around here?"

Wilkes's face went gray. Lucinda Moore's lips tightened. She would have a traitor on her staff, he thought, almost certainly. Her old-fashioned politics of openness made her an easy target.

Henry Kerry stared down at the notepad before him. Here was another candidate, not because he was in any way weak—he wasn't—but because the State Department was just too damn big not to be vulnerable. So Fitz had traitors close to him, of that he felt sure, some kid carrying coffee and listening to every word, some secretary, affable and trusted, who left her reports in a back alley somewhere.

"Anybody wants to cry, do it outside." He chuckled a little. Lay it on. They needed to leave here thinking he'd lost it. Tell their staffers, make him seem weak, a little mad. If he was lucky, the enemy would hear and become overconfident, and make some sort of mistake.

"It's surrender," Secretary of Defense Ryland said. He was loud, his voice challenging. There were murmurs around the table, heads nodding.

Now it was time for the president to lie. This was his prerogative. The greater interests of the country always came first. "We have firm intelligence that the threat in the latest document is damned close to being real. There are at least thirty-five bombs planted around the world, and probably the fifty he claims is a true number. And mark my words, if I don't go out there and get on my knees, we will see them all detonated within a week."

"Like Washington? We've survived."

"Like Rome, man! Rome!"

"Are you sure of this?" Ryland asked.

Coming from a man who should certainly have been in the loop on this, it was a fair question. Fitz's answer, however, was not fair. "We have acquired a hard disk from Pakistan. It's being decoded, but slowly."

"What hard disk?"

"Need-to-know, Mike," he told Ryland smoothly.

"I have a need to know!"

Fitz would never say, in this room, that the hard disk had belonged to the Mahdi, and that the Mahdi had been killed. Because that would become news. They would leak it. And it was both true and false. The Mahdi was dead. Long live the Mahdi. Plus, the disk was proving a tough nut.

"Mike, I'm sorry. You're out of the loop and I can't say why."

Ryland came slowly to his feet. He leaned over, got his briefcase, and slid the pad into it. "You have my resignation," he said.

"No! No, I won't hear of it! Not now!"

"You have my resignation!"

"You sit down. When this is over, you can do what you want, but I can't have cabinet officers quitting now. How would it look, for God's sake!"

"It's gonna be over as soon as you say that damn prayer out there. So fine, I'll resign after that. One minute after, I'm done."

Kerry stood, then Ryland, then the rest of them. Total rebellion.

Fitz laughed; he walked to an arched window, gazed out toward the gathering press. "I've got quite a crowd," he said. "Maybe I'll do a little soft-shoe." He danced a bit. "Yes, Sir, that's my baby. . . ." He flashed his professional grin, purposely did it too bright. He laughed a little harder. "You're like kids who threaten to run away, but you're scared to leave Poppa. Well, hell, Poppa's got thirty-five cities full of people and treasure and the life of a goddamn civilization to worry about, so either *get out or sit down*!"

As he shouted at them, he kept the grin going. It must look wild. Absolutely bonkers. He'd done drama at Yale, but only a little. Too bad he hadn't tackled Lear. Always wanted to, but he'd been a satisfactory Chance Wayne in *Sweet Bird of Youth,* also a well-reviewed Captain Warrington in *Little Mary Sunshine.* He laid his hand on his heart and sang, "In Izzenschnooken on the lovely Essenzook Zee . . ." Chuckled again. "I'm gonna become Muslim in English," he said. "If I mispronounce the Arabic, we're liable to lose another city."

"Mr. President," Mike Ryland barked, "I'm not sure you're well."

"You know, you've got a point. I've got a headache, and I've had a little gas. Actually, I could be coming down with something. Nothing very serious, though. Death, maybe?" He barked laughter, then cut it off by wiping the air in front of his face. "Never laugh at your own jokes, son. Wise advice." He glanced at his watch. "Time to go and fuck the world to the wall." He started out of the room.

Ryland followed him, strutting along like a mechanical man, his bald pate as red as an apple. "Fitz, they can't hit Washington! We know they're not hidden in a building and they're not in one of the tunnels, so they have to fly like they did in Vegas and Rome. They have to fly, Fitz! From Boston to Houston, any unauthorized aircraft has thirty seconds of airtime, Fitz! They cannot take us!"

"Whoop-de-do," Fitz replied. "So, we've given them Rome; let's give them Paris and Venice and Berlin and Tokyo."

"Fitz, don't do this!"

Fitz stopped. "Do you know what they're smelling right now in Athens? Roast. They're smelling the Romans literally cooking to death. In *Athens*!"

He could not say more. He could not face his cabinet any longer. He blamed himself for all this. He'd known how vulnerable the security services were to penetration. He'd known how few it would take on the inside to do this damage. But he had not pressed the inspector general, had he? He should have been shouting down telephone lines, forcing the bureaucracy out of its massive inertia.

They had restricted Muslims in the intelligence services. So how hard was it to simply abandon your religious affiliation, especially if you had family and friends to help you? It was like the Cold War, when it had been so difficult to keep the communists out. But worse, there was the matter of money. A lot of cash, just to glance away for a few minutes, what did it matter? It was probably just a marijuana shipment, anyway.

Oh, God. He was the accursed president. This was the worst.

He went out into the Rose Garden. Approached the podium. Faces, camera lenses, microphones. "Good morning, Hugh. Selena. Hi there, Cokie. Okay, folks, we have a very brief time here." He swallowed. Wanted water. There was no water. "All right." As never before, he was aware of the silent presence behind the machines, of the billions who were watching this. The thirty or forty feet between him and the cameras, he imagined, was filled with angels. He allowed himself a little smile, a private moment in what was certainly the most public place in the history of the human species. He wouldn't have been surprised to find that every man, woman, and child on the planet was watching or listening.

"First, I would like to express my belief that there is no God but Allah, and Mohammed is his prophet."

Even the clicking of still cameras came to a halt. From deep within the crowd there was a sudden sound, a cry, instantly stifled. There it was—the end of this age, not a bang, not even a whimper, just that little sigh.

Fitz thought, *What a species we are, that a few words could mean so much.* Then further, but deeper and more insubstantially, he reflected that the great curse of religion was that it tempted people into believing that the story of their deity was more important than the lives of human beings. It came to seem morally right to kill on behalf of the story.

"Now, before Allah and our blessed Mahdi, our guide given to us by a loving God, I say this. Allah in his infinite mercy has allowed the Mahdi to see into our dark hearts, here in the West, and has revealed to him that we were indeed planning a maneuver—an attack—that would have killed the faithful. That's right; we would have killed the faithful. I know you are wondering what that means. It means that we were ready to cause the death of hundreds of millions of people. Their lives were dangling at the end of our great and terrible Crusader sword. But no more. I have this day ordered the American Air Force and all the American military all through the world to stand down. Even as I speak, the planes are returning to their bases, and the missiles are being stowed in the holds of the ships that were about to launch them. And now, I call upon the Mahdi to bring forth new officers to help us enact the holy law of Allah in our land."

There were tears on faces, other faces disappearing into hands. How ironic that, of all that Fitz had learned and seen in life, the thing that had most truly defined his largest moment, in the end, was his experience as Chance Wayne. The truth was not the word of God. There was no word of God. It was the silence.

Fitz turned and went quickly back into the White House, ignoring the voices wailing out their questions. The Roman emperors might have had problems with assassination, but they hadn't had to worry about the press. Still, turning his back on the questions shamed him.

But then again, there comes a time in every big hand when a player with good cards feels a tinge of conscience. As Fitz crossed toward the elevator, people rushed forward. "I know that every world leader, every major CEO, every big banker, is on hold. Tell them this. The president says that Šarī'ah law is clear. Follow it."

Linda and Dan and Logan tried to enter the elevator with him. He held up his hand. They stood, staring out of red, devastated eyes, as he closed them out of his world. They could not follow him, not now.

He did not return to the residence. Instead, he went down to the old Cold War–era White House shelter.

The moment the doors slid open, he heard voices and the clatter of keyboards. An enormous job had been done here in just a matter of hours.

The two Marines on guard duty confronted him. "Sir, the sequence."

If he got it wrong, they would shoot him immediately, and by his own order. But he would not get it wrong. He had created the sequence himself. "Dulcinea," he said.

"Sancho Panza," the master sergeant replied.

"Mahdi."

They stood aside, and Fitz stepped out into the transformed space. Gone were the elaborate electronic maps that had made this secret chamber one of the wonders of the Cold War world. What was left was raw concrete walls and people working at plastic tables brought in just hours ago. Power lines and fiber-optic cables ran out and down the long tunnel to the Potomac, where four more Marines manned a guard station that bristled with makeshift antennae.

What he had here was a highly sophisticated signals acquisition and communications center that completely bypassed the whole intelligence-gathering infrastructure. It had limitations, of course, but surprisingly few. Jim Deutsch and Nabila al-Rahbi, and Nabila's group leader, Margaret Pearson, had handpicked the minimum number of people essential for the work. They were from the National Reconnaissance Office, the CIA, the National Security Agency, and the National Geospatial-Intelligence Agency. Even so, there were just eleven people present and two Marines.

Fitz went straight to Deutsch, who huddled with a group of technicians, staring at a laptop.

"Where are we?"

Nobody answered. Nobody stopped working. Fitz could smell the sweat of desperation, the stink of it mingling with the sour damp of the concrete.

Jim Deutsch glanced up. "They have the disk contents uploaded from Pakistan pretty well decoded," he said.

Fitz's heart literally bounded in his chest. A rush of blood made the world sway. "That's wonderful!"

"It doesn't look good."

Elation, then the cliff. "Oh?"

Marge Pearson said, "We're looking at sixteen target cities."

"It's not fifty, at least."

"We have no idea where the bombs are or how big they are, or even if there's really a bomb present in all the cities."

"Which cities?"

"Think world tour. Us, of course. Then New York, London, Paris, Brussels, Berlin, Moscow, Beijing, Tokyo, Riyadh, Los Angeles, Seattle, San Francisco, Dallas, Chicago, and, of course, Jerusalem."

"They got a bomb into Israeli territory?"

"This one is going to be delivered from outside. From Syria, we think. A small plane or missile. In general, delivery is by small planes that are capable of using city streets as runways. In Rome, it was a racecourse."

"Okay, so my next step is to warn the Syrians."

"I wouldn't do that," Deutsch snapped.

A paladin, for sure. Nobody talked to the president of the United States like that. Still, he forged on. "Why not, Mr. Deutsch?"

Deutsch just shook his head, went back to whatever he was doing on that laptop. But Fitz didn't care, because this tiny operation down here represented, however faint, the only chance of winning this war. It was Deutsch who had suggested that he bring in people who had been close to the known traitor, on the theory that they would be most angry and thus the most highly motivated. It was as counterintuitive as all hell, but Fitz had to hope that Deutsch was right and traitors didn't run in packs.

Nabila al-Rahbi, also, was almost certainly loyal. She had the credibility of her religion to save, and Fitz had seen that she was a faithful Muslim of the deepest, truest kind. In fact, her Islam reminded him of his mother's Christianity. Her faith, also, had not been simple, and her intelligence had also tested it constantly, and driven it deep. "Trust grace," Mother had said. "Just trust grace. Faith is nothing but that."

Deutsch had suggested that he bring in Mark Chambers, Rashid's supervisor, and Carol Wilkie, his closest coworker. They had been working hour after hour, without sleep, running drones, pulling data from satellites, all the time cloaking their activities so that other elements in the intelligence community would not be able to detect their mission.

The more information the disk from Pakistan gave up, the more they could zero in on specific target cities, and perhaps isolate the location of the damned bombs.

"What about the specialist teams?"

"Operating in every known target city," Nabila said.

"What're you working on, Deutsch?"

"Our backyard."

"Do you not want me here?"

"No."

The president felt anger flush his face, but Deutsch was too valuable to fire, or even snarl at. Fitz told himself that this wasn't like being slighted by some senator or prime minister. The man was just some professional killer, after all, a guy from the depths one preferred would remain hidden. After this was over, he'd slip back into the shadows. Fitz knew the type.

"If I don't communicate with the Syrians, we risk the loss of Jerusalem, Mr. Deutsch."

Deutsch didn't even look up from his work. "Think," he said absently. "Sir."

"You don't like me, do you?"

Now Deutsch did stop. "That's a typically American question, you know that? We're obsessed with being liked. Most people in most cultures don't give a rat's ass. So forget that and consider this: if the new Mahdi discovers he's being drawn into a bluff, the world blows up."

"If he finds out. And I might save Jerusalem, for God's sake."

"You take that risk, you're a fool."

"You don't care if you're liked by me? That could matter."

"Look, what's happening in here is war fighting, okay, so I don't have time to stroke you. Thank you. Sir."

"Do you have anything for me?"

Deutsch seemed to freeze. "Sir, when we do, you will be called. Obviously. Thank you!"

"In other words, get out."

"Go upstairs and do your crazy-man routine. Lay it on. The weaker you look, the more lives get saved."

"I'll do Lear. I've always wanted to do Lear."

"Fine. Good-bye."

Fitz nodded to Deutsch. Stepped back. "Thank you. Everybody." He might as well have been in an empty room, for all the reaction he got.

He left, off to do his duty and range the halls of the White House, smiling and muttering for the listening devices that might be there, and hoping to God that the plan that had been evolved mattered.

31

THE OCCULTATION OF THE MAHDI

No man might know how Allah, in the infinity of his wisdom and the limitlessness of his power, hid his guided one, only those who received the ancient spirit of the Mahdi into their unworthy bodies. The great secret of Inshalla was that for hundreds of years the Mahdi had moved in spiritual form from one human receptacle to another, each chosen by heaven for Allah's own reasons. Aziz had been Mahdi, but now Aziz was dead, killed by women who had been invaded by demons, and who had themselves been killed by corrupt policemen greedy for Crusader gold.

So Eshan had come to this old madrassa, to this old man, Syed Ahmad, following a prearranged instruction.

There were vines here, which Eshan thought were more ancient than this city but not more ancient than its founders, who had come down from the Kush carrying the vines of the blue flowers. They had called this the City of Flowers, and he could imagine them, in their silks and their furs, the fragile, cloudlike clothing of the ancients, tending their blossoms.

Syed Ahmad was not a sophisticate, as Aziz had been. He was not a lover of luxury. He knew the Book, though, far better than Aziz had. When Syed Ahmad spoke, there was music in it, the secret music that only the greatest scholars could ever express, and here he was in this little school, the master of a few boys, who would sit about only half-listening to his genius, their eyes flickering like all eyes to the glitter of life and the lure of the West.

Eshan watched him chew his food and wag his head, his dirty clothes reeking of tobacco and unwashed years. Eshan did not want to serve him, but he could see that the Mahdi was indeed in Syed Ahmad. So he was, literally, the embodiment of the Mahdi now. None knew how the choice was made. Somehow, Inshalla did it . . . and perhaps, Eshan thought, the Russians had a hand in it. He was not blind to political reality. He understood that Allah worked through men, and therefore also through their politics.

The Russians were more clever than the Americans, certainly, but they could not begin to understand the workings of Allah in the world, could they? This was why the assassins they had sent after Aziz had been, themselves, assassinated. It was because God had needed Aziz to come here to the City of Flowers—thick today, though, with smog, and clattering and roaring with vehicles leaving, with demonstrators and police speeding around in trucks. Shots echoed up and down the streets, disturbing the quiet of this ancient place, too.

"Now," Syed Ahmad said, standing up from his table in his dining room with its dangling bulb and dirty carpet, and its blue mosaic ceiling a memory—faint—of the dome of the sky. "Here we are when the great event comes to pass." He went across to a sideboard made of black, fragrant wood, and pulled a small banana from a bunch that lay there in a brass bowl. "And banana trees, with fruit—do you know it? Ah, Eshan, you shake your head. The Book must be in your blood, in your body. People of the Book, my son, that's what it means. Your discourse must be filled with the Book; thus you only speak from your true heart, which is Allah's house in you."

"I have not memorized the Quran."

The new Mahdi wagged his head from side to side, reminding Eshan of a great ship swaying on the sea, his white beard its sail. But sails were not stained with tobacco, were they? "Then you're illiterate," he said.

"Oh yes, in the Book. But I can read. I speak and write in English, too."

The Mahdi shook a blunt finger. "Useful, useful. Were you, then, schooled by the English?"

Eshan smiled. "They were before my time, Master. Actually, I'm an American. I went to school in New York. Brooklyn, New York."

"Your faith has been well tested. Have you done hajj?"

"I have. Master, may I now ask you a question?"

Syed took off his glasses and rubbed them with a small blue cloth. For such a dirty man, this new Mahdi was surprisingly fastidious. An orderly nature, as befitted a scholar. He smiled, then, his beard bobbing beneath his long nose. "What is your question?"

"Did you feel it, when you became Mahdi?"

He laughed. He laughed loud. So loud, it began to make Eshan angry, causing him to feel as if he was being mocked. "You do not become Mahdi. The guided one simply opens his eyes. Within me, within you. It doesn't matter. Look at Aziz. He had business suits and hair pomade, I hear."

"Until we went to Pamir, he had a Mercedes convertible. He was the toast of Tehran." Eshan paused for a moment. "He drank. He smoked hashish."

"Allah is merciful."

"But . . . how are you chosen? Why did I have your address? Why did you expect me?"

"What do you think? That this would all happen by virtue of the breeze? But speak no more of it."

When they came down to Peshawar, a boy had brought Eshan this name and address, so he had done as he had been instructed, and come to this place as soon as he saw that Aziz was being killed. But . . . had the women been ordered to kill Aziz? Perhaps that Persian catamite was involved, that wretched child, sent as a spy from who knew who? He was no student, apprenticed to Aziz by a loving father, that shadow-slipping boy with his seductive hands.

The women and the catamite had, in their turns, been killed. Somebody cleaning up after themselves, Eshan assumed, in this world where nothing was as it seemed.

On the way to Syed, Eshan had passed through the street of the shoemakers, as the note had instructed. He'd felt nothing but had afterward discovered something in his pocket. An Olympus recorder with a full tape in it.

"I have the recording, Master."

"Oh, that's good. And is the trap lying open? Have they stepped in?"

Eshan had no idea how to answer this, so he turned on the recorder to let the Mahdi listen. There was the usual creaking and popping. Syed Ahmad raised his eyebrows.

"He puts on the suit jacket. The transmitters are located in the jackets. Woven into the cloth by—"

The master held up his hand. "I do not need to know this."

President Fitzgerald's voice came through. "Better," it said. "Now I look like a corpse that's pretending to be alive."

"What is this?" the master asked.

"How is your English, Mahdi?"

"My English is from school, but I still don't understand this sentence. How is he pretending? He is alive."

"It's not important. He talks only to his wife."

Then, more faintly, Linda Fitzgerald's voice: "Where's that paladin of yours?" Then the daughter's voice came, speaking of the "guy with the Muslim wife."

"And all of this means?"

"'Paladin' means a hero or champion. He must have an operative that he trusts who has a Muslim wife."

"But not himself Muslim? How strange, to be so close to the faith and not desire it."

"Americans are strange."

"This faithless husband needs stoning."

Then the president's voice came again: "Are the spiders in the web?"

"What does he say?"

"He refers to his viziers. He does not trust them."

There was a clunk, then the sound of shuffling. "He enters the Cabinet Room. They come to their feet. Now, listen."

The president spoke for a moment, saying that he would do the "Allah two-step."

"The Allah two-step? That is a term of respect?"

"It is not a term of respect."

"Then his acceptance of the faith was not sincere?"

The entire world had seen his acceptance of Islam. "That I cannot say. Certainly he is angry. But that's to be expected. Islam becomes very quickly a habit of soul. This is why, once converted, so few fall away from the faith. But it's hard for them at first. You know."

"Yes, Eshan, very well. What is next?"

"The acceptance, which you saw."

"Yes, and then what did he say in his privacy?"

"For twenty minutes, nothing. The signal was lost for a time."

"Ah. Why is that?"

"You hear him walking, then a whirring sound, then static. Ten minutes later, the whirring again, then he walks, speaking . . . some sort of declamation."

"May I listen?"

Eshan sped the tape forward until he heard the peeping of speech again. When he slowed the machine, the president's voice returned: " 'Come, let's away to prison: We two alone will sing like birds i' the cage: When thou dost ask me blessing, I'll kneel down, and ask of thee forgiveness: so we'll live, and pray, and sing, and tell old tales, and laugh at gilded butterflies, and hear poor rogues talk of court news . . . ' " Then he laughed, muttered, and went on declaiming.

"This means what?"

"Master, this is unknown to me. It's in a old form of English. Perhaps a poem."

The master looked at him, then stood and went across the broad room, his stockinged feet whispering on the weathered blue mosaic. "It is said that the devil is a mule, Eshan. Do you know of that saying?"

"No, Master."

He chuckled. "This American devil is indeed such a creature—stubborn without cause, mean out of his deepest nature, habitually cruel." He pointed a finger at Eshan, a long finger, the nail pale sculpted ivory. "Mind me, he knows very well that we are listening, and I tell you this—what we want to hear is what he said when the static was on. This is when he spoke the truth." He waved the hand, opening it as if freeing a bird to the air. "All we have heard is a lie."

"He has not embraced the faith?"

"He has not."

Eshan tried to understand. "Then, Master . . . is he mad?"

"But of course, mad not to take the hand of Allah when it is extended to him. In his madness, I am afraid he leads the world further down the Crusader path, and all else is lies."

"What is to be done?"

"All things come to him who waits."

"That is a saying of the Jews."

"Who respects the Jews has their measure. We will now punish Washington."

"We cannot accomplish this at present."

"Ah, no? You think not? I think that Allah has fixed that which was broken, my son, because Allah knew that the time to punish the Crusader capital was not two nights ago. It is now."

His dark eyes twinkled, and Eshan knew that the Mahdi truly had entered Syed, for how otherwise could he possibly have such insight?

Syed laughed. "You wear your puzzlement so clearly, Eshan, you of the hopping eyebrows!" The laughter extended, then faded to a gentle sadness. "A carpet, Eshan, is woven of many threads. You are but one thread."

"Then we are proceeding against Washington, Master?"

"It saddens my heart, that so many must suffer for the obstinacy of so few."

Eshan tried to contain the explosion of joy that came up within him, but the sheer intensity of it caused a ripple of delighted laughter—whereupon the master gave him a slap with a hand as soft as a woman's. There was no real pain, but he turned his head aside, bowing to the shame. "Forgive me, Master."

"Tell me, do you miss Aziz?"

This question frightened Eshan, because there could be no right answer.

The Mahdi gave him that charming smile, then touched his cheek. "Sometimes he worked for Mr. Deutsch, you know. Sometimes for the Russians. Did you know?"

Eshan struggled to quell his hammering heart. If there was the slightest suspicion of him, his life was over. "I killed the Russian contact with my own hands," he said. "I slit his throat."

Syed Ahmad smiled brightly. "Now come and help me pack and move, for it is certain that the Americans will unleash Dream Angel the moment that our beloved bomb detonates. We must hide among their running dogs, or we will be burned with the faithful."

"Do we not desire martyrdom?"

"Of course we do, but we have work to do for Allah; we cannot yet allow ourselves to inhale the sweet scent of heaven."

Eshan remembered the death of Aziz, and for the first time the thought touched his mind that this man might have been behind it, somehow. When the eyes twinkled again, Eshan saw something behind the merry glitter, a stillness of a sort he had seen just once before, but unforgettably. It had been in India. He had been walking along a path by a stream. It was twilight. In a field nearby, children were playing soccer, their voices echoing. He'd seen, beyond the path, something so still that he thought at first that it was a statue. Another instant, though, and he realized that the gold he was seeing belonged to the eyes of a tiger. It was watching the children. They were only Hindus, so he had hurried on.

Syed Ahmad of the tiger's eyes stood. "Nowadays there is never enough time for tea!" He swept off into the deeper parts of the house, Eshan going quickly behind.

32

A LEG UP

As Rashid entered Alexandria, he became careful, and then very careful. There were few people about, most of them either gone or respecting the curfew. He did not doubt that there was a bulletin out for him by now. Once they lost him, they would be beside themselves, putting all of their resources to work. Would his own supporters keep him safe? They were salted here and there, two in the FBI that he was aware of, certainly a few more in the CIA, in Homeland Security, in the National Intelligence Office, cutting false orders, diverting real ones.

He'd spent the day sitting in his car listening to the radio news and watching to see how the local police patrols were organized. When he'd heard Fitzgerald sniveling about his conversion, Rashid had instantly known that Allah had granted Washington these additional hours precisely so that the cowardice of the Crusader king could be revealed to the whole world. Allah, beloved father, was always a step ahead of the devil.

Rashid drove until he found an indoor parking garage, then went in deep. He parked the car and climbed the stairs to street level, where he watched the sparse traffic for a time without stepping out. When he did so, he kept his head down. It was a long chance, but a skilled analyst could come close to identifying a specific individual, if the target was looking up at just the right moment. He had personally made Osama bin Laden four times. Nothing had happened, though.

Rashid had never met Bilal and Hani Aboud, the Moroccans who were responsible for this most important of all the bombs. How it was that Inshalla had chosen them, Rashid did not know. Obviously, though, something was not right.

He walked out into a ghostly quiet. Stores were closed, some of them with steel shutters. This was actually helpful. Although he was the only person on the street, which obviously made him a target of the police, it was also true that it would be easy for him to spot the opposition.

He walked steadily and quickly, keeping as close to buildings as he could, taking advantage of any overhead cover that presented itself. In tracking, he knew what he was capable of, and Mark was even better, and he would be highly motivated, for sure, Mark who was facing weeks of interrogation about the mole who had worked for him, and probably would see his career go into terminal decline. So Mark was up there in the sky looking right now, as were they all.

In addition to worrying about what might be happening overhead, Rashid had to think about the police. There were few squad cars, thankfully, and the National Guard was not deployed in this death trap, so his chances of encountering anybody were not great. Still, he stayed off of short streets as much as possible. He didn't want some damned cop to come swooping around the corner before he had a chance to conceal himself.

He had been walking for three blocks when he heard a faint sound, perhaps a car engine. For a moment, he saw no place of concealment, but then he noticed that one of the stoops of the row houses he was passing had a small space under it. He slipped in, forcing himself down among the garbage cans that were kept there, making as little noise as possible.

The sound became more distinct, an engine nearly on idle, coming closer. Automobile, he thought. No lights, though. The police, then, being very stealthy.

This did not seem like a routine patrol. This seemed like what might happen if they had been sent here to look for somebody. Rashid forced himself not to look, not to even think about moving.

Something tickled his ankle. Then he felt a pinch. Of all things, a damned rat was biting him. He loathed filthy creatures like snakes and rats. When he moved, though, the garbage cans immediately rattled, and the guttering of the engine was now distinct, so he had to simply hold his breath and bear it, an awful sensation, stinging, then tickling as the creature licked at the blood it was drawing. He was sickened; his skin crawled.

Then he heard voices, soft, intent, and a shaft of light appeared, shining along the wall. He watched it play carefully around the stoop. A glow filled the cul-de-sac. He pressed himself hard against the back wall . . . and the light moved slowly away.

He begged God to make them leave, because the rat was tearing at the skin now, sending excruciating waves of pain up Rashid's leg. He tried to move the garbage cans, but again there was sound—a scraping. And again the light returned.

Click. The car door had been opened. There were steps on the sidewalk, and the scuff of feet on the two steps down. Rashid could hear the cop breathing, in and out, in and out, a slight wheeze to it. Crashing, then.

"Shit!"

"What?"

"They got every garbage can in town down here."

The pain in his leg stopped and the flashlight beam wavered as the rat sped into the pool of light that ended just an inch from Rashid's crouching body.

"It's a rat," the cop said, his voice now uninterested. A moment later he was back in the car and the danger had ended. Still Rashid crouched, trying to get his heart to slow down. Allah, he knew, had done this. What rat bites through a man's trouser leg and chews at living flesh? No, it had been a miracle, God making sure that the rat would be present when needed. "Thanks be to God," he breathed. He waited, though, until the guttering of the engine had entirely faded and been gone for a time. Then he came out, allowing the cans to clatter a little. At first, he stood in the shadow beneath the stoop. Then he stepped back up onto the sidewalk. With the streetlights out—and they had been turned off earlier all over the Washington area, presumably to make it more difficult for any pilot to locate his target—the street was now far darker than it had been. But even so, just before this Rashid had been able to see. Then he realized, of course, the moon had set.

It had been over a year since he had gone online to find this house on a map. He had done it from a computer at a public library in Bethesda, and mapped a nearby location, not the actual house. He had also concealed his search in a series of other searches for local Wal-Marts and Target stores. This made him fairly sure that his tracks were covered, but again, he knew the skills of the analysts in Nabila's department. Somehow, they might be able to uncover his search, although he could not imagine how.

He moved through the silence and blackness, no longer bothering to keep close to walls. There was no point. That sort of maneuver made it harder to get visuals, but a single man walking the streets on a cool night had an unconcealable infrared signature. If the cops were being directed from above, they would be back very shortly, and this time he would not escape.

He walked quickly, moving down one block and another, past houses, then bleak-fronted apartment buildings, their lobbies dark. A dog followed him for a time, a gray, panting shadow. "Come," he murmured, "come along," but the dog went off. Too bad; it would have appeared less suspicious.

Here and there, he saw a parked car, but never one that looked as if it could be easily used. And then it hit him like thunder from the hollows of his soul: You are here to die. If you are successful, you will not see another dawn.

He stopped, held his hands before him, two pale claws. His tongue felt his teeth, his skin the cool air. His mind was filled with images, memories, thoughts—and suddenly he saw inside himself a truth that he had been denying for years or, rather, covering with an increasing elaboration of prayer. This was that the Muslim promise of a heaven stocked with virgins seemed boring to him. More than that, he did not, he had to admit, believe in heaven at all, or hell, or anything, really, except the night air that surrounded him now, and the fact of death. So, why did he do this? He had no answer. He was face-to-face with the mystery of the soul.

Then he came to the critical block. The house was just around the corner. He could not assess the situation by walking to one end, then doubling back, or going around the block, or anything like that. Anything except going directly to the house and quickly letting himself in would be immediately suspect. So he walked down the sidewalk, crossed in the middle of the street, and approached the door of the red-brick row house. The street was so quiet that the only sound was the whisper of his sneakers on the pavement. Although the Air Force planes cruising above showed no lights, he knew that they were there, too high to be heard, knife-edge planes piloted by magically skillful men who would swoop after him the moment he became airborne. He had no illusions about this. The flying of the plane would be his responsibility. The only question was, what had happened to the Aboud brothers? They had not been captured, of that he was certain, because his unit at the NGIA would have been among the first to know and he had not been discovered until after they had failed to detonate their bomb.

He reached the front of the house and went up the steps. In his training, he'd learned the particular locks that were installed on all of the buildings that were in use for this project. Simple locks had been chosen intentionally, and the tongues had been filed to allow easy entry to anybody who knew the secret. Their security did not rest in things like locks. A lock couldn't keep out the authorities, and they were the only threat that mattered.

He drew his American Express card out of his wallet and pressed it into the doorjamb, an act that he had practiced many times in camp but never again, certainly not at home, where he had left the locks alone. Nabila's department had installed the locks, the alarm system, and her safe room, and he did nothing but use what he was cleared to use.

He slid the card but encountered no resistance. Odd. As he was sliding it again, he heard a distinct sound, very faint. He froze, listening. Was this a jet engine, perhaps, very high? A fighter, perhaps an E-4B . . . or no, a drone.

But it was none of these things, and he knew instantly that a car was drawing near, was not a block away, was moving slowly along the street. Had he been spotted by an infrared system?

Again, he slid the card. Again, no resistance.

The engine noise became distinct. He slid the card—same result. Then he had a thought—perhaps the door was unlocked. He pushed at it . . . and it opened. Not a good sign.

The blackness inside was so absolute that he could see only the faint sparks generated behind his eyes by his own nervous system. With this blindness came the unsettling feeling that somebody might be standing in front of him. He stepped forward, feeling with his hands. How might the house be laid out? The garage, he had seen as he came in, was to his right. That would be where the plane would be kept, presumably also the bomb. He felt in that direction but kept swiping air. Finally, he turned that way. There was no wall; therefore there must be a large room.

He stepped once, twice—and his foot hit the leg of something. Glass shattered, and there were blue sparks. He had knocked over a floor lamp. From somewhere there came a sighing sound, as if somebody who had been holding their breath had tried to cover a sharp inhalation under the noise and not quite succeeded. For some time, Rashid stood motionless, listening to the house. Faintly, water ran in a toilet, the steady gurgle of a bad valve. There was an odor of cumin-seasoned food, old and stale. He took a step into what he knew now was the living room. Behind it would be the dining room and, somewhere on the far wall, a door into the kitchen. There, he hoped, he would be able to find a flashlight, which he would use to enter the garage. He knew how the plane would work, and he thought he might be able to extend the wings on his own. If not, he would detonate the bomb right here. Despite the fact that it would not be an airburst and it was ten miles from Washington, the destruction would be gigantic. Certainly the Pentagon would be completely destroyed. The Capitol's dome would be smashed, the Washington Monument knocked down, the White House set ablaze. Alexandria and Arlington would be devastated and Georgetown set alight. Radiation would be everywhere, and the American government—what of it remained intact—would be forced to permanently relocate. The shame of it would haunt America for generations to come. The ruins of Washington would become a permanent symbol of America the powerless.

Forcing himself to move slowly, to use his hands like eyes rather than flailing them, he found the far wall, which was bare. In fact, except for the one lamp he'd had the bad luck to hit, the room itself was almost empty. This was a mistake. A safe house should look in every respect like a home; that was what they had been taught, and it was good teaching.

He found that he could see the outlines of windows faintly, and was soon able to guide himself into the kitchen. Then the door was under his hands. He took the knob and opened it.

At once, there was a smell, and he knew that it was blood, raw blood, and not yet decayed. What was here? What was he finding? He fumbled down into the garage itself, into a complicated mass of protruding obstacles. Tools clattered on a workbench as he drifted his hands along it. And then he felt something else, a softness, wet and dense, like a soaked sponge, but large. Gingerly he felt its rough edges, its damper center, then along the smoothness of it, feeling farther and faster, the cold, elastic quality under his fingers.

Frantic now, afraid of what this was, he felt for some sort of light, found a string, and pulled it, but uselessly. All the power in the region must be turned off.

But then he had something in his hand—a metal tube. Yes—he found the button; he pressed it, and found himself shining the flashlight beam on a man's severed leg.

Gasping, forcing back his cries, he stumbled away from the workbench. Flashing the light around, he saw that there was blood everywhere, most especially on a green chain saw that had obviously been used to do this horrific thing.

But why? Who?

And then he understood. To be certain, he swung the light toward the bulky shape of the plane. It stood complete, the wings folded back. They had only to be drawn straight, he saw, and hooked down.

In the cockpit was exactly what he expected to find, the slumped body of Balil Aboud. He had cut off his own leg to make himself light enough to get the plane off the ground. His brother, therefore, had either run away or died. Balil's hands clutched the stick, his fingers skeletal claws. His face was twisted with concentration, his teeth bared in a grimace of rawest agony.

Somehow, this man had sawed his own leg off, had dragged himself to the plane, had gotten in. But how? And why bother, given that he couldn't hope to get it out onto the street, let alone open the wings? Then Rashid saw the prints of shoes in the blood on the floor, and they made what had happened here quite clear. Hani had faltered in his courage, and Balil had tried to replace him. The plan had been for Hani to push the plane out and lock the wings opened. But it had not happened that way, obviously.

Had Balil died here and then Hani run away? Or had Hani been a traitor from the beginning, in the pay of the Americans, perhaps, or the Saudi king, who paid bribes to jihadists all the time, the filthy dog? In any case, what Rashid saw here was the reason that Washington still stood.

"I have a gun."

He turned, shining the light in the direction of the voice. In the doorway stood what was almost a human skeleton, a hollow-eyed, sunken shadow of a human being. Held in both clenched fists, his arms shaking so much it seemed as if he would drop it at any moment, was a .38-caliber revolver, a Police Special. The man was so weak that he could barely lift the small weapon. With its short barrel, it was not particularly accurate, but Rashid would not take that chance.

"Hani, Allah forgives. Allah is merciful."

"There is no Allah! Allah is a lie!"

"Now, you know that isn't true. You know that Allah is in your heart."

The pistol began to shake more. He was trying to fire it, to pull back the trigger, but he was very weak. To make him light enough to fly, his brother must have starved him.

Rashid leaped at him, throwing him back into the kitchen. He hit hard, his head thudding against the floor. Rashid straddled him, no longer knowing where the gun was. He lifted Hani's shoulders and slammed his head against to the floor. There was a grunt, and he lay still. When Rashid shone the flashlight on him, he cringed away from it.

Rashid smiled at Hani. "It's nothing. I understand. There's no shame in this."

"There is shame."

"You still have a chance."

"I cannot fly the plane."

"But I can, Hani. I'm within the weight range."

Hani gave him a careful look. "I thought you would kill me."

Rashid wished dearly that he could. But never mind, Hani would get his justice along with the rest of the devils in this evil place. "No, no, there's no shame. There's no blame, Hani. You must do for me what your brother was going to do for you, and help me run the plane out."

"Who are you? How did you come here?"

"I'm nobody from nowhere. Now come."

As he returned to the garage, Hani followed. Shining the light into the plane, Rashid saw, for the first time in his life, one of the legendary bombs. It was stowed in a carrier just behind Balil's ruined body, a steel darkness. Rashid couldn't make out the exact shape, except that it was a rough ball covered with what looked like blasting caps. There were many wires, which appeared disturbingly delicate.

He followed the wire harness around beside the pilot's seat to where it ended in a covered switch. He opened the switch cover. In tiny Arabic script were written below the silver toggle the words "Courage for the heart" and above "God is great."

He touched the switch. That was all that was necessary, simply to flip that toggle a quarter of an inch. That would forever change the world. Forever. "How great you are, O God," he whispered, fingering it.

"I thought of triggering it here. Right here."

"But you couldn't even do that?"

"I've never seen anything. I have never made love. I have no children."

"Help me now," Rashid said.

Balil's body had stiffened, and as they forced it out of the plane, the garage was filled with the sound of cracking bones.

"At midnight," Rashid said, "I will fly."

"And will it . . . wreck this house?"

For an instant, Rashid was going to tell him the truth. Just in time, though, he caught himself. "Oh no. The house will shake. Be damaged. But the explosion will not carry this far." He gave Hani what he hoped was a believably reassuring smile. "It's safe here for you. Safe enough."

As Rashid embraced Hani, he continued smiling, but to himself. *May this devil burn in the firestorm that will be triggered by the bomb. May he burn slow.*

33

A NIGHT-BLOOMING FLOWER

"You've never done operational work, Nabby," Jim Deutsch said to his wife. "Stay cool. Things can happen fast. Just rely on me; this is my office."

"Jim, I'm cool."

"No, you aren't."

They were sitting together in the tightly confined space of an FBI surveillance van, which had been modified for radiation detection. The space was packed with technology, maybe useful, maybe not.

"We could see action and I want you to *not* get involved. You cannot handle a gun."

"I can, and I've got one."

She showed him her little Backup.

"That's for close-in work. It feels like protection in a firefight, but it's not protection. Too inaccurate."

"Should I not use it?"

"Keep it close to hand, but don't get ambitious."

They had now been working Alexandria for four extraordinarily tense hours, moving slowly down each street, watching their screens and drinking endless cups of coffee. So far, they had detected eleven medical X-ray facilities and one dental office with what turned out to be a damaged X-ray machine. Now they were methodically covering every residence that was close to a medical X-ray facility, on the theory that the bomb had been hidden inside the radiation signature of such a facility.

It was now eleven forty. Fitz had capitulated in order to buy time, but the Mahdi's latest message had been quite clear: all of his demands had to be met or Washington would die tonight.

Few of his demands had actually been met, though. Certainly, no bankers were being rounded up, and the worldwide *hijab* rebellion continued.

At least there had been a certain mercy, in that the time gained so far had enabled more orderly evacuation of the region. The president had personally asked the demonstrators to leave, and many of them had, including all of those with children. Still, though, a certain number remained around the White House, singing and praying, their voices echoing through the darkness that had descended with sunset. There was not a single light, not a cigarette, not a penlight, in all that crowd.

The White House, the Capitol, all of the monuments were darkened as well. Only deep inside the most secret places was there light and activity, such as the White House bunker where Marge and Mark and the others were making progress only by agonizing inches.

Despite the security issues, the original disk had now been flown to the United States. It was at a classified NSA facility, with another team working on it there.

As they passed down a long street, an indicator spiked. "Stop, please," Nabila said. The driver braked. "What have you got?"

"Go, now," she murmured.

The van moved off, bouncing a little as it accelerated, the equipment bays rattling.

"We have it," she said simply. "Back there, the third house. The bomb is there."

"You're certain?"

"Oh yes. Western X-ray is across the alley, right behind the house, but their signature would not extend this far. And yet we have a good signal. It's there."

"Invisible from above, though."

"Completely hidden, yes, thanks to Western X-ray. The only place to find it is from the street. But we have found it."

He got on the horn. "We have a hit. It is a full positive. Please set the deployment well back, and deliver a blueprint of the property pronto."

As Nabby listened, her eyes grew moist. Jim understood that he could not know her emotions. Her family had been extremely close. Rashid was like an extension of her own soul. She loved him that deeply.

"Nabby, when it's somebody you love, it does things to your judgment. Be careful."

She shook away her tears. "I can do this."

"It might come to him dying."

"Jim, Rashid is not my brother. My brother has died already. The man in there is the Dajjal, as are they all, all the ones who do this. It has stolen their bodies and killed their souls."

The Dajjal was the Muslim equivalent of the Antichrist. Ideas like that didn't resonate with Jim, but if they gave her the courage she needed, then fine. If Rashid was here, she was going to face some terrible moments. To Jim, people who could kill for ideas were always the same—narcissists unable to empathize with others, their hearts killed by their ideas. As far as he was concerned, a person who was willing to murder another because they disbelieved some story was not a fully developed human being, and that included all religious fundamentalists, all political ideologues, all fanatics.

"You sigh," Nabby said.

"Remember this: even if this bomb is detonated right here, inside that house, it's going to cause incredible damage. We have only one mission: prevent that bomb from detonating, no matter who dies." He reached out to her, drinking in her wide, soul-rich eyes in the amber glow that filled the tiny space. Both of her small hands took one of his great paws. "I'll go in first," he said. "If he's there and I need you, I'll call you."

"The house plans are downloaded."

He turned in his seat and viewed them. He noted the date, August 13, 2002. No legal alterations had been recorded since then. But if there was a plane in there—and he was certain that there was—there were going to be major internal changes. He concentrated on the basic outlines, the street-facing rooms. What was it like deeper inside? Too bad he couldn't know.

"I'm as ready as I'll ever be," he said into his radio.

There was a brief silence while the coordinator checked the many levels of response. There were four SWAT teams on the ground, which would now all move to drop-off points just out of sight of the target location. Overhead, the entire airborne response force was targeting this immediate area. Bomb neutralization teams from Homeland Security and three police forces were deploying.

And, as Jim knew perfectly well, it was all pretty much useless, because no matter who was in there, all they had to do would be flip some switch or push some button and the entire region would go up in flames, centered on the crater that would be all that was left of Alexandria.

The radio beeped. "This is the president," came Fitz's familiar voice. "I wish all of you the very greatest success in this endeavor. May God be with us all."

Then, a young man's voice: "Radio silence now, please."

The frequencies they were using wouldn't be picked up by even the most sophisticated retail scanning equipment, but who knew what these people might possess? Fitz should have kept off the damn horn.

An image flickered onto one of the screens that lined the packed walls of the van. It was a bright shot of the house in full color, looking like day.

Jim busted radio silence. "Pull that damn Global Hawk out *now*!" he snapped.

"Global Hawks are invisible from the ground," Nabby said.

They were indeed equipped with transference technology camouflage, which displayed a continuous picture of the sky above the plane off its lower surfaces, but at low altitude a small amount of engine noise would reach the street. Normally, not enough to matter. "The city's too quiet," Jim said.

The image flickered off. The Hawk was gone.

Jim took a deep breath, let it out. He did not want to take Nabby with him, but he saw no choice. If Rashid was in there and he had his finger on the button, she was the only hope—and a faint one—of getting him to change his mind. "Eleven forty-six," Jim said. "Are we in place?"

The FBI explosives team was there. These men had suppression equipment that could prevent blasting caps from detonating. Wonderful technology, but they would need to get close to the bomb, and they would need time.

Jim opened the door of the van onto what had become a cold, windy night. There was a suggestion of rain in the air. Low overhead, clouds had begun racing down from the north. Jim would have liked night-vision equipment, but there was no use in calling further attention to the operation.

He'd hoped for alternate entry to the house, but there were only the two doors. Nabila came out beside him.

"I'm going to need to go in through the back," Jim said.

"I can distract him. Knock on the door."

"No! The least sign of activity, that bomb is going off."

As he began to move away, Nabila grabbed his arm. "Don't just leave me here!"

"Nabby—"

"I can help you. I have to, Jim." Her fingers tightened around his wrist.

"You job is here. You control these people. You do it right."

Her eyes bored into his. "It's not going to work. Any of it. And you know it, don't you?"

Drawing away from her, he stepped out into the alley.

SISTER AND BROTHER

The SWAT teams that surrounded this place had already confirmed that there were no spotters or snipers posted anywhere. The house was meant to seem totally innocuous, and so was unguarded.

The house was a different story, though. The house would be bristling with guns.

He moved down the alley, staying close to the walls of buildings, careful to never expose himself to a sight line from one of the back windows. In his life, he'd done hundreds of entries like this, but never with stakes this high, of course. Not only did an entire city depend on this working, but that city was Washington, D.C.

He came to the back door, which was approached by two concrete steps. As he mounted them, he kept below the line of the window in the door. He crouched, listening against the wooden door. The urge to just smash the damn thing to kindling and get in there and try to kill the guy was almost more than he could suppress.

The lock was simple enough, but it would need a lock pick, not a credit card, which meant that there was going to be a slight click. He listened harder, pressing his ear against the wooden door. There was dripping, that was all. Of course, there could be a guard in there, somebody with the skill to remain silent. Could be Rashid, even. He wasn't a man easy to anger, but he found himself eager to kill Rashid.

He inserted the lock pick, felt for the slight resistance of the tumblers, was momentarily stopped by a shield in the cylinder, then got past it. The lock dropped open with a noise so loud it actually echoed. The damn thing sounded like a bullet!

Or rather, this was one very quiet place—of course, it would be, a safe house in an evacuated city that was waiting to die.

Nothing happened, so he pushed the door open. In the stuffy fetor that emerged, he smelled the unmistakable odor of blood. It was not brand-new but not old, either. So violence had been done here. He thought he was about to find out why the bomb had not been detonated.

He penetrated deeper into the kitchen. The clock on the microwave oven offered the only illumination. He watched it change to 11:47. Vegas at midnight. Rome at midnight . . .

Jim closed his eyes, inhaled deeply. Blood, the dressing of salad eaten sometime this evening, still full of the volatile scents of seasonings . . . more faintly, oh yes, that would be aviation fuel, and the fuel can would have been opened within the hour or the fumes would be gone.

The blood was older, so whoever had cracked the fuel can was probably still very much alive. They would be with the plane, and he did not think it likely that he could reach them in time to prevent their flipping their switch. In fact, the moment they detected the least sign of his presence, this city would be destroyed.

The door to the garage, he recalled, would be on his left. It was so dark, though, that he couldn't be sure of his bearings. He moved ahead with extreme care, sliding his hands along the floor as he proceeded. All he could do here was get as close to them as humanly possible. To try.

Explosives suppression was a difficult business. There were no ray guns; that was for damn sure. To prevent a cap from detonating, it needed to be surrounded by a group of devices with highly specialized properties. This was slow, careful work for experts. If they were looking at a plutonium implosion bomb, it would be a sphere arrayed with many such caps, all timed to explode at precisely the same instant and compress the plutonium core so that it would go critical—and the rest would be history.

He found the door and slid his hand along it until he grasped the handle.

The knob was cool beneath his fingers. Very carefully, he moved it slightly. The door was unlocked.

He closed his eyes, took a deep breath, and let it out slowly, preparing himself for what was beyond question the most important moment he had ever known or would probably ever know. It was a warrior's moment, and he forced his attention to leave his screaming, jabbering mind and focus on the beating of his heart, the sensation of his muscles, on his hearing and his eyes.

He turned the knob until the tongue was fully retracted.

His life was punctuated by moments like this, which involved sudden, violent movements into dangerous places. He did not allow himself to consider death. That was for peaceful nights under the stars. He was aware, instead, of every muscle wound tight. You needed to be ready to act faster than thought, like an animal.

To minimize any squeal of hinges, he drew the door open fast, causing a gust of fuel-soaked air to hit him in the face.

He found the place lit thin blue by a fluorescent lantern, and also found that there was nobody immediately visible. Quickly he scanned the space. The wall of the family room behind the garage had been knocked down to create a makeshift hangar.

Before him stood a small airplane, its broad wings folded back against its fragile fuselage. He thought it was kit built, perhaps even specially designed. From its configuration, he could see immediately that it was able to take off in a very short distance.

The evacuation had played into their hands, because on a normal night pulling this thing out into the middle of traffic, setting the wings, and taking off would have been all but impossible.

They must have counted on a curfew, even an evacuation. This was a symbolic strike, after all. They weren't after people here; they were after a way of life, and the city that organized it and enabled it to unfold.

Wreck Washington, break the will of America . . . and, icing on the cake, throw the country into political and economic chaos from which it would never recover, not in its current form.

What the evacuation had done was give them their runway. Poor old Fitz had been so proud of it, too. "All those lives being saved," he had said. For what? To people who had lived in freedom, death would appear better than the life the Mahdi was going to force on them.

Jim was beside the tail of the plane, standing in the doorway from the kitchen. The room was entirely silent, or so it seemed at first. But rooms were never silent. No place was silent. He looked from the bloodstained workbench and the meat-encrusted chain saw lying on it to the garage door. He listened for breathing, heard none.

There was what seemed to be an earsplitting click and the garage door began to open. For the first time in his professional life, Jim was so surprised that he almost cried out.

An instant later, the plane's engine screamed into shattering life. He hadn't heard anybody because the pilot was already inside the plane, invisible behind its folded wings. Jim stepped down into the garage proper, went to the plane, and grasped the tail.

Then he felt weight—somebody on his back. The weight didn't stop him; it felt like a child. Jim shifted, intending to scrape the kid off him. In that moment, the plane bounded forward—and the kid was gone. Jim started after the plane, which had gone down the short driveway of the row house and was now in the street.

He jerked to one side and ripped at a thin shoulder, tossing the skeletal child off his back. The kid hit the wall hard and slid down it. He was a human skeleton. Horrible. Had he been a prisoner? Or no—the bomb probably ate up all the lift the plane had to offer. He had starved himself so that he could fly it.

Had he gotten cold feet? Was he somehow incapacitated? And who was the pilot?

None of it mattered. What mattered was preventing that plane from taking off and at the same time not allowing the pilot to see him.

But how could it take off? The wings were still folded. There was a two-man job ahead, but now there was only one man.

The plane idled. The pilot was waiting for his accomplice. A glance at the kid told Jim that the accomplice was done.

The only problem now was the surrounding mass of personnel. If anybody made a mistake and showed themselves, that pilot was going to detonate his bomb immediately. The only chance they had was to disable the plane just as it was taking off, to crash the thing before he could push the button.

The plane's engine continued to idle. The pilot wouldn't wait long, and indeed the fuselage began to rock, as he twisted and turned in the cockpit, trying to see behind.

Jim stepped back into the shadows, dropping down beside the tool bench.

The pilot came out, bending low under one of the folded wings. He looked back toward the garage. "Hani!"

Jim saw that it was Rashid. Nabby would see this, too, on about four different monitors in the van. Moving with the greatest care, Jim drew the M9 he'd been issued at the White House. But Rashid was at least two hundred feet away, standing just behind the folded wing. If Jim missed and hit the bomb, Rashid would earn his heavenly virgins and so would everybody for twenty miles around. Normally, Jim would have no problem, even though the pistol's rated effective range was about 150 feet. But he had never fired this particular weapon, and if you were going to stretch range like that, and at night, you needed to know your pistol very, very well.

Rashid turned to the plane and quickly unfolded and locked the wing. Then he walked around the fuselage.

Taking advantage of fact that the bulk of the plane hid him, Jim moved quickly across the garage. Now he was perhaps eighty feet from Rashid. Close enough, no question. As soon as the head appeared in the cockpit, Jim could squeeze off a shot that would not miss.

He knelt and braced the pistol.

Rashid appeared in the cockpit.

"Rashid!"

The voice blasted in Jim's ear. Instinct swung him fast. Before he could stop himself, before he could think, he squeezed off four fast shots, sending Hani crashing against the back wall of the garage in a haze of blood and smoke.

The plane was on its way down the street, its wingtips just clearing obstacles such as light poles and a public mailbox.

Jim ran, his legs hammering. There was no longer any chance of preventing Rashid from pushing his button. He was going to detonate the bomb, no question. Now all that mattered was that he do it here on the ground and not achieve a far more damaging airburst.

The plane gathered speed slowly, and Jim gained on it. Closer. Closer still. He aimed the pistol. It didn't matter anymore what he hit. Keep the damn thing on the ground; that was what mattered.

He'd done four rounds. He had eleven left. Properly placed, they could tear the little aircraft apart.

Then he saw, coming from ahead of it, another running figure. He saw white clothing; he saw black hair.

"Nabila! Nabila, get down!"

He had to shoot. There was no choice. And what did it matter if he hit her or not? They were all dead, anyway.

Incredibly, the plane rotated. Just like that, its nose turned skyward and it seemed to dance off the pavement and into the sky, and Nabby was hanging in the landing gear, her feet kicking as she struggled for purchase.

He stood there, his pistol raised, as the plane's engine screamed and the aircraft wallowed, then heeled badly. He saw the rudder snap far to the right, saw the flaps work—and then the plane's left wing struck a streetlight, and the fuselage wheeled, smashing into a house. The rudder hit Jim hard, causing him to lose his footing and topple forward, arms windmilling.

He regained his balance, then froze.

The plane was still now, the engine silent. The reek of aviation fuel mixed with the smell of smoldering wires from the tangle behind the ruined dashboard.

When Jim tried to step closer, a searing blast of pain made him fall forward instead. From the lack of control and the waves of fiery agony, he thought he'd burst a tendon, or smashed his ankle altogether.

Grabbing an edge of the wing to support his weight, he peered into the twisted cockpit. Rashid was not only conscious; his hand was fumbling for something, undoubtedly the critical switch. Jim's gun was gone, though, lost as the rudder hit him.

Then everything was black. The world was upside-down, turning slowly, slipping into the distance. He was losing consciousness; he must have taken a head injury as well. He fought it as hard as he could, but his hands would not work. He couldn't get to Rashid. He had no strength. He felt as if his muscles were turning to water.

He was used to controlling his body. He could absorb a lot of punishment, handle a lot of pain. He was concussed though, maybe losing blood. Forcing himself, concentrating all his energy, he raised his right arm, and suddenly somebody else was there, a flash of white—he realized that it was Nabby and she had dived into the cockpit with her brother.

The reek of fuel filled Jim's nostrils as the whole scene was flooded with light. Low overhead, a helicopter was lighting up the entire street. There were voices then, and the sound of big engines—fire equipment coming closer.

An F-16 howled overhead at low altitude, waiting to pounce if the plane somehow managed to take flight. But this airplane was dead.

A single dot of consciousness remained, and it was telling him that Rashid could still detonate the bomb.

Rashid smashed his feet against the windscreen, which popped out of its housing with a loud, cracking protest.

He was out, just like that, supple as a panther. He staggered, stood—and suddenly, in the blazing floodlight, held up a remote control. Round and round he turned, holding it high. He was grinning, his teeth flashing.

Nabila, her clothes ripped, her body covered with blood, leaped through the broken windscreen and flew at him. She embraced him, also embracing the remote, and for a moment they were dancers, graceful in the steel-white light from above, dancing to the rough beat of the helicopter's rotors.

Nabila had Rashid's wrist in her right hand, bending his fingers back and tearing at it with her teeth, trying to get the remote from him. Her left arm was twisted in a way that could only mean it was broken. At any moment, Rashid was going to press the crucial button.

Breathing deep, Jim opened himself to his pain, accepted that it was now part of him, and began moving toward them.

Nabby cried out, "Why are you doing this?"

"Islam converts by the sword! Face it, Nabby!"

"Daddy sees you from heaven! Think of that! Daddy sees this; he sees you killing the world!"

They went down together, Nabby throwing her head back and screaming with agony when she rolled across the broken arm. Jim saw the white of bone protruding from her elbow.

As he forced himself forward, his eyes were on that remote. The light from above was too blinding for him to see much beyond the pool of it where Rashid and Nabby struggled, but all around them Jim could hear the clatter of deployment.

Then Nabby was on top. She grabbed Rashid's shirt and slammed his head against the pavement, growling through bared teeth. His eyes registered surprise, but the remote did not leave his hand. She did it again, the growling louder now, and this time Jim saw that Rashid was stunned.

Jim came to Nabby, and found himself beside a savage being, somebody he did not know, and he understood for the first time what it means to say that somebody has blood in their eye. She glared at him, teeth bared, cheeks sucking, and the growls turned into tears, bitter, agonized. She raised her head and stared up into the light of the churning helicopter, into the blasting wind of its rotors, and the sound that came out of her was the pain of love denied, a sister's tortured heart, and the agony—even deeper—of women across the world. He heard the vast history of frustration that was in that cry, the despair of women denied the only things they want, which are an equal embrace and equal partnership on the human journey.

She had killed her own brother, and this was how it sounded when a woman's heart tears itself apart.

But the remote, *the remote*—

Jim threw himself across the pavement, grabbed it, blood covered but intact. So why were they all still here? Why hadn't Rashid used it?

Then Jim saw why. This remote wasn't going to trigger a bomb. It was just an infrared TV remote with a range of maybe twenty feet, assuming no obstacles. A remote trigger for a bomb would emit radio frequencies that could broadcast farther than infrared.

So this was a decoy. His eyes snapped to the wreckage of the plane.

Screaming to make his pain easier to bear, he dragged himself to his feet and headed toward the wreck. "Timer," he said, but his voice was not loud enough, would not carry over the crashing echoes of the rotors above. "Timer . . ."

He beckoned the darkness until he saw men come into the light at last, men in blast gear and reflective face guards. Had there been time, he would have laughed.

He crawled into the blood-soaked cockpit through the shattered windscreen. The dashboard was ripped open, wires pulled out. Rashid had been trying to repair the manual firing mechanism, and when he couldn't do it he'd produced this TV remote and used it to gain time.

He'd thought to bring it with him. Rashid was a careful man. Chess, not poker. He didn't trust luck. He was always many moves ahead.

The bomb was a darkness behind the seat. Jim pulled its bent frame aside and saw it, black, about the size of a beach ball, hidden in a mass of wires that led to the detonators, each one a black plate plastered against the blue steel of the bomb's housing. The plutonium core would be positioned in the center, surrounded by the triggers that would almost instantaneously compress it. But you would never see that. That would happen in well under a second . . . and it could happen any second.

Where was the countdown timer? It had to be running or Rashid wouldn't have bothered to decoy it.

Then Jim saw it, a tiny plastic square no larger than a watch face. Its wiring was concealed under the black tape that held to the body of the bomb. The counter was reading down. He saw it go through 58, on its way to the end of its final minute.

There was no time to disarm this. That sort of thing could only be done in the movies. Actually running down the wiring of a timer like this and safely neutralizing it took hours.

He backed out, turned, and grabbed one of the explosives experts who were now crowding in behind him. "It's on a timer," Jim shouted above the din of the rotors. "Get explosives suppression on this thing! *Now! Now! Now!*"

They tried to pull him out, but there was no time, and he slid over the bomb and into the tiny space behind it. Here he could be of help. He could place charge suppressors. If they did enough of them in the right pattern and they worked, the plutonium wouldn't be compressed correctly and the bomb would never go critical.

They knew what they were doing; they had probably simulated this a thousand times. One after another, the suppressors went onto the firing mechanisms, covering them like gray beetles.

A hand thrust three at him. "Where?"

Twenty-two seconds.

No time. He simply placed them at random, forcing them down over the explosive caps, hoping for the best.

Darkness.

35

A QUESTION OF TIME

Ahead, the light. This was death, then. So quiet! The light . . . beautiful. Calling him, a silent, sacred song. Then an angel looking down at him. God's good angel.

"Jim!"

Pain, then, sweeping dreams of heaven away. It surged up and down his chest, running in his guts like a pack of starving rats.

This was not heaven and the light was just the damn chopper and the angel had a busted arm because it was Nabila. "Oh," he said, and heard his own voice displace the ringing in his blast-shocked ears.

"Medic," she shouted. Then she stood up, sweeping out of Jim's field of view. "*Medic!*"

Vans came, and a larger truck, a SWAT vehicle.

He felt himself being moved, heard voices speaking quickly, saw an IV appear, and a needle, and knew that the needle was going to shut him down.

Nabila would not let them give her any pain medicine, not with Jim in such grave condition. His chest and stomach had been laid open when the detonators fired. He'd literally been cradling the bomb.

A colonel came into the meat wagon as the doors closed. "Is he gonna make it?"

Only a miracle would keep him alive, even this very powerful man. All bodies have their limits. She put her hand on his gray forehead. It was cold, dry. It felt as her father's had felt when he lay in his coffin.

She looked at Jim. Closed her eyes.

The colonel came up beside her. "He pulled this thing out," he said. "Those suppressors he placed were the key."

Ignoring the pain that her every movement sent surging through her own broken arm, she bent close to Jim. "Jimmy, you hear that?"

The vitals monitor's faint, slow beeping was his only answer.

From in front, she heard: "Hey, lights!"

She turned, looked between the drivers, out the front windshield of the windowless ambulance.

The lights of the city were coming on, flickering at first, then erupting in long, glorious streams of street lamps, in dancing signage, in traffic lights, store windows, and houses. And in the light, cars began to appear honking their horns in joy, people who had been hiding came out from their houses, police cars whooped the delight that the young men and women inside felt.

Then, a high-pitched sound. Instantly both medics leaped into action in the careening ambulance, and Nabila knew that Jim's heart had stopped. She threw herself onto the floor beside the stretcher on which he lay, and gave to Allah the greatest, the strongest, the most heartfelt prayer of her life, that her life be one with God's will, and vowed to always be faithful, and to raise her and Jim's children in faith, if only she could have this chance.

On and on, the screaming, empty whine continued. One of the medics did CPR, his breath interrupting the deadly wail. Then they had paddles, and they got her to go back to the bench in the crowded space, and they shocked Jim. His body hopped, and there was a stench of burning hair, and they shocked him again.

He's gone, she thought. Just when she had finally found a way to love him, to accept what he had to offer, which was the toughness and compassion of a true soldier, his soul had departed.

But then the beeping started. Not slowly, not dramatically, but all at once.

"Oh, wow," one of the medics said. He looked toward her. "This guy's hard to kill."

"He's alive?"

"Lady, right now, the answer is yes."

EPILOGUE

Six months later, Nabila's arm was long since out of its cast, but Jim was just get-ting up on a cane, and would be on one for a while. His internal injuries were healing well, but the ankle hadn't been broken. He had somehow walked with a severed Achilles tendon, and healing that was going to take time.

Nabila drove them to the White House for the presentation.

There was still a great deal to be done, but an enormous danger had passed in these months. Beyond the bombs in Washington, Rome, and Las Vegas, there had been five other actual devices. The owners of this particular hard disk had also been in control of bombs in Paris, Madrid, Moscow, London, and Los Angeles.

Of course, there could be more still out there, and the penetration of the U.S. intelligence system was far from resolved.

Inshalla was harmed, though to an unknown degree, as the hard disk had given away few secrets about its personnel.

But for now, the full catastrophe was averted.

Italy remained in political chaos, and the European Union was striving to assist it in reconstructing some sort of functional central authority. Virtually every organized country in the world now had a continuity-of-government plan that addressed the danger of sudden decapitation.

Helped out of the car by a Marine in formal uniform, Jim was still getting used to the idea of being alive. Waking to find Nabby with him had surprised him, and he was still not absolutely sure that this new life that they were sharing was not, after all, some outpost of heaven.

He sucked in the sweet air of spring. "Smell the roses."

"Yes, Sir," the Marine said.

"I didn't mean you."

"No, Sir."

As they moved toward the entrance, Jim saw that a Marine honor guard was saluting them. He snapped one back. They did not lower their hands.

Jim and Nabila entered, and as they crossed the lower hall, Marines in their dress uniforms and Secret Service in their black suits came to attention. "I thought it was supposed to be classified," Nabila whispered, her shoulders hunched.

"Better keep our traps shut, then."

They were conducted down to the West Wing Lobby, then immediately into the Roosevelt Room.

The long table had been removed, and the president, the vice president, and the secretaries of defense and state and their wives stood before the fireplace and the dramatic Tade Styka painting of Teddy Roosevelt as a Rough Rider.

When they began applauding, Jim at first thought somebody was behind them, and caused a ripple of laughter when he instinctively began to turn to see who it was. The two of them walked to the small podium, and the president stepped up to it.

He looked from one to the other. "I didn't think we'd make it," he said.

"Have we?" Nabila asked.

He cleared his throat and turned to the audience. "Not often in the history of mankind has there been so much owed to people who must remain hidden. I know that these medals are only a small token, but they are, nevertheless, the little we can offer you for a job well done."

Traditionally, there was little said at the presentation of the Intelligence Medal. Some of the people in this room were not even cleared to know exactly why they were receiving it.

The president pinned Jim's medal to his suit, and presented Nabila with hers. A few moments later, the ceremony was concluded and the medals were placed in their black felt boxes, to remain there until they would be buried with the recipients.

Afterward, the president, Jim, and Nabila went into the Oval. "Jim," the president said, "I'll get right to the point. You know that we've been making some changes in intelligence operations."

"I noticed." It wasn't just change, though, not this time. There was a revolution under way. The whole system of classification was being revised, and stovepiping of information now carried with it serious penalties. Whole agencies and departments were being disbanded and reconstructed along new lines. The gigantic outsourcing process, so fraught with danger to the nation, was being ended, and the two private mercenary armies, as well as the various private intelligence operations, were being dissolved. Jim himself was no longer a contractor but once again a direct employee of a currently leaderless CIA.

"Jim, I'd be grateful if you'd accept the Directorship of National Intelligence. Could you do that for me?"

"No, Sir, I could not."

Nabila sucked breath. She knew that no such offer would be made to her. Muslims had work to do in the West, a lot of it. Repairing the damage would take generations. She was lucky her clearance hadn't been pulled.

"There oughtta be a law against that—declining your president."

"Sir, I'm needed in the field. It's going to take years to identify and roll up this group that calls itself Inshalla. They've been hurt, but they're still out there, and at last count, we're looking at nearly a ton of plutonium still missing. Plus, we're penetrated. I don't think I'm competent to deal with that. I'm a frontline guy."

"You underestimate yourself, Jim." He turned to Nabila. "I hope you don't."

"I know my skills, Sir."

"Good, because what I want you to do is build something for me. We're starting a new directorate. Secret. We're going to repair the damage done to the interdiction infrastructure. We're going to find the people we can't trust, once and for all, and get rid of them."

She was silent. "It will be a secret directorate, so it's politically safe to appoint me, is that it?"

The president smiled a little. "I can't get you through a public advise and consent, obviously, Nabila. But if you'll let me, I can help you serve in a capacity that's worthy of your abilities."

"I will accept the directorship."

They left then, and while they were returning to their house, Nabila's phone rang. It was the White House. A meeting was scheduled at seven tomorrow morning. Orientation and a discussion of policy.

"You've never had any operational training, have you?" Jim asked her.

"No Camp Swampy for me. Guns in the hands of Islamists—bad idea."

"Then you should have some. Defensive driving. Neck breaking, perhaps."

"Is this funny? Should I be laughing?"

"It's funny. You should be laughing."

"It's not Arab humor." Then she did laugh. "First Arabs blow everything up and the CIA director is fired. Then the new CIA director comes along and it's an Arab. That's funny."

"You're not getting that directorship."

"Not officially, but you know that's what it is. What it amounts to. Actually, it'll have higher priority than CIA. Which is funny. Arab funny."

"Why so?"

"Don't you see? It's purdah for me when I am rejecting purdah. My face is naked; my legs can be seen. But in my work, I remain in purdah. The woman is hidden!"

"It's not American humor."

"I was born here, remember! I am an American, Jimmy. Never forget it."

"You're an Arab-American." He kissed her cheek.

"Careful, I will forget I am driving."

That night, they lay discreetly together. Very late, she whispered to him that he must wait for her to bear him his children. She wanted this work. She wanted it very badly.

He held her, felt her strong heart beating against his, and loved her more deeply than he had thought it was possible for him to love, and went with her in the ship of the night, always now with her.

Syed Ahmad sucked his water pipe and watched the television. For the first time in history, Muslim leaders were in attendance at the investiture of a new pope. All eight Grand Muftis were there, part of what was said to be the greatest procession of religious leaders ever assembled, moving through the streets of Florence to the huge Basilica di Santa Maria del Fiore. Ahmad smoked and watched with the others in the small coffee bar. Soon enough, there would be a new Mufti in Saudi Arabia, also, and it was already being said that the pope would attend his accession.

Blasphemy. Apostasy. God would curse them all.

But when there was applause, Syed also applauded and smiled. Secretly, though, he sent constant prayer to Allah, begging that the fire be put to their skin, and again, and again.

As God made all, God also made this. Inshalla had failed God, so God was repaying them by allowing this obscene blasphemy to be spat in the faces of the faithful.

Or perhaps there was another way to look at it. Perhaps this was purification. After all, Aziz had been corrupt, had he not, with his fast cars and his liquor? Who knew if he had truly given up his sins? Perhaps others besides Aziz had angered God also.

Syed was careful in his prayer and full of love and devotion. He could not be the reason that there had been this failure, and he did not think he was blamed. No, he was not blamed; otherwise he would never have been allowed to escape from Pakistan.

His journey had been harrowing, but at least its possibility had been contemplated and there had been planning.

He had initiated it by sending Eshan on a certain errand into the center of the city, one from which it was not intended that he would return. His identification, however, had come back, but now it had Syed's picture where Eshan's had been.

That easily, Syed had gone from being an Arab of fifty-three years to an American of forty-one years. A little dye had turned back some years, and he had left Pakistan using the American passport of his own clerk. So Syed was here in the United States as a proud citizen—or rather, Eshan was.

He had come a long way, flying first to Karachi, then to Paris, now here. There was nothing against Eshan. This was his homeland. There would be no questions here.

The customs officer had asked him, "What were you doing in Pakistan for two years?"

He had replied, "My mother was ill. I was helping her until she died."

"For two years?"

"She died at once. I was settling the estate."

"You have an accent." He was looking at a computer screen, seeing that Eshan had been born in this country.

"I do?" He had laughed. "I've been gone too long!"

"Two years just to settle an estate? Must have been a big one."

"Not big. Arab."

He'd laughed then, the hard young customs man. "Welcome home," he had said.

And so it was. The new Eshan would start his old life over. He had no living relatives here, his father having met with a tragic accident just before they were to be reunited at last. Indeed tragic.

Even under this new name and in this unholy place, he still bore the idea of the Mahdi in his soul. He would start everything again, yes . . . but slowly and carefully. Go back to putting a grain beside a grain, the way it had been with them always.

Perhaps there would be no further attempt in his generation. But there was the future, and God had all the time that existed.

God had all the time, but Ahmad was tired. His body and his bones felt stripped of life, exhausted, and he thought that death was not so far in his future. The truth was, the failure had broken him.

Perhaps he shouldn't even be watching this. Perhaps his rage and disgust would weaken him even more.

Another round of applause. Was there not a single faithful man in here? Not one sitting off, keeping to himself?

Not one.

It was early yet here, but the sun was shining in Florence, on all the great men of the world, kings, presidents, prime ministers, and all those apostate and faithless religious leaders, strutting their lies.

Even so, Ahmad was at one with God's will. Not at peace inside himself, far from it, but certain, still, of heaven.

In fact, as the smoke relaxed him, he put on a smiling face for those around him. Agents, he assumed, were everywhere among the Arabs, noting everything. *Why is that one not smiling? Give us his name. . . .*

On the far wall there was a faded portrait of the old Saudi king Faisal, may God forgive him. In the back, a mural of the Arabian desert. But Ahmad was not really Arab; he was Baluchi, a man used to seeing his wealth stolen by others.

He listened to the fawning voice of the Al Jazeera reporter, a slick-looking Kuwaiti, grinning in his ridiculous Western suit of clothes. Why wear such things, the clothing of barbarians?

"The new pope has taken a name out of a famous prophecy. Cardinal Arinze, the first African pope, is to be Peter the Roman, Petrus Romanus. In the prophecy of Saint Malachy, Petrus Romanus is the last pope, but Peter the Roman has a message to add from the words of the Christian Book of the Revelation of John 'I am Alpha and Omega, the First and the Last.' He says, 'The last is also first, and the last Roman pope shall also be the first pope of a new church, in a new era of peace, that will be everlasting in the world.' This is the message he gave upon his triumphant restoration of the ancient Catholic papacy."

That was enough. Ahmad left. He could bear no more. You break their city, you leave it burning—and here they are!

Ahmad had no television in the small room he had taken above the shop of a leather-goods seller, but he certainly didn't want to see more of this. When he needed news, he looked in the papers or listened to the radio.

He had some dates and cheese from yesterday, and would take this for breakfast, with an orange soda.

He went slowly up 3rd Street, in a whipping morning wind, and saw that the trees were touched by buds and there were petunias lifting their heads in the small flower boxes that so many people kept in their windows, here in Bay Ridge. He thought that he would like Brooklyn, despite the cold. He had crossed many borders, and passed through many lands, and dark. This one, though, smiled its innocent American smile, and hoped only that the traveler would accept the welcome that was offered at every turn.

Yes, Brooklyn was a good place for him to be. He would be safe here.